RULED BY A ROGUE'S DESIRE

"If I were a gentleman, I'd leave you be, Sabrina. I'd leave this town, this state, and never see you again. I'm not the kind of man you need."

"No!" The thought of him carrying out his words, of leaving, instilled her with an aching emptiness. "Don't leave."

"I said *if* I were a gentleman, Sabree." He stared at her. His voice was so gentle that she shivered. "I've lived a hard life. I'm a wanderer. You deserve pretty words and flowers. I'm not that kind of man."

"I don't care!" She wanted him just the way he was.

". . . and I'm not the kind of man content with hand-holding," he said as he pulled her closer. For a heart-wrenching moment Ross looked deeply into her eyes.

Sabrina glanced toward the bed then back at him. A fine madness seized her as he lowered his lips to hers and she opened her mouth to him. There were so many things she didn't know about him, but suddenly she didn't care. All she knew was that without him she didn't stand a chance of being happy.

CHEROKEE'S CARESS

KATHRYN HOCKETT

ZEBRA BOOKS
KENSINGTON PUBLISHING CORP.

ZEBRA BOOKS

are published by

Kensington Publishing Corp.
475 Park Avenue South
New York, NY 10016

First printing: November, 1990

Printed in the United States of America

Author's Note

In 1883 East at last met West when a frontier scout nicknamed "Buffalo Bill" took to the road with his first Wild West show. Buffalo Bill was a man who could do many things, one of them was put on a good show. He presented to each audience three action-packed hours of marksmanship, horsemanship, and frontier daring that symbolized the West.

Soon he had competition from "Pawnee Bill," "Tiger Bill," "Tim McCoy," "Charles Tompkin's Real Wild West," and other such shows which featured cowboys, cowgirls, war-bonneted Indians, and exaggerated stagings of life beyond the Mississippi river. Buffalo Bill Cody inspired more than a hundred imitators anxious to make a profit on the fascination the East held for the bold daring of the cowboys. These shows, heralded by bright, gaudy show bills that promised excitement and entertainment, soon flooded the country.

"Buffalo Bill's Wild West Show" traveled all over the United States and Europe. Everywhere he went kings and queens, grandparents and children flocked to see those his show made famous. The age of the rugged real Wild West with sweat-stained ranch hands and marauding Indians was ending and a new era of cowboys and cowgirls in spotless ten-gallon hats, furry chaps, and silver spurs was beginning.

Part One

Gentle Surrender
New England, 1884

Chapter One

The sun rose in the cloudless blue sky gilding the leaves of the trees and turning the early morning dew to diamonds. Autumn in New Hampshire was an enchanting time, Sabrina James thought as she pushed at the rickety back door of the Four Horsemen Inn with the handle of her broom. The leaves always turned a bright golden color as October gave way to November. For just a moment, as her eyes scanned the beauty, life at her father-in-law's shabby old tavern did not seem quite as dismal. As long as she still had her dreams, she was afforded some escape from the drudgery.

Sabrina had lived with her father-in-law, Rufus James, since the death of her husband, a whaler who had been swept overboard in a storm on the North Atlantic coast. Left penniless and homeless with no family of her own, she had sought out her husband's father for help. He'd shown her little sympathy, quickly putting her to work with little time to mourn. In return for board and lodging, Sabrina kept the Four Horsemen Inn clean.

One month had blended uneventfully into the other, each day an all-too-familiar routine. Often times she would think of her dead husband, Seth, and reminisce about their marriage. She had known happy times then. It was perhaps the most contented period of her life, for her husband had been loving and gentle, a contrast to his father. She couldn't help wondering how Seth could have been sired by such a man as Rufus, a penny-pinching tyrant who was always grumbling.

Recently Sabrina had been given the added task of serving in the inn's tap room, a chore that she detested. She wasn't lazy, far from it. She hated working in her father-in-law's tavern because of the pawing hands, the bawdy, suggestive remarks, and the bold stares his customers granted her. Instead of protecting his daughter-in-law, Rufus James seemed to approve of the ogling she was afforded by the paunchy gentry and sunburned sailors. Sabrina knew that Rufus was using her as bait to lure men and thus their coins to the taproom.

Sabrina's moments of warm contentment were indeed brief as the Portsmouth, New Hampshire summers. Her cold miserly father-in-law treated her more like a servant than family, never ceasing to remind her that she was living on his charity. There really wasn't much she could do about the situation, though, as long as she was eating his bread and living beneath his roof. Until she could think of a way to be independent of his grudging generosity, all she could do was manage as best she could. She would continue reading her dime novels and dreaming that someday things would change for the better.

Her many dreams put her in a pleasant state of mind. Without them she would have lost her sanity. Sometimes she imagined that a handsome frontiersman or cowboy would come riding up on his horse and carry her away from all of this. A man who would bring her the happiness her husband had. A man with which to share her life. She was so very lonely, achingly so.

"Let it be soon . . ." she sighed, pausing to listen to the trill of robins resting on a branch of the old oak tree. One robin brought a smile to her face as he cocked his head from side to side as if to ask, "Shall I stay here awhile longer or head south for the winter?" Just like Sabrina, he wanted to move on.

It was Sabrina's dream to go West, to that area of the country where a person could make a fresh start and with hard work and courage make her fortune just as the heroines in her dime novels had done. Her novels she thought. Oh, what a godsend they were, for they gave her hope and took her mind off her own problems.

The old oil lamp by her bed glowed long into the night. Reading was the one luxury Rufus James allowed her as long as it didn't interfere with her work. Stories such as *Hurricane Nell* and *Mountain Kate* were a welcome escape from her own heartaches. The stories never ceased to amaze her. Women of the West braved hordes of Indians, outlaw bands, and fearsome wild animals for the sake of the men they loved. Their reward was always a happy ending. Hurricane Nell had given up fighting outlaws to marry a lawyer from Philadelphia named Cecil; Mountain Kate had likewise found her perfect mate. And so would she eventually find another man to love.

Sabrina was determined to find a man with an occupation as unlike her husband's as night was from day. Her husband Seth had been a strong, dashing, adventurous, always smiling man, but she needed a man who did not follow the calling of the sea. The next time around she wanted a man who kept his feet firmly planted on the land.

That was not to say she hadn't loved Seth. She had loved him for his faults as well as his virtues. At first, after Seth's death, when Sabrina was alone in her room, she would look through Seth's spy glass out to sea as if in so doing she could bring him back to her. The thought of his even white teeth smiling at her behind a well-trimmed mustache made her cry and cry until there were no more tears left. That twirling, foaming ocean had swallowed up the dearly beloved husband who had always wanted a better life for her.

Seth had known every inch of the ship and even took on duties that were not his own such as pulling the halyards when sails were raised or spending long hours at the huge wooden wheel. The pushing and pulling kept his arms and shoulders in good shape he used to proudly tell her. He would pick her up, throw her over his shoulder, and race through the town of Stanford, Massachusetts, where they were living at that time, to their small cottage. There, he would make love to her for hours. Oh, how she missed him! Two years had passed now. She had finally realized that nothing could ever change the fact that he was never coming back. She simply had to get on without him.

Indeed, resigning herself to his departure had been nearly impossible in the months after his accidental death. She used to envision his tall muscular form striding up the beach in his blue striped turtleneck, the long sleeves rolled up above his elbows, and his light gray pants rolled up above his knees. Her daydream was so real that she would have to put her hands over her mouth to keep from calling out to him and hold herself back from running down the beach to meet him.

It was all a mistake, she would tell herself. Somehow Seth had found the strength to swim to shore somewhere and at this very moment was waiting to be rescued. She fantasized that he would come back to her, but the recovery of her husband's body had shattered all her dreams.

As she gazed out, letting her thoughts take full command of her, she saw ships of every size along the horizon. There were whaling ships, merchant vessels, small schooners, and other tiny fishing boats. The art of being a sailor was hard work, but Seth had loved it. She still treasured his captain's log book and his brass spyglass in a brown leather case that had been given to her by his first mate after the accident. They were really the only two things belonging to him that had been saved.

Sabrina leaned on the handle of her broom enjoying the fresh early morning air. She loved the mornings. They were peaceful. Quiet. Her father-in-law's scolding voice was silenced to sleep. He would be abed at least until noon and though she was expected to clean the inn from top to bottom, make all the beds, wash the mugs, cups, tankards, and plates, she was able to enjoy her solitude.

A soft breeze filled with the scent of the Piscataqua River, stirred the red, gold, and green foliage on the trees. Sabrina let the soft wind caress her face and stir her hair for a long moment. Tomorrow was her birthday. That thought caused her to stiffen. Twenty-four. It sounded so old. She'd spent two years here with her father-in-law. If she had known what a stern, calculating, manipulative person Seth's father really was, she would never have come here. He had never crossed Seth nor shown his true personality in front of his only son when he visited them in Stanford. Only when she had been in need had he revealed his true self.

"I want to be far, far away from here and from him," she whispered.

If she were quite frugal with the coins the patrons sometimes gave for a job well done, she might make her dream of leaving here a reality. With that hope in mind she had been carefully saving each and every penny, stashing it beneath her mattress in a small leather purse. A nest egg. A chance for freedom.

What a beautiful word—*freedom*. If she were fortunate, she would not have to spend another winter beneath this roof, listening again and again to her father-in-law's complaining. That he resented having to take her in was obvious in every look he cast her way, every word he said to her. No matter how hard she worked or how much she tried to please him, he never smiled or showed her any kindness. What was worse was the way he talked about her husband as "a romantic fool" who had brought about his own self-destruction. Rufus James never ceased to jabber on about how he had told Seth not to go to sea. Nor had he looked favorably on his son's marriage to a girl who had grown up in an orphanage.

"Your looks are your only value," he had said on more than one occasion, "and all they will do is get you into trouble." It seemed he was not above using her prettiness for his own ends, however.

He had made a similar remark just last night, Sabrina thought as she stared into the diamond pane of the mullioned window. She had been told by the inn's patrons that she had a flawless complexion. She could see for herself the high cheekbones, large copper-colored eyes, and teeth that were perfectly straight. Ha! Little good such blessings did her. Her face and the gentle swell of her bosom were her mother's only legacy. That and hard work. Sabrina couldn't remember a time when her mother, likewise a widow, hadn't toiled at housework or as a seamstress to keep food on the table and a roof over their heads. Even when she had been stricken with illness she had pushed herself beyond endurance, finally leaving Sabrina all alone in the world. Now she was gone and Sabrina could only pray that at last she had found peace. It was Sabrina's turn to labor now.

With a sigh of resignation, Sabrina went indoors, wrinkling up her nose in disgust as she stepped inside. After the freshness of the salty, morning air, the odor of the taproom was all the more noticeable. It smelled of smoke, grease, stale wine, and beer. Although she would mop the floor and clean from floorboards to ceiling it would smell the same tomorrow morning. It was a thankless task, yet one that needed to be done.

With a shrug of her shoulders Sabrina sent her dust rag skimming over the scarred wooden tables, then filled a bucket with water and soap. As she worked, her thoughts soared beyond her earlier doldrums and her drab surroundings. Her imaginative mind soon made her forget her drudgery. Her mop wasn't a mop at all. It became a rifle. Her dress was not made of a dull brown cotton but of buckskin, tastefully fringed and ornamented with Indian beads. Her long golden blond hair wasn't drawn back in a bun, but braided. For a moment

14

she was Malaeska, the Indian wife of the white hunter, saving her husband from a marauding band of Indians, savages that were hiding menacingly behind each and every barrel in the taproom. Raising the broom to eye level she took aim.

"Come on out of there or I'll fill you full of lead!" she shouted, mimicking a scene from the latest dime novel she had read. A creak and a thump answered her words.

"Whoa! Don't shoot." With a deep throaty chuckle, a tall dark-haired man rose from behind the largest barrel with his hands up. "I'll come peaceable like, ma'am."

"Wha . . . what are you doing here?" Sabrina's face flushed with embarrassment. She had thought herself to be all alone in the room. Now she felt foolish. "The taproom is closed!" she said curtly, hiding the mop behind her back.

"It wasn't last night when I . . . uh . . . fell asleep here. Too much whiskey," he explained with an apologetic grin. "A celebration of sorts, you see." He stood perfectly at ease as if he and not her father-in-law owned the establishment. He made no move to leave.

"Well, you shouldn't be here." He shrugged but didn't budge. "We don't serve wine, beer, or whiskey until afternoon. My father-in-law's rules," she said, studying him intently as he moved into the glare of sunlight streaming through the mullioned windows. Realizing she was staring, she said quickly, "I . . . I don't remember seeing you last night." He was the sort of man that no one would forget. He was tall and muscular with the bold look of a desperado despite his well-tailored tan suit which was a bit rumpled from the night on the floor. The firm lines of his jaw and upper lip were shadowed by at least a day-old beard. Wisps of dark tousled hair fell into his eyes and brushed against his collar. He was badly in need of a haircut, yet somehow the length of his dark brown hair added to his good looks.

"Nor do I remember you . . ." His eyes swept over her appraisingly, lingering on the rise and fall of her breasts, then touching on her face. "Pretty. Very, very pretty." Ah yes, she was, he reflected. With her soft golden hair drawn back from her face, a few tendrils curling about her temples, she looked like a seductive angel, one who had fallen from grace. Serene as a cameo, yet with a sensuality in her full mouth and long-lashed eyes.

Sabrina smoothed the wrinkles from her apron, hastily checking her appearance in a small mirror. There was a smudge of dirt on her nose; her hair was coming undone from the confines of her hairpins; the skirt beneath her apron was threadbare and badly in need of mending. His scrutiny suddenly made her aware of all such flaws. Blue eyes, as clear as the morning sky, looked back at her. There was a self-assurance in those eyes, as if he were a man who knew his self-worth.

"You most definitely weren't around when I arrived last night," he was saying. "Only that frowning, bespectacled tavern keeper."

"I . . . I was in bed." When the tavern was sufficiently full, the money and whiskey flowing freely, Rufus James at last permitted his daughter-in-law to retire and tended to the customers himself.

"In bed!" He grinned again. "I envy your husband."

Sabrina's face burned as she realized what he meant. "I . . . I was alone! I'm a widow."

"A widow . . ." He clucked his tongue in sympathy. "For how long?"

"Nearly two years. My husband drowned." She saw no need to relate the whole story to a stranger.

"I'm sorry." He sounded sincere, but one of his dark brows suddenly quirked suggestively. "And have you found another to take his place as your protector?"

"Certainly not." She quickly lowered her eyes from his piercing gaze. "I live here and work for my father-in-law."

He could well imagine after seeing that man how stimulating an experience that must be. Clearly this young woman was in need of a companion, someone

16

who would make her feel alive again, for by the sadness in her eyes this beauty was not content. Loneliness was written all over her face. Always one to speak his mind he came right to the point. "A woman as pertly pretty as you are should never be without tenderness or sleep alone."

His bold manner shocked her. "My dear sir!" She stepped back quickly.

He eyed her hopefully, then shrugged his shoulders. "Just an observation and an invitation if you find yourself with a hankering."

Sabrina was incensed by his behavior. A "hankering" he called it! He was cocksure. "It would be a cold day in hell before I—"

Again he laughed. "Aha! A spirited filly." When she made it a point to ignore him, he took a step closer and said in her ear. "I like a woman like you, little gal."

"I can assure you I don't care if I meet with your approval." Ah, but in truth she did. This bold rascal had caused a funny little quiver to dance up and down her spine as she felt his breath tickle her ear. What's more, there was a certain excitement in verbally sparring with him. "You are sadly lacking in manners, sir!" she said, trying to hide any telltale signs of her real feelings. Her heart was pounding so loudly she was certain he could hear every beat.

His hand tightened on her shoulder, halting her departure. "I meant to give you a compliment. I'm sorry if I offended you." His voice quieted to a rumbling seductive whisper. "I was merely telling the truth. A woman like you should be cherished against a man's heart. Comforted. Loved." His tone was a low rasp that touched every nerve in her body. "Never lonely."

He had touched upon her vulnerability. She *was* lonely. Terribly so. It was true, she did long for a man's arms around her again. There were times when she did long for the kisses and caresses she had shared with her husband. Nevertheless, she shook her head and answered tartly, "I am not lonely!"

He turned her around to face him. "No, I don't suppose a woman as lovely as you would be." She found herself close to him, so close that her breasts lightly brushed against his hard chest. Close enough that one flyaway lock of her hair tickled the sandpaper of his beard and then slid free. "Men undoubtedly hover around you like bees to a honeypot."

"Yes. No!" She thought of her father-in-law's leering patrons and grimaced. "That is, I don't want them to." She was suddenly aware of the rippling muscles in his thighs as his legs moved against hers, but though she could very well have pushed him away she didn't do so. The contact of their bodies was much too pleasant. She looked at the chiseled strength of his lips and found herself wondering how his mouth would feel upon her own. It was a contemplation she quickly pushed from her mind.

He looked deep into her eyes, trying to delve into her thoughts. Was she telling him the truth or just being coy? He had to know. "Then you haven't set your sights on another man?"

It was such a forthright question that she gasped. "No! I most assuredly have not." He was audaciously brazen.

Her answer pleased him. "Good, for that means I won't have to fight any man to lay my claim." Tipping her chin up with one lean finger he kissed her mouth before she could sense his intentions. It was a surprisingly gentle kiss for all his strength, and though she tried to ignore the flicker of warmth that spread from her mouth to the core of her body she could not. It was an enjoyable sensation, a pleasurable tingle.

Sabrina closed her eyes, pressing close to him. Her lips trembled beneath his. This man knew exactly what he was doing. The gentle caress of his mouth moved against hers in a way no other lips had never done. Clinging to him she relished the sensations as his lips and tongue explored hers. She could feel his heart pounding against her breasts as his kiss deepened. How long he kissed her she didn't know. All she could think about was the singing in her heart as she felt his masterful strength. His mouth seared hers and for just a moment she feared she'd allowed herself to come too close to the flame.

"Mmmm." His arms went around her waist, pulling her even tighter against him. "I was right about your mouth. It is every bit as soft as it looks," he said at last when he lifted his lips from hers.

With an enormous effort she lifted her eyes to meet his gaze, knowing that if he hadn't been holding her she would have fallen. She could feel her heart beating so loudly that it seemed to shake her whole body. She couldn't think, couldn't breathe. Her ears filled with a soundless rushing. What was happening to her? Kissing this handsome stranger was very pleasant and yet there was something else. Something she sensed could be dangerous. With that thought in mind she found the willpower to pull away.

"Oh no, sweetheart. Don't pull away!" He grasped her by the shoulders again, sensing her response to him. He'd soon take her mind off toiling in this godforsaken tavern. She needed him, even if she didn't realize it. "Let's not waste one precious moment of the morning." In all his associations with the fairer sex he'd learned that they more often than not adored a strong, compelling man. One who would literally carry them off. Well, he was more than willing to do just that if need be.

"Sir . . ."

He silenced her, touching his finger to her lips. "Lovemaking can be very enticing before breakfast. It stimulates the appetite." He accompanied his words with a bold caress. Then, with a self-assured grin, he positioned one arm behind her knees the other at her hips to sweep her up into his arms.

"Sir!" Sabrina said again, struggling against him. A

19

kiss was just a kiss, but she was outraged by his assumption that she could be bedded so easily. Even her father-in-law's most daring customers had never been so impudent. "Leave me be!" Though she meant what she said he seemed amused by her angry outburst as if he didn't take her answer seriously. Soft laughter met her protests as he tightened his hold. Though the touch of his hands set her blood afire, Sabrina pushed hard against his chest until he set her down.

"Don't tell me no. There's no sense in playing coy." He was tiring of her game when he knew she felt otherwise. Even the pounding of her pulse at her temples betrayed her. "I want you. By your response to my kiss, I know you want me too." Taking her hand he led her towards the stairs. "Come, I've already paid for my room. I might as well make good use of it. We'll spend the whole morning making love."

"No!" Sabrina dug her heels into the wood of the floor and resisted him with every bit of strength she possessed. She'd not be treated like some tavern whore. Since she was a child she'd been cautioned against men such as he, men who thought they could have anything or anyone they wanted. Hadn't any woman ever told this rogue "no" before? Apparently not. She delighted in being the first. "No!" she said again. "Can't you understand English? N. — O. No! I have work to do if I want to keep a roof over my head."

So that was it. She was worried about money. Reaching deep into his pocket, he brought forth a handful of banknotes. "All right, if you insist on being stubborn, I'll pay you, though it's not usually my practice." At the moment she fired his blood so heatedly that he knew he had to have her at any cost.

"What?"

"Most women come quite willingly to my bed but—"

Before he could continue, Sabrina completely lost her temper. Without reflecting on her actions, she took the mop, aimed it at his head, and struck him full across the face with the sopping cloth. Then she ran from the tap-room as fast as her legs could carry her without once looking back.

Chapter Two

It was smoky inside the Four Horsemen Inn. Ross, Sheldon sat with his feet propped up on the table. The roasting mutton sizzled on a spit over an open fire giving forth a tantalizing aroma. It teased his nostrils and made him acutely aware of his hunger. He hadn't eaten breakfast and was impatient for the noon hour. His growling stomach only added to his foul mood. He was of a bad disposition at the moment. Having one's ardor cooled so abruptly by a wet slap in the face did that to a man, he reflected bitterly. And yet in all earnestness he couldn't really blame her. He had been less than gentlemanly. It was just that the pretty little gal had enchanted him. How was he to know that when she'd said "no" she'd meant it?

Closing his eyes he remembered the kiss they'd shared. Potent was the name for it. Hell, one would have thought he'd never kissed a woman before, when in truth he'd kissed a hundred or more. Even so, his reaction to her nearness had been nothing short of intoxication. Like being drunk on too much whiskey. Far more powerful than he might ever have imagined when he initiated the seduction. Her soft, yielding mouth had tasted sweet and had unleashed his desires the moment his mouth had touched hers. Oh, he had known desire before, had carelessly slaked his passion, but no young woman had ever stirred him quite so strongly so quickly. The more he thought about it, the more confounding it all became

22

and the more enticing. Forbidden fruit was just all the more desirable he supposed.

I should have moved on, he thought. He had no reason to stay at the inn any longer. His business transaction had been completed last night. Why then was he still here? The answer was simple. The woman. The golden-haired tavern keeper's daughter-in-law. Though she had scampered from the room like a wounded rabbit he had hung around the taproom all morning in hopes of catching sight of her. To make amends? Or was he more deeply drawn to her than even he would admit?

Ross shrugged it off with the reason that she was the only woman who had ever told him no. Not just told him but given her answer in such a convincing way. Even now he smarted under his humiliation. Imagine being hit in the face with a mop! He, "Cherokee" Ross Sheldon. Second only to Buffalo Bill, he now owned the largest Wild West show in the United States. He was nigh onto becoming a legend, one he hoped would not include this morning's incident.

Ross's life had been filled with adventure, since the time he was a headstrong young man rebelling against his father's stubborn domination. The youngest son of an impoverished Southern plantation owner he had left home at thirteen to make his own way. He'd spent time in the U.S. Cavalry, been an Indian fighter, a ranch hand, a gambler, and a scout. It had been a life of varied pleasures, vices, and dangers.

Then one day Ross had discovered that there was money in words. He had put down on paper the same tall tales he'd often told around a campfire. "Dime novels" they were called by snobs who looked down on them because they weren't scholarly. Ross preferred to call them just plain exciting stories that gave these Easterners a chance to live vicariously. God bless the steam press—it had enabled him to turn quite a profit from his imagination. With a character he'd called "Logan

Hunter," a latterday Robin Hood who dressed all in black and "Clem Vickery," a sheriff from Colorado, he'd soon saved up a reasonable amount of cash. Most men would have been satisfied, but not Ross. It was just the horns, and he wanted the whole steer.

Ross had decided to become a publisher, to have complete control over the characters and plots he'd scribbled down so enthusiastically. That he had an instinct for the marketplace many of his rivals lacked made him a fearsome competitor. He had a sense of fair play that earned respect. He paid authors promptly when many of his fellow publishers virtually stole manuscripts that arrived in the mail without paying the writer even a penny. He used placards and sandwich men to advertise. He bound his books with bright colors—orange—yellow, so that the buyer could easily recognize them from as far away as fifty yards. His instincts had made him a wealthy man. Entrepreneur was what he called himself now.

Ross had come to Portsmouth on a new business venture: to give his old friend, Buffalo Bill Cody, a run for his money—competition in the form of a Wild West show. Last night he had made the transaction legal by signing his name to a contract and giving Apache Ed a sizable sum for his collection of sharpshooters, cowboys, and Indians. He planned to change the name of the show to "Cherokee Ross's Wild West Show." Regardless of what it was called, he was determined to turn a losing proposition into a success. If anyone could do it, he could. And he would. It was a challenge he couldn't turn his back on, just like the yellow-haired woman. He meant to have her, to taste of her charms before he left this old New England inn.

As if his thoughts conjured her up, he looked up to see her walking slowly down the stairs. With a laugh, he leaned back, obscuring himself in the shadows. Oh, he could be a sweet-talking devil when he wanted to be. He'd win that pretty little gal's heart yet or his name wasn't Ross T. Sheldon. She intrigued him.

24

Sabrina hastened into the taproom, dust rag in hand. She had heard her father-in-law rustling about in his room and knew he'd soon be about his grumbling. How could she explain to him that the reason she'd neglected her duties this morning was because of her wariness toward one of the inn's patrons? She'd stayed upstairs making the beds as long as she could for fear she'd have to suffer the man's odious behavior again. Rufus James would never understand. He wouldn't even try. Pleasing his patrons was all he cared about. All he would do would be to scold her for her actions. And yet she was less afraid of his sharp tongue than her emotions.

The tumultuous meeting she'd had this morning with that dark-haired scoundrel had left her shaken to the core. For just a moment her defenses had been breached. The man's warm lips on hers had awakened a host of sensations she didn't want to feel, had made her remember happier days. She soothed her mind by convincing herself that it had been Seth she had been thinking about when her heart had fluttered like a bird's wing, Seth she had succumbed to, or at least his memory. Anyway, hopefully by now that dark scoundrel was gone and she would never have to see him again. With that wish on her mind she cautiously entered the room.

"Good morning!" The husky male voice startled her. "It is such a pleasure to see you again."

Sabrina whirled around. "You!"

Ross's generous mouth curved in a smile as he stood up and made a polite bow. "Allow me to introduce myself. Mr. Ross Theodore Sheldon. Just plain Ross as I prefer to be called."

Sabrina stiffened, eyeing him warily as she tried to relax the muscles of her stomach. They suddenly became knotted with tension. "Mr. Sheldon," she said icily, little caring that his name sounded vaguely familiar as it tripped from her lips. Sheldon. The name rang a distant bell. She couldn't say why nor did she care right now. Her only thought was to get away. She moved briskly towards the door, but Ross Sheldon moved with the grace of a panther to block her exit.

"Please, I know I frightened you this morning, and unknowingly and unthinkingly insulted your . . . uh . . . virtue. I just want to say I'm sorry." Though his eyes twinkled and his mouth held its usual smile, he sounded sincere.

"You're sorry."

"Doubly so if it means that every time you come into a room and I'm already there you'll run away." He held out his hand as men usually did to one another. "Can I make amends?"

What good would it do to tell him no? Obviously he didn't know the meaning of the word. Besides, Sabrina had never been one to hold a grudge.

"All right. I'll accept your apology, if you promise that it won't happen again."

"I promise not to ravish you." His teeth were a glow of white, contrasting sharply with his sun-bronzed face and his dark brown hair. "You have my word."

Ravish her? By his tone he was making light of their encounter, angering her anew. She did not like his teasing manner. "Indeed you won't, as you put it, 'ravish me.'"

Once again his infuriating self-assurance fired her temper. Moving toward the fire she grabbed up a large poker and wielded it like a weapon.

"Whoa! I'm seeking a peace treaty not war." Taking out his white handkerchief he waved it like a flag of truce.

Why did she feel compelled to fight with him and yet at the same time longed for . . . By the devil's fire, he unnerved her, confused her with contradicting emotions. Her instincts warned that he was dangerous. Even so, she put down the poker. It would not do to cause a stir in the inn by wounding him. And he had apologized. If one were to penalize every rogue and scoundrel in the town there'd scarce be anyone left to talk to.

"All right, we'll make peace. For the moment." Her hand was grasped by long, hard fingers caressingly.

26

Those fingers stirred something deep within her as he held her hand.

"There, that's much better." He'd been an impatient lout, but now that he'd been given a second chance all would be different. He would woo her with finesse.

Struggling to appear poised, she betrayed herself as she lowered her eyes from his gaze. "I'm not . . . not the kind of woman that you took me for. I . . . I don't . . ."

"I merely saw a very beautiful but lonely woman. I meant well." He stroked the palm of her hand with his fingers.

She was conscious of the redness and blisters that marked her hands. "I work very hard for my father-in-law, keeping the inn clean and serving his customers." she said, trying to explain.

He saw the evidence himself and he damned that toilmaster beneath his breath. "Your father-in-law must surely be a villain to condemn such a lovely young woman to drudgery." He meant every word he said. Were she a relative of his, he would never make her work, but would pamper her instead. Bending low, he pressed his warm mouth into the flesh of her hand in a gesture he'd learned from an English earl. It always worked to charm a lady, he thought.

Sabrina's heart pulsated as rapidly as the wings of a trapped butterfly. Though it was her hand he touched, she found herself remembering the pressure of those knowing lips against hers. She tried to ignore the sensations running down her arm as he caressed each finger with his lips.

"Surely your father-in-law has to be a dolt to underestimate the rare, beautiful jewel he is guarding." As she brought her hand down to her side, the soft material of her dress tightened across the firmness of her breasts. Ross fought against the urge to take her in his arms, knowing well at this point that too bold a gesture would rekindle the old battle.

Despite herself, Sabrina felt the corners of her mouth

turn up in a smile, wondering how Rufus James would like being called a dolt. "I'm not a jewel really."

Slyly, his voice was a caress. "I think that you are."

Sabrina put her hand up and stepped farther back. "Enough!" Oh, what a sweet-talking rogue he was. She knew his kind. Chasing after every woman he met. Hadn't he already proven to her just what he was?

Ross shrugged his shoulders. Perhaps this one was going to take more time than he thought. "I've told you my name, but you've not told me yours," he said conversationally.

"Mrs. James." She tried to effect a proper, respectful tone.

"Missus. Now that's an unusual first name. Don't know as how I've heard it before."

His grin was infectious. Sabrina felt her resolve to maintain an icy aloofness thawing. "Sabrina. Sabrina James."

"Sabrina! Sabrina." The name tripped smoothly from his tongue. "Sabrina. I like it. Somehow it suits you."

"It's my mother's middle name." The light from the window danced on his strong cheekbones and Sabrina stared, fascinated at the way the sun played across his boldly carved nose and hard jawline. A ruggedly handsome face. She couldn't help but be curious about him, but she didn't want to ask prying questions.

"Your mother's name." He hadn't counted on her having a meddling mother nearby. That might throw a cog in the wheel of his plans. The father-in-law was bad enough but a mother . . . "Tell me about her." He winced. "Does she live here at the inn?"

"No." She let out her breath in a long-drawn-out sigh. "My mother is dead. She died eight years ago of a fever."

"Oh!" He felt a twinge of guilt at his prior thought. "I'm sorry." He really was, knowing how gut-wrenchingly sad it was to lose one's mother. Perhaps if his mother had been alive he never would have left home. "Your mother as well as your husband lost to you. Poor little gal."

"I have no family."

"So you live here with your father-in-law, or so you said."

"Yes." Sabrina's brows drew together in a frown, an expression Ross couldn't help but notice. "He took me in when my husband died because I had no place to go." She had too much pride to tell him any more. Even so, the slight frown tugging at the corners of her mouth gave her away.

So, she isn't happy here, he thought. After seeing the sour face on her father-in-law he wasn't surprised. I bet the old bastard is hell to live with, he mused. "How kind of him," he said. He couldn't keep the sarcasm from his voice.

Sabrina answered simply, "Yes, it was."

"Mmmhmm . . ." Ross was having some thoughts of his own about the situation. There was no doubt that that long-nosed innkeeper father-in-law of hers made her work her fingers to the bone. He had already seen evidence of that. Knowing that, however, just might make it easier for Ross to win this lovely young woman. Oh, he didn't want a permanent relationship. He wasn't ready to settle down and get married just yet. He had too many things to do and too much money invested to take on a bride right now.

Buffalo Bill Cody had made that mistake and his wife had become a thorn in his side every hour of the day. She didn't want him to do this and she didn't want him to do that. That's the way women were once they'd put a bridle on a man. Bill's wife cried and carried on every time he had to be away from her and his daughter. Ross was sure that Cody's marriage would eventually end in divorce and he wanted none of that. When he married he wanted to be sure that it would last and that he and his bride would be compatible. She had to be an easygoing sort of woman without even a sign of a temper.

Ross smiled as he remembered Sabrina James hitting

him with that wet mop. Even-tempered? Didn't seem so. This young woman was certainly pleasant enough to look upon, however, and he had a sneaking suspicion she could thrill him to death in the bedroom if he could ever convince her that she really needed his lovemaking as much as he needed hers. He knew enough about women to recognize the ones that were liquid fire when they were aroused. He'd spark that fire he saw smoldering in her eyes. Looking up to appraise her he suddenly was reawakened to their conversation.

"He could have turned me away," Sabrina was saying. Despite the harsh treatment she sometimes suffered at her father-in-law's hands she felt the need to defend him. "But I don't want to talk about me." She didn't want him to know how bleak and uninteresting her life had been the past few years. Waiting, always waiting for her husband's return. Strange, but as she looked back on it now she realized that she had often been lonely even when Seth was alive, for he had spent many months away from her, out at sea. Then his death had thrown her into such depression that she had taken to her bed for weeks, until finally the landlord had thrown her out and she'd had no place to lay her head. She didn't even want to think about that now. "Tell me about yourself."

"Okay!" It was just the chance he had been waiting for. Ross Sheldon was not a man of feigned modesty. Never had been. He figured if a person didn't "toot his own bugle" no one else would do it for him. Taking Sabrina's hand, Ross pulled her toward a row of chairs. "Sit here." When she hesitated, eyeing him warily, he said, "I made a promise and I always honor my peace treaties. Have from the days when I was an Indian scout. I'll be as circumspect as a Sunday school teacher."

Pulling up the back of her skirt just enough to make sitting more comfortable, Sabrina settled herself beside him. "Let me begin by asking you where you are from." she said softly.

"Georgia originally. I was born there. I was only thirteen when the war broke out and did nothing but carry the flag and beat a drum for a while. Eventually I moved on to the Dakotas, Wyoming, Colorado, Texas and some other territories in between."

"Out West!"

The excitement in her voice made him chuckle softly. "Yeah, out West. I've gambled, scouted, driven cattle, ridden horseback for so many days that its a wonder my legs aren't bowed. I've been shot at, done my share of shooting, and even ducked Indian arrows."

"One sunny morning another man by the name of Sam Sutton and I were out scouting along the Upper Platte River in Colorado Territory with William Cody, better known now as Buffalo Bill."

"With Buffalo Bill?" Sabrina's copper-colored eyes were as large as silver dollars. She had been listening intently, wanting to know as much about him as she could. She was truly impressed. He was certainly the most interesting man with which she had ever come in contact.

"Sure. He's been a friend of mine for a good many years. Anyway, to get on with the story . . ." He cleared his throat and continued. "This frontiersman by the name of Sam Sutton, Will, and I were mounted upon our horses with rifle, knife, and revolvers ready for any trouble we might encounter. Sam had just been hired on as a scout a few days earlier but he knew the countryside like the back of his hand. He was no upstart, but a seasoned riflemen."

"I wish I knew how to shoot a rifle. I can ride horseback, but I'm not too good with firearms."

Ross smiled. "Oh, I don't know about that. You were doing a pretty good job of sighting that broom handle a little while earlier." They both laughed. "Now where was I?" he continued. "Oh yeah. I remember now. We had been traveling for about twenty miles or so when we saw a band of twenty-five or thirty Indians emerge from a clump of trees. They were about a half a mile away from us, but riding fast. We found ourselves in a desperate situation. To surrender meant sure death."

Sabrina sat spellbound.

" 'Load up again, Sam,' I shouted as they began to circle our little trio. We had taken cover in a deep ravine." His vocal inflection made the story spring to life. "We kept up, dropping pony after pony and an occasional Indian as well. After about two hours the Indians got tired of fighting and lit fire to the prairie grass then rode off, leaving us to our doom. Or so they thought." He paused and looked her straight in the eye. "What do you think happened then?"

"I . . . I don't know."

He savored her anticipation, maintaining silence.

"Ross! Ross, don't keep me in suspense. Please tell me what happened next."

The excitement in her voice made him chuckle. "Luckily the grass near the ravine was short and not very dry, even though the smoke caused us to cough and our eyes to burn and water. Anyways, we beat at the flames with our coats and hats, praying heartily all the while."

"I can imagine."

"We formed a path for ourselves and were lucky enough to escape the encounter. The grass burned right up to the edge of the ravine then flickered and burned itself out. And here I am to tell the tale."

"Oh, my!" She couldn't help but be impressed.

"Each and everything I have done is a story in itself." He winked at her. "As a matter of fact, I have written many of them down and sold them."

"You are a writer?"

"You might say that." He squared his shoulders in a show of pride. "Have you ever heard of Logan Hunter?"

"Yes, I have. I read a book about him once. *The Daring Deeds of Logan Hunter*." Ross Sheldon, she thought, running the name over and over again in her mind. Now she knew why she recognized his name. She'd seen it on the cover of a book. "Logan Hunter's a very brave man. But you must know that, having recounted his adventures."

"Not recounted. Made up." Tapping his temple, he exclaimed, "He's my creation."

"No!" She had thought Logan Hunter was a real man and the knowledge that he wasn't disappointed her. "Then he isn't really helping the ranchers keep their lands, fighting against injustice in the West?"

"Nope." Reaching out he gently tugged at a stray golden curl. "But don't you worry your head about that. Someone is. I based him partly on fact, partly on fiction, and added a few of my personal experiences to the tale."

A sudden thought struck her. Maybe they were all fictitious characters. "And Mountain Kate and Hurricane Nell. Are they . . ."

"I'm afraid not." She wasn't the only one who took all the tall tales seriously and believed that some purely imaginary heroes were real. Perhaps because people wanted to believe in the romantic West. People needed illusions.

"Oh . . ." It was as if for just an instant he had shattered her dreams. It was nothing but a dream after all.

"Buffalo Bill is real, however, just as I said. And a friend of mine. Really." She looked so downcast he had to add that. He didn't have the heart to tell her that although William Cody existed, the stories of his prowess and heroism weren't always true to life. In fact, in his opinion, Cody could be a real pain in the ass on occasion. Stubborn. Moody. Set in his ways.

"Do you also write about Buffalo Bill?"

"No. I've let other writers carry on that legend."

She thought about that for awhile then asked, "What brought you to my father-in-law's inn?"

"Business. I just bought myself a Wild West show, one to compete with Bill's. Even though he is a friend of mine, since I bought the show he will now become a rival as well." His voice hushed to a throaty whisper. "But you would have been the reason for my trip if I'd have known you were here." He leaned towards her and might have lapsed into more sweet talk if not for the intrusion of her

33

father-in-law into the taproom. Like a windstorm blowing through paradise, Ross thought, swearing beneath his breath.

"I have to go." Sabrina bolted to her feet, looking in the direction of Rufus James. She didn't want him to embarrass her with his tongue-lashing in front of this man. Lifting up the hem of her skirt slightly, she moved in her father-in-law's direction, but she paused to look over her shoulder at Ross just long enough to bask in the warmth of his smile. She wouldn't have admitted to herself for the world how his grin affected her. Most certainly not. But it did. Nonetheless, lifting her chin, she walked with dignified grace across the room.

Sabrina could feel two pairs of eyes riveted on her as she went about her cleaning, her father-in-law's and the dark-haired scoundrel's. She tried to tell herself that the newcomer's attentions were unwanted, but she knew that to be a lie. His presence was stimulating and put a tinge of excitement into her routine day. Certainly he was a fascinating man, one who brought to mind the kind of hero she found in her books. Handsome. Bold. Daring.

"I wonder if I could convince him to take me out West with him?" Sabrina thought to herself. Everyone was looking to the West as an outlet for the landless, an escape from the law and taxes. Americans were taking to heart the tales of how bright the moon was and how far one could see from the top of the peaks on a clear night. There was no doubt about it. The west sounded like a romantic place to be alright.

And yet, a man like Ross Sheldon could mean trouble. She doubted that he had a loyal bone in his body or knew the meaning of the word *fidelity.* Tensing her lips together, she took out her frustrations on a dirty part of the floor.

"Somethin' ailing you, woman? You've scrubbed at that same spot for more than ten minutes now."

Sabrina started as her father-in-law pinched her

shoulder. "It wouldn't come out," she said quickly. As always, when he fixed his small, beady, bespectacled brown eyes on her she felt a flutter of nervousness. There was something unwholesome in the way he looked at her at times, an ugly leer which made her flesh crawl.

"Well, let it go. It's a big floor. Land sakes, woman, if you took that amount of time with every smudge you'd be here all day."

"Yes . . . of course, you are right." Sabrina didn't want to argue with him, especially not with Ross Sheldon watching. Clutching her mop she tried to sidestep her father-in-law, but he purposefully maneuvered so that they would collide. "Excuse me."

"You need to keep your head out of the clouds, Sabrina dear," he said with a forced smile, using the accident as a reason to touch her. Pretending concern, he brushed at her clothing, letting his fingers linger on her a bit too long.

Sabrina pulled away. "No harm done." The garments she was wearing were little better than rags and she scorned his miserly ways beneath her breath. "As you have said, I need to be about my work." Purposefully, she put as great a distance between them as she could, throwing all her attention to her task.

Chapter Three

Ross Sheldon watched the pretty blond tavern maid work for a long, long while. He could not help but feel a twinge of admiration. That odious ogre of a father-in-law made her toil endlessly, yet she never uttered one word of complaint. She had even defended him, for heaven's sake! If it had been up to him, he would have dumped the contents of the mop pail over the man's head. It seemed that one thing Sabrina James had was plenty of patience. He smiled, however, at her audible sigh when at last her father-in-law tired of watching her and left the room.

The old goat had eyes for her, he thought, feeling disgust at the very thought of the pockmarked man putting his hands on a woman so lovely. Father-in-law or not, there was something in the man's eyes that revealed all too clearly his true nature. He wondered how much longer Sabrina would be able to avert the innkeeper's advances.

It is none of my concern, he growled beneath his breath, and yet somehow it was. Somehow he had already marked Sabrina as his own and meant to keep it that way. If it was the last thing he did before he left, he'd see a smile turn up the corners of that soft rosebud mouth. From what he could make of her life, she needed more than a lover. She needed a guardian angel. And yet even that cadaverous father-in-law of hers hadn't been able to erase her spunk. That and not just her beauty was what interested Ross most of all.

What an unusual young woman she was, he reflected. Most women would have sulked and frowned at this life of drudgery, but not this feisty beauty. She went from room to room cleaning, washing, waxing, and dusting, humming a tune as she worked, tackling the dirt and grime as if it were a personal enemy. Moreover, she managed her tasks with a certain grace and dignity. His gaze was drawn to her slender body as she rose up on her toes, extending her reach to dust off the mantel, or bent over the mop pail. What a delightfully curved backside she had, he observed. He was aware of her grace and beauty with her every movement. She was proud. Whenever their eyes happened to meet, she squared her shoulders and lifted her chin as haughtily as a queen, as if forbidding Ross to feel sorry for her.

Lighting a cigarette, Ross watched her for a long moment. Just what kind of a woman was she? Though she had been married, there was a certain innocence in her demeanor. Her vulnerability made her all the more alluring somehow. Even so, there was a certain unaffected sensuality in the way she moved. She was a compelling combination of siren and saint.

He wondered what her husband had been like. A fumbling lout who demanded his husbandly rights when he came to her bed, or a good lover? He opted for the latter, it would make it so much easier for him if her memories of making love were pleasant. Had she loved her husband? Somehow he supposed that she would have. Sabrina James seemed the type to give her whole heart. Certainly she seemed bereft at his death. Damn the man for dying and leaving her to this.

When the cigarette had burned down to a nub, he

snuffed it out and found himself striding towards her. Damnedest thing, he thought, but he felt a sudden urge to help her, he who never put himself out unless for a profit. "Allow me," he found himself saying as he hefted a heavy pail and carried it across the room.

His sudden assistance startled Sabrina. "Thank you," she said softly, looking at him from the corner of her eye as she carefully smoothed her apron. She was going to tell him that she didn't need his help, but the words just didn't come. Maybe because she'd been hoping he'd seek out her company.

Their fingers brushed for just an instant as she reached for the handle of the bucket to regain her burden. "We must look like Jack and Jill," he said. She laughed softly, a sound he'd been waiting to hear again. He doubted she knew just how truly lovely she was when she smiled.

"Just as long as we don't fall," she answered, wondering if it was not too late for her. The magic of his masculine, commanding presense was making it harder and harder to keep her resolve. Although she knew she should have been shunning his companionship, she found herself welcoming it.

"Fall? Don't worry, I always look where I'm going," he answered with a deep-throated chuckle. Indeed, he was cautious in all facets of his life, including those of an amorous nature. That's how he'd escaped the bonds of matrimony for so long.

"Good. For I am equally cautious." Her eyes sparked with determination, giving him a silent message that she was prepared to fend off any attempts he might make at seducing her. Despite her bravado, however, she suspected that it would be all too easy to fall in love with him. He was bold, exciting, and more than just a little mesmerizing. She was already feeling the pull of his charm in that most secret place in her heart. She would have to be wary or so she told herself over and over again.

Throughout the rest of the day into late afternoon, Ross gave aid, carrying buckets, emptying out the dirty water and filling them with clean. He even located another broom and moved it briskly over the wooden floor. He told himself that his sudden act of gallantry was because he had tarried with her this morning and thus was partly responsible for her tasks not getting done promptly, but that was an untruth. Damned if it wasn't just because he liked her company and would garner that luxury even if it meant helping her work.

Hoping to amuse her, Ross told her stories about his travels as they spent the time together side by side. He basked in the warmth of her laughter.

"A smile becomes you, sets your pretty little face all aglow," he whispered. "You should smile more often."

"Haven't had much reason to until —" She blushed, realizing that she had nearly said, "until you came along." Certainly he'd transformed today into something special. The only thing that saddened her was the knowledge that his being here wasn't permanent. He could leave tomorrow and she would never see him again. Unless . . . Once again the thought of going with him tugged at her brain, but she quickly rejected it. No, if she was going to escape her father-in-law's domineering presence it would have to be on her own.

"Haven't had much reason to smile," he was saying, "then I guess I'll have to change all that." Though he spoke lightly, there was a seriousness in his eyes that caused an odd quaking in the pit of Sabrina's stomach. For a long moment she stared at him in disconcerted silence, not knowing exactly what to do or say.

I should tell him I do not have time to be in his company, tell him firmly and be done with it, Sabrina thought. Hadn't he proven to her at their first meeting just what it was that he wanted from a woman? Ross Sheldon wanted more from her than just companionship, of that she was quite sure. She was not some foolish, untried woman who didn't know the workings of such a man's mind. Joining together in bed was foremost on a man's thoughts when he was with a woman. Even Seth had been driven by such urges.

I must be wary of spending too much time with him. He wasn't the kind of man to give her any permanency in her life. Exciting though he might be, he was a wanderer. If she wasn't careful he might break her heart. Sabrina gave herself some very good advice. Still, when they parted and Ross told her that he would see her in the taproom later on in the evening she didn't protest. She felt decidedly light of heart.

Chapter Four

The taproom was thick with smoke. Firelight danced and sparked, illuminating the faces of the inn's patrons as if through a fog. The room was filled to overflowing with the typical boisterous Saturday night crowd. The laughter and chatter was so deafening that Sabrina could barely concentrate on her own thoughts. It was just the kind of evening she detested, for she knew what was to follow. The assemblage of louts would grope, fondle, and stare, yet she would not be allowed the privilege of slapping their wandering hands. The only thing she could do was to try to stay out of their way.

Her father-in-law scurried from table to table then back to the door, personally greeting his most favored customers. "Sabrina! Girl, don't just stand there gawking! Bring our special wine for my friends," he barked out by way of a command as he led a trio of well-dressed men to their favorite table near the roaring fire.

Sabrina took a deep breath, filled several glasses with the pungent-smelling red liquid, and, balancing them on a tray, glanced apprehensively towards a table of thirsty, rowdy men. As she passed their table, she managed to dodge their pinches and pats and came unmolested to her father-in-law's side.

"Here, sirs." She recognized one of the men at once,

a particularly loathsome man of wealth who had given her a devil of a time when last he was in the tavern. Tonight he was watching her with more than usual intent, so much so that one might have thought he'd never seen her before. It made her very uneasy.

"You are my very best patron, John Travers. There isn't anything I won't give you if it is in my power," Rufus James was saying. From his tone of voice and the way his eyes touched on Sabrina, it seemed as if she was included in the offer.

"I know exactly what I want and I will have it later." Though he was not specific, Sabrina knew exactly what the man meant. Because of her father-in-law's words this man was going to be troublesome tonight. She just knew it. As she walked away, she cast a worried glance over her shoulder to find her father-in-law staring after her with a speculative expression.

Cups, mugs, and glasses were filled and refilled. Throughout the evening as she carried the trays back and forth she could feel the Travers's gaze on her, but purposefully ignored eye contact with him lest she give him any kind of encouragement. And all the while she looked for Ross Sheldon, disappointed at not seeing him. She felt a flicker of thwarted expectation as the thought came to mind that he might have taken his leave of the inn. Would he? Without saying good-bye?

"You foolish girl," she scolded herself. "Did you really think he cared?" Ross Sheldon had his own exciting life to live. He would never give a second thought to some tavern maid. That opinion only reinforced her notion that the only person one could count on was oneself. Such a view on life had kept her strong during the days at the orphanage, through the turbulent years after her husband's death, and now during these times when she had so few coins to rub together. Hard times had made her a survivor.

Tonight Sabrina was too busy to succumb to her emotions and disappointment at not seeing Ross. As usual, the taproom's patrons kept her busy. Not only were wine glasses, ale glasses, tankards, and whiskey mugs washed and refilled over and over again, but there was food to clean up from both the floor and tables.

Half the evening had passed, and the dark-beamed taproom was already in a shambles. Spilled liquor and food was everywhere. Patrons warbled lewd songs, sprawled upon their benches, or snored as they cradled their heads on their hands. Then, temporarily awakened, they lapsed into their revelry again. The only time Sabrina felt relief was when she watched patrons drag themselves from the tavern. She tried to amuse herself by keeping track of the most annoying customers.

The one she thought of as the Pincher had thankfully passed out beneath one of the tables. The Belcher was on his seventh tankard of ale, making another loud show of appreciation. The Slosher had spilled another mug of whiskey. The Giggler was laughing uproariously at another whispered tale. The Miser was arguing once more with her father-in-law over his bill.

Soon there were only a few patrons left. Sabrina was about to retreat to her haven upstairs when a golden-haired, immaculately dressed gentleman deterred her as she sought to leave.

"Come, sit beside me. Just for a few minutes," he said, taking her hand as she brushed by his table.

"I have much to do, sir—" Sabrina was wary, leery of his intent. Hastily she pulled her hand away.

"A penny for your ear. That's all I desire of you. I want someone to listen." The man's words were a bit slurred. "By the look of you, it appears you might be a girl with a bit of sympathy for a man wounded by life's arrows." Before she could protest he had thrust a handful of coins into her palm and she, seeing the lonely look in his eyes, did not move away.

"Well, perhaps I can spare a moment." Though she tried to return the coins, he shook his head. Sabrina clutched it tightly. Every bit of money meant she could leave her father-in-law all the sooner. A welcome boon. She smiled in appreciation, noting how pleasant this fellow was to look upon. Not handsome really, but pleasing to the eye in a boyish way. She sat down with the gentleman and prepared to listen.

"Allow me to introduce myself. I am Jonathan Colt. The same family as those of the gunmaker." He raised his finely arched golden brows in expectation.

"Sabrina. Sabrina James."

"A lovely name which suits you to a T. His eyes swept over her, from the tips of her shoes to the top of her blond hair, but with gentle appraisal. "What is a young woman like you doing here?"

"My father-in-law owns the inn."

"I see." He looked deep into the depths of his glass, swirling the liquid around. "I have been watching you, my dear miss. The expression on your face reveals my own misery. That's why I called you over. To spill out my own pain and in turn listen to yours. Please tell me why you are so sad."

Sabrina didn't understand why, but she opened up to him. "I am a widow, dependent on my father-in-law for my very sustenance." Clenching her hands, she couldn't hide her tears. "I hate working here, but I have to. And that, Mr. Colt, is the reason for my frown." Remembering that he had spoken of his own unhappiness, she added, "And you?"

"I've spent my life living up to my father's ideals and have fallen far short, I fear. So many wasted years. Only now have I realized my mistake and the revelation makes of me a morose man." As if seeking comfort, he took her hand and squeezed it, "And now I feel cheated, though it was my own foolishness and cowardice that was the cause. I always let him tell me what to do. I do not want to manage a firearms factory."

"It is never too late to change one's mind." Reassuringly Sabrina returned the pressure of his hand. "You are still young with a great many years to be lived, just the way you want to live them." She might have said more if not for her father-in-law's shout.

"Sabrina! Sabrina!"

Anxious to avoid a scene, she hastily left Jonathan's side to answer Rufus's call, but as soon as Sabrina came to her father-in-law's side, he grabbed her hand and pried her fingers open none too gently. "So, holding out on me." The coins were an obvious sign of her supposed guilt.

"The money is not for ale, wine, or whiskey but for—"

"Whoring!" At that moment his face twisted in anger. She wondered again how a man such as he could have ever sired a son as gentle and peaceful as Seth had been.

"No! Never that, but since you seem to feel free to promise my services to others, I thought it only wise to take a few coins to listen to a man's woes," she answered coldly.

"It is my taproom and thus my money." Rufus James's eyes hardened into two heated coals as he glared at her.

"Your money be damned. I know what's stirring in your head, you panderer. Do you think I am so stupid that I did not sense your meaning to that fool in there?" She gestured to Travers. "Well, I'm not for sale."

"These coins say differently," he rasped.

"They are for a few moments of conversation and nothing more." Sabrina put her hands behind her back, determined that he would not have the coins.

"Hand them over. I handle all of the money in this place." Grasping her wrists, he tried to wrench the money free.

45

"No!" Sabrina clutched the coins tightly. It was the principal of the matter and not the money that made her stubborn. "Not until you treat me with the dignity and respect that's due the widow of your son."

"Widow! How you play up on your circumstances as if you were a saint. Well, I'm not at all certain that you are as innocent as you pretend."

Gripping her with both hands, he brought her jarringly against his bony frame. As she struggled in humiliation, close to him, Sabrina freed one hand and gave him a resounding slap, then without waiting for his reaction, she turned on her heel and hastened for the safety and solace of the wine cellar. It was the one place she could be alone until she could gather her wits. She looked nervously back over her shoulder several times to see if her father-in-law were in persuit. That he did did not pursue her meant she'd won the battle, but only for the moment. No doubt it would be war with him from now on.

She almost stumbled on the last step as she looked back to reassure herself that she had not been followed. She then heard a low throaty laugh.

"Ah, so there you are . . ."

Turning abruptly, she saw Travers hovering in the doorway. "Yes, here I am, she answered, adroitly dodging his grasping hands. John Travers obviously knew she'd have to come here eventually. "Now if you please—"

"Old Rufe giving you a bad time of it, girl?"

"Girl! Oh, how she hated to be called that. As if she were nothing more than an indentured servant. But perhaps in her father-in-law's eyes that was exactly what she was. Trying to maintain her poise, she said, "I do not mean to be rude, sir, but it is none of your business what transpires between my husband's father and myself." She turned to leave, but his hand barred her way. He gripped her arm tightly. "Let me go!" she commanded, but he wouldn't release her so easily.

46

"You're a real little beauty, do you know that?" he said in a low tone. "Much too haughty, though. It wouldn't hurt you none to be a little more friendly. After all, I do put more than a few dollars in old Rufus's coffers." His hand sneaked up quickly to pull the kerchief from her head, sending her golden hair tumbling around her shoulders. He used her shining tresses to hold her captive, moving his face closer. "Yet, I guess as beholden as you are to your father-in-law, you can't afford to be too uppity."

Sabrina's cheeks burned at the insinuation that she was a charity case. Though she lashed out at her captor, however, he held her so tightly that she was as helpless as a mouse cornered by a tabby.

"Once more, I ask you to let me go. I'll shout for help if you don't leave me be." Her unease mounted, but she tried to keep her shaky voice calm.

"I'm not hurting you, honey. Just want to enjoy myself, that's all. A little kiss . . ."

The very idea was revolting. "Please!" His breath reeked of whiskey and tobacco. Sabrina twisted and turned in his punishing embrace, but couldn't break free.

"Way I look at it, you don't have much choice. Lord knows old Rufus doesn't give a damn. No one to come to your rescue as I see it."

"Is that so?" asked a dangerously low voice. "Well then, mister, you had better think again."

Sabrina gasped at the sound of Ross's voice slicing through the darkness. She felt a rush of relief.

"Turn her loose." Ross's gaze remained locked on Sabrina, even as he spoke to her tormentor. "Let her go or so help me I'll break every bone in your slimy body." His fury was barely suppressed. "I'll count to three. One . . . two . . ."

Something in Ross's eyes must have given the other man warning, for he loosened his hold, putting his hands at his side. Instead of leaving peacefully, how-

47

ever, he made the fatal mistake of putting up his fists. Lunging out, he connected with Ross's chest, but the punch seemingly harmed him more than it did Ross. He rubbed his fingers with a wheeze of pain, a squeak that got much louder as Ross lashed out with a blow to the chin, sending the other man back against the cellar wall.

"That's just a sample of what I'll give you if you ever bother this lady again. Do you understand me?" Travers nodded, his eyes frightened. "Then get your fat ass out of here." To help him along, Ross aimed the toe of his well-polished boot at the man's backside, sending him scurrying up the wooden steps. He turned to Sabrina. "Are you all right?" His strong fingers brushed her arm, as lightly as a night breeze.

"Yes."

No one had ever fought for her honor before, not even her husband. How could she help but feel grateful and—if the truth be known—flattered? Any last shred of doubt she might have felt about him at their first encounter disappeared as quickly as the morning mist.

"He was a downright unpleasant fellow. Didn't seem to want to turn you loose." A low whistle escaped his lips. "Hmm. I'm beginning to see why you hit me in the face with the mop, Sabrina. Now that I understand what you're up against I don't blame you. Fact is, I made myself look just about as oafish as that bloated bullfrog I suppose."

"Yes, I suppose you did."

He chuckled at her blatant honesty. "I did, and I am sorry." He gathered her into a protective embrace. "Well, with me around, little gal, he won't come near you again."

She shivered inadvertently against him. He felt so warm, so strong, that she melted into his embrace, putting her arm around his neck and laying her head against his broad chest. For the moment she hovered

48

in the security of his arms and marveled at just how right it felt.

As to Sabrina's attacker, John Travers gulped and moved with some difficulty, almost falling over his own feet in an effort to get away from the man he thought must surely be insane. The toe of Ross's boot to his backside had brought more humiliation than pain, but he still rubbed that injured part as he looked back.

As silently as possible, he staggered up the cellar steps, pulled his coat collar up around his throbbing jaw and disappeared into the dark night without stopping to say anything to Rufus.

The inn's patrons were all gone now. Rufus stood with his back to the fireplace, rubbing his hands together as if gleefully appraising the evening's profits. He had not seen John Travers slip silently out of the side door, nor Ross and Sabrina as they slowly made their way to where he stood.

"Ross!" Sensing his intent, Sabrina knew a moment of hesitation.

"I'll handle this." Ross was adamant. He had a thing or two to say to Sabrina's father-in-law. With a nod to Sabrina, who was standing near the staircase leading to the second story of the inn, he said, "You stay here." Ross did not want to wait until tomorrow to confront Rufus. He figured the time to take care of this situation was right now.

Walking briskly over to Rufus, he got right to the point. "I have something to say to you!"

Startled by the sound of a voice behind him, Rufus James whirled around. "What the devil? Where did you come from? Out of thin air?"

"Let's just say I materialized at an opportune time."

"Sneaking up behind me is what you mean!" Rufus didn't even try to hide his dislike of the brash young fellow. "Well, say your piece and then leave me be. It's late."

"All right, I'll get right to the point. I saw the way

you treated your daughter-in-law tonight. What the devil is going on around here?"

"None of your business!"

Ross took a threatening step forward. "I'm making it my business. Why are you treating Sabrina in such a shabby manner?"

Rufus's eyes focused on the floor. Without looking up, Rufus mumbled something Ross did not understand, then proceeded to talk very rapidly.

"What has Sabrina been telling you about me? Her words are all lies. They are lies I tell you! Rufus's face and neck were beginning to turn a bright red. His eyes darted to where Sabrina stood, and he sneered.

Ross touched the tavern owners arm in a not-so-gentle squeeze. "Sabrina has never complained to me. Don't be looking at her. I watched you. I saw you manhandle her."

"You saw?" Rufus paled.

"I saw!"

There was a long moment of silence. "I've been good to Sabrina. I took her in after my son's death at sea. I give her food, a bed, the warmth of a fire. What more can I do?"

Ross squared his shoulders. "You can start treating her like the lady she is." A lady who guarded her virtue. A wry smile passed momentarily over Ross's lips as he almost felt the wet mop against his face.

"Lady? Lady!" Rufus James guffawed suggestively. "She's been sneaking off at night, lifting her skirts and gathering a few coins for herself." He paused to lick his thin lips. "That's what she's been doing while I pay the bills and do most of the work. I was only trying to get my fair share."

"Bullshit!" Ross raised his hands into fists. "Why in the name of God are you trying to convince me that white is black?" Only by the greatest of effort could he maintain his self-control. "You know perfectly well that Sabrina is not a whore."

"She is! She is."

"She's a proper widow woman who behaves exactly as society expects her to behave."

Sabrina moved from the foot of the staircase in the kitchen which led to the second story of the inn closer to the pantry door. From her new position, she was well out of sight but could hear every word the two arguing men uttered. Her heart jumped with joy at Ross's next statement.

Taking Rufus by his coat lapels, Ross lifted the man halfway off the floor, forcing him to look into his eyes. "Now, you listen to me, Rufus James, and listen well. From now on I am appointing myself Sabrina's protector. I'll not be far from her and I'll be watching you every minute. If you don't start treating her with the respect she deserves, you will personally answer to me, and I will take Sabrina so far away from here that you will never find her." Placing Rufus's feet once more upon the floor, he concluded, "Do you understand?" He punctuated each word with a stab of his index finger against Rufus's chest.

From Ross's statement, Sabrina concluded that Ross intended to stay for a very, very long time. Her protector. It had a nice ring. Perhaps he could be the man with which she spent the rest of her life. Certainly she experienced quivering feelings every time he touched her. Was she in love with him? Not yet, for love was a thing that sprouted and took root, growing and growing with the years. But she was well on her way.

Putting her fingers to her lips she softly spoke his name. "Ross!" She had been wrong in thinking that he was a scoundrel. He couldn't be, then fight for her this way. Not once but twice. He had simply not understood the kind of woman she was. Now that he knew, however, he had appointed himself her guardian angel.

She would bet that Rufus would be as obsequious as

a lap dog from now on. At least while Ross was around. Nor would her father-in-law turn Ross out. He'd be too intimidated. After all, Ross had a room at the inn and had placed a lot of money into Rufus's pocket. He was also a published author and the new owner of "Apache Ed's Wild West Show"—a respected and famous man. Rufus never crossed a wealthy patron. Ross would be no exception.

Sabrina knew that as long as Ross was around she would be safe and secure and that gave her a warm glow. Now she had to figure out a way to keep Ross here as long as she could, at least until their feelings for each other had time to grow. It was the first time in a long time that Sabrina had felt truly happy. When Ross reached Sabrina's side, once more she was leaning against a post at the foot of the stair leading to the second floor where he had left her. He had no idea that she had overheard every word he had said to Rufus, but he did notice her smile.

"You look mighty pretty when you curve up your lips that way. Mighty pretty."

He put his hand beneath her chin to to turn her face upward. They silently stood there for a moment looking into each other's eyes. Then one of her most delightful smiles dimpled up at him and a matching grin spread across his face from ear to ear. He kissed her on the cheek.

"Care for an escort, ma'am?" he asked.

"I'd like that, sir," she responded immediately. Like two people walking in a dream, they climbed the stairs hand in hand.

Tonight there would be no need for Sabrina to be carried away vicariously. She would have no reason to read a dime novel. She had the writer of such novels right here beside her.

Chapter Five

Ross and Sabrina sat on the top step of the long flight of stairs, his arm securely wrapped around her slim shoulders. "You're really quite a woman, do you know that, little gal?" He gave her shoulders a gentle squeeze. He was thinking what a treasure she would be for the right man. "I'll bet old John Travers will think long and hard before he gets smart with you again."

"I couldn't have held out much longer if you hadn't shown up when you did." Her copper eyes grew wide with admiration as she laid her head gently on his shoulder. "I really didn't do it all alone. But I still haven't figured out how you knew that I was being attacked in the wine cellar." Her face flushed as she looked up at him. "Anyway, thank you for rescuing me."

Her hair tumbled into her eyes and he reached up to brush it away, enjoying the chance to leisurely touch her. "When we parted earlier in the day I told you I would be at the tavern later in the evening."

"Yes, I remember." His fingers were doing delicious things to her temple, the slow stroking sending warm shivers up her spine. "I must confess that I was very disappointed when you didn't show up."

"Oh?" Ross was pleased by this admission, his mouth twisting into a grin at her slight confession. "I had to go to town to sign a few more papers to close the deal on the Wild West show. On the way back the carriage broke an

53

axle. By the time I got to the livery stable to rent another, it was getting late. I arrived at the inn just in time, however, to see Rufus treating you so roughly. He was trying to extract the coins from your hand." He swore beneath his breath as the picture flashed before his eyes. Damn the man! It was all Ross could do to keep from kicking the hell out of the arrogant bastard. "When you slapped him and started down the stairs, I almost shouted out loud."

"He accused me of trying to cheat him. I wouldn't —"

"Of course not!" Indignation that she had been so wrongly accused roiled in his belly. "He had no right to say those terrible things to you."

"He feeds me and gives me a bed. It makes him think he has the right. I suppose most people would think that it does."

Ross clenched his fists. "I don't!" If only he could take her away from here, he thought, quickly banishing such a dangerous thought from his mind. He was a loner, always had been, always would be.

Sabrina sighed, leaning her head on his shoulder. "He always has been a bully and a miser, but he kept it hidden until after my husband died. Then when I was helpless he showed his true colors."

"A real gentleman!" Ross said snidely. "Well, I'm glad you slapped him, Sabree. If you ask me he's deserved that slap for a hell of a long time." With a surge of protectiveness, he held her close against him. "Anyway, when he stormed out of the kitchen I had a sneaking suspicion that something was afoot. I saw that fat little man on your trail and followed you down the stairs."

Sabrina raised her head from his shoulder. It had been so long since she'd had someone who cared. "Oh, Ross, you will never never know how glad I was to see you." She lowered her eyelids shyly. "Thank you . . . thank you again for that daring rescue."

His now-familiar grin slashed from ear to ear. "Oh, it was nothing." Even so, he puffed out his chest with pride. Certainly she made him feel masculine and very, very needed. "You need a man to protect you, Sabree. There are too many coyotes rovin' loose out there, just waitin' to get into trouble. A woman as lovely as you are should have someone around," he blurted, then stiffened. Damned if this woman didn't bring out dangerous feelings. "You . . . you need a husband," he quickly amended.

A husband. Sabrina was startled. She could hardly believe her ears. He was talking marriage. He certainly was revealing a new side to his character that she hadn't glimpsed before. A gentle, protective side. Was it possible that all Ross Sheldon needed was a good woman to round off some of his rough edges? For just a moment she wondered what it would be like to have him by her side forever and found the thought very pleasing.

"Every woman is looking for the right man," she whispered, hoping he would carry on with the subject.

"Yeah. Well . . ." Ross swallowed so hard he nearly choked. He hadn't been thinking of himself as the bridegroom when he'd made that statement. He could have kicked himself in the backside for opening his big mouth. What he had meant was that a pretty single woman working in a tavern was bound to have problems with unscrupulous men if there wasn't a man to answer to.

"Ross." Seeking his warmth, Sabrina snuggled even closer into his arms.

"Sabree . . ."

Ross recognized the dangerous situation he was in. A few more moments of this and he'd do something foolish. Say something silly. Get himself in a hell of a pickle. Do something he would regret for the rest of his life. Hell, no! He wouldn't be tied down. With determination, he reached out to take her hands in his. They were cold as ice.

"It's chilly out here in the hall." Being here alone with her was giving him strange ideas. They'd damn well better go somewhere else. "What you need is a nice warm fire. We'll go downstairs."

"No. Please." Sabrina was quick to protest. "I just don't feel like being under my father-in-law's scrutiny again."

"Then I'll escort you to your room."

Ross had gained Sabrina's trust by his heroic rescue and gentlemanly manner, otherwise she wouldn't have said, "We could go to yours. You could tell me some stories and we could just talk." She didn't want to be alone. She wanted his company for at least a little while.

"My room?" He stiffened. For a woman who had hit him in the face with a mop for even daring to make such a suggestion she surprised him. He appraised her, but finding no coquettishness in her eyes, no hint of a seductive smile, he realized she just wanted company. Even so, he was hesitant. If he was smart he'd run as far away as he could. "Don't think it would be a good idea."

She misunderstood. She'd made such a show of thinking him to be a cad that he was going overboard to prove his gentlemanly qualities. But how could she doubt him after tonight? "Oh, Ross, I trust you. I do."

But did he trust himself? He wasn't at all sure that he did. How ironic he thought, that a few hours ago he would have been about as happy as a bear in a honeycomb if she had made that same suggestion. He'd wanted to bed her right from the moment he'd laid eyes on her. But now, knowing her situation here, the way she had been mistreated by her father-in-law, made everything different. He didn't want to hurt her. And yet, he did relish her company.

"Well now . . . honey." He dropped her hand, stood up, and fumbled in his pocket for his key. Funny, but his fingers were trembling. Because he could feel the magnetism that seemed to be pulling them together? "Ah, here it is." He effected his usual bravado when trying to hide his true feelings. "I was afraid I might have lost it when I delivered that uppercut to old butterball's chin."

Dangling the key between his first finger and thumb, he paused for just a moment, wondering if he ought to have second thoughts about this. His manly pride wouldn't let him back down. "Come on, we'll take a stroll. It's the third room on the left."

"Yes, I know." Sabrina also knew exactly what that room looked like even before they entered. She made it up every morning, admiring this particular room which now took on a special warmth to her as she stepped through the doorway. Ross's things scattered about gave it a homey touch. Several hats, boots, and a decorative saddle on a stool by the fireplace.

"Well, here we are."

It was a spacious room with a stone fireplace at one end, a big brass bed at the other. There was a gold-patterned overstuffed sofa and matching chair, a round table, and two chairs. The carpet was soft and warm beneath her feet as she gave in to Ross's invitation and took off her shoes. The red-striped wall paper gave the room a warm glow.

"I'll put another log on the fire." Ross tried to keep his eyes from looking in the direction of the bed. From the moment they had entered the room he had been strangely nervous. He'd have to be certain to keep at least an arm's length away from her. And keep his mind on other things besides her gentle curves. "Make yourself comfortable."

Sabrina did, slowly lowering herself upon the gold sofa, which felt like heaven after a long day and night's work. As Ross busied himself, she let her eyes scan the room. Each and every time she changed the sheets on that big brass bed she remembered sleeping on just such a feathered mattress with Seth. She had felt so secure then, so content. A voice whispering in her ear told her she could feel that same happiness again.

"I've always loved this room." Her room was just a hole in the wall, a converted broom closet, as a matter of fact, with furniture that consisted of a cot with a cotton-stuffed mattress, a chest for her clothing, a nightstand with an oil lamp, and two crates that acted as a make-shift bookcase. Her cubbyhole was nearly too small for all the books she had collected. Her uncle had threatened to throw them out, but to Sabrina they had been treasures that she just wouldn't give up. She had solved the problem of space by stacking them under the bed.

Ross finished his putterings by the fireplace and smoothed the cushions on the stuffed chair. Brushing off his pants, he took a seat. He cleared his throat. "Well, here we are," he said, leaning back.

Son of a gun! If he didn't suddenly feel tongue-tied. He, Ross Sheldon, the best damned talker in the West. For the life of him, he didn't know what to say. Just what the hell did a man say to a woman to make conversation? Only time he'd done much talking to the fairer sex was when he was wooing them into bed. But he didn't want to do that to Sabrina, at least not tonight. She'd had quite an evening and he didn't want to add to her woes. And much more than that, she had said she trusted him.

"Yes, here we are . . ." Sabrina had wanted him to sit beside her, but instead he had distanced himself. He was a strange man, she thought. Snuggling and handholding one moment, aloof and circumspect the next. A bold, brash talkative adventurer in one instant, withdrawn and quiet within the blinking of an eye. A complex man. How could she have ever thought to judge him so quickly?

"The fire. It's warm." Ross crossed his arms across his chest, figuring it to be the safest place for them. His hands itched to touch her. He was aware of her nearness in every nerve, every sinew in his body. So much for his self-control.

"It makes the room cozy." She wanted him to come sit beside her, to hold her close again, but didn't want to seem brazen. "I suppose you have a great deal of experience, starting fires that is. Must get awfully cold out on the prairie."

"Damned cold at night. So cold that there are times when you have to cut a hole in the ice for a drink of water. Times when it gets so chilled you find yourself hugging your horse just for body warmth. Times like that a man swears off the roaming life. Yep, it gets cold."

"Then you must appreciate the comforts of the inn."

"Yes and no. There's a certain freedom to be had out on the prairie. A man finds himself missing it the moment he's left." He had a faraway look in his eye as he remembered the rocks, grass, trees, and mountains he'd left behind. He wasn't sure he could ever be happy living in the East.

"Then you want to go back?"

Nodding his dark head, he crossed one leg above the other knee. "Yep!"

"But not too soon, I hope." She knew she shouldn't reveal her feelings this quickly but she couldn't help it.

"Not too soon."

They chattered away. There was a blossoming, easy relationship between them as if they had never had that first confrontation. At first, Ross told a few stories, but then the mood changed to a more reflective one. Sabrina revealed to Ross the difficult days at the orphanage after the death of her mother, and he, relating to her emotions, told her about the death of his own mother when he was little more than just a boy.

"Strange. You're the first person I've ever told that story to," he whispered. Opening up his heart was not a thing he did often or easily, and yet he had with her. Now why was that?

"Perhaps because you knew I'd understand." For the first time since she'd met him, Sabrina sensed the little boy inside the man. Oh, he was brave and strong, but there was a vulnerable side to him as well. A side he hid beneath his glib talk and swaggering.

They continued to bask in the warmth of each other's companionship for a long time — longer than either one of them realized. Neither one was willing to break the

59

spell. Ross knew he was playing with fire, knew it could prove to be sheer insanity to allow himself to have such feelings for this young woman, but somehow he couldn't keep away from the flame. He should have sent her off, but he couldn't take his eyes off her. He watched her hungrily, noticing the way her smile lit her whole face, the way her copper eyes would shyly meet his then flicker away. He was absolutely mesmerized by her.

"Sabrina . . ." He rose lithely to his feet to stoke the fire. When he finished, he sat down on the sofa beside her. For a long moment he stared down at her, his eyes moving tenderly over her thick lashes and full mouth. Unwillingly, he felt desire stir. Aware of the potentially dangerous, combustible situation, he reached out to touch her face. "It's late. I'd better take you back."

The look on his face thwarted any argument. Sabrina had seen that look on Seth's face often enough to know what it meant. It was time to go. "All right." Slowly, regretfully she rose to her feet. Oh, how she hated to leave and yet there wasn't any other choice. She had the feeling if she stayed a moment longer Ross's determination to remain a gentleman just might be strained to the breaking point. And yet, perhaps one day there would come a time when she wouldn't have to leave. It was a tantalizing thought as she walked side by side with Ross down the long narrow hall.

Chapter Six

From the moment the day dawned, Ross Sheldon knew it was going to be a fine one. Warm. Sunny. No hint of rain. He felt decidedly happy. There was a spring to his step as he walked across the room to put on his clothes, an intoxicating burst of happiness as he dressed. Last night with Sabrina had given him a feeling of contentment that was with him even now. It made him anxious to see her again.

Hurrying down the stairs, Ross sat down and lingered over breakfast, his eyes scanning the room for Sabrina's familiar form. When he didn't see her, he panicked, thinking the worst of old man James. His thoughts wandered down an unpleasant path whereby he envisioned that some harm had come to his lady love. Bounding to his feet, he sought out the surly man only to be coldly informed that Sabrina had gone to church. Sunday, it seemed, was the one day the old goat gave his daughter-in-law off.

"Church, huh?" Ross snorted his approval then buried his nose in a cup of coffee, waiting patiently for Sabrina's return. He wanted to spend time with her, do something to make her forget her troubles. He wanted a return of the closeness he'd felt blossoming between them when they were alone.

Drumming his fingers on the table, pacing a path across the hard wooden floor, Ross tried his best to keep himself occupied. Barely twenty-five minutes later, his patience was rewarded when Sabrina walked through the inn's front door.

"Good morning!" With a smile in his direction, Sabrina pulled off her black bonnet and coat. She looked stunning in a black skirt and stiff white blouse closed at the throat with a broach. Her hair was piled in curls atop her head with a tendril falling just in front of each ear. "What brings you downstairs this early in the day?" Ross Sheldon usually stayed abed until noon.

Ross smiled back, his eyes roaming appreciatively over her slender form. "You! Your lovely self."

"Me?" She couldn't hide the fact that she was pleased.

"Thought you might concede to spending a little time with me today," he said, casually strolling towards the door.

"Sabrina!" Rufus James seemed to materialize out of thin air, moving forward to stand like a gargoyle just a few feet away from his daughter-in-law. "It's Sunday!"

Ross was unruffled. "Indeed it is, sir. A day of rest." Ross winked at her, as if to say that he'd take care of the old fool. "By your own admission, it is Sabrina's day away from the drudgery you measure out to her." He took Sabrina's arm. "Come on, little gal. It's much too nice a day to stay here."

"Just a moment." Drawing himself up as stiffly as any preacher, Rufus James scowled. "She isn't going anywhere with you!"

Out of habit, Sabrina hesitated, used to obeying her father-in-law's commands. She wanted to go with Ross, wanted to laugh with him, be with him, but for just a moment all she could focus on were Rufus James's beady eyes which were bright with anger. Somehow he would find a way to punish her if she disobeyed him. And yet . . .

"Ah, but she is. Unless you feel that you are man enough to stop me from walking right over you if need be!" Ross took a step forward, but Rufus drew away. "Just as I thought. Come on, Sabrina." Ross walked jauntily as they pushed through the door.

Beside him, Sabrina was vibrantly aware of the hand on her back. He had wanted to be with her. That thought gave her a warm sense of well-being that chased away all fear of her father-in-law. She had been so lonely here with Rufus, but now she knew that someone cared.

It was a quiet morning without any of the usual sounds around the inn's yard. Ross was whistling as he matched Sabrina step for step. She was a damned pretty sight, he thought, noticing how the rich morning sunlight filtered through her hair turning it the color of spun gold. He noted how the bright light cast their two forms into shadows, blending into one as they turned a bend in the pathway.

"Well, now. And just what would you like to do?" Involuntarily Ross's eyes strayed towards the stables. Oh, how he would love to impress Sabrina with his daring. He always felt at his best when he was on the back of a horse.

"It's such a nice day I'd like to go for a ride," she answered, her cheeks dimpling as she made the suggestion.

It seemed like the answer to Ross's prayers. They'd go out riding and it would give him a chance to show her all the tricks he could do on a horse. He'd learned a whole string of things when he'd met up with a band of Indians traveling in Bill's show. And who could say? Perhaps he could persuade her horse to run away so that they could ride back home together. The idea sounded very pleasing.

"Sounds like just the way we should spend the day." Ross headed for the stables but Sabrina went in the opposite direction. "Sabrina?"

Her laughter was melodious. "Not horseback riding. Bicycle riding. It's how a lot of us get around here in the East." She led him to where a peculiar-looking machine lay in wait.

"I wonder if riding a bicycle is anything like riding a horse," Ross muttered beneath his breath. He had never ridden the newfangled contraption and he experienced a brief moment of insecurity. Ross's pride meant everything to him and, he didn't relish the thought of making a damn fool of himself. "Never ridden one before," he ventured cautiously.

"I have. More times than I can count." Sabrina laughed softly at his wry expression. "Whenever my father-in-law sends me far away on errands and if the weather is favorable I ride his bicycle. He tells me it's cheaper than hiring a carriage. We can borrow the neighbor boy's bicycle for you."

"Oh!" He circled the vehicle warily. It looked ominously ridiculous with a large wheel in front and a small one behind. He'd heard a great deal about the damn fool thing and read a few articles in the newspaper but never thought he'd have to ride one. Still, if the neighbor boy could do it, how could he legitimately refuse?

"Shall we?" Sabrina's eyes issued a challenge.

"Yeah, why not?" He followed her as she walked across a weed-infested field to knock on a large brown door. Amiably, the young lad that lived there gave up his bicycle for Ross's use, though Ross could have sworn he was guffawing behind his hand.

Ross carried the monstrosity back across the field, setting it down by Sabrina's machine. He contented himself in just watching her for a moment. She was using two beltlike straps of leather to secure the folds of her skirt to her legs, a bit like a man's trousers. It afforded him a brief glimpse of her ankles. Slim. Shapely. He waited as she climbed up on the contraption, surprised that she managed to be quite graceful.

64

Ross's own ascent was anything but easy and once he'd plopped down upon the seat he didn't stay there for long.

"Are you hurt?" The encounter had turned into a catastrophe for Ross.

With a violent oath he got to his feet and brushed off his clothing. "If I fall off this damned thing one more time I'll . . . I'll . . ." He didn't know just what he would do but it would be desperate. Oh, how he wished he could vent his frustration on this object of his humiliation but he wanted to keep his calm for Sabrina's sake. It certainly wasn't a bit like riding a horse. He could not inflict his will on this conglomeration of hard rubber tires and metal.

"One more time!" He felt more than a bit foolish and clumsy as he straddled the contraption again. If it was the last thing on earth he did, he would master it! After all, he'd broken the wildest, stubbornest horses. How much different could this really be?

He was soon to find out. Again and again he lost his balance and tumbled to the ground, falling on his backside, but not being a quitter, Ross got up, brushed off his pants and tried again. Patience seemed to win the day as he finally managed to stay on the bicycle for a long jaunt down the road. By the end of the afternoon he had almost become an expert.

"Care to race me to that tree and back?" He was feeling daring.

"All right!"

"I'll even give you a head start."

Sabrina felt the corners of her mouth tilting up. She was enjoying herself, having fun for the first time in ages, since Seth's death in fact. It was as if she too had been dead. There had been too many months and too many tears in between her smiles. Now things seemed to have changed. She felt different. It was as if suddenly she was coming alive. Now she had hope.

Cranking enthusiastically at the pedals, Sabrina

raced across the wide meadow that stretched in front of them. It was familiar ground to her, perhaps that was why she was more than just a bit reckless. Her eyes sparkled with competitive spirit. She wanted to win!

Ross was just as determined. The only way to make up for his humiliation earlier was to beat Sabrina to the two trees marking the finish line. His long well-muscled legs pushed the pedals in powerful bursts of energy, closing the distance between them.

"Loser forfeits a kiss," he yelled out gaily, realizing he couldn't lose on such a bet.

He was gaining on her, only a foot behind, when Sabrina looked over her shoulder. At that moment, the large front wheel of bicycle hit a bump, sending her flying.

"Sabrina!" Ross acted instinctively, hurling himself to the ground to act as a cushion. It knocked the wind out of him when she was flung into his arms, but it was a successful rescue.

"Ross!" Sabrina could hardly believe that he would risk injury to himself just to see to her safety.

Though she was a bit bruised, there was nothing broken, and she realized that this was due in no small part to Ross's daring.

"It was nothing. I've taken much worse falls from horses during Indian attacks," he quickly said, then there was silence.

They were both suddenly aware of their position, her full breasts crushed up against his chest, her hip pressed into his groin. Though his arm ached like the very devil, he was all too conscious of her slender body so close to his own.

"Sabrina!" His eyes lingered on the rise and fall of her bosom, then moved upward to the fullness of her provocative mouth. For a long moment he looked at her, then with something that sounded like a curse, Ross bent his head and his mouth claimed hers.

66

Sabrina was stunned. Not by his action, but by the potent reaction she had to his kiss. A sweet fire swept through her veins as she reached out to cling to him. She was giddily conscious of his warmth, and the faint scent of tobacco that clung to him. His touch evoked a deep longing within her. The world seemed to be whirling at a hazardous pace. With a sigh she gave herself up to those feelings.

Ross, too, was stunned. His reaction to her nearness, the acquiescence of her mouth was far more potent than he could have imagined it to be. Her mouth was so achingly soft against his that all he could think of was that he wanted to pleasure her, to share with her the tumult of his feelings. For one wild second he nearly lost his head completely.

"Sabree! Sabree!" He wanted to part her lips and explore her inner sweetness, but as reason slowly returned he reluctantly lifted his mouth from hers. "I won and that was my reward," he said, a rueful grin tugging at his lips.

"Won? You did not." Sabrina looked towards the trees. "You didn't reach the finish."

"I won just the same." If looks could start a fire she knew in that instant she could have ignited into a flame.

"Ross."

His name sounded stirringly intimate on her lips and he felt a surge of blood course through him. He wanted her so much he was aching from the wanting. It was the first time since he'd grown to manhood that he'd been with a woman for so long without it ending up in bed. He was more than a bit surprised at himself. He was the one who had drawn away.

Taking a deep breath, he tried his damnedest to keep his expression from registering the sensations she unleashed. He didn't want to pounce on her or frighten her. She was beginning to feel comfortable with him and he didn't want to disturb the balance of friendship and passion between them.

"Oh, woman!" His breath was shaky. If she only knew what she did to him. Keeping his hands to himself was just about the hardest thing he ever had to do.

Sabrina was a grown woman, a widow, not some untried girl. She should have been well past the blushing stage. Yet Ross Sheldon, this dashing rake with bold challenging eyes, made her face glow red with a mere glance, and set her heart pounding. She felt giddy in his presence. Certainly his kiss had been a most welcome experience, shockingly different from Seth's. But what did she feel? Love? Passion? Sabrina wasn't certain. She had thought she knew what love was like. Hadn't she loved Seth? Loved him so strongly that his death had nearly destroyed her? And yet that wasn't the same emotion. Her feelings for her husband had been gentle; what she felt for Ross Sheldon was like standing at the edge of a cliff and looking down. Whatever it was, however, she knew that from then on there would be a change in their relationship.

Chapter Seven

The next few days were extrordinarily happy for Sabrina. She skipped through her work like a sea nymph skimming over the water so that she could spend precious moments with Ross. An hour, a half-hour, even just a few minutes near him made her feel rejuvenated. Ross made her feel as though she were the only woman in the world. How then could she help herself from falling more than a little bit in love with him?

As to her father-in-law, since his last encounter with Ross, Rufus had steered clear of her whenever possible. It was as if he knew that Ross was watching his every move, and would make good his threat. Even so, there were times when she could feel his angry stare burning into her back. In those moments she was doubly thankful that Ross was there, for she knew that if he hadn't vowed aloud to be her protector, her father-in-law would have made her suffer severe retribution.

But he is here, she thought as she washed and dried the tavern glasses. And when he leaves, if he leaves, he'll take me with him.

Hurriedly she moved through her tasks, for when the day's cleaning was done she and Ross could be together before she had to return to the inn for her nightly duties. They took buggy trips throughout the New England farm country, visited the wharfs, had their picture taken by an Eastman Kodak salesman. They

69

witnessed some of the mechanical marvels that were being shown at a fair, hitherto undreamed of products — hydraulic pumps, steam engines, new farming equipment, and a machine that played music. They even saw pictures of the Brooklyn Bridge in New York that had just been completed. Ross bought Sabrina a bottle of imported French cologne and hair ribbons in a rainbow of colors. He spoiled her with more than a dozen presents.

Sabrina felt a warm sense of companionship with this handsome, daring man. She never knew just what surprise he had in store for her or what they were going to do. It made being with him all the more exciting.

"Sabree!"

Sabrina looked up, smiling as she saw him crossing towards her. "You're just in time. I'm all through," she said. Tonight had been slow because it was the middle of the week thus she was finished sooner than usual. Hurriedly she dried her hands on the towel, then reached up to straighten her hair. Fumbling with the ties of her apron she had soon peeled it off so that she looked pretty for him. He didn't take his usual time to notice.

"Got something to show you," he said instead, smiling at her mysteriously. Taking her hand, he led her towards his room.

Sabrina hesitated for just a moment. They hadn't gone to Ross's room since that night they had retreated there to talk after John Travers had come upon her in the cellar. But she was being foolish. Ross's conduct had been above reproach. She didn't want him to think she didn't trust being alone with him now. The truth was that she wasn't certain she trusted herself. Ross Sheldon unleashed emotions deep within her that she was finding harder and harder to control.

"Something? Well, let's just see what it is." Without another thought she walked hand in hand with him up the stairs.

Ross exhibited the exuberance of a little boy as he bounded into the room and lit the lamp. There on the small table was the strange invention that had so fascinated Sabrina at the fair. "The phonograph. Remember. I couldn't help noticing how fascinated you were by it. You said you loved music and wished you could listen to it whenever you wanted."

"The music machine . . ." Sabrina ran her hands over it in wonder. It was so hard to believe that a song was created by the tiny needle, but she had seen it demonstrated. Strange. Magic. But it worked! A revolving wax cylinder grooved with wavy lines contained the song, or so Ross had told her. When the handle was cranked a needle pressed against the rotating cylinder. As the needle vibrated, the music was released through the horn.

"I bought it for you." It was Ross's hope that the phonograph would bring a little joy into her life, give her something to look forward to when she had finished her chores. He had something else in mind as well, however. He would have been lying to himself if he hadn't admitted that another reason he had purchased the contraption was with seduction in mind. Though he'd been above approach the last several days his patience was wearing thin.

"For me?" It deeply touched Sabrina that he would buy it for her. She'd received very few presents in her life, even from Seth. Times had been hard and they'd had to save every penny for the necessities.

"Yeah, little gal." Just seeing her eyes glow made it worth every cent. Ross was all smiles as he turned the crank several times and put the needle in place. A soft, soothing waltz filled the room. Sabrina closed her eyes and contented herself listening.

"It's as if a magician found a way to put a tiny orchestra inside that box," she softly. "Oh, Ross, it's glorious!"

Ross's breath caught sharply in his throat. "Yes, glorious," he whispered, but he was talking about her hair,

71

a soft gold in the fading sunlight. She was so lovely, he mused, his eyes moving tenderly over her thick lashes, the sculpted planes of her face, her generous mouth, her neck, and what lay below. Oh, how he wanted to feel her nestled in his arms. His gaze slid slowly, lingeringly, over her body, resting on her full bosom and he felt his desires stir.

Ross Sheldon, slow down! he thought. Sabrina was vulnerable, he knew that. She was a woman in need of protection against just such men as himself. He'd been that kind of protector, held himself back, but a man could just stand so much temptation.

"The music is wearing down. Here, let me crank it up again," he said, trying to take his mind off the potency of this situation. His smile was wry as he said, "Now we can dance." It would be a test of his will power if he could be alone with her like this, holding her, touching her.

"Dance?" She stiffened, not wanting to admit that she didn't know how but her expression gave her away.

"You've never been to a dance, Sabree?" That thought made him sad. A woman as beautiful as Sabrina James should have been the toast of the town. He moved forward, towering over her.

Sabrina tilted her head back to see the expression on his face. "Never. I've never danced before." Suddenly she felt so awkward, so silly.

Beneath his breath he damned that curmudgeon of a father-in-law. Did he allow her any pleasures? "Then it's about time you did."

"But . . ."

Before she could mutter a protest, he had one arm around her waist and the other lightly grasping her hand. She felt small and fragile when she was in his arms. Ross Sheldon made her feel very feminine. When his eyes swept over her she saw herself through his eyes and relished that he obviously thought her to be pretty.

"Put your hand on my shoulder." He smiled encouragement as she complied. "That's right." Pulling her along with him in a gliding motion, he moved in time to the music. "Move your feet in the shape of a box like so . . ." He demonstrated.

Sabrina felt as if suddenly her feet were huge clumsy appendages to her body. They wouldn't move the way they should. She tried to relax, but her body seemed to stiffen each time she took a step.

"Let me count it out. One-two-three, two-two-three . . ." He pulled her closer, touching her, guiding her through the motions of the waltz. The soft whisper of his breath tickled her ear, sending tickling sensations all through her. His legs brushed against hers with every step, making her vibrantly aware of how close their bodies were. An intimate embrace.

The light in Ross's room was dim. Sabrina was overwhelmingly conscious of how alone they were. There would be some who would decry the intimacy of being together like this but tonight Sabrina didn't care. She was bewitched. The music was weaving a magic spell, an enchantment that she didn't want to break.

"One-two-three. That's right. You've got it now, Sabrina." He could tell that she was enjoying herself and that pleased him.

As she became more accustomed to the steps, he increased the tempo, whirling her around and around until she was dizzy and out of breath. Sabrina clutched at his shoulder for balance, laughing all the while.

He loved the sound of her laughter. "Oh, Sabree . . ." Damned if he wasn't having just about the best time of his life. She was so light in his arms. The music stopped. He stared into her eyes for a while, his gaze softening as he looked at her. "You're a lovely woman, Sabrina," he whispered huskily. "Very lovely."

Sabrina could feel a blush heating the skin of her face, rising from her chin to forehead. She had dressed for Ross tonight, taken special care with everything from her stockings to her hair, debating over wearing the bright blue calico or the green and white checked cotton dress. She had chosen the calico, remembering Ross had said it was his favorite outfit. She wondered if he knew. "Thank you, Ross."

Though he tried, he couldn't take his eyes off her, but watched her hungrily. He was playing with fire, he knew it, but how could he resist? This was meant to be, he felt it. "Your neck and shoulders look as soft as velvet. Inviting."

Before she could even think his head had dipped down. His mouth, warm and hard, touched the soft, bare curve of her shoulder, igniting a hundred sparks that pulsated through her body. It had been so long since a man had made love to her. Seth had initiated her into this glorious experience. His death had left her cold. Unfulfilled. She wanted to live again, feel cherished and loved again.

"Sabrina!" Everything within her was responding to him. Totally. Uncontrollably. She found herself wondering how his mouth and hands would feel if he did to her what Seth used to do, but instead of initiating any lovemaking, Ross moved away to crank the phonograph again.

"Now that you're an expert, let's try it again."

Sabrina's senses were spinning as he molded her body against his, instigating a pattern of dips, turns, and sways. She was more comfortable with the dance, able to concentrate on something besides her feet. She sensed his strength in the hand that clasped hers, relished the wide expanse of his chest, felt the rhythm of his heartbeat. Looking up at him she felt all fluttery to see how his eyes were glittering with desire.

Ross was totally entranced with her, the way her smile lit her face, the way her wide copper eyes shyly met his then darted away. But most of all he liked the feel of her body next to his, the texture of her skin.

"Oh, darlin' . . . I love to touch you." His arm tight-

74

ened about her waist possessively, as if he were staking his claim. Sabrina could feel the rippling muscles in his thighs as his legs moved against hers in the dance.

"And I love to have you touch me." Sabrina took a deep breath, hoping to regain her calm, but it was impossible now.

"Sabree, you feel so good." He made her burningly aware of how tightly her breasts had flattened against the hard planes of his chest. For just a moment he stiffened. "If I were a gentleman, I'd leave you be, Sabrina. I'd leave this inn, this town, this state, and never see you again. I'm not the kind of man you need." It was a truthful admission. He wasn't the kind of man to settle down. Never had been, just never could be.

"No!" The thought of him carrying out his words, of leaving, instilled her with an aching emptiness. She couldn't bear the thought of life returning to the way it used to be. She had been so lonely. "Don't leave."

He grinned. "I said *if* I were a gentleman, Sabree." He stared at her, his jovial mood turning to one of reflection. His voice was so gentle that she shivered. "I've lived a hard life. I'm a wanderer. You deserve walks in the moonlight, pretty words and flowers. I'm not that kind of man."

"I don't care!" She wanted him just the way he was.

He had to be blatantly honest with her. "I'm not the kind of man content with handholding." His hands tightened on her waist, biting into her flesh. "I've held myself back because I know what you are going through here with your father-in-law. But I'm a man with hungers—"

"Ross!" Her lashes dropped to veil her eyes. She didn't have the nerve to tell him that she had hungers too.

"You make me even hungrier!" He pulled her closer. A mixture of alarm and pleasure sang inside her veins. "I want to strip off your clothing slowly, sensuously, like the petals off a flower and see what lies beneath. I want to cup your breasts in my hands and caress them until—"

"Stop. Ross," she whispered. "Please . . ." Her voice lacked the element of command to make him take her seriously.

"I want to feel your legs wrapped around my waist, want every inch of our naked flesh to mingle in one long caress. And I feel that you want me too." He had made a vow that he wouldn't seduce her but if she were willing . . . "Do you want me?"

"No! I don't . . . I . . . I . . ." But she did. The way he was talking should have infuriated her, should have made her flee from him, the way he was talking only seemed to inflame her desires. Her body was alive, aching, throbbing for him to do exactly what he wanted to do. Oh, what kind of a woman was she?

"Then if you don't want that, you'd better leave. Now. While you still can." He waited expectantly, but she didn't go.

"I don't want to run away, Ross." She wanted to give him her heart, her soul, and with it the soft, burning passion of her body.

Locked against him as she was there was no mistaking his arousal. And it fueled her own desires. To be loved again. To join with a man in that most glorious show of love. At that moment it was all she wanted, all that she desired.

"I've been patient, Sabree. Astonishingly so." He was looking at her through narrowed, passion-filled eyes, imagining how it would be between them.

"I don't know what to say . . ." She felt weak. Shivery. Her fingers clenched his shoulder for fear of falling.

"I'm not apologizing for telling you the truth." He smiled rakishly, with no show of embarrassment. "Or for my body showing you how much you mean to me. I'm a man, and I'm reacting as such."

He took satisfaction in the fact that he had given her the chance to deny him, but she'd stayed. It gave him a heady confidence. Leaning down, he lifted her into his arms. He couldn't remember when he'd ever been so impatient to taste the charms of a woman. Oh, he was crazy about her all right. Dangerously so.

"Please. Tonight." His voice was a low rasp that caressed her body, touching every nerve.

"Ross . . ."

A fine madness seized her and she felt light-headed, like she'd drunk too much wine. She wanted to be Ross's woman. His wife. Wanted him to make love to her.

She glanced towards the bed then back at him. Their eyes met and her heart began to hammer wildly. There were so many things she didn't know about him, but suddenly she didn't care. All she knew was that without him she didn't stand a chance of being happy. No, she wasn't as wild and carefree as he was, but did it matter? She was willing to take the chance that she could make him care for her. She had to take the chance. Now. Taking a deep breath she gave Ross the answer he longed for.

Chapter Eight

Wisps of flickering lamplight danced over the quilt of the bed as if beckoning the two lovers, yet Ross didn't hurry. He wanted to take this slow and easy, wanted to enjoy every moment. It was as if time didn't exist, at least not for him. Then slowly, with even strides, he moved in a manner that prolonged the expectation.

"Sabree," he murmured. At last she was in his arms, was soon to be in his bed. It was where she belonged, he thought. She was his now and before this night was through she would know it too.

It was very still in the room. The phonograph had long since quieted. All that could be heard was the sound of their breathing. The soft flame of the lamp cast a soft, golden glow, intensifying the web of enchantment that surrounded them. For a heart-wrenching moment Ross looked deeply into her eyes, then slowly he lowered his mouth to hers, fusing their lips together in a kiss that left her breathless.

Sabrina's mouth opened to him, her lips trembling. This was what she had wanted despite her protestations. Perhaps she had secretly wanted this right from the start. Maybe that was why she had reacted so strongly against him. But oh, it felt so right. Closing her eyes, she pressed close to him, her lips parting as she sighed her surrender. Only now did she realize the depth of her own need.

Shyly at first, then with increasing boldness, Sabrina kissed Ross back with all the hunger in her soul, her tongue moving to meet his. She loved the taste of him, the feel of his passion. Following his lead, she kissed him deeply, her exploring tongue mimicking his. Slowly her arms crept around his neck, her fingers tangling in his thick dark brown hair.

Without disrupting their kiss, Ross slowly lowered Sabrina to the bed, then took his place beside her. Gently he pulled her down until they were lying side by side, his muscled length straining against her softness. He cherished her in deep searching kisses. With trembling fingers, he unlaced her bodice, pulling it down around her shoulders, seeking her naked breast.

"God, you're beautiful!" Ross had been with many women but Sabrina's beauty touched his heart. She was as soft and as delicate as a rose, yet he knew her strength and determination. A special lady. Yes, a lady was what she was. He wanted to make this beautiful for her, something to remember.

Slowly her shyness thawed. "Am I, Ross?" She wanted him to think so.

"Yes." Pushing her onto her back he slid his hands down her throat, across her chest, to the breasts he had bared, in light circular motions of adoration. "Just about the most beautiful sight any man could behold!"

Beautiful, she thought. Strange, but in all the time they were married, Seth had never told her so. In fact, he had never spoken much at all when they were making love, but had remained shyly quiet. Ross was anything but silent and his moans of appreciation acted strongly on Sabrina's own passions. She wanted to be naked against him, to be cherished all over by his questing touch.

Ross seemed to guess at her thoughts. With infinite slowness he continued to undress her, taking the deepest pleasure in looking at the smooth, creamy flesh that he had exposed, the firm breasts jutting proudly under his gaze, the deep coral peeks full and erect. Her waist was just as slim as he had imagined, her legs just as long and shapely. Taking off her shoes and stockings, he saw that even her feet were pretty. Slowly his eyes swept up and down and back again. He lay looking at her for what seemed to be an eternity of time, letting out his breath in an audible sigh.

Sabrina watched the expressions that moved across his face and felt a hot ache of desire coil deep within her. "Oh, Ross—"

"Hush, darlin'." He silenced her with another kiss.

For a long while they lay so entwined, contenting themselves just in kissing and caressing. Sabrina relished the yielding softness of the bed, the texture of the coverlet beneath her, warm and sensuous against her bare shoulders. But most of all, she gave herself up to the sensations Ross was creating with his questing hands, kneading the soft skin of her breasts, teasing the very tips until his touch made her tremble. An ache was building deep within her, becoming more and more intense as his fingers fondled and stroked. Strange, she thought, but Seth had never touched her breasts like this nor taken the time that Ross was taking just to caress her.

Ross lay stretched out, every muscle in his body taut with expectation. The fabric of his trousers couldn't conceal his arousal, nor did he seek to hide it from Sabrina's searching gaze. It seemed to be just about time for him to get comfortable, really comfortable, he thought.

"Mind if I—" He sat up slowly, tugging at his boots.

"No." She knew what he was going to do, but nonetheless couldn't keep from blushing, the burning color flaring high on her chiseled cheekbones. Shyly she turned away as she usually did when Seth had bared his body, but Ross cupped her chin in his hand.

"I want you to appreciate me just the way that I did you. I'm proud of my body, Sabree. I want you to see me." His eyes never left her face as he tossed his boots to the side with a thump. His socks followed and then his shirt. He had to leave her for just a moment to remove his pants. Standing up, he unfolded his tall, muscular frame, unfastening his belt and releasing it with one firm tug. The button at the waistband was undone with a flip of his wrist, as if he were used to undressing in a hurry. Moving his hips he shrugged out of the pants then stood there silently for her view.

Sabrina was surprised that he wore no underwear. She didn't have time to close her eyes or even to blink before the full glory of his maleness was presented to her. And a glory he was. His shoulders were broad and a golden brown, his chest perfectly formed with a dark mat of hair that seemed to beckon her touch. Her eyes traced the line of his hipbones, exploring the cavity of his navel, then ran down the length of his well-muscled thighs and back again. But it was what lay between his legs that stunned her. Once in a while she had sneaked peeks at Seth during the preliminaries of their lovemaking, and compared to him, Ross was quite the magnificent specimen. It was frightening and exhilating at the same time and for just a moment Sabrina was tempted to pull away.

"I know what you're thinking—and I won't," Ross whispered huskily.

"Won't what?" Realizing how she was staring, Sabrina tightly closed her eyes.

"Won't hurt you. I'd never do that, Sabree." With a low groan he came to her. "Ah, darling . . . Don't be afraid of me." As if to give her reassurance, he gathered her into his arms, then his mouth covered hers in fierce possession. It seemed he enjoyed kissing and so did she, so very much.

Sabrina gloried in the closeness of their bodies, her palms sliding over his muscles and tight flesh to know his body as well as he knew hers. He had said that she was beautiful and yet so was he. He reminded her of a stallion she had seen at the fair. Sleek and trim and magnificent. Being so close to him made her feel alive. Soaring. She trembled in his arms, her whole body quaking as she thought about what was to follow. She moved against him in a manner that wrenched a groan from his lips.

"Sabree. Oh, what you do to me." She could feel exactly what he meant as his manhood stiffened even more. Like a fire, his lips burned over her. He teased her breasts with a devilish tongue turning her insides molten, her body liquid with the flow of desire.

Moving his hand down her belly, he touched the soft hair between her thighs, smiling as his fingers came away wet. Tremors shot through him in rocketing waves. He lifted his hips, his hand burrowing between their bodies to guide himself into her.

"Oh, Ross!" It had never been like this before. Never. She had loved Seth with all her heart and yet he had never instigated such pleasure. She arched against him in sensual pleasure. Wanting.

Ross supported himself on his forearms as he moved with his hips. Sabrina opened herself to him like a vulnerable flower. Slowly he slid inside her, sheathing himself completely in the searing velvet of her flesh.

"My God," he whispered in a low moan. No other woman had ever affected him quite as deeply as this. It was heaven! More so! As if he had suddenly died and gone beyond the limits of this world. He couldn't get enough of her. It was as if he wanted to bury himself so deeply inside her that they would be permanently part of each other. His deep moans of pleasure filled the room.

Sabrina couldn't help the whimper that escaped her lips. There was nothing compared to the intense pleasure of being filled by him, loved by him. A shock wave catapulted through her body. Her lips parted, her breath rasping.

"No. Don't stop!" she cried out. She knew she would die if he left her now. But he didn't pull away. As she clung to him, he moved back and forth in a manner that nearly drove her crazy. Spasms of exquisite feeling flowed through her like a dance, like a roaring wind, like the ocean's tide. She arched her hips hungrily, blending with him. In his arms she wasn't the demure, well-mannered Sabrina James, but a wild thing. Clutching at him, calling out his name, clinging to him with desperate hands. There on the bed she gave him her heart, her soul. An aching sweetness became a shattering explosion, an escape into a timeless, measureless pleasure.

Then, in the silent aftermath of passion, they lay together. Gradually their bodies cooled, their pulses slowed down to a normal rate. "Are you all right, my love?" Ross was all tender concern for her.

"Yes . . . Yes, I am," she answered shakily. She tightened her arms and her body, holding him inside the warmth of her embrace. For a long, long time they held each other, as if neither one really wanted to face coming back down to reality. They didn't speak, for there was no need for words.

Ross gazed down at her face, gently brushing back the tangled hair from her eyes. "Sleep now," he whispered, still holding her close. With a sigh, she snuggled up against him, burying her face in the warmth of his chest. She didn't want to sleep, not now. She wanted to savor this moment of joy, but as he caressed her back, tracing his fingers along her neck, she drifted off.

Ross watched her as she slept. He cuddled her against him. She would never know the feelings she inspired. Dear God! He hoped with all his heart that she would never regret what had passed between them. The devil damn him for a bastard if he broke her heart. And yet there would come a time when he would have to go. What then?

Chapter Nine

Soft rays of sunlight fluttered through an opening in the curtains. From beneath the window the sound of the first cock's crow reminded Sabrina all too jarringly that morning had come yet again — one of several mornings she had awakened to find herself in Ross's arms. Rising up on one elbow she looked at him now with aching tenderness, for he looked so much younger as he snuggled up against her in sleep, his powerful body sprawled across the bed as if he didn't have a worry in the world. She contented herself in watching him as he slept, her eyes roving eagerly over his features — the thick dark brown hair, his long, curling lashes, his full lips. The dancing sunlight shadowed the hollows beneath his high cheekbones and accentuated the hard line of his jaw and the well-defined shape of his nose. A very handsome man.

Lover. Once Sabrina might have thought the word to have a tawdry ring to it, but feeling as she did about Ross she couldn't believe that the pleasure they found together was wrong. He knew just how to touch her, the right words to say, how long to caress her, how to bring her again and again to a heart-stopping crest of pleasure. Once she might have blushed at the thought of a man learning every inch of her body, yet with Ross it just seemed as natural as breathing. She gave herself to him without reserve, looking forward to the stolen moments

84

they found together. It was a sweet secret that made her smile even under the most scathing of her father-in-law's scolding.

Ross. Ross! Just the whisper of his name on her lips made her heart sing. She gave to him her whole heart because she was incapable of holding the tide of her feelings in reserve. She granted him all her love, her strength, her devotion, because it just wasn't in her nature to give him less. Sabrina was a one-man woman. First there had been Seth. Now Ross was that man.

And I'm his woman, she thought. Though she longed for a firmer commitment from him, wanted with all her heart to be his wife, it was enough for now. Besides, during their times together she was really coming to know him. Ross Sheldon's life had been anything but perfect. A combination of disappointment and cruelty had made him a loner, a man who lived on the edge of danger. He had known coldness, hardship, and pain before erecting that thick shell of bravado around himself. Sometimes to stay alive he had been forced to live by his wits and his strength. Sabrina wanted to heal him with tenderness and the soft, burning worship of her body.

I guess I do want to tame you, my love, she thought as her lips curled up in a smile. She wanted to protect him. From what Ross had revealed to her, the West could be a dangerous place and she didn't want to even think about him being hurt. But she didn't dare let Ross know that.

Leaning forward, she touched his mouth lightly in a kiss, laughing softly as his lips began to twitch. She thought surely he would awaken, but when he didn't, she let him be. Ross was a late sleeper, she'd allow him that luxury. As for herself, she had to be up and about before her father-in-law came looking for her. She'd already been late to begin her chores twice this week, unleashing his anger.

Quietly, so as not to awaken him, Sabrina rolled to the edge of the bed. Putting first one foot, then the other on the floor, she stood up, missing him the moment she looked over her shoulder. But there was tonight. It was a thought that made her sigh.

Bending over, Sabrina picked up her clothing which was scattered about the hard wooden floor where Ross had left them. Slipping into her chemise and petticoat, she pulled at the drawstring at the waist allowing herself to dream. Sabrina Sheldon The two names fit so perfectly together. Would it ever be? Would Ross ask her to marry him? She had to believe that he would, for the thought of his ever leaving was decidedly painful. It was a thought she put far from her mind as she hurried to dress in a plain pink cotton dress, then tiptoed to the door. Soundlessly she opened the door and stepped out into the hall, then closed the door behind her.

"Sabrina!" Her father-in-law's voice startled her as he came up behind her. "Where have you been? What have you been doing?"

Putting her trembling hands behind her, Sabrina tried to maintain her calm, though she could feel a blush staining her cheeks. "Making up the room, sir."

"This early?" His eyes darted from Sabrina to the door and back again, his faced etched with suspicion.

"I . . . I have a great deal to do today," she stuttered, self-consciously fashioning her flyaway hair into a bun. "If you have forgotten, the brewer will be here with the kegs of wine, ale, and beer." One of Sabrina's added duties was to take inventory.

Rufus James grunted. "Well, don't just stand here dawdling. Get on with it, girl. For a truth you've been little use to me of late. Always ogling that—that—" He couldn't seem to think of a name vile enough to call Ross.

Sabrina didn't take the chance of her father-in-law beginning an argument. Picking up her skirts, she hurried down the stairs, nearly tripping in her haste.

The taproom smelled of vomit and spilled ale again, renewing Sabrina's wishes that she could get far away from there. Even so, she set about the tasks at hand, cleaning and scrubbing. Then she opened the door, and looked out into the courtyard for the brewer's wagon. Her eyes lit upon something else instead. A piece of paper with colorful pictures of Indians and cowboys was tacked to the door of the inn. Upon closer inspection, Sabrina saw that it was a handbill, one advertising the last performance of "Apache Ed's Wild West Show" before it was transferred to a different owner.

"Ross's show!" Her eyes glistened with anticipation. She felt a thrill just reading his name in the lower right-hand corner. Ross Sheldon, new owner. It was said that he was to make a guest appearance that afternoon. Sabrina was determined to go with him. She'd always wanted to see a real Western show.

Sabrina had the chance to ask Ross when he came downstairs much later to have a bit of breakfast.

"See the show?" he said with a smile. She was so excited how could he turn her down. "I'll do better than that. Not only will we go to the show, but you will have a ringside seat. Only the best for my girl." He planted a kiss upon her brow. "Don't forget, it's soon to be mine. The new name will be "Cherokee Ross's Wild West Show" How do you like that?" Although he smiled, it was a painful reminder that soon he'd have to go. He'd already spent far too long here. But how could he have ever realized where their lovemaking would lead?

When the show left town I'll have to go with it, he thought sullenly. The die was cast. There was no turning back. But how was he going to tell her? Tonight at the Wild West show he'd have to find a way. And yet he reluctantly had to admit that there were times when he actually thought of taking her with him. Their lovemaking had proven to be a soul-stirring experience that he had yet to get over. Oh, yes, she was something all right. Pure fire beneath her quiet allure. He was a man of strong physical hungers who had never been satisfied with one woman before, but with Sabrina it was different. She was a woman with which he could share his life and heart.

"That kind of thinking will cause me no end of trouble," he muttered beneath his breath.

"What?" Sabrina's eyes were wide and questioning as she looked up at him.

"I said I hope tonight doesn't end in trouble," he replied quickly. Several wisps of her hair had come down from their pins and he reached to secure them again. As he did so, a wave of tenderness washed over him. How could he ever think of leaving her behind? Well, he'd have to sort it all out in his mind and come to some conclusion.

Chapter Ten

The late afternoon was crisp, colder than usual for November, due to the snow that had fallen high in the mountains the night before. Even so, a huge number of people had turned out to see the show. The air crackled with sound as Sabrina and Ross arrived at the fair ground. Voices chattered, howled, and shouted their excitement. Horses neighed. Scattered snaps of gunfire shattered the air. A variety of smells, both pleasant and acrid filled the air as they elbowed their way through the crowd. Ross put a protective arm around Sabrina's waist and maneuvered her to the front gate, smiling at her reassuringly when the doorkeeper reached out for their tickets.

"We don't need any tickets," Ross proudly stated, wanting to show off a bit for her.

"Everybody needs tickets," the man countered.

Ross sauntered forward, frowning his annoyance. "I am Ross Sheldon, the new owner of this show." He crossed his arms over his chest. "The young lady and I are guests of Apache Ed tonight on his *last* appearance as owner."

"Ross Sheldon!" the ticket taker repeated.

The name was taken up and twittered by those standing nearby. Sabrina could hear several people in the boisterous crowd ooh and ahh as they got up on tiptoe to take a look at the famous author. Two young girls giggled and remarked on how good-looking Ross was as they tried to get his attention, but Ross was oblivious to their adoration. He only had eyes for Sabrina. It made her proud to be with such a celebrity. It was a bit like being with Buffalo Bill himself, only she reasoned that Ross must be a whole lot handsomer.

"I'm . . . I'm sorry, Mr. Sheldon. Sir. I just didn't recognize you dressed as you are in a suit," the ticket man said by way of apology. "I've only seen you in buckskins and . . . and with a lot of hair on your face."

Ross suppressed a laugh. For the sake of his image he had grown a beard when he had posed for publicity pictures for his books. It made him look thoroughly Western with no trace of the Southern boy that he really was. "No harm done. Just open the gate and let us through."

The gates for the remainder of the crowd wouldn't open for another ten minutes, but Ross and Sabrina were allowed entrance. With a cocky smile, he led her to a bench in the first row.

"This is the best seat in the house, Sabree. You won't miss anything from here." He squeezed her hand tightly. "I'm sorry I can't sit here with you, but I have to get dressed in my buckskins."

"You can't stay?" A strange sense of shyness and panic overcame her. Being here like this was new to her and for a moment she feared being alone in that stampeding crowd waiting just outside the gates. They reminded her a bit of the strange, dark woolly beasts called buffalo she had seen in the pens as they had walked through the gate.

He winked at her. "I'll be looking at you from the arena, though, and feeling very proud."

She forced herself to smile. "I hope so, Ross." Sabrina reached up to adjust her brown feathered bonnet and brushed at her bright green and brown dress. Usually she wore such finery to church, but this afternoon she had wanted to look special. In truth, she nearly had to move heaven and hell to get her father-in-law's approval for her to leave the inn early today. Only her promise that she would be back by the time his patrons arrived had secured his agreeing nod.

"You're a very beautiful woman, Sabree. Always remember that. And that no matter whatever happens, you are very, very special to me." With that he turned and dashed away toward a large tent. His huge strides were just short of a run.

Sabrina busied herself by looking around. The arena was set with the replica of a fort in the wilderness, complete with cabins and trees. There was a steady stream of wagons, horses, carts, and riders on horses. It was like reliving a page out of history. In fact, she recoiled as she saw a group of Indians passing right in front of her. They looked frightening in their war paint, feathers, and fringed leather leggings. She stared at them in awe as vivid images from the stories she read flashed through her mind. "Savages," they were called. Hostiles. Heathens. She felt nervous to be all alone within the arena and sighed with relief as at last the gates were opened and a throng of people came pouring in. It didn't take long to fill the empty seats. There were even those who stood in the aisles.

Along with the onlookers were reporters carrying pads and pencils, and photographers setting up cameras. Young men were busily passing out programs and autographed copies of Ross's latest novels.

Amusing herself by watching the crowd, Sabrina was suddenly startled by the noise of a bugle. Her eyes darted in the direction of the sound to see that a large procession had begun at one end of the arena. Several men dressed in cavalry uniforms led the parade, the American flag they held aloft flapping in the breeze. Next came men on horseback, followed by others on foot, all garbed in various hues of buckskin or denim. Some wore beaver hats, others large-brimmed Stetsons. Sabrina's eyes searched for Ross, but she didn't see him.

"Isn't this something?" A bespectacled, white-haired

lady sitting next to her, poked Sabrina in the ribs. "You know, my husband was a soldier. Fought in the war a long, long time ago." She sighed as if the sight of the blue-uniformed men brought back memories.

Next came the Indian braves on horseback, the same ones who had passed by Sabrina. With haughty pride they pranced down the field on their chestnut Indian ponies. Their squaws and children walked behind leading dogs and ponies. Whereas the crowd cheered for the soldiers, they booed the Indians, taking particular joy in taunting the tallest brave.

"That's Crying Wolf," the woman by her side informed her. "The Indian chief. Almost as famous an Indian as Sitting Bull, or so they claim."

Sabrina remembered Ross telling her all about this Indian chief. He wasn't even an Indian at all, but a Mexican dressed in paint and feathers. She remembered Ross proudly telling her his plan of putting a real Indian chief under contract for the period of two years. White Feather was the chief's name and Ross was determined to get him for his show. He wanted real Indians. Ross had said that it was a stroke of genius on his part, for Indians were always good on their word and would give him far less trouble than the pretenders.

The Mexican vaqueros resplendent with silver saddles and bridles were last in line, then the trick riders appeared. With whoops and shouts they rode by exhibiting their skill and prowess. Some practically stood on their heads, hanging from the saddles, others took great delight in balancing on one leg as they rode by.

As soon as all the members of the show were assembled on the field, a blast from the cavalry bugles gave a signal. An announcer stood upon a raised platform, shouting through a megaphone, a coneshaped device used to direct the voice, or so Ross told her.

"And now, ladies and gentlemen. May we introduce Apache Ed and Cherokee Ross Sheldon."

A gasp of awe and anticipation passed through like a

gust of wind. The crowd stood on their feet and cheered as two horsemen rode from the end of the field. They galloped behind two men on horseback carrying a banner with huge letters. "Apache Ed's Wild West Show," it read. On the other side was written "now owned by Cherokee Ross Sheldon." The wooden benches vibrated with the throng's exuberance.

Sabrina stared in awe as Ross came riding forth on a white stallion with gold and silver saddle and bridle. How could she help it? He looked so handsome in his beaded and fringed buckskins and wide-brimmed hat — like a hero out of one of the books he had written. The fringed sleeved jacket, tight hip-hugging trousers and knee-high boots clung to Ross like a second skin, emphasizing the physique that she now knew so well.

"Yahoo!" he shouted, obviously enjoying his popularity. As he passed in front of Sabrina's seat, Ross flashed a gleaming white smile and tipped his hat. His eyes sparkled as if reminding her that she was "his lady."

His lady! Just the thought caused a shiver to flash all the way up and down her spine. Ross Sheldon's lady. Oh, how she wished she could shout it out loud.

Ross rode round and round in a circle, followed by the former owner of the show, stopping as the staccato beat of Indian drums echoed like a heartbeat. The show had begun.

The crowd was poised on the edge of their seats. Those not fortunate enough to have front benches stood on tiptoe or craned their necks to catch a glimpse of the drama enfolding. It was a reenactment of life on the frontier. When a farmer needed a new house, all of the neighbors would gather for a frolic and house raising. Amidst dancing and singing, the walls of the log cabins were quickly raised, but Sabrina wasn't really watching what was going on. She was looking to see where Ross had gone and spied him in serious discussion with another man. He looked angry. He was waving his arms around and seemed to be swearing. Sabrina was curious, wishing she knew just what they were arguing about, but her attention was diverted when a sharpshooter made his appearance to shoot at clay pigeons being tossed in the air. Sabrina could imagine herself standing there. Oh, how she would love to be able to perform like that. For the moment at least, Ross was forgotten.

Ross, meanwhile, was besieged with problems. He had wanted to run a good, clean, honest show but now since talking to Tom Kirkland, one of the cowboys, he could see that he had been taken in. Several of the performers were threatening to quit because there wasn't enough money with which to pay them. Money was owed on the costumes, backdrops, and feed for the animals. Ed had run the show into debt and was buried in bills up to his eyebrows!

Ross had inherited a show that was quickly losing money, or so Ed and his friend Hawthorne were trying to make him think. Ross, however, had the suspicion that someone was skimming money off the top and putting it into their own pockets. Well, that was quickly going to stop now that he'd bought the damn show, which was exactly the message he was trying to relay to Tom in hope that it would be carried to the right person.

"But I have a friend who would be more than happy to buy himself in to the show," Tom was saying. "He's had experience with such things—"

"Not only no, but hell no!" Ross thundered. He was nearly in a rage. So that was the game being played. Well, he wouldn't take the bait. He'd bought the show in good faith and winning money or losing it he'd handle the business alone.

"No? You can't mean that." Tom Kirkland was taken by surprise, obviously having expected Ross to capitulate to a most generous offer. "Hawthorne is—"

"I can and I do." Ross's eyes narrowed. He clenched his jaw. "So, that's why Ed wanted me to make this appearance tonight. To set the likes of you upon me."

94

"No, I rather suspect it was to point his creditors in your direction." Tom Kirkland clucked his tongue. "Better think seriously about my friend's offer. You can still have the glory of having your name attached to the show."

"No!" Ross's anger was near the boiling point. "You can tell Ed that and that man you call Hawthorne and any other damned idiot who thinks me to be a fool. Sink or swim, this show belongs to me. I'm owner, manager, and my word is law. Understand?"

"Yes."

"And tell Ed that if I ever see him anywhere near this show after tonight, I'll have him thrown out," Ross grumbled. Seemed that whenever Ed left a town, it was never quite the same. He was scheming, conniving, and about as crooked as a dog's hind leg. He should have known better than to have had any dealings with such a man, but he had wanted this show so badly.

Well, he could certainly see that he had his work cut out for him. He'd have to stop thinking about Sabrina and concentrate upon his show. Could he pull it out of debt? He had his writing career and the money from that and he certainly had his share of friends from San Francisco to Denver and back East in the publishing world. He'd sure as hell give it a try.

"Damn!" He was incensed that suddenly his new-found empire seemed to be crumbling, but it was a thing he couldn't concentrate on right now. It was time for another dashing ride. He'd forget about the show's troubles for awhile and give this crowd their money's worth. Besides, it was worth it to ride by Sabrina, just to see the glitter of pride in her eyes. "Sabree . . ."

Ross urged his stallion into a trot, taking a position behind the marksmen to ride in a circle. Once again the audience clapped and shouted giving him a taste of just how exciting this all could be. Riding tall in the saddle, Ross was all smiles as he raised his arm to sweep off his hat just as he passed Sabrina. Their eyes met and held

95

for just a moment before he galloped on. All too soon she was out of sight again. Even so, Ross found himself glancing back. He didn't see the rifle that was aimed at him from the end of the stands, didn't notice the shot as it mingled with the other gunfire, but he felt the searing pain as the bullet struck his shoulder. How he managed to stay on his horse he didn't know, but he did, following the other horsemen as they left the arena to take refuge at the north end. Ross felt himself sliding, falling off his horse, but somehow he found the fortitude to fight his pain and stay mounted. He didn't want to start a panic and have a stampede in the stands because he'd been wounded. It would be bad for business. Watching play-acting was one thing, but seeing the real thing was just a mite too scary for Easterners.

Besides, Ross had too much pride to let it be known that he'd been shot like a clay pigeon. He wouldn't let this ruin his debut. Ah no! Quickly he sought out his tent, slipping inside before anyone noticed the blood seeping from his arms and started asking questions. Let whoever planned this think they had missed.

Planned. Had this been a scheme? Was his shooting an accident or an ambush? He wasn't sure which. But he was aiming to find out at the first opportunity.

Chapter Eleven

It was getting dark. The setting sun caused the chill in the air to be more pronounced as Sabrina sat amidst the crowd. The show was drawing to an end, already some of the onlookers were deserting their seats to make their way toward the exit. Anxiously she scanned the field for sight of Ross, but there was no sign of him. It was as if he had just vanished. Tapping her fingers on the hard wood bench she couldn't dispel her nervousness. Her father-in-law would be fit to be tied if she didn't return to the inn on time. And yet what could she do? She didn't want to leave without Ross. In helpless frustration she tried to concentrate on the show, but the yahooing Indians were anything but soothing.

"Excuse me, miss, but is this seat taken?"

Sabrina looked up to see a young man pointing toward the seat recently vacated by the elderly woman. She started to say that it was, hoping Ross would come back soon and sit beside her, but when she recognized the familiar face she shook her head. "No." It might do her some good to have company. She remembered the blond man at once as the man who had given her payment at the inn for her conversation. "Please. Sit."

He didn't have to be invited twice. Brushing off the bench he sat down, humming a lighthearted tune. "Johnathan Colt. Remember?" he said between hums.

"Yes." She couldn't help but smile. He was so likeable somehow. Amiable. "The gunmaker's son."

"The gunmaker's disinherited son," he corrected. "And I remember you. Sabrina! Lovely copper-eyed Brina." He swept off his Stetson in a gesture of greeting. "I looked for you that night but couldn't find you to finish our conversation. You had retired for the night no doubt."

Remembering John Travers's advances and Ross's rescue, Sabrina nodded, not wanting to explain. "It was late," she said, instead turning her eyes towards the field. The Indians were circling a wagon, setting it on fire, and for just a moment it looked so real that Sabrina was transfixed with horror.

"Looks authentic, doesn't it?" Jonathan squeezed her arm reassuringly. "They have to have an Indian attack in all these shows. They're standard. Just playacting, but sometimes a body or two can get hurt."

"Really?" Sabrina's eyes were as round as coins.

"Yeah. I saw a young cowboy get trampled once at a show in New York City." He shuddered. "An unpleasant memory all right."

"I can imagine." Sabrina's focus turned towards the field again, worrying about Ross. She had been so caught up in the excitement and glitter of the show that she hadn't realized the risks there might be. Oh, where in the world could he have disappeared to? The situation was beginning to concern her. She stood up with the intention of going in search of him, but Jonathan Colt grasped her hand and pulled her back down.

"You don't want to go down there or anywhere near the field. In a moment there will be a finale and then such a stampede that you'll be certain they've set all the buffalo loose." He flung one arm out. "People will be running all around, pushing, shoving, trying to get out that gate." Seeing Sabrina shiver, he squeezed her arm again. "Just stay here with me and I'll protect you."

"But you don't understand!" Sabrina was beginning to

98

feel desperate. She had been so anxious to come to the show tonight, but now all she wanted was to find Ross and get out of here. The noise of gunfire, war whoops, and loud chatter was beginning to cause her anxiety. She had a sixth sense that something had happened, but didn't know just what to do about it. It wasn't like Ross to desert. "I've got to find him."

"Him?" His golden eyebrows shot up in question.

"Ross," Sabrina said by way of explanation. "Ross Sheldon. He owns the show now. I came here tonight with him."

He regarded her thoughtfully for a moment. "And he's left you stranded." Jonathan Colt clucked his tongue sympathetically. "What a churlish thing to do."

"No, he wanted me to wait here for him," Sabrina instantly contradicted. "He's coming back for me." She wasn't at all certain she liked this man who judged Ross to be a scoundrel.

For just a moment Jonathan Colt looked as if he would debate the point of Ross's return, then he merely shrugged his shoulders. "We'll see." Sabrina flashed him such an indignant look that it made him laugh out loud.

That chuckle prompted her to say again, "He'll come back for me."

But Ross didn't return. Sabrina settled impatiently back in her seat, clutching her skirt so tightly that it was soon crumpled. And all the while the show went on, ending amidst gunfire and bugles as all the Indians, cowboys, settlers, sharpshooters and every other assortment of Westerner made a last grand sweep of the arena. Ross was noticeably absent.

"Where is he?" A worried frown crisscrossed her brow as she debated what to do. One thing was certain. She would never forgive herself if something happened and she wasn't by Ross's side. Ignoring Jonathan Colt's advice, she hurriedly left the stands to go in search of him, chastising herself for not having followed her own advice sooner. She was pushed, pulled, and elbowed so fiercely that she was certain she had received at least a dozen bruises. Though she wanted to go in one direction, the press of the retreating crowd forced her to go the opposite way until she found herself outside the gate. All she could do was seek shelter behind a large tree until the swarm of people had thinned out. Only then could she push back through the gate.

"Excuse me, I'm looking for Ross Sheldon," she announced, approaching a man dressed all in white buckskin — one of the sharpshooters.

The man shrugged. "Haven't seen him since he came out riding beside Ed."

Two other men insisted that Ross must have already left. "Ain't seen him," said another. Though Sabrina pushed through the gathering of performers asking the same question over and over again, it seemed that there was so much confusion that she couldn't get the right answer. Everyone had seen Ross's triumphant ride around the arena but he seemingly had disappeared after that. "Gone celebrating," a few cowboys insisted. At last in defeat she left the arena, looking back over her shoulder just one more time in hopes she would catch sight of him. When she didn't, there was no other choice but to return to the inn all alone.

Ross peered out through the tent flap, watching her go, clutching at the scarf wrapped tightly around his arm to stop the flow of blood. He'd been bushwacked. There was no other word for it, but the question was by whom? Tom? Ed? Or some other son of a bitch? he thought sourly.

He wanted to follow after Sabrina and explain, but he had an uneasy feeling. He didn't want to involve her in any of this until he found out exactly what was going on. Truth was, he didn't want anyone to know just yet. He didn't even want the members of his show to know he'd been shot lest it ruin their morale. Too many things had been going wrong. He'd promised it would all come to an end, that he would fix it. It just didn't fire up confidence in a man to know he'd been shot like a sitting duck! So much for his bravado.

Ross winced at the pain in his shoulder, yet he didn't utter a sound. With all the gunfire and people pretending to be wounded, not even one of his troup had guessed he'd been hit and he aimed to keep it that way. He didn't want some damn fool reporter to get word of this, that's why as soon as he was hit he went into hiding until he could stop the bleeding and change his clothes.

Someone wants to ruin this show or else see me dead, he mused. Was it Apache Ed? Certainly he had a motive. If Ross were dead he could pocket the money he'd been given and keep the show as well. Tom? He certainly didn't seem to be a man with fierce scruples. But would he stoop so low as killing? There was only one way to find out and that was to ask a few questions.

Chapter Twelve

The moon peered from behind a dark mass of clouds, its muted light flickering on the form moving stealthily across the fair grounds. Anger turned Ross's face a mottled crimson as he went in search of Apache Ed. He came upon him as silently as an Indian stalking his prey, pushing through the tent flap, grabbing him by the shirt front. Ross's eyes blazed with the intensity of his anger. "Someone took a shot at me tonight," he hissed, clenching his teeth at the pain which shot up his arm from such exertion. "Now who do you suppose it might have been?"

Ed's dark eyes widened in fear but he didn't say a word. It was as if he were suddenly struck voiceless.

"I asked you a question!" Anger poured from Ross. "Dammit! Tell me who it was."

"It wasn't me!" At last Ed seemed to find his voice, but it came out in a squeak. "I swear to God I didn't have anything to do with it."

"You're lying!" Ross shot back. Ed's expression seemed to confirm his guilt. Using every reserve of strength that he had, Ross lifted the shorter man up in the air until his feet were dangling. "Now, tell me what's going on or I swear I'll choke it out of you." Just to demonstrate that he was in deadly earnest, Ross tightened his hold, tugging at Ed's shirt so violently that the other man's eyes bulged.

"All right! All right . . ." Ed choked. "I'll tell you everything if you just let me down."

Ross did, with a force that sent Apache Ed sprawling, but this action cost him, for it reopened the wound he'd so carefully tended, sending a flow of blood coursing down his arm. It stained his white shirtsleeve a vibrant shade of scarlet.

"So, you did get hit after all." Ed's lips curved with satisfaction.

"A scratch. Nothing more," Ross said quickly. He fought the urge to clutch his arm, and hovered over Ed threateningly. "It hasn't slowed me a bit. I've still got the strength left to beat the shit out of you if you don't tell me what's going on."

Something in Ross's tone or his expression must have convinced Ed because he shook his head. "I will. I will." Slowly he got to his feet, running his fingers through his thinning brown hair. "We weren't trying to kill you or anything like that. Just frighten you a little."

"Frighten me." Ross laughed sarcastically. "If you weren't such a dimwitted son of a bitch you'd know such a tactic wouldn't scare me. It just makes me as mad as hell!" Seeing Ed's hat next to his left foot, he took his frustration and anger out on the inanimate object, kicking it across the room.

"I know! I know! That's what I tried to tell him."

"Him? Who? Who put somebody up to taking a shot at me?" Ross was in a hurry to finish the interrogation so that he could tend to his arm. He didn't want to play any games. Clenching his jaw, he guessed. "Hawthorne!"

Ed nodded. "He wants to continue getting his cut of this show's money."

"Never!"

"He's an important man with connections in all the high places." Ed smiled weakly. "Come on, Ross. Don't shoot yourself in the foot. If you don't play his game he'll hurt you in more ways than one. With his influence he could pester you and pester you until you have to shut the show down."

That threat struck a sour note in Ross's belly. "If he does he'll have made himself a powerful enemy. One he'll wish he'd never tangled with. You tell him that, Ed. And you tell him something else as well." Jutting his chin out as he spoke, Ross squinted his eyes. "If anything else happens to this show, to me or to anyone else, I'll expose this Hawthorne for what he is. I'll see that the story is run in every newspaper in the country. You tell him that for me."

Oh, he knew the kind of man Hawthorne was all right. A crook! Well, he was going to run an honest show. There was no need to be a faker and deliberately cheat people. Ross felt that if he played fairly with his people they'd give him their all. He wouldn't let someone like Hawthorne hover in the background pulling all the strings.

"Tell him to keep the hell out of my affairs. The show is mine now! Mine alone." Squaring his shoulders and whirling around, Ross stalked away, pushing through the tent flap and walking halfway back across the field. Only when he was out of sight did he allow himself to cringe in pain. The wound was worse than he'd first thought. He'd have to see a doctor before he left town. Shrugging out of his shirt, he tied the bandage tighter hoping to slow the trickle of blood. He'd rest a moment; that would help.

Sabrina, he thought. What was going to happen between them now? It was the first question that popped into his head, proving to him, as if he didn't already know it, just how important she'd become to him. Sabrina. She was the soft spot in his armor. His Achilles heel. He'd always been a loner, but now she inspired dangerous thoughts. Thoughts he forced from his head. No. He wasn't the kind for a permanent attachment. Besides, with this trouble with Hawthorne bubbling, it just might get Sabrina into trouble if it were found out that he had a hankering for her.

But leave her? He closed his eyes to the twinge of pain that that thought caused. Knowing her was the closest to love he'd ever come. Or perhaps he did love her. How then could he just walk away? Turn his back on the happiness and contentment they'd shared? Could he really be that big a bastard?

You have to be, a voice answered inside his head. It's either walk away now or become permanently entangled. As difficult as it was to even think about, it wasn't going to become any easier. The longer he stayed, the harder it would be to leave. And he had to leave. He couldn't keep the Wild West show here, especially now after what had happened.

But what about taking her with him? That thought played over and over again on Ross's mind. He'd seen the awe, the thrill, the excitement on her face tonight at the show. He could find a place for her in the troupe. Certainly it would be much better than leaving her to the mercy of that father-in-law of hers.

Take her along with him to be his mistress? That thought turned to ashes in Ross's mouth. A kept woman. Was that what Sabrina deserved? A woman traipsing after her lover as they made the rounds from town to town. A wanderer. A nomad. A woman without a permanent home. No, Sabrina deserved more. She was the kind of woman who would make some man a very good wife. Some man. The right man.

"Damn!" Ross hit a fence post with the palm of his hand. If only he were that man. But he wasn't. He wasn't the kind of man to have a prim white house with a picket fence and flowers in the yard. He had always been a man in search of adventure. It was as if he had gypsy blood driving him on.

"Sabrina." Her name escaped from his lips in a breathless gasp. He had to do it. For her welfare much more than his own. All the cards were stacked against their ever knowing happiness. They were just too differ-

105

ent. He was like a tumbleweed and she like a rosebush. For all her hard work, Sabrina had been sheltered from the harder realities of life. She just wasn't a rover, but he was. He had to face that fact and deal with it. But how? What was he going to do? One thing he didn't want was Sabrina tagging along after him, following him and trying to convince him to change his mind. Therefore, he had to make a clean break of it, had to find a way to let her know beyond a doubt that it was over.

Every muscle in Ross's body stiffened as it suddenly came to mind just what he had to do. He would return to the inn for his things tonight. He'd leave behind a letter telling Sabrina good-bye as gently as he could. Pray God that he could think of the right things to say, he whose fortune had been made by writing. Good-bye. Such a sad word and yet it needed very much to be said.

Chapter Thirteen

Never had an evening moved so slowly. As Sabrina moved about the inn, it seemed that everything and everyone was moving in slow motion. And all the while her line of vision was fused on the door waiting for Ross to come back. Again and again the door opened and her heart stopped in anticipation, but again and again it was someone else, this patron or that. At last, in disappointment, she turned her attention to her work, trying to hide her anxiety behind false smiles. But, oh, how she wanted the night to be over.

Certainly the evening had begun very badly. Just as she knew he would, her father-in-law had given her a severe tongue-lashing when she returned late from the Wild West show. In penance she went without supper, hurling herself into cleaning and waiting on tables without even taking time to breathe. Hoping to soothe Rufus James's anger, she was doubly attentive in her duties of filling and refilling the customer's tankards, but her thoughts were elsewhere. Where was Ross? Why hadn't he come back for her? When was he going to return?

Listen to me. I sound like a nagging wife, she thought in self-condemnation. She had to be patient. Ross would have an explanation. Perhaps he and Apache Ed had decided to go somewhere and talk business. There would be a good reason for his quick disappearance from the fair grounds. She didn't want to scold. That was the best way of all to lose a man.

Tonight, just as in all the other evenings, Rufus James watched over her, insisting that she linger in the taproom to give the patrons something at which to ogle. It always bothered Sabrina, but now doubly so. She wanted to be away from here, longed for the privacy of her own thoughts. Was it stuffy in the taproom or was it nerves that made her so uncomfortable? Pausing beside the window, she lifted her thick hair from her neck to cool her skin, taking time to peer out the window. Though men came and went, there was no sign of Ross.

At last, just when she was certain she could stand his surveillance no longer, her father-in-law stepped outside with two favored customers. Sabrina took advantage of the diversion to slip upstairs. Making her way to Ross's room she peeked inside, hoping against hope that somehow she would find him there. The room was empty.

Sabrina checked his room again and again, hoping that he would come back and explain. But he didn't come back. She refused to listen to the voice in her head that whispered he wasn't coming back at all, that he had moved on. He wouldn't leave without saying good-bye. He just wouldn't! Not after what they had shared. He loved her. Ross Sheldon loved her. He proved it with his gentle hands and soft words. No, he would return, of this she was certain. That his belongings were still scattered about was proof of that. It was only a matter of time.

The flames engulfing the huge logs in the hearth sputtered and burned low. One by one, the smoking candles hissed and died out. Darkness gathered under the high ceiling, shadows hovered in the corners of the taproom. At last, the night was ending. Very few guests lingered at the tables. Sabrina was relieved that at last she could retire. Checking Ross's room one last time, she made her way to her own tiny chamber. There she lay down on her cot without taking the time or trouble to undress.

Sabrina attuned her ears to the noises of the inn, tossing and turning on her narrow, lumpy mattress. From down below in the taproom she could hear the faint rumbles of laughter as the few remaining patrons shared a jest or two, There was the sound of clinking glasses, then after a few moments there was only silence. Closing her eyes, Sabrina intended only to rest for a few minutes, but against her will she fell asleep. Awakening to the sound of her father-in-law's snores, Sabrina sat up in bed with a start. How long had she dozed off? She could only wonder.

Tiptoeing to the door, Sabrina found the darkened corridor deserted. Slipping out into the hall, she moved carefully and quietly so as not to set the floorboards creaking. Just like a homing pigeon, her footsteps took her to Ross's door. Taking a deep breath, she reached for the doorknob and tugged, opening the door wide. It was dark inside the room, thus she fumbled in her pocket for a match and lit the oil lamp just inside.

"Dear God!" The room was empty of Ross's things. His boots, hats, shirts, pants, and satchels were missing. Sabrina gasped in surprise. He had come back but the heartbreaking evidence was clear to see. Sabrina had to face the truth. Ross's room was picked clean of his belongings. Sometime while she had slept he'd returned, but not to stay or say good-bye.

"How could he?" Tears stung her eyes. Her disappointment and heartache threatened to choke her. The thought that she had been left behind without even a second thought nearly destroyed her, her sorrow turning to anger, a burning rage as hot as the flames of passion he had inspired. All too abruptly her dream world had come to a shattering end. "No!" She couldn't let him leave. Picking up her skirts, Sabrina fled down the stairs, hoping against hope to catch up with him before he left the inn.

The moon had risen high, teasing the inn yard with faint pulsating light. A huge chestnut tree stood like a sentinel, spreading its limbs like arms. Sabrina looked around, but the inn's grounds were deserted. There was no sign of Ross.

Sabrina was chilled by her emotions. She'd never felt so alone, so desolate. "Ross!" Her voice was a croak against the night air. The night breeze stung her eyes, blending with her tears. He'd left her behind without even so much as a word. "Ross!" Turning around, she realized that she wasn't all alone, a figure stood outlined against the wooden walls of the tavern. "Who's there?"

The figure did not answer. Even so, Sabrina took a step forward. Hope leaped in her heart as she made her way towards him. "Ross! Ross!" He'd changed his mind, he couldn't leave her after all.

"Not Ross, my dear."

Sabrina recoiled as she recognized her father-in-law's voice. His tall form cast an ominous shadow across her path. "You!"

A menacing smile lurked about his mouth as he stepped toward her. "Yes, me. Not your lover, Sabrina dear. He has taken his flight, it seems." With a trill of gurgling laughter, he held up a piece of paper, dangling it teasingly. "He left you behind with only this to console you."

Ross had left her a note. Just the thought eased Sabrina's pain. "Please. Give it to me." She reached out, but Rufus James snatched it away.

"Oh no! Not so easily." His eyes hardened as he grabbed her arm. "There's a price to be had for this."

"A price?" Sabrina's blood ran cold. Just what did he mean?

"A kiss." His thin lips curved upward to reveal crooked teeth.

"No!" The very thought was revolting.

"It's little that I ask." His eyes narrowed in anger. "A kiss!"

"No! Don't touch me!" Sabrina put up her hand to fend him off, but he was much stronger than he looked. With an oath, he pulled her to him. "Please!"

"Please," he mocked. "You ungrateful little whore. Don't you think I know what has been going on? You've been fornicating with that . . . that cowboy right beneath my roof. Well, now he's gone. Your self-proclaimed protector has left without you."

"He . . . he's coming back!" Struggling against him, Sabrina tried to break his grip, but he held her securely.

"Coming back? Not according to his little note."

Rufus James took great satisfaction in reading the words printed there. Ross said that although he enjoyed their moments together and found her most desirable, he must leave her behind. He wished her happiness in the future with a suitable husband which he most certainly would never be.

"He's gone." He imprisoned her wrists in one hand as he fumbled with the waistband of his pants. "Ah, no. He's left you all to me, my dear."

Sabrina shuddered as she deciphered his meaning. "Don't do this!" With every ounce of strength she had, she tried to break free from his grasp, but he was a deceptively strong brute despite his thin physique.

"Don't do it? I've wanted this right from the first moment I laid eyes on you, only all your protestations of being so bereaved, so virtuous fooled me. But all this time you've been giving yourself to that buckskin-clad bastard, so why not to me?"

Sabrina stared at him in horror. "You . . . you're my husband's father." It almost seemed like incest.

"And you are my dead son's widow. So what?" With purposeful motions he undid the top button of his breeches, pushing Sabrina violently to the ground. "I'll teach you who you belong to. Right here. Right now. Oh, I'm going to enjoy this!"

"Don't! If you touch me, I'll . . . I'll kill you."

In answer Rufus James laughed, then dropped his pants, looming over her with a leer on his face. "We'll see." He landed with a thud on top of her, knocking the wind from her lungs, pawing and pinching. Sabrina cried out in shock and humiliation, lashing out at him with her hands, kicking at him with her feet. Rufus James only laughed again. "You can't fight me off all night."

"I can and I will!" Working one of her hands free, Sabrina clawed frantically at the ground, searching for anything to use as a weapon. With a sigh of relief she gripped her fingers around a large stone. "Please . . ." she said again.

"Please," he repeated in a falsetto. He fumbled with the lacings of her bodice, reaching down inside to greedily fondle one of her breasts with a touch so rough that she winced in pain. "Soft. Ripe." His sweating, lewd hands invaded the territory only his son and Ross had ever caressed.

"Don't!" Sabrina warned him once again.

"Let's see what else you have to offer." Rufus James's hands moved lower, tugging at her skirts. It was the final insult.

Sabrina's fingers tightened around the stone. She raised her arm, the weapon poised with deadly aim. Mustering all her strength, she brought the stone down upon her father-in-law's head. The contact of rock and skull made a sickening thud and in that moment she was able to roll out from underneath him.

Rufus James howled in angered pain, rearing back like a lion a ready to spring. "You bitch! Hit me will you?" He rose and lunged for her, but Sabrina ducked aside. "You'll pay. By God you will!" Stealthily he stalked her as she hurried towards the inn's back door.

Sabrina searched for another weapon, one more substantial, and found it in the heavy iron poker leaning near the door. She brandished it threateningly, hoping to frighten him into curtailing his attack. Instead, he growled threats of how he'd make her pay.

"I'll brand your hide with that! You'll be sorry!"

When he lurched towards her with obvious intent, she brought it down full force upon his head. Rufus shuddered from the impact. Sabrina felt the vibration all the way down to her toes, watched her father-in-law stumble, but in a moment he was up on his feet again. Sabrina was certain that all was lost, but just as suddenly her father-in-law staggered, crumpled, then fell. He stiffened as he grasped her tightly, then his body went limp. This time he did not rise.

Sabrina knelt beside him for a long moment, then with a shudder she moved away. "Rufus! Rufus!" He didn't answer her, nor did he even move. Not an eyelid, not a finger, not a muscle. He was out cold. Or was he dead? Sabrina was fearful that she might have hit him too hard. Bile rose bitter in her throat as she took note of the blood seeping from his head. "Rufus!" Dear God, what if she'd killed him?

Putting her ear to his chest, she listened for a heart-beat, but all she could hear was her own heart wildly thumping. "No!" He couldn't be dead. Sabrina drew back, trying to control a fit of sudden trembling. He'd tried to rape her, that was his intent. No one would blame her for defending herself when she told the story. No one!

Clasping her hands together, Sabrina tried to think rationally. She had to fetch a doctor. First and foremost that was what she had to do. Rising shakily to her feet that was her intention.

"What has happened here?" The voice shattered Sabrina's already taut nerves. "What have you done, Sabrina?"

John Travers. There was only one man she loathed more than her father-in-law and that was the fat little man.

"My father-in-law struck his head," she said by way of explanation. It was none of Travers's business just what had happened here.

"Struck his head? You mean that you hit him." He grinned evilly, looking like the devil incarnate in the moonlight. "I saw the whole thing, Sabrina. I'm a wit-

113

ness."

"All right, I hit him, but . . . but only to protect my honor." Surely he must understand. Any woman would have done the same thing.

"Yes, I know." He chuckled. "But that's not what I'm going to say."

"What do you mean?" Sabrina was uneasy.

"Let's just say that I owe you one, my dear, for the humiliation you caused me." As he walked forward, he limped, giving proof that Ross had caused him more injury than she had suspected. "I'll tell anyone who will listen how you cold-bloodedly assaulted your father-in-law. With a poker of all things."

"But I didn't do it purposefully. You wouldn't . . ." Sabrina turned pale.

"Indeed I would unless . . ."

Sabrina didn't wait to hear his terms. Every instinct screamed at her that she had to get away. Quickly. With an outcry of revulsion she ran to her bedroom where she knew she only had time to grab the little purse under her mattress, her nest egg. Clutching it to her breast she took to her heels, pushing past Travers and through the door. Running towards the bushes, she fled the inn.

Chapter Fourteen

Fear goaded Sabrina to run and run until she was exhausted. A wave of sickness washed over her as she thought about her father-in-law and what she had done. Murder. She had taken another life. It little mattered that there had been provocation. No one would believe her when John Travers told his lies. Rufus James was a respected citizen with a hundred friends and patrons. What chance had she? As soon as her father-in-law's body was found, a cry would be raised and she would be hunted down unmercifully. What then?

Her emotions welled up inside her, ready to burst at any moment. At last they did. Tears which she had been holding in check now rolled down her cheeks. Fiercely she swiped them away, sobbing as she stumbled and fell headlong in a heap upon the grass. Huddled in a ball of misery, she gave vent to her fear and grief until her tears were spent. She felt like a lost soul, torturing herself with memories of Ross. Nausea churned in the pit of her stomach as she thought of his betrayal. She hadn't meant anything to him. Not really. If she had, he never would have left her with just a piece of paper to explain his feelings. Left her to her father-in-law's mercy.

Bastard! Unfeeling scoundrel! He was that and worse, but she loved him still. "Fool. I am such a fool!" Slowly rising to her feet, she wandered aimlessly for a long while, running in a circle, lost in her broken dreams and memories. What was she going to do now? She didn't really know. Where could she go? There was no one who would take her in. Where could she hide? She was all alone and friendless.

The sound of running feet and curses was carried to Sabrina's ears by the wind. Undoubtedly John Travers had already raised a fuss. Hysteria would possess the townsmen. They'd cry for her punishment when the lie was told.

"Oh, let them take me to prison, I don't care," she whispered. She felt numb. Tired. Even so, the instinct for survival was stronger than she might have imagined. Strong enough to push her into seeking out a hiding place behind a large discarded ale barrel. There she watched the goings on with strange detachment.

"Where is she? Where is the murderess?" she heard a large-boned man thunder.

"We'll find her. She won't go far," John Travers answered. "All the roads leaving town are blocked, thanks to my warning."

"She won't get away . . ."

Cautiously, Sabrina peered out from her hiding place to view what was happening. The square courtyard of the inn was the scene of total pandemonium. Holding torches aloft, several of the townsmen were pacing about the inn yard. The night's events had drawn an angry crowd who hovered about John Travers. It was obvious by his frantically waving arms and shouted expletives that the scheming, rotund little man would not stop until she was found. Sabrina was frightened. She was trapped like a fox by that cur and there was nowhere that she could go. And all for the sake of petty revenge.

Every doorway and gateway of the inn was blocked now to her escape as townsmen searched the premises. She would soon be discovered, for even now they were searching the grounds. But where could she hide? Where would she be safe from detection? If only she had gone farther instead of giving vent to her sadness she might have had a chance, might have gotten away. As it was she was cornered. How could she escape the snare they were laying? Indecision fueled her frustration until her eyes lit upon a brightly painted wagon in one end of the courtyard. The horses were harnessed and ready for travel. In all probability the wagon would soon be wheeling its way out of the courtyard, towards some unknown destination.

"A wagon. A covered wagon." How convenient! If only she could reach the open end of the wagon without being seen, perhaps she might yet have a chance of escape.

Although the wagon was shrouded by shadows, Sabrina knew that she could not take the chance of her movements attracting attention. Needing to create a diversion, therefore, she fumbled about for a large rock and took aim, hurling it towards the rooftop several feet away.

"Someone's over here!" she heard a voice shout as all eyes looked in that direction. Stumbling through the darkness, Sabrina headed in the opposite direction, darting in and out between crates and barrels as she made her way toward the intended hiding place. Upon reaching the wagon, she pushed aside the curtains behind the wagon seat and climbed inside, pausing just a moment. Feeling relieved that there were no sound of pursuit, she smiled, but she knew she was not safe. Not yet. She might still be caught.

"Never!" she breathed. Somehow she would outwit them. She wouldn't let John Travers, that slimy rat, win! Covering herself with a large piece of canvas, she moved her lips in a silent prayer, a prayer that was seemingly answered as the minutes passed in silence.

Sabrina was quite pleased with herself, certain now that John Travers would search for her in vain. How sly she had been to hide herself right under that bastard's nose. She would prove herself more than a match for him.

It was surprisingly comfortable inside the wagon and Sabrina whiled away the time by looking around her. The sides were paneled, the semicircular top covered with characteristic ornamentation both inside and out to attract attention. It was much like a house on wheels. The top was rounded and made of painted canvas, stretched over wooden hoops. Added wood to the top and sides made it completely weatherproof to guard the treasures inside — guns. Loads and loads of guns!

The back had two large hinged doors for easy loading and unloading, the front was open with curtains drawn across to give a small measure of privacy. Whoever had built the wagon had done so with a loving hand. For the moment she felt safe.

The security she felt was soon threatened however. The sound of angry voices and shuffling feet warned Sabrina of danger as a group of men passed by the wagon. Fearing discovery, she clutched at the tarp, covering her head, determined to go down fighting if necessary, but no such problem occurred. Instead, she heard a jovial voice arguing his need to get his wagon on the road.

"I've been here much too long already," said the voice. "I just want to get out of here."

"Why are you in such a hurry to leave?"

"I've got business elsewhere, an important appointment. A load of guns that I've at last found a customer for."

"Guns?"

"That I'm taking to upstate New York."

"Well then, go on. We'll suppose you've paid your bill, though if you haven't we'll soon track you down."

The wagon was was going to pull out. Sabrina felt a wave of relief! New York. It was so far away. She feared the unknown, but it was her only chance to escape. Escape! The word had a pleasant ring. She would go as far as the owner of the wagon would take her. By that time the search would have died down somewhat, she reasoned, and she would have time to plan her next course of action. Then she could come back, hire a lawyer with the money she had saved, and clear her good name. Or perhaps she'd go far away and never come back. This wagon offered her a haven from those who sought her and at the same time offered her a chance for adventure. Hadn't that been what she had wanted all along. A chance to live the kind of life she read about in her books?

Sabrina held her breath in anticipation, exhaling in relief as she felt the floorboards jiggle and sway as the man jumped upon the wagon, settling himself on the front seat. Soon the wagon was bouncing and creaking as it moved down the bumpy road.

Sabrina was exhausted and for the next few hours the rocking of the wagon as it moved along nearly lulled her to sleep. Closing her eyes, she listened as the driver lapsed into song. It was a familiar voice, low and soothing. Maneuvering herself towards the front of the wagon, she pushed aside the curtain just an inch and peered out, not in the least surprised by what she saw. The driver of the wagon was none other than Jonathan Colt.

"Jonathan!" she whispered to herself. She had the urge to confide in him, to tell him what had happened, but she held herself back. It was too early to trust anyone. Perhaps she never really would again.

The sudden jolt of the wagon wheels jiggled her bones and reminded Sabrina that she had been in one position too long. Her arms and legs felt cramped and stiff and without a second thought she stood up, trying her best to stretch her aching limbs and bring back the blood to her feet and hands. Unable to stretch to her full height, lest she bump her head on the top of the wagon, she contented herself with a stooped posture, hanging on to two support beams to keep herself upright. As the wagon rolled and bumped down the road, she familiarized herself with her surroundings.

Guns, guns, guns! Of every shape and size. There

119

were rifles, pistols, and handguns. Guns with pearl handles and those of a less decorative style. Some had short barrels, others long, skinny barrels.

Sabrina was so intent on her exploration that she did not see the curtain pushed aside, nor the eyes which peered through the curtains of the wagon, widening in surprise as they caught sight of her.

"Well, well, well. In truth, I am a blessed man." The voice startled her so much that she rose up and bumped her head. "Easy, pretty little lady. Easy." The wagon screeched to a halt.

"I can explain!"

"I'm sure that you can." Jonathan's grin split his face from ear to ear as he waited.

Sabrina was afraid to tell him the truth, so she conjured up a fanciful tale that she was on her way to join a Wild West show. It seemed to be the first thing that popped into her mind. "Any show will do."

Jonathan's golden brows popped up in surprise. "You want to join up with a Wild West show?"

"Yes. I do."

"Just like that?" He seemed puzzled yet pleased at the same time.

"It was seeing that Wild West show this afternoon. It put ideas in my mind." Sabrina shrugged. "I don't want to stay at the inn forever. I want adventure."

"And you think you'll find it with me?" He seemed to be amused by her chatter.

"I wanted to get far, far away. The wagon was here and I remembered you saying that you had some guns to deliver. I just took a chance that you'd be going in the direction I wanted to go and ducked inside." Sabrina was afraid she might not be a very good liar. Though she managed to make her voice convincing she couldn't look him in the eye. Lying just didn't come easy to her.

Jonathan, lonely himself, seemed very agreeable to the idea. "Well then, since you intended to stow away anyway, I'll issue you an invitation. I can indeed help you fulfill your dream." Jonathan bowed low. "I, Jonathan Colt, do most humbly invite you, Sabrina James, to come with, me on my journey to join up with Buffalo Bill Cody."

"Buffalo Bill?"

"Yep! I once did a stint as a sharpshooter in his show."

"A sharpshooter!" Sabrina was notably impressed. First Ross and now Jonathan. It seemed to be a very small world. "Oh, how I wish that I could do such a thing. I wish I knew how to shoot."

Jonathan puffed out his chest with all the pride of a strutting rooster. "It's not difficult. I could teach you."

"Teach me to shoot?"

He laughed softly, charmed by her enthusiasm. She was such a refreshing change from the other women he had known. She was open and honest in expressing her feelings. "So well that you can put a bullet between the eyes on the face of a nickel." Seeing her look of doubt he rambled on. "If a person believes strongly in himself, anything is possible."

"Anything?"

"Hell, you can touch the moon if you think you can." He touched his temple with his finger. "It's all in the mind, Sabrina. All in the mind. If you think you can, then you can. I've seen proof of that over and over."

"Me, shooting in a Wild West show and meeting Buffalo Bill."

In all her wildest dreams she had never supposed she would ever meet up with *him*. A real Wild West show. The father of them all. Had it not been for the severity of the situation, Sabrina might have laughed out loud. Her dreams were just about to come true, but at a devastating price. For just a moment a smile creased her brow as she thought about her father-in-law. But no, she mustn't think about that. What had happened had happened. Sabrina was determined to leave her old life behind her.

Part Two

The Buckskin Temptress
On the road: 1884-85

"I can resist everything except temptation."
Oscar Wilde, *Lady Windermere's Fan*

Chapter Fifteen

The wind brought a stinging mist to Sabrina's cheeks and hands as she sat on the wide board at the front of the wagon taking her turn at holding the reins. The mud-covered earth from a recent rain had dried into a dull sludge that slowed down their progress as the wagon ambled down the road. But as Jonathan said, a man just couldn't wrestle with the elements. They'd get where they were going soon enough. Buffalo Bill would just have to wait for his guns.

Sabrina had grown used to the rough ride in Jonathan's wagon as they meandered along the New England roads. She was determined to leave her old life behind her, though there were times when cherished memories of Ross intruded into her thoughts, pushing contentment aside. A lump would rise in her throat then, causing throbbing heartache that took a long time to subside. She would never again feel the firm pressure of his lips against hers, nor enjoy his strong protective arms. Never again know his touch, hear his laughter.

There was something else that bothered her as well. Always at the back of her mind was the memory of her father-in-law lying so still and John Travers waving his arms as he set about weaving his web of revenge. She had little doubt that her fate would be precarious at best were she to return to the inn. That knowledge gave her the fortitude to endure the often long and tiring journey. The trials, tribulations, and sufferings were preferable to being locked up behind iron bars. She had a strong will and determination that convinced her that she could bear even the harshest conditions.

As the days passed she found out that she had an inner strength as strong as steel. Sabrina began to see that life was not so much what happened to a person, but how they accepted their circumstances. A person could either see the flowers or the weeds, the sunlight or the shadows, the dark in the clouds or the silver lining. She was determined to view only the positive aspects of her life and try to forget the bad. There was no turning back, no purpose in thinking of the "what ifs" or the "what-might-have-beens." She had to accept her life just the way it had turned out and hope for the best.

Not only did she change her attitude, but her looks as well, just in case anyone happened to be searching for her. She knew she had to make certain that she would not be recognized, thus her only recourse was to react as if she were being pursued by the law until she knew for sure. With that purpose in mind, she bought a dark brown wig from a costume supply company and coated her eyelashes and eyebrows with charcoal to darken them. She had never worn any kind of make-up before, but now she applied bright pink to her lips and cheeks. Sabrina knew that even her own mother, God rest her soul, would not have recognized her.

As for Jonathan, he had proven to be a perfect gentleman and an understanding friend, as well as a most pleasant traveling companion. Although she didn't give him any explanation for her change in appearance, he didn't question it but remained his amiable self. If she chose to be a brunette for a change, well that was her business and to tell the truth, he rather liked her new look. Moreover, he wouldn't let her "worry her head," he said, about the trip's expenses. Jonathan had enough money to put them up in separate rooms at the various hotels and inns they frequented along the way. True to his word, he was taking her to meet Buffalo Bill, though they did detour from time to time on their route so that he might give in to his one vice—gambling.

"We'll get you a bit part in Bill's show," he promised with a wink. From time to time during their journey, they'd stop by the side of the road and Jonathan would give her a lesson in shooting. She shot at bottles, tin cans, and apples Jonathan threw into the air, using pistols, revolvers, and rifles. Jonathan insisted that she had a real aptitude for handling a gun as well as the steady hand and keen eyesight that was needed. "One of these days you'll be able to shoot with the best of them," he would say.

Sabrina soon made up her mind that this would be so, a vow that was doubly impressed upon her when one afternoon they attended the Sells Brothers Circus. Along with many other interesting acts—jugglers, tightrope walkers, mimes, dancing bears, prancing horses, and animal trainers, was a husband and wife sharpshooting team billed as "Butler and Oakley." Sabrina was hypnotized by Annie Oakley's shooting and now knew for sure that she simply had to learn how to shoot like that.

"I mean it, Jonathan. I intend to be just as good a shot as her some day." If Sabrina could learn, perhaps Buffalo Bill would let her perform in his show just as Annie Oakley was doing for the Sells Brothers Circus.

At first Jonathan had looked at her skeptically. "I don't know. From what I've heard, Annie Oakley has been shooting for a long, long time. Had to learn to be a crack shot so that she could bring in fresh game to feed her family. She was practically born with a rifle."

"I don't care. If I have to practice every morning and night I'll do it." Such a skill seemed to be the only avenue open to the better life for which she longed. Buffalo Bill was just the person who could provide her with the necessary opportunity to better herself. If Annie Oakley could do it, so could she, Sabrina James. She even picked out a stage name, inspired by a combination of the garb Annie wore—buckskin—the pet name for one of the circus lions—"Kitty"—and the brand name of Jonathan's favorite whiskey—Tremaine. Buckskin Kitty Tremaine. The more she spoke the name aloud, the better she liked it.

"Buckskin Tremaine," Jonathan repeated when she told him. "Kitty Tremaine. I think I like it."

"Then that's who I'll be from now on!" The change in names gave her added security from being apprehended by any of John Travers's cronies. "And you can call me Kit."

"Kit!" Jonathan said the name with special emphasis on the *t*. "Kit."

Sabrina's mother had taught her sewing long ago, thus she passed the days on the road by sewing her own costumes—leggings under a short skirt and a jacket, all buff-colored leather. She added a special touch by decorating the outfit with beads, much the same as one of Ross's decorative buckskin suits. Little by little Sabrina was changing from an Eastern girl into the woman she had dreamed of one day being. But even so, a day didn't go by when she didn't think about Ross at least once or twice, wondering where he was, what he was doing.

Ross was in fact doing more than a bit of traveling himself, guiding his company of wagons along a road that ran parallel a mile from the one Jonathan and Sabrina had chosen. His arm was still a bit tender, though the doctor had put in a few stitches and cleaned the wound to help with the healing.

Ross had packed up his old Wild West show the very next day after the shooting, in fact. He had collected his things from the inn and written the note for Sabrina. The troupe had left long before sunup, for he knew they couldn't take a chance on staying a moment longer with all the threats being bandied about. Even now his belly coiled at the thought of what Hawthorne had done. Someday he'd see the man paid.

Now they were headed for the company's winter quarters and the journey had been uneventful. Relatively peaceful. "So, it's all worked out for the best," he told himself over and over again.

At this time of day Sabrina was undoubtedly mopping the floors of the inn, a grueling job and yet a safe one. There was little harm that could come to her from that, whereas journeying on the road was fraught with problems. He had done the right thing in leaving her behind, or so he tried to convince himself. If he kept looking behind him, well, that was just to make certain that everybody was keeping up. If his eyes misted once or twice, that was from the dust of the road.

"Just where are we headed, boss?" A young kid named Joe Kenny had just joined with the show and his excitement was obvious.

"Straight on up this road."

Ross had made up his mind that Buffalo Bill needed his comeuppance. That was why he'd decided to make his camp only a short way from where Bill was quartered. He'd give old Bill a run for his money, force the old billy goat to be competitive. It would make for an interesting time.

Chapter Sixteen

The jingle of the harness and the rumble of the wagon wheels was music to Sabrina's ears. Before them was a beautiful view of rolling hills and well-painted farmhouses. The air was filled with the noisy sounds and acrid smells of the country, the early morning crowing of barnyard roosters, the squealing of pigs, the mooing of cows awaiting their milking. Some of the farmhouses seemed deserted, but soon the farm folk were up and about like so many bees in a beehive, going about their daily chores, waving at Sabrina and Jonathan when they read the letters on their wagon as they passed by. Large draft horses with strong necks and flaring nostrils were soon hard at work pulling plows, wagons, or other farm equipment.

"It's just such folks as these that have made Buffalo Bill a celebrity," Jonathan declared, waving back. "That's why I put Bill's name on the side of the wagon. Insures us of special treatment as we go along." Indeed, Jonathan had painted a large circle in red with yellow letters that read: "Gun supplier for Buffalo Bill — J. T. Colt Esquire."

Seemingly it had worked, for during those nights when no hotel was within sight, Jonathan had managed to con more than one farmer and his wife into letting him and Sabrina stay for the night. Usually they were treated to a tongue-pleasing home-cooked meal both at night and in the morning, then it was off on the road again.

Sabrina was enjoying the journey more and more as

time went along, for in truth Jonathan was an entertaining companion who always treated her like a lady. He was the complete opposite of Ross in more ways than just his looks. He was cautious whereas Ross had been impulsive, somewhat self-effacing where Ross was self-assured and a bit egotistical at times. Where Ross talked a lot about himself, Jonathan seemed more concerned with Sabrina's opinions and abilities. Ross was adventuresome and ambitious, but Jonathan seemed to take life more in his stride. The word *hurry* just didn't seem to be in his vocabulary. Being with Ross had been exciting, being with Jonathan was soothing.

It had been an interesting journey so far, a time of just looking out at the countryside and pleasant conversation. Sabrina had learned that Jonathan's full name was Jonathan Thaddeus Edward Platton Colt. "Quite a handle," Jonathan said with a grin. "As if my father expected quite a lot from me. Is it any wonder I shortened it to just Jonathan T. Colt?"

Though he treated the matter with humor, Sabrina had sensed hurt behind his words, as if Jonathan perceived himself as a failure. From his talk it seemed that though Jonathan had tried his luck at many ventures, he had not been as successful as he might have planned. He had traveled just as extensively as Ross, indeed to nearly all of the states and territories, yet had not been able to turn his ideas into money. Still, as Jonathan himself was the first to admit, he was certain that if he just continued following the rainbow he'd find his pot of gold.

"Well, looks like we're getting closer and closer all the time," Jonathan teased. "Are you anxious?"

"Very much so." Sabrina had thought about meeting Buffalo Bill all along the road, going over and over in her mind just what she would say. She'd call him Mr. Cody, just to give him a proper show of respect and then she'd ask him in a polite way if there was anything she could do to earn her way in the show.

As they traveled along, getting nearer and nearer to the

upstate New York town of Albany, the rumble of other wagons could be heard even before they were sighted. It wouldn't be long now. Sabrina tried to calm the butterflies in her stomach, but they seemed to be having a riotous time.

"Our destination is just on down the road, Kit," Jonathan confided, lapsing easily into using her new name, "near a pine grove beside a creek. Buffalo Bill has a winter camp there at Albany." Flicking the reins, he urged the horses into a faster pace.

They were nearly there when they spotted a black shiny carriage approaching. Upon the seat, driving the horses, was Buffalo Bill himself. Sabrina knew him right away from both Jonathan's and Ross's description, and her eyes widened as he came closer. Even sitting down it was obvious to see that he was extremely tall. His dark blond hair hung down to his shoulders, whipping about his neck as he tugged at the reins. He had a well-trimmed mustache and a beard, long but carefully trimmed so that it grew only from his chin and not his cheeks.

Bounding from the seat, Buffalo Bill grabbed Jonathan's hand, cranking it up and down like a pump handle. "Jonathan. It is you. Glad to see you, my boy. Mighty glad. I've been impatiently waiting for you to bring my cargo." He paused for a moment, his line of vision focusing on the wagon. Seeing Jonathan's sign he chuckled. "Good. Good. I can use all the publicity I can get. Good for business." He cocked his head and paused as if suddenly remembering his manners. "How was the trip? Not too unpleasant I hope. You're a bit late. Hope there weren't any problems."

"Nope! A bit of rain and wind made the going a bit rough and slowed us down a mite, but nothing serious."

"Good. Good." Spying Sabrina he inquired as to who the beautiful lady was and in that instant Sabrina turned as red as Jonathan's sign.

"Why, this is none other than Kitty Tremaine." Jonathan smiled mischievously as he helped Sabrina down

132

from the wagon. "Kit, this is the famous Buffalo Bill Cody."

Sabrina let out her adoration in a sigh. "Yes, I know . . ."

Bill nodded, smiling from ear to ear, his gray eyes twinkling. "Pleased."

"I've read so many stories about you . . . about all your . . . your acts of bravery, Mr. Cody." Ross had inundated her with detailed tales about William Cody's early days.

"Oh, you have." Bill threw back his head and laughed, a sound that seemed to come upward from his belly in a deep boom. "Lies all!"

"What?" Sabrina was confused by his laughter, fearing she might have said the wrong thing.

"Never mind." Bill quickly sobered. "And please, call me Bill, young lady. Mr. Cody sounds just too formal. Out West most people just don't bother with last names or formalities."

"Bill . . ." His dapper, down-home personality drew her to him instantly. Somehow she envisioned that she and this man might well become friends.

Jonathan looked from Sabrina to Bill and back again. "Kit's a female sharpshooter," he blurted out.

"Sharpshooter?" Bill's eyebrows shot up in surprise. "You don't say." The information seemed to doubly spark his interest, for he circled Sabrina three times, eyeing her up and down. "Interesting."

"Imagine the possibilities." Jonathan winked conspiratorially "Why, Kit here could bring in a bigger crowd than you can imagine."

"Jonathan—" Sabrina was aghast. Pursing her lips, she tugged on his sleeve. She certainly couldn't be called a sharpshooter, at least not yet. Why, she had just begun her learning. Undoubtedly she'd be all thumbs were she even to try to shoot in front of an audience.

"Now, now, little lady, don't be modest." In a gesture of genuine affection, Buffalo Bill took her hand, patting it gently. "It's my business to know about special talents.

133

That's what's made my show what it is."

"And Kit can make your show very successful." Jonathan seemed determined to keep the subject alive. "She can shoot backwards over her shoulder while sighting into a mirror and aim at targets while riding bareback." It was an out-and-out lie.

"Jonathan!" Sabrina was certain he must have suddenly lost his mind. She couldn't do any of that. She started to tell Bill that, but Jonathan lightly touched her lips with his index finger.

"We'll talk about all of this later. Right now we got a whole load of guns and ammunition to unload." Putting his arm around her waist, Jonathan led Sabrina back to the wagon then took his familiar seat beside her. He urged the horses on as they followed Bill's carriage.

When they reached the encampment at the bottom of the hill, the view was magnificent, the air clear and clean, and even the distant tent village looked gleaming white in the distance. To the right the land sloped to a sheltered valley through which a bubbling stream made its way. Drooping willows grew along the bank mixed with tall straight sugar maples. The encampment included one hundred acres of good farmland, complete with corral, cultivated fields, and pasture. It was an ideal spot and Sabrina was hoping she could stay here a long, long time. Now she knew why people from the city spoke so enviously about the country folk. Even the farmland around Plymouth could not match this for beauty.

Bill proved to be a cordial host. He showed Sabrina to a tent that she would occupy with another woman, a dog trainer. Jonathan would lodge with the ringmaster for the time being.

"Just try to think of this as home," Bill had said.

"Home . . ." Sabrina had never really had any kind of permanent home, not with her mother, her father-in-law, not even with her husband. Looking around the tent, she wondered if she could ever think of this place in such a manner. Well, at least it would give her a sense of permaᴡency for a little while.

There was a large wooden tub in the center of the tent, a reminder of the long, dusty, tiring journey. The first thing Sabrina did was to have the tub filled with water. As warm as she could possibly make it. Cleanliness was next to godliness, or so her mother had always said. Certainly as she lowered herself into the water it seemed as close to heaven as she had come since setting off with Jonathan.

Her new roommate, Sadie Pender, seemed to understand, for she left soap and towels in a pile by the tub with an all-knowing smile. "That handsome hunk of a man you been traveling with would inspire me to soak for a long, long while too," she said. "Anyone can certainly see that he's smitten with you."

"Smitten?" Sabrina was quick to shake her head, feeling the need to dispel any such rumors. "No, no, Jonathan is just a friend."

Sadie giggled. "A man doesn't look at a friend the way he looks at you."

Sabrina started to protest but before she could get the words out of her mouth, Sadie had already ducked through the tent flap to help the others with the meal preparation. There was no one to talk to except herself, so perhaps it wasn't any wonder Sabrina started mumbling.

"Jonathan isn't smitten." At least she didn't want him to be. She liked him, really, truly felt a great deal of affection for him, but it didn't even approach the feelings she had for Seth and Ross. She felt grateful to Jonathan because he had been there when she needed him. It wouldn't be right to repay him by hurting him. She knew all too well what it felt like to love someone when he didn't love you back.

Lingering over her bath, scrubbing her body, and lathering her hair, she was troubled. "He isn't smitten. He isn't." She didn't want to admit it because she didn't want him to care for her in that way. It would complicate things too much. And yet, the more she thought about it, the more she remembered that Jonathan always did seem to have a special glow in his eyes when he looked her way. His fingers always seemed to linger for an extra amount of time when he touched her shoulder or her hand. Whenever he talked about the future, he always spoke as if they would be together for a long, long time.

"Oh, Jonathan." She closed her eyes, but all she could see was Ross's face. How was it possible that the same man could have brought her such happiness and at the same time such pain? Ross Sheldon. Ross Sheldon. Pressing her fingers against her temples, she sought to force him from her thoughts. Somehow, someway, she had to forget him. She was determined to regain the air of aloofness that up to the time she had met Ross had been her shield and armor. Yet was it possible? Ross had come into her world with all the suddenness of a thunderbolt and she wondered if she would ever be the same again.

Sabrina lay back in the wooden tub for a time, troubled by her contemplation. Then at last, when the water grew tepid, she stood up, stepped from the tub and wrapped herself in the large flannel towel. There was only one answer to her dilemma. From now on she had to take a firm hand in her own destiny. She had to be strong and not rely on any man. Untouchable. That was what she had to be. And ambitious. She had to make a place for herself in the world so that never again would she be dependent on a man for her well-being and happiness. As to Jonathan, he had to be shown that her feelings for him were strictly platonic. Friendship. Business. It was the only way that Sabrina could find any peace of mind.

Chapter Seventeen

The weather was warm and often sunny for the time of year, with little snow and cold. An Indian summer, Jonathan called it. Even though it was winter and there weren't any performances, there was something to look forward to: Spring.

For the first time in a while Sabrina had the sense of belonging. She was content with her new life in Buffalo Bill's show, happy with what she was doing. Since she had always been good with animals, she was put to work caring for the smaller caged animals at her own suggestion. Though she was always busy either practicing her shooting or doing her share of the necessary chores, it was a far cry from the drudgery of her father-in-law's inn. What's more, she was complimented for her efforts.

She soon found that everything went according to schedule, including eating and sleeping. There were approximately six hundred people all gathered together. Many of the men had their families with them, the Indians their squaws and papooses. She soon found that there was a variety of nationalities, dialects and costumes represented in the miniature city. One thing she could say about the show was that the people were certainly a friendly lot. For the first time in a long while she felt as though she were part of a family.

Sabrina had never really had any female friends before, but now she had not only her tentmate, Sadie Pender, to talk to, but other women as well. There was Sue Anne Roberts, a woman known for her skill riding bareback, who taught Sabrina more about a horse than she could ever hope to know. Mrs. Clara Williams, who was the costumer of the show, was as well-meaning as any mother and took Sabrina under her wing like a protective mother hen. Sabrina also became friends with Sadie Thompson, an opera singer who was rumored to be Bill's paramour.

Then there were her male friends. Jonathan, of course. "Arizona John" Burke, who acted as press agent for Buffalo Bill and promised her he would make her a star. Adam Bogardus and his sons, who had been temporarily assigned the place of sharpshooters in the show and they opened themselves up to Sabrina's gesture of friendship. They added diversity to Jonathan's teaching and made her lessons in gunmanship doubly interesting. Day by day, the list of Sabrina's friends grew, including a tall, large-boned giant of an Indian called Strutting Wolf. Despite the fact that he could not speak English, they somehow communicated. Sabrina could tell that he had appointed himself her guardian, and kept his eye open for any danger in which she might be.

"Winter is passing. Won't be long until you get your chance," Jonathan whispered several times in her ear.

Though at first Sabrina had been a bit wary of Jonathan's bragging of her ability, she soon perceived it as a challenge. She would learn to be just as good as he boasted so that when Buffalo Bill gave her the chance he promised, she'd be up to the task. With that thought in mind, she forced herself to practice at least four hours a day, even when she was exhausted. In time she could shoot while holding the rifle up in the air, hitting everything Jonathan tossed up. She could shoot bent over backwards and even between her legs. Little by little she was developing her self-confidence and determined to put her past behind her, to do everything possible to advance her new career.

If every once in awhile Jonathan would give himself a pat on the back by suggesting that he had been the one responsible for her ability, it was to be expected she supposed. It was true that he had taught her how to shoot. "Remember that gal at the circus. Annie. You're as good a shot as she was, Kit. Perhaps even better," he would say. That would make her beam with pride. "Course now, she and that Butler fella were a husband-and-wife team. Think we might be a team someday, Kit?"

"We're already partners, Jonathan," she responded hesitantly.

"A sound business decision on my part," he said with a smile. "You're going to make me a rich man at last, Kit. But I want to be more than just that."

"We're partners and *friends*." She had to make that clear to him. They were good friends to be sure, but certainly not in a romantic way. She remembered Sadie's words that first day she had arrived. So Sadie had been right.

"Sure, friends!" He couldn't hide his disappointment. "But maybe someday . . ." She started to protest, but he silenced her with his fingers. "It doesn't hurt to dream. Give me that at least."

"Jonathan. I don't—"

"Hush. Please."

Sabrina was touched by the look of adoration on his face. If only she could love this man. He was good to her. Oh, why couldn't the head rule the heart instead of the other way. For the moment at least, the subject was put to rest.

Buffalo Bill had established a comfortable winter quarters for his entertainers. Life there was much like in a small village, self-contained and self-sufficient. The tent city on the outskirts of the town was complete with a community mess hall, similar in style, Jonathan said, to an army encampment. Sabrina couldn't make the complaint that she wasn't well fed. There was usually beef— with beans, in a stew or sliced with vegetables; or chicken—boiled, broiled or fried; and potatoes fixed in a variety of ways. The cook was fond of desserts, so there was always some kind of pie or cake, including pumpkin. She had to be careful lest she burst all the seams in her buckskin, she joked to Sadie.

Despite the hiatus in the show, the *Weekly Sentinel* had all sorts of stories about Buffalo Bill and the show. No one experienced more popularity than this bigger-than-life hero, as the journalists who were always hanging around professed. And then suddenly Sabrina found herself to be the talk of the area. Someone had leaked out the information that when the show opened in a few more months there would be a female sharpshooter with the show. "Buckskin Kitty Tremaine," the posters read.

"Jonathan, I'm not ready." Sabrina's hands went cold as if all the blood had drained from her body. She'd never realized she would feel such fear at the very thought of shooting before the crowds.

"Of course you are." Jonathan seemed to be attuned to her emotions. Grasping her hands in his, he rubbed them gently between his own, warming them. "You'll be just fine."

"What if I can't shoot a thing?" It was a worry that plagued her. Practicing was one thing, performing before hundreds of people another. She'd be all thumbs. "What if I miss?"

"Then you bluff, Brina. Showmanship is only thirty percent talent. The rest is bluster!" Before she could react, Jonathan bent down and lightly kissed her on the lips. "Oh, Brina . . . Kit!"

"Jonathan! Don't." Every muscle in Sabrina's body tensed. Shaking her head, she stepped away.

He looked as wounded as if she had struck him. "I'm sorry! I only meant it as a kiss for luck." He forced a

140

laugh. "But then, maybe you don't need any such superstitious nonsense. You're good, gal. Very, very good. I have every confidence in you. You'll show them all."

Despite Jonathan's confidence in her, Sabrina was nervous anyway. Her first touch of anxiety crept over her. She was experiencing what Jonathan and a few of the others always termed "stage fright." Try as she might, her stomach was tied in knots at the very thought of being watched by so many people. Bill had poured a great deal of money into the advertisements and expected record-breaking crowds when the show opened. How then could she not be a nervous wreck? She was a fake. A phoney. She'd never shot before a crowd before, despite what Jonathan tried to tell Buffalo Bill. What if she failed?

The newspapers promised "scenes from the Wild West that few had witnessed." "Two hours of entertainment that will keep you on the edge of your seats!" Posters large enough to cover the entire side of a house and handbills small enough to put in a pocket were plastered on barns, silos, telegraph poles, and the brick walls of banks. The bright ink splashed yellow, green, and red everywhere, lending a false sense of spring to the area. "The amusement triumph of the age," the posters declared. "Miss Buckskin Kitty Tremaine will astound you with the accuracy of her aim!"

Sabrina was unaware that "Cherokee Ross Sheldon's Wild West Show" was playing in a neighboring upstate New York town, nor that he had seen one of their posters. "So there will soon be a showdown of our companies," he said aloud.

Ross was very pleased with himself. He had evaded further trouble by moving farther east. He also posted two men to stand guard over his campsite, although they had lost one crate of wild coyotes in the crossing, which he suspected had been stolen. Not letting that event rile him, he had assembled new workers and contracted several bookings including Brooklyn, New York. What's more, he now had an authentic Indian, Chief White Feather of the Arapaho nation, in his employ. A real Indian chief whose reputation preceded him. That was something even Buffalo Bill did not have. Indians, but no authentic Indian chief. Even better, Chief White Feather had brought a troupe of warriors and women with him, resplendent in their feathers and beaded leather finery.

Ross knew that the New Yorkers loved pageantry, especially Western display. Never in her life had America been more interested in entertainment. He had put together a show that would keep the people of the country standing in the aisles. He had assembled a variety of cowboys and Indians to enhance the true image of the West. In addition, he had boxes of Indian relics to display. In cages he had a large prairie hen and some talking magpies to display along with a large black bear. He was sure that he was on the road to success and need not fear any competitor, not even Bill.

"Well, let's just see what Bill has up his sleeve," he muttered. There was the usual list of performers he'd seen last year: Captain A. H. Bogardus and his boys, a shooting exhibition; Con T. Groner, the cowboy sheriff of the Platte, noted for capturing part of Doc Middleton's gang and foiling their plan to join up with Jesse James to rob a Union Pacific train; Jim Lawson, a distinguished lassoist with roper, Utah Frank; Bill Bullock, leader of the cowboys and part Sioux; Bud Ayers and Dick Bean, who were to appear in feats of horsemanship. It looked like the same old show until something caught his eye. Well, he'd be damned!

"Buckskin Kitty Tremaine," he scoffed. "Bill will sink to anything, even using a woman to promote his show." Competition was the name of the game. Each Wild West show was trying to surpass each other with gimmicks, costumes, Indians, and dazzle.

Well, he'd soon show him that he didn't have the field to himself anymore. Ross intended to be a real competitor. "A *woman*," he exclaimed beneath his breath again. He'd have to find something that would be just as big a drawing card. He wouldn't take this sitting down. But what? An Indian attack? No, that was standard in all shows. He wanted to get something different. But first perhaps he'd visit this "amusement triumph" and take a look at the female sharpshooter for himself. Perhaps he might even try to steal her away from Bill. That thought was amusing. With a chuckle, he made his plans.

Chapter Eighteen

The March sky was an azure blue, nary a cloud anywhere. The weather heralded Buffalo Bill's opening show with a glorious sunny day. For days now Sabrina had tried to prepare herself for her first appearance with the show. She had spent long hours practicing her trick shots, earning Bill's hearty approval, and had tried on all the costumes she had made for herself. She decided on the light fringed buckskin jacket and skirt with leggings to match. Since she had to do a lot of bending over she had no desire to show her underwear to the public.

Over and over again, Sabrina had practiced how she would enter the arena, smiling, bowing, and waving to the crowd. Buffalo Bill himself had taught her to ride sidesaddle and shoot from the back of a horse. Now if she could only retain her air of confidence and not let herself fall apart, perhaps she had a chance of pulling off this daring deed. Perhaps when all was said and done she wouldn't make a total fool of herself.

Since early February, every day had had its curious or enlivening incident. There was never a dull moment. Everyone had an assigned job to do and made every effort to get it done. Carpenters had worked from early morning until late night constructing the bleachers and set for the upcoming performance. Jonathan had helped paint the sets, Sabrina had taken on the task of helping the Bogardus boys clean the guns. Sadie Pender carried trash, sorted and arranged costumes, and busied herself with general chores.

There was a sense of anticipation among the troupe. Singing, laughter, and incessant chatter accented the days. It was a bit like the cast and crew were coming out of hibernation, blossoming, leaving their cocoons. Sabrina was caught up in the excitement. With a sense of awe, she stood alone viewing the scene before her. In the arena was a replica of a fort, just like in Ross's show. There were seven log cabins, intricate in their detail, even to the plank door with leather hinges and log steps; three two-story blockhouses used for activities such as dancing; even a one-room schoolhouse with clapboard roof, all linked together by a ten-foot-high log stockade.

Soon she would be standing in the middle of that setting with an audience of hundreds looking on. She was a novice in this business, a beginner, but oh, how she loved it. Somehow she felt as if this was where she belonged.

"Buckskin Kitty Tremaine," the flyers read in letters that matched those on the red and yellow banners fluttering in the breeze. The attention she was getting put a heavy burden on her shoulders, for Buffalo Bill was relying on the publicity of a woman shooter to bring in a huge crowd for the opening. How could that not make her a nervous wreck? And all the while Jonathan strutted about like a rooster as if it were his name and not hers emblazoned for all to see.

"You're going to be a star, Brina." He sometimes slipped and called her by her given name.

"Kit!" she quickly corrected. Now particularly she couldn't afford to have anyone guess at her identity.

"Kit." He beamed with pride. "You'll dazzle them. Just remember what I told you and, most importantly, keep your hands steady and your eye glued to the target. No distractions."

"No distractions."

That was easier said than done, for nearly everything Sabrina looked at reminded her of that moment she'd have to prove that she was worthy of Jonathan's bragging. The unhitched gray ticket wagon stood just down the hill from the arena looking a bit like a house on wheels. It particularly made her aware that soon the show would be more than a dream. Later today it would be hitched to four gray horses and sent on its mission down one of the avenues.

Sabrina's stomach was filled with butterflies, her head pounded as if there were war drums inside. Oh, why had she let Jonathan get her into this? Why hadn't she just settled for being one of the women who dressed up like pioneers and be done with it? Why was she trying to be something that she wasn't? With a groan, she put her hands over her face and flung herself to her cot.

"Why, Kit, you look as pale as General Custer's ghost!" Bending over her, Sadie was extremely sympathetic. "Are you ill?" Her hand was cool as she placed it on Sabrina's brow. "You're not hot. No fever." She stepped back, assessing the situation, then breathed out a long, drawn out, "Ohh."

Sabrina opened her eyes wide, staring up at her friend. "Sadie, I . . . I've never shot before an audience before. Jonathan was telling tall tales when he told Buffalo Bill that I had." Telling the truth seemed to soothe her. "The truth is that until I met Jonathan, the only shooting I even knew about was what I read in books." She waited for her confession to cause Sadie's scorn but she received a smile instead. "I'm a phoney!"

"Do you think yourself to be the only one here?" Sadie's voice lowered conspiratorially. "Dick Butkus isn't really a frontiersman. Never was."

"He wasn't?" Sabrina was amazed.

"He was a farmer who gambled his property away. Bill took him in and gave him a new identity. And there are dozens in the show who are the same." Taking a deep breath she proceeded to rattle them off one by one. "Even Bill isn't quite the Indian fighter you perceive him to be."

"He isn't?" The revelation was more than a bit shattering, though she remembered that once Ross had alluded to the same thing. It was just that Bill had become one of her heroes.

"Nate Salsbury, Bill's partner, is responsible for a lot of the whoopla concerning our dear Buffalo Bill. But the point is not in what he really is, but in the image he creates. That's what the audience wants. They want to believe." Sadie sat down on the edge of the cot. "Most of the people sitting out there live dreary lives, are trapped in a dull routine. But we make them happy. For just a few hours we touch their hearts and make their lives special. Someday they'll tell their grandchildren and great-grandchildren that once they actually saw the great Buffalo Bill and his company."

Sabrina remembered that it had been that way for her. The legends had created another world and brought a ray of sunshine to her unhappy life. "We bring them magic."

"Each and every girl and woman out there is going to be secretly dreaming that she's the one pulling the trigger. Every time you hit the target it will be she who is triumphant because at that moment she'll see herself in that buckskin skirt, holding that smoking gun."

After Sadie had left, Sabrina gave the matter a great deal of thought. In a manner of speaking she was like Hurricane Nell and the female heroines of her books. Hadn't she gotten great joy from pretending? And now she would be able to give back a bit of that contentment and share it with others. The idea was soothing, taking away her trembling and headache. She would, she could do it for Bill, for Jonathan and for the audience. With that thought in mind, she gave careful attention to her toilette, braiding her dark-haired wig, adding a touch of color to her buckskin outfit with a few red and yellow feathers. If she was going to be "Buckskin Kitty," she'd look the part.

Sabrina quickly gathered her courage. She would be a success! If the audience wanted to see shooting, then she'd give them a hell of a show. With her new-found confidence, in she left her tent, accepting a handbill a young boy was handing out at the gate. Expecting it to be one announcing Bill's show, she gave a start of surprise when she looked down and saw that it was an advertisement for another show instead.

"Cherokee Ross Sheldon's Wild West Show," she breathed, her contentment suddenly shattered. The name echoed over and over in her head, reminding her of things she'd wanted to forget. So, Ross Sheldon's show was playing in a neighboring town. So what? She wouldn't let that upset her. It was over! The feelings she had once held in her heart for him were a part of the past she had buried. And yet, dear God, the very thought of him being so near made her feel weak, shaky.

"Break a leg, Kit!" one of the cowboys said. In the theatre it was a tradition to express oneself that way. Wishing someone good luck was supposedly bad luck.

"Break a leg, Bob." Folding up the handbill, Sabrina took a deep breath, determined to gain control of her emotions. She felt like crying all over again, but she wouldn't break down. She had the show and her friends. Now was not the time to let them down because she had once so foolishly given herself to a man who hadn't cared a wit! Besides, the odds of her ever seeing Ross again were achingly slim. That thought was foremost in her mind as she tossed the handbill

148

over her shoulder and went to join the others for their march into the town.

Buffalo Bill led the parade astride a white horse, followed by an open wagon which held the show's band. The tooting of the trombone, the steady beat of the drum, gave the members of the show a vibrant accompaniment as they made their way along the road. Next came Adam Bogardus surrounded by his marksman sons. Following the Bogardus family rode Buck Taylor, a six foot five cowboy who was advertised as being able to "throw a steer by the horns or tail and tie him single-handed, pick up a handkerchief from the ground while riding a horse at full gallop, and master the worst of bucking broncos. Sabrina was twenty-fifth in the parade, astride a solid black gelding. Riding by her side on a gaudily saddled pinto was Jonathan.

"I tell you, darling Kit, you will be a sensation. You'll see," he exclaimed as several of the gawking crowd broke into applause as she rode by.

As they rode he treated her to a barrage of compliments which couldn't help but turn her head. Above all, Sabrina knew she had to remember that without Jonathan her fate might have been a very different one. Now she was riding in a parade to the rousing sound of cheering, she had a roof over her head, more than ample food, a weekly salary, and she was on the verge of becoming a star in a Wild West show. More than enough to satisfy any young woman.

The parade reached the fairgrounds at precisely eleven o'clock where it was fittingly received by one hundred mounted Indians from the encampment. Jonathan was right when he said that Bill really knew how to put on a show. Early indications were of a large, enthusiastic crowd. Soon people were pouring in from all directions, stirring up the dust like a dark storm cloud.

Ross Sheldon tried to blend in with the onlookers as he pushed his way through the throng. As the members of the company passed by, he saw only one. With a keen eye he appraised this dark-haired, petite markswoman billed as "Buckskin Tremaine" and quickly assessed her as a fake. No frontierswoman this one, she sat on a horse too much like a lady with her hands delicately grasping the reins.

"Hell, I wonder if she can even shoot," he scoffed aloud, wondering just where Buffalo Bill had gotten this one. A woman sharpshooter, indeed! The very idea was amusing. In truth, the little lady hardly looked strong enough to even handle a gun, unless it was a small one. Well, he'd soon see just what entertainment was to be offered. Undoubtedly when the day was over he'd have had himself a good belly laugh. It just might very well be that Buffalo Bill had made a real mistake this time.

Carriages, wagons, and buggies funneled into the streets, disgorging the eager spectators who quickly made their way to the gates. Men in everything from overalls to three-piece suits led their families towards the wooden walls of the stockade. Ladies in flowered hats and a myriad of brilliant colors made the fairgrounds look more than a bit like a garden. Boys in knickers and girls in ribbons and pinafores squealed in excitement. "A thief's delight," Ross said aloud, knowing very well that pickpockets, scalpers, and peddlers would be right among them, working their way through the gates to obtain their own profit.

Voices cried aloud hawking souvenirs — tomahawks, leather pouches, and autographed programs with Bill's likeness on them. Ross secured his money clip next to his bare chest, just to insure its safety, then moved towards the parade of mounted performers as they entered the open portal. He wanted to get as close a look at this Buckskin Tremaine as he could.

"Probably as homely as sin up close," he chuckled, imagining her to have a slightly long nose and weak chin. Rouge, powder, and paint could only work so much magic. But he was wrong. Though he only caught a glimpse of Bill's famous female shooter he knew in an instant that she was beautiful. Fascinating. But it was much more than that. Something bothered him about her appearance, something he just couldn't put his finger on. As he elbowed his way through the onlookers to take a seat, Ross was deeply troubled.

Chapter Nineteen

It was so quiet in the arena that Sabrina could almost hear the roar of the silence. Then the twitter of anticipation began. People knew instinctively what was about to happen and craned their necks for a sight of Buffalo Bill, resplendent in white Stetson, bleached doeskins, and shiny black boots that went all the way up to his knees. He was an arresting figure, a symbol of the untamed West with his long blond hair falling in slight waves. He gave the signal for the grand entry to begin, then, to the toots and whistles of the uniformed regimental band, rode forward.

Indians in feathers and paint, scouts in buckskin, vaqueros in silver and black, cowboys wearing woolly chaps mounted on horseback or driving coaches and wagons followed, circling inside the bleachers while the cheers and applause swelled and receded, then rose to a peak. The enthusiastic show of approval drowned out the drums, tubas, and flutes of the band as Buffalo Bill took off his hat and made a deep bow from horseback.

Sabrina felt all fluttery as she and Jonathan took their turn to make the grand sweep. For just a moment, the noise died down as every eye in the arena seemed to turn her way. Dear God, if she made a mistake now she'd surely die of humiliation, she thought, somehow calling forth some special reserve of courage to keep her from succumbing to a swoon. How could she have ever imagined what it would really be like to make her first appearance before the crowd? It was a bit like the feeling she had when she and Ross had reached the climax of their lovemaking. Exciting. Exhilarating.

The first event was a display of shooting put on by Captain A. H. Bogardus and the young boys who had become Sabrina's friends, a show of skill she knew would most certainly be a difficult act to follow. Nine-year-old Henry started the exhibition by shooting a glass ball out of his father's fingers with a .32 caliber rifle. Peter, not quite as skilled as the others, lofted the targets up in the air while Edward took his turn to shoot. The grand finale of the act was one of skillful daring. The oldest Bogardus boy carefully aimed his pistol, shooting at his brother as he stood in front of a canvas-covered backdrop, outlining his brother's body with bullet holes. The audience roared their approval.

A facsimile of an Indian attack on a stagecoach followed. As the vehicle rumbled across the field, a large band of screaming Indians emerged from hiding to make pursuit. With his whip nearly crackling as fiercely as gunshots, the driver made pretense of a valiant flight from the rifle-toting band, but in the end the rocking coach glowed with red fire. A gasp and then a bloodchilling blanket of silence spread over the crowd. Sabrina was caught up in the action, though she'd seen it a dozen times or more during the practice. Even so, she found herself cheering as the scouts arrived to drive away the savages and rescue the coach's passengers.

A half-hour of action-packed Western entertainment followed, with cowboys, war-painted Indians, and exhibition of exceptional horsemanship. Sabrina appeared early in the show, in the sixth spot. Taking a deep breath, she made her entrance, not marching in as some of the others did, but walking in with a slight spring to her step, bowing, waving, and wafting kisses. Jonathan followed, wearing a dun-colored Western-cut suit and carrying a rifle and a leather pouch. From the pouch he withdrew a sparkling blue glass ball, walking around the arena, holding it aloft for all to see.

"Ready, Kit?" he asked aloud, making great show of dangling it in front of her.

Sabrina tried to pretend that she and Jonathan were all alone, that this was only a practice like any other. Taking a long, deep breath she said at last, "Ready!"

Jonathan tossed the ball up into the air with an underhand throw just as Sabrina withdrew one of the twin colts she wore on her hips. She cocked it and took aim quickly, trying to remember all he had taught her. She fired just as the ball reached the top curve of its trajectory. In a shattering burst, it broke.

Her first few shots brought forth a few shrieks of fright from the women, but soon they were lost in round after round of a most enthusiastic handclapping as she targeted and hit two, three, and four more glass balls. Holding her hands up she made a gesture of appreciation.

From his seat in front of where Sabrina stood, Ross snorted skeptically. An easy feat, he said to himself, that any beginner could master. Why, when he was just seven years old he'd managed to hit just as many glass balls, only to come under his father's wrath when it was learned what had happened to the Christmas tree ornaments. This young woman still had to prove herself to him.

Sabrina called upon all her playacting skills to create the mystique expected of her. It was as if for just a moment she was transported into one of her beloved dime novels and actually became the heroine therein. She proved herself to be a consummate actress, convincing not only those in the audience but herself as well. She *was* Buckskin Kitty Tremaine, if only for a little while.

When one Colt revolver was empty, she holstered it, then drew its mate, this time shooting at the brightly painted tin cans Jonathan threw up in the air. Next came the cards from a pack of Jonathan's playing set.

154

The cards that had been hit were thrown into the audience as souvenirs by Jonathan who made great flourish of the act.

"How am 1 doing, Johnnie?" Sabrina asked, feeling triumphant and more than a little cocky as she switched to a rifle. She had done it, pulled it off without a hitch.

"Terrific, my darling. Absolutely perfect." Sabrina bowed low, thinking it to be the end of her act, but Jonathan shook his head. "The mirror trick."

"What?" Sabrina was certain that he had lost his mind. It was something they had only attempted once, a feat much too daring.

Suddenly all her poise vanished. In a moment of panic she headed towards the bleachers with the thought of making as hasty a retreat as she could. It was in that moment that she came face to face with Ross, her eyes nearly bulging in her head as she recognized him. Frantically she backed away. No, it couldn't be! Not here! Not now. She wasn't prepared for the shock of it. Dear God! And yet in was. Even from the distance of eight seats away, she recognized him. Ross Sheldon was the kind of man who would stand out in any crowd. It was him all right.

Ross noticed how the dark-haired woman was staring and smiled to himself. He was used to female adulation, but this time it especially pleased him. A smile tugged at his lips. What if he wooed this little filly away from Bill's show, made her his own star? The idea had great appeal to him. For a hundred mischievous pranks played upon him by the show's owner, he owed it to Bill. Besides, there was something about the young woman that greatly appealed to him. She was most definitely his type. Long-legged, slim-waisted, she was built with an hourglass figure. Boldly he waved to her.

Sabrina was horrified. He recognized her! What was she going to do? She never wanted to see him again. Never. Surely if he even came anywhere near her she'd fall all to pieces. Damn her silly, foolish heart, she couldn't forget the love she'd felt for him. Not now. Perhaps not ever.

"Kit! Kit!" Jonathan hissed, seeing her nearly crumble before him. "Get hold of yourself!" Taking the megaphone from Bill's hands, he made the daring announcement, whereby he promised that Buckskin Kitty Tremaine could split a playing card from forty paces with her back to the target. "She will accomplish this feat while looking in a mirror."

"What?" Even Buffalo Bill was amazed.

"Jonathan, no!" Sabrina was certain she'd completely fall apart. She couldn't do it, especially not after seeing Ross. "Please!"

There was an uncomfortable twitter in the audience as everyone sensed her disquiet. A buzz of whispering ensued as if everyone in the crowd was asking what was wrong. Sabrina tried to steady her nerves, but it was nearly impossible. Even so, Jonathan had made it impossible for her to back down now.

Trembling from head to toe, Sabrina balanced the barrel of the rifle on her shoulder, cocking it, then putting her thumb on the trigger. Hesitantly she took the mirror from Jonathan's outstretched hand. Slowly she raised it to her face, watching as he took a card from the deck and carefully placed it on a long stick. With a great sweep of his hands he held it out and nodded.

It was totally silent in the arena as the crowd waited in anticipation. Sabrina's hands trembled and she couldn't steady them no matter how hard she tried. A minute went by, then another, stretching out like an endless ocean as the tension increased in the arena.

"Come on, lady. Shoot!" called out a voice from the crowd. Sabrina did, missing the target by more than a foot. A whisper of disappointment flowed through the crowd like a giant wave.

Jonathan scowled, as if doing such a difficult trick shot had been her idea. "Once more," he said aloud. "Kit won't miss this time."

Sabrina cocked the rifle, taking as much time as she possibly could before raising it to her shoulder again. Taking a deep breath, she took aim, but before she could pull the trigger a shot rang out. In confusion, she looked around as cheers filled the arena. The card had been split in two, but not from her bullet. As she looked towards one of the wagons Edward Bogardus winked at her. Unknown to the audience it was a bullet from his gun that had hit the target and saved her reputation.

"Good, Kit. Very, very good." Even Jonathan seemed to be unaware of the deception. Taking her hand, he bowed while she curtsied as the seats swayed under pounding feet and clapping hands. Though Jonathan and Sabrina exited, they were called back for another round of applause.

"Jonathan, don't ever do that to me again," Sabrina growled, feeling a fit of ill temper.

"Why not? You made it."

"No, I didn't. It was Eddie."

"Eddie?" Instead of being properly chastened, he broke out into a grin. "Then we'll have to have him do the same thing again."

"No!" Any attention she gained would be on her own efforts, not by deceit. Pulling her hand away, Sabrina stalked off ahead of Jonathan, to fume in her tent as the members of the company playacted a buffalo hunt. Drums accompanied Sabrina as she left the arena.

From his seat, Ross was amused. A lover's quarrel, he speculated. Well, it was just as well. He'd never been a man who liked competition. Besides, the more he thought about it, the more determined he was to win the pretty little dark-haired lady. Even if she wasn't all that spectacular a shot. He laughed to himself. Perhaps she'd fooled everyone else in the crowd with her antics, but he for one had seen that young boy raise his gun and pull the trigger. Cheap theatrics, that's what it was. But what the hell, he'd teach her how to do that trick honestly. And besides, knowing her secret just might give him a bit of leverage when he went to court the fair cowgirl.

Ross hardly noticed the rest of the performance, he was too busy planning his seduction. Besides, Bill's show wasn't really all that noticeably different from his own. A bigger cast, more elaborate props, but that was about the only thing. When the grand parade began he looked for Miss Buckskin Kitty Tremaine, hoping to corner her in the arena, but she was noticeably absent. Ross shrugged his shoulders. It didn't matter. He had a different plan in mind.

As the spectators filed out to fall victim to the hawkers, he moved amongst them, smoking his cigarette thoughtfully. He knew very little about this buckskin-garbed, braided markswoman so he would have to make a guess as to how to win her attention. Flowers? Why not? There probably wasn't a woman alive who didn't swoon under a barrage of blossoms.

Feeling cocky, Ross soon found a flower seller, purchasing not one bouquet, but five. Scribbling a complimentary note expounding on Miss Tremaine's beauty, daring, and surefire nerve, he signed his name with great flourish—Cherokee Ross Sheldon. He added a postscript that she should meet him at the ticket wagon at six o'clock so that he could take her to the finest restaurant for dinner. Then, feeling delightfully sure of himself, he gave instruction that the flowers be delivered at once to Miss Tremaine's tent.

Chapter Twenty

Sabrina was a star! Despite the mirror shot failure, the newspaper reporters praised her as they rushed to talk to her. "Unusually attractive," one wrote down, making liberal mention of her charms. "She takes to shooting as some women gravitate to ballrooms and teas," another reported. "She has made a conquest of their hearts," said still another. She created a sensation with her expert marksmanship. Some hinted that she must have Indian blood, that she was the daughter of an Indian chief. One reporter speculated that she was a man in disguise.

"My little lady," Bill called her, so pleased with her debut that he gifted her with a palomino pony. "When the next posters and flyers go out, I'm going to put your name in big red letters," he promised. "Maybe even a sketch of you holding your rifle."

Jonathan was quick to take advantage of Bill's good mood. "Yep, Kit's a star all right. Seems to me she deserves a lot more than the pittance you said you would pay her." It was one of Jonathan's shortcomings that he was greedy. "I'd say if you were wise, you'd double her salary, just to make certain someone else doesn't run away with her."

Buffalo Bill's eyebrows furrowed, his gray eyes darted fire. "Now, see here, Colt!"

"Pshaw! You can afford it and you know it," Jonathan insisted, pushing the matter, now that he saw it to be mutually advantageous. "I've heard rumors that the Bogardus

159

family is thinking of leaving the show after this season. That they are thinking of going to Europe."

"Damnation!" Bill's oath was a deep rumble. For just a moment, Sabrina feared he might tell both her and Jonathan to go to the very devil but then his brow smoothed. "All right! All right. As long as Kit does as well as she did today, I'll pay the price. But not a penny more."

"Agreed!" Jonathan had the look of a cat who had just swallowed the family canary.

"But Jonathan, I missed the target," Sabrina protested, taking him aside. She didn't like living a lie. Besides, it only meant that even more would be expected of her next time.

"Hellfire, it doesn't matter. People want to believe." He gave her cheek a playful pat. "Remember what I told you about bluff. It's the mystique of being a heroine. These newspapers did you a big favor. Now there isn't one person out there who won't see you as a perfect marksman."

Indeed, Sabrina was inundated with cards, letters, and gifts from several admirers, including candy and flowers. Feeling like a little child at Christmas time she sat in her tent, opening up each and every paper-covered surprise.

"I thought I was just going to die when Jonathan announced that I was going to do the mirror trick," she confided to Sadie. "I was afraid that I would be cause for Buffalo Bill's humiliation in addition to my own."

"But everything went well." Sadie giggled knowingly, then quickly promised that she would keep Kit's secret.

"I'll be eternally grateful to Edward, but I won't let him save my hide again. I'm going to learn that trick. I'm determined." Opening up a box of her favorite bonbons, Sabrina offered Sadie some. "I want to be worthy of the money Bill is paying me and of his trust. He's a man I truly respect."

Sadie snickered, then stuffed one of the candies into her mouth. "That's because you don't know the scoundrel as well as I do. Bill doesn't wear the halo you think he does. He's got more than his share of vices."

"I know that he used to drink a great deal, but Nate has put an end to that. Or so it seems." Sabrina didn't like to criticize this man who had been so very kind to her. Somehow it seemed like a betrayal.

"Yeah, he's limited himself to one drink all right. A slug of whiskey from a bucket!" Sadie grinned evilly, chocolate sticking to her teeth.

Shaking her head in mild irritation, Sabrina sought to change the subject quickly. "I can't believe all these cards, Sadie. From people I don't even know."

It was unbelievable. Only a few months ago she was toiling away at her father-in-law's inn, now she was a celebrity. Yet there were times when that fact troubled her. She didn't want to become too well known. She couldn't afford to have her picture grace any of the posters that floated around the various towns. Even with her dark wig there might be someone from the inn who might recognize her and eventually put two and two together.

"Flowers for Miss Tremaine!" A young lad that Sabrina recognized as one of the hawkers' sons entered the tent carrying an armful of bouquets.

"Soon you'll have so many flowers someone will think there's a funeral," Sadie teased. She took it upon herself to relieve the boy of his burden, sniffing the blossoms appreciatively. "I think I should switch from dog training to shooting."

"If you want to trade places, I'm agreeable," Sabrina said quickly. It would certainly be less nerve-wracking to work with the two little spaniels than to do what she was doing.

Sadie thrust the flowers into her hands. "I'll think about it." She cocked her head. "Does that include Jonathan? If so, then I might seriously consider it." She had never made a secret of the fact that she thought Jonathan to be an extremely attractive man.

"I have no ties to Jonathan," Sabrina said peevishly, still more than a little irritated at him. "We are partners and friends. That's all."

"Mmmm?"

"That's all!" A flush stained her cheeks, which Sadie seemed to take as contradiction. She busied herself in find-

161

ing glasses and tankards in which to put the various bunches of flowers. Red, pink, blue, and yellow petals made her tent as colorful as a field in spring. Someone had been very thoughtful.

"They are all from the same man. I looked. He must either be secretly in love with you or he's a very rich man." Sadie giggled again. "Or else he owns a flower shop."

Sabrina was curious. It was certainly an extravagant gesture. After opening the note which accompanied the flowers, she gasped. "Ross Sheldon!" The name stung her eyes with tears. "It can't be." But it was from him. Every single flower.

"Kit?" Sadie was surprised at her outburst. "Do you know the man?"

"Yes!"

At first Sabrina suspected that Ross had recognized her, but as she scanned the words he'd written, her anger flared. He was flirting with the mysterious Miss Tremaine, not renewing their love affair. It seemed an all-too-strong reminder of his perfidy. He was a bastard! After every woman he saw. And so smugly self-confident. The note reeked of arrogance. He wanted her to meet him like any little trollop so that he could get to know her. Well, the devil take him! It would be a cold day in hell before she would give him that satisfaction. She would scorn him most forcefully. It would do him some good to see that not every woman succumbed as easily as she had!

Running to the opening of the tent, Sabrina hailed the lad who had brought the flowers. "I want none of his gifts!" she told the startled flower boy.

In a voice tinged with outrage, she instructed the boy to return the flowers at once to the man who had bought them. Oh, he would be met at the ticket wagon all right, but not by her. That thought should have made her smile, yet somehow it left her feeling quite empty and more alone than she had ever felt in her life.

Chapter Twenty-one

Ross was all decked out in a three-piece gray business suit, tapping his foot impatiently as he waited. Reaching up, he straightened his blue string tie, adjusting the brass bull that kept it in place. He felt a bit like an organ grinder's monkey all duded up as he was. Hell, he'd even put on men's cologne for the occasion. The last time he'd done that was that night he'd seduced Sabrina in his room.

"Sabrina . . ."

Strange how even after four months she popped into his head when he least expected it. There were moments when he felt regret, wondering if he wasn't the world's biggest fool not to have gone running back to her father-in-law's inn at the first opportunity. But it was too late now. She was a beautiful woman who always got plenty of male attention. Undoubtedly she'd forgotten all about him and was keeping company with some marriageable fellow. Well, he sincerely wished her well. She deserved happiness.

And what of him? He'd spent all of his free time, every waking moment, trying to whip his show into shape. He didn't want to be second best to Buffalo Bill. Hell, he didn't want to be second best to anyone. It was his intent to put his own show on an equal with Bill's, at least. He had spent, therefore, a great deal on advertising. More so than any rational man would have put out for a new show. But he had a feeling it just might be worth it. He certainly hoped so.

Ross had proven to be canny when he had hired a publicist to assist him in making his Wild West show known. The man had, like himself, written several dime novels and seemed to have a talent for prose. Hopefully it could be used to good advantage. So far his pen had been useful in writing the souvenir pamphlets which were scattered around the town. But would it bring the crowd in? Ross knew he was taking a chance. Gambling. It made him all too aware that he had to watch over the proceedings carefully.

Certainly this week had been an organized man's nightmare as he had gone over the final few hectic details of his show. First the mayor had threatened to withdraw his license, making it impossible to perform, then an impatient stallion had battered his way through the side of one of the wagons. Then again, Apache Ed had seemed to have a penchant for hiring men for jobs wholly unsuited for them. It had taken Ross weeks and weeks to straighten it out, but he had, shuffling some of his people around to responsibilities for which they had the skills.

Money was tight. It had taken imagination and ability to conjure dollars out of the tight wallets of some of his friends. Then there was the usual problem of drinking and gambling among those in the show. One of his bronc riders had turned up dead drunk when it was time for his act. Ross had quickly sobered him up, making him promise that from then on he would avoid whiskey when the company was due to perform. There had been the usual run of bad luck, things to be expected, but for some reason or other his top sharpshooter had just up and quit, leaving a vacancy — which brought him to the reason for this meeting. Would he be able to woo the young lady away from his competitor? Only time would answer that question.

"Paper, mister?" A passing newsboy held the evening's news.

"Sure." Ross tossed him a quarter, telling him to keep the change.

"Well, I'll be damned!" He chuckled as he read the front

164

page story, concerning the adulation being given to Buffalo Bill's female sharpshooter. So, his instincts to try and win her to his own show had been sound after all. For just a moment he had wondered if it wasn't a personal attraction that had drawn him to Miss Kitty Tremaine. There had been something about her that had intrigued him, made him want to get to know her better. He would have been lying not to admit that he was looking forward to this evening.

He wondered what she was like. There were certain mannerisms which she displayed that marked her a lady, and yet what on earth would such a woman be doing in Buffalo Bill's Wild West show? A country girl, then? He had watched her and knew for certain she wasn't from the West. Such women had a certain way of walking, a bold stride that gave them away.

What if she was married? That sudden thought caused his jaw to twitch. Certainly it would put a monkey wrench into his plans. No. He'd looked and hadn't seen a gold band on her finger. That yellow-haired fellow had acted like more of a lover than a spouse, which suited Ross very well. He didn't want to deal with any irate husbands.

Impatiently, Ross checked his pocket watch. She was late! Ross was always a man who appreciated punctuality. Even when he was out West he stuck to a schedule. He grumbled beneath his breath. She was more than thirty minutes late. If he hired her for his show, he'd have to see that she learned to keep a better eye on the time.

Ross squinted against the setting sun, looking towards the area where the tents sprouted from the ground like mushrooms. It was then that he saw the walking flower garden coming his way. "Damn!" It was the young man from whom he had bought the flowers. No wonder Kitty Tremaine hadn't come to meet him.

"You! Boy!" Ross's voice was a growl as he gestured the lad towards him. "I told you to deliver those flowers to Miss Tremaine's tent."

"I did!" The boy winced under the scrutiny of Ross's

gaze. "She told me to return them."

"What?" It was the last thing Ross expected him to say. "There must be some mistake. Turn right around and take them back to her." The boy did as he was told, only to return once again. "Well?"

"She said to tell you thank you, but that she never accepts gifts from overly forward men." The boy recoiled as if afraid he would be boxed.

"What?" Ross's overeager pride burst like a bubble. "Perhaps you didn't make her understand."

"I did! I told her you most sincerely wanted her to have these, that you didn't want them back. She told me that in that case I should take them to one of the hospitals so that some of the patients might enjoy them."

"She said that?" He shook his head, not believing the boy's words at first. Then slowly it dawned on him. She didn't want to see him. More than disappointing, it was like a slap in the face. Ross gritted his teeth. "So, then I would say there is only one thing to do."

"Yes, sir?"

"Take them to the hospital. At least there will be someone there who will appreciate my generosity." Oh, how her response irked him. He'd never really had anyone scorn him before. Women always were anxious to capitulate to his manly charms. Except for Sabrina. How could he ever forget that day she had hit him with her mop when he had been too bold. Sabrina. And now this haughty miss.

Ross felt his blood boil. He'd meant his gesture as a show of friendship, but now he felt it was something akin to war to be so brutally rebuffed. It fired his frustration. At that moment, he made a vow. If it was the last thing he did in this life, he would change her mind. If she thought he was going to give up, then she was a terrible judge of character. He'd do everything within his power to make her want him, fall in love with him. It was a vow he made in earnest as he left the ticket booth to return to his own encampment.

Chapter Twenty-two

Sabrina awakened to the sweet fragrance of flowers. Sitting up in bed, she let her eyes scan the room and thought for a just a moment she'd somehow been transported to the greenhouses of the city. "Roses!" White, pink, and red flowers met her eyes.

"Yes, roses, Kit." Sadie was skillfully arranging the bouquets. "Not one, but four dozen of them. My, my, my. It seems you have quite an avid admirer. One who just won't take no for an answer."

"Oh dear!" She had been so certain that when she had scorned his attentions, Ross Sheldon would just go away. He surely was a stubborn brute. Every time she sent a present back, he sent something else in its place, each with a card that said how much he wanted to meet her.

"And yesterday the bonbons! And the day before oranges — a whole basket full of them. And perfume." Sadie giggled. "Even a pair of lace garters. Oh, how I wish . . ." Blushing, she turned her face away from Sabrina's avid stare. "I mean — well, wouldn't you just like to at least meet him? Doesn't your curiosity nearly drive you insane?"

"No! I know very well what he is like. What all men of his kind are like, for that matter. Takers, every last one. Don't let the gifts fool you, Sadie. He's trying to buy me." Sadie had a trunk made into a makeshift dressing table. Bounding out of bed, Sabrina put on a blue satin robe and sat before the mirror, brushing her long blond hair so vigorously she nearly tore it out.

"Maybe he just admires your skill. The notes say that he has seen several of your performances." Sadie aided Sabrina in putting her hair in a bun so that she could more easily slip her wig on for the performance. "I think you're rather fortunate."

Fortunate, Sabrina thought. Hardly that. Just the opposite in fact. Ross Sheldon was playing havoc with her life and her emotions. *Stay away from Ross Sheldon, forget him.* It was much easier said than done. Certainly he had no intentions of letting her elude him, or so it seemed. The past few days he had wooed her with a vengeance, making it all the more difficult for her to be firm in her resolve to keep her distance. And yet she *had* to. Succumbing to his charm would only bring heartache and possibly dire consequences.

"Bonbons are certain to make one quite fat. And . . . and as for roses, they make me sneeze. You can have them if you want them, Sadie. But I don't want them in here." She wanted them out of her sight for they were a painful reminder of what might have been. What hurt her most was that Ross Sheldon didn't even know who she was. He was trying to win the heart of another woman. A dark-haired sharpshooter.

"Take them away?" Sadie looked at Sabrina as if she had suddenly lost her mind. "But . . . but Kit . . ." She fondled the soft petals lovingly. "They are so beautiful."

"Please!" Sabrina's voice was sharp, and she regretted her peevishness. She was hardly one to give orders to Sadie. After all, it was just as much Sadie's tent as Sabrina's. "I give them to you. Someone should appreciate them. But please, keep them on your side of the room."

"I'll make a necklace of them, perhaps to wear at this afternoon's show. It will be very colorful." She looked at Sabrina as if positive she would change her mind. "Ooh, what a face! Pshaw, girl, I don't understand you one wit. If a man were as crazy as a loon over me, I'd be smiling, not frowning."

"You wouldn't understand." She'd wanted Ross's affections once, had dreamed about it night after night. Now that dream had turned sour for she was caught in her own trap and wasn't quite sure what to do about it. She didn't dare reveal who she was, lest she put her very freedom in danger. What then? One of these days Ross Sheldon would be tired of her hard-to-get act and might very well corner her.

After Sadie left, Sabrina dabbed at her rouge and powder, and thought of all the reasons why she should hate Ross Sheldon. He was a man who was much too fond of women. That alone made loving him out of the question. He had left her, with only a scribbled note as his goodbye. And now he was casually pursuing someone he hadn't even met. What better proof did she need that he was the worst kind of cad?

"The only reason Ross Sheldon is sending me flowers is that he has something up his sleeve," she whispered to her image in the mirror. But what? Was it because of her notoriety? Or that she was just another conquest? He seemed to be a collector of women. And oh, how easily she had been won! The very thought caused her the greatest humiliation.

Closing her eyes, Sabrina tried to forget him, but his face hovered in her mind's eye. The way his hair brushed his forehead, the shape of his nose, the width of his shoulders, the way he walked and talked all haunted her. And his mouth — full and artfully chiseled, possessing a sensuous curve when he smiled. Touching her lips, she remembered his kiss and felt a warm glow flicker through her.

"No. I won't let him bother me this way," she murmured. "I won't let him turn me into a lovesick ninny!" In aggravation, she stood up, only to see that Sadie had forgotten one solitary red rose in her hurry. Lying all alone on the dirt floor, it beckoned her touch and though she knew she should ignore it, she bent to pick it up. It was too fragile, too lovely to be crushed under foot. With trembling fingers, she touched the velvety petals and sighed. It was then she saw the note Sadie had left behind.

"Kitty,

These flowers are pretty, but they pale beside your beauty. You haunt me night and day. I must see you, if only for a moment. Perhaps we have more in common than you know. Just a minute, that's all I ask. I promise you that you will not regret it — Ross."

And she wanted to see him again, too. Dear God, but she did! No matter how stubbornly she might try to convince herself that she hated Ross Sheldon, she never would, never could.

He left you alone. He won your heart and then he deserted you. How can you even think of seeing him again? Her mind screamed a warning that was answered by her heart. She tried to tell herself again and again that Ross Sheldon was a cruel, unfeeling man, yet how could she forget the gentleness he had displayed whenever they made love. There had been concern in his deep blue eyes when her father-in-law had scolded her. And he had fought John Travers for her honor. How could she forget?

"I must see you, if only for a moment," she read again. Oh, if only she could confide in him. Tell him the truth of who she was and all that had happened. He would understand the circumstances that had forced her to kill her father-in-law. He had seen firsthand just how harsh and cruel Rufus James could be. She'd tell him that she had run away. He might even help her clear her name. If they couldn't be lovers, perhaps they at least could be friends. Maybe there was a chance for happiness after all, if she were honest with him, trusted him.

"No!" She had trusted him once, had opened up to him and all she had gotten for a reward was pain. Ross wouldn't help her. Ross wouldn't care. When he found out that she was Sabrina James, he'd undoubtedly laugh, then just as quickly walk away.

Sabrina viewed the rose through a mist of tears, knowing what had to be done. There was really only one answer. She had to cool Ross Sheldon's desire by making him believe she was interested in another man. Jonathan. In her way, she did care for him very much. If she showed him more attention and affection while they were performing, perhaps it would discourage the bold and brash Mr. Sheldon. Certainly he thought he was God's gift to all women. She'd prove to him that he was not, that someone else held her heart. And maybe, when all was said and done, she could really convince herself to love Jonathan. He was a good man, a gentle man, the kind of man she would choose for herself if she were rational, if love hadn't turned her brains to pudding.

Jonathan had saved her life by offering her a journey in his wagon. He had taught her how to shoot. Love and affection were obvious in his eyes. From now on she would try to return the feelings he so openly displayed for her. She would fight fire with fire! Who could say where it might lead?

Chapter Twenty-three

Traveling the show circuit was hectic, tiring, but, even so, Sabrina loved it. It gave her a chance to visit places she had never seen — Boston, towns in New York State, even all the way to Connecticut. The weeks were a jumble of street parades, of two or three performances a day, and of railroad excursions to cities booked for the show. How strange it was, she thought, that she was being lauded as a Western heroine, but had never even traveled West. Instead, Bill's caravan was concentrating on the Eastern towns, where anything that even hinted of the lands beyond the plains was celebrated.

Bill's partnership with Nate Salsbury truly seemed a stroke of genius with Cody providing the showmanship and Salsbury the brains. Once she heard them talking about Ross Sheldon, however, with a tone akin to awe. Both men were amazed by the changes he had made in Apache Ed's "losing proposition." Sabrina detected a note of worry that Cherokee Ross just might be something to reckon with in time.

Certainly Ross Sheldon was a stubborn man, Sabrina thought as she stared out at the Trifield, Connecticut, audience. She was beginning to feel like she had a shadow. Just when she thought he had given up, that she would never be bothered with him again, low and behold, she would spot Ross in the audience.

"The nerve of the man," she mumbled, trying to concentrate on her routine. She would never have admitted for the world how her eyes strayed to that same place in the bleachers time after time through her performance, but they did. "What a rogue he is!"

As their eyes met and held now, he was even so bold as to grin at her as he tipped his hat. Tossing her head, Sabrina quickly turned away, making an exaggerated show of affection towards Jonathan as she took his hand to acknowledge the crowd's applause. Then, standing up on her tiptoes, she brushed his cheek with a kiss, which caused a glow of pleasure to spread over Jonathan's face.

"Mmm. Whatever it is I did to deserve that, just tell me and I'll do it again." Jonathan's smile was tender. He held onto her hand as if he would never let it go.

"That's just for always being there," Sabrina answered. In truth, the more Ross Sheldon pursued her, the more frightened she became, clinging more and more to "Johnnie." "I'll never forget that you were there when I needed you." She made a sweep of the audience with her hand. "None of these people would be here clapping for me if you hadn't taken the time to teach me how to shoot. I'll never forget that, Jonathan."

Hand in hand, they left the arena and once beyond sight of the audience, Jonathan put his arm around her waist for a squeeze. "How about you and me going for a buggy ride as soon as the grand finale is over," he inquired, tickling her ear with his whisper.

"A buggy ride?" It had been a long time since she had known the luxury of a leisurely jaunt. Whenever she traveled with the show, everyone was always in a hurry, the roustabouts striking the tents and booths for shipping to the next location.

"We'll pack a picnic basket and just take our time. How about it?"

"It sounds heavenly, but Bill was counting on us to go to the barbecue." Bill had invited the press to an authentic Western cookout in the arena after the show where the journalists could mingle with the cowboys and the Indians. Good public relations, or so Nate and Bill said."

"To hell with Bill. We have a right to some time on our own. Together." Jonathan's look was so earnest that Sabrina just couldn't refuse.

"All right." Once she had vowed to think of Jonathan only as a friend, but Ross Sheldon's intrusion in her life changed all of that. Though she was still in love with Ross, Sabrina was adamant about not to succumbing to his charms again, no matter how hard he tried.

Standing side by side, they watched from the wings as Buffalo Bill recreated his desperate duel with the young Cheyenne chieftain named Yellow Hand, who in reality had been Yellow Hair. It was a bit like some tale straight from the Middle Ages, Sabrina thought, with Buffalo Bill in the role of the heroic knight. Riding towards each other, the two champions played out a tense pantomime. Bill fired from the saddle and made a great act of killing the Indian's horse just as his own mount went down. Yellow Hand toppled and Cody leaped upon him. The sunlight caught the gleam of their knives as they grappled. Pretending to stab his opponent in the ribs, Bill wrenched off Yellow Hand's war bonnet, amidst grunts and groans.

"First scalp for Custer," Bill shouted out as he bent over the body of his vanquished enemy, alluding to Custer's Last Stand. To add to the glory of the moment, the band broke into a rousing song that brought the audience to their feet. Tonight it was even more clamorous than before as the crowd celebrated their hero. Bill was so enraptured over the attention he was receiving that he surprised the company by forgetting the grand parade and claiming the arena all alone to the beat of the band.

"Well, I'll be . . ." By his smile, Jonathan seemed amused. "He really can be an egotistical bastard after all. Hope he doesn't begin to believe his own myth."

It was obvious that he was, though, for as the barbecue spits were erected, Bill strutted among the throng of reporters, firing off several of his tall tales. Sabrina knew

174

that the headlines would surely be praiseful tomorrow when the newsboys peddled their papers.

The tantalizing aroma of roasting meat mingled with the stench of manure. The strange combination riled Sabrina's stomach and made her thankful that she and Jonathan had decided to get away from here.

"It promises to be quite a party." Sabrina looked up to find a tall, cigar-chomping, bespectacled reporter looking avidly at her.

"Bill always knows how to do things right," she answered, a bit edgy under his probing stare. There was a photographer with him, which made her even more uneasy. One thing she could not risk was having her picture appear anywhere. Even with her dark-haired wig she might be recognized by John Travers.

"P.T. Barnum charges that Bill Cody stole the idea of the show from him. Is that so?"

Sabrina was amused by the question. "Not at all. Buffalo Bill is one of a kind, just like his show. We're nothing at all like a circus. More like a family, I suppose."

"And how about you, do you do your own shooting or is there a gimmick to the act?"

Tensing her jaw, Sabrina remembered the time Edward Bogardus had helped her out, and she winced. Well, that was then and now was now. She had practiced and practiced until she was blue in the face, and did all her own shooting now. "I'm for real. Care to join me in a shootout?" she challenged.

The reporter shrugged his shoulders. "Heck no. The closest I ever got to guns was today." He shuddered. "Ghastly things — all that noise. Unsettles one." Hastily scratching with pen on pad, he wrote down a few notes then moved along, this time interviewing one of the Bogardus boys.

Sabrina looked around her, marveling at how quickly the arena had been transformed. Kegs of foaming beer dotted the open field.

Smoke drifted up from the many campfires. Trestle

tables bulged under the weight of the food the company's cooks had prepared. Soon it seemed that just about everyone had a spicy red hunk of meat in his hand, which was rumored to be buffalo. Sabrina glanced over her shoulder with a smile, then quickly went to her tent to change her clothes. She'd wear something feminine, her lilac-colored gingham. How tired she was of buckskin and leather. Sabrina knew she'd made a perfect choice by the look of appreciation on Jonathan's face. He was hard put to keep his eyes on the road. Again and again, he looked over at her and she got a warm feeling inside.

Jonathan wore a tan Western-style suit embroidered in black, red, and gold, and a fawn-colored Stetson with a wide brim. Since her success he had taken to dressing fancy. Sabrina knew that something was afoot, however, because he reeked of expensive men's cologne, the kind he had purchased when the troupe had visited New York City.

The afternoon was quickly turning to dusk, a fading purple glow that turned the sky a deep violet. As they traveled along, Sabrina let her eyes feast on the view. It was a romantic setting, the kind that turned the mind towards kissing and cuddling, but, strangely, Sabrina's heart was cold. She wanted to love Jonathan, willed it to be, yet she couldn't force her emotions. She leaned back with a sigh against the leather cushion of the buggy, her hands resting in her lap.

At last, when Jonathan thought he had picked just the right place, he stopped. Helping her from the buggy, he picked up the picnic basket and led her towards a spot beneath the trees, then sat beside her. "Well, here we are all alone." His eyes gleamed, catching the last thread of sunset. Turning to her, he studied her face. "Or are we?"

"What do you mean?"

"He's here with us." At her startled look, he said softly, "He's still there, in the back of your mind. I know it, Kit."

"I don't want him to be."

"It's all right." He inched nearer to her, his hip meeting

176

hers as he took her hand. "I've noticed him in the audience. Ross Sheldon." As he mentioned his rival's name, a slight look of pain flickered in his eyes, which Sabrina deeply regretted. She was indebted to Jonathan for his kindness, his faith in her, and so many other things, and yet she had wounded him. "I remember the two of you were quite a duo at the inn."

"He left me!" Putting her hands over her face, Sabrina tried to control her emotions. "Oh, Jonathan, I don't really want to talk about it. I want to forget."

"Then I'll help you do just that." Slowly his head turned towards her as he leaned forward. Sabrina lifted her face and their lips met in a soft, open-mouthed kiss. Jonathan took her hand and placed it on his breast and held it there for a long time. "Marry me!"

"What?"

"I said, marry me." Sensing the tenseness in her body, he moved his free hand down her back, caressing her. As if hoping to relax her, he reached in the picnic basket and pulled out a bottle and two glasses. As the dusk turned into late evening, he plied her with more and more wine. "Marry me," he said again and again.

Sabrina felt delightfully tipsy. Warm. Floating on air. "Are you trying to persuade me to say yes by making me drunk?" she asked with a hiccupping giggle.

Jonathan answered quite truthfully, "Yes!" He smiled and could not look away from her full silken mouth. "You are beautiful, Kit. Your hair, your eyes." Putting her hand to his mouth, he kissed it. "Please say yes. I adore you!"

"Jonathan . . ." What kind of wife would she be? Could she ever truly forget Ross Sheldon? Sabrina sincerely doubted it. Ross was branded upon her soul.

He studied her for a long moment, not even bothering to hide the fact that his ego was more than a bit bruised. "You like me."

"Very much!"

"But you don't love me. At least not yet." He kissed her

hand again in lingering kisses, his lips moving from her palm to her small-boned wrist. "But you will. Marry me. Give me a chance to show you how truly wonderful being together can be."

She couldn't say no, she didn't quite say yes. "Give me time, Jonathan. Please. A week. Let me have just seven days to make my decision, and then I will give you my answer." Closing her eyes, Sabrina hoped with all her heart that when the time was up she could keep her promise.

Chapter Twenty-four

For a man who was usually wise with a dollar, Ross Sheldon shuddered as he sat scanning his ledgers. Double-entry bookkeeping did not lie. By trying to compete with Buffalo Bill Cody, he was spending far too much money. He'd thought it would be easy to earn a quick profit, thought that all he had to do was wrap up the West into a marketable package and take it from there, thus he'd commissioned brightly inked lithographs depicting his stars. His campaign made the most of his passion for authenticity. His cowboys were sweat-stained ranch hands, not fancy pants. Beneath their fiercely painted faces and gaudy, feathered war bonnets, his Indians were real braves and not graying men from a reservation. Not one of his performers had ever seen the inside of a circus tent.

For weeks before his show came to town he'd send out advance men to blanket the area with posters and flyers. All he'd gotten for his efforts was that the advertising bills for his relatively new show were high. So far the proceeds had not been big enough to make him feel comfortable. He had enough money from his novels, it was true, but he didn't want to take that for granted and then end up impoverished. It took a lot of money to run a show, particularly when his investment had started out being in the red. And then there was all that money he had been spending on Miss Kitty Tremaine.

She has yet to even agree to meet me, he thought, tensing his jaw. She acted as if he had the measles. He had set out to gain her attention, but no matter what he did she rebuffed him. It was puzzling. His head swam with a dozen angry questions. He'd never in all his life had a woman act like that. What bothered him, though, was that with each box of candy she sent back, every bouquet that was returned, each haughty look she gave him as he sat watching her performance, she only intrigued him more. The unobtainable Miss Tremaine had become an obsession. He wanted her to join his show, that was true, but it was much more. He wanted her!

Ross ran his ink-stained fingers through his hair. Damn! The whole situation was getting on his nerves. The woman was on his mind all the time of late. Hell, he'd even booked his own company into towns he might have avoided, just to make certain he was within riding distance of the irritating little chit. Following after her like some silly puppy.

"I've been a gentleman, Ned," he said to the small, thin old man with gray hair whose job it was to clean his guns. "I've treated her as if she were royalty, trying to make an appointment."

The old man scratched his chin. "Mayhap that's where you've been wrong. There are some women who don't much reckon to politeness. They like their men bold and brash."

"Bold. Daring." Instead he'd acted like some banker going courting. Not like himself at all. Even with Sabrina he'd gone after what he wanted.

"Hell, when I lived out West in Colorado Territory, the women there welcomed a man who knew what it was he wanted." Spitting on Ross's Colt revolver, the one with the swing-out cylinders, he chuckled as if he seemed to remember something from his earlier years. "Yep, a man has got to show a woman who is boss if he wants her respect!" Taking off his bandana, he wiped and wiped at the barrel of the gun until it shone like silver.

Ross was thoughtful on the matter. If Kitty Tremaine wouldn't come to him, then he would go to her. It wouldn't be very difficult to find out which tent she occupied. He'd follow her and when she was alone he'd corner her and speak his mind. What did he have to lose? If she didn't like what he had to say, well let her spit in his eye!

Ross bided his time until early afternoon, then in his slow, relentless manner he took a leisurely carriage ride to Bill's campgrounds, just to the east of the Brooklyn train tracks. On a flat, dusty, tree-scattered plain, circled by protecting hills, there were rows of cone-shaped structures that reminded him a bit of duncecaps—objects of humiliation he had worn all too often as a mischievous boy.

Finding the perfect spot to leave his buggy, he jumped down and contented himself with a slow stroll through the grounds. He could hear the familiar blare of trumpets announcing the grand finale and watched as the horses and riders rode single file through the gate to dismount. He had no trouble at all distinguishing Kitty Tremaine's petite form. After all these weeks of watching her, he recognized her graceful gait in an instant. And just as he suspected, she was headed towards the tents. He had only to follow her and then once and for all they'd have their confrontation.

Sabrina began to undress as soon as she pushed through the flaps of her tent, hanging her buckskin dress in the scarred trunk against the wall. She sat down then in her chemise and underdrawers and pulled off her boots, exhaling with pleasure as her feet were released from the tight, pinching confinement. Rising, she padded on her stockinged feet to the table and poured water into the basin to wash her face and hands. Only then did she take off her wig, setting it carelessly aside. It had been such a long day. Reaching up, she unpinned her hair, letting it fall almost to her waist in a vivid, shimmering waterfall of gold. Picking up her worn hairbrush, she began to brush her luxuriant waves with measured strokes until her hair crackled.

Sabrina was tired. Her arms ached with tension. Her hands were sore from the weight of the guns she had hefted in the arena. And yet, it was worth it, wasn't it? Certainly her fame was spreading more quickly than she might have ever imagined. Her reputation as a sure shot, as a woman of cool, uncharacteristic nerve, was preceding her from town to town. She was pleased, Jonathan was happy, and Bill was ecstatic. Why then did she have such an empty feeling inside?

After putting on a blue satin dressing gown, she sat down in front of the large mirror that acted as her vanity and studied herself in the glass. She ought to be happy. Jonathan had professed his devotion to her just fifteen minutes ago. As Sadie always said, he was a fine man, a handsome man. He was the reliable type. Gentlemanly. The kind of man who would take care of her all the days of her life. Why then couldn't she feel even a spark of love for him?

"Time. It will just take time."

To remind herself how very much Jonathan adored her, she reached down, fumbling in one of the drawers of the trunk for the little reticule that was hidden towards the back. Withdrawing it, she took out a heavy golden chain from which hung a locket. Inside was an inscription that read simply, "To Kit from Jonathan with never-ending love." She slipped it over her head, letting the satiny weight of gold nestle in the valley between her breasts. The metal was cold. As cold as her hands were as she thought about her future.

"Oh, Ross!" Putting her elbows on the vanity, she rested her forehead on her hands.

At first Ross was certain he had gotten the wrong tent. A young woman occupied the tiny room, sitting at a trunk folded out to make a dressing table, but she had long, glossy blond hair and not Kitty Tremaine's dark braids. One glance at the dark wig hanging on an old whiskey bottle, however, changed Ross's mind. So Buckskin Tremaine was no brunette after all. Interesting.

"Excuse me." His voice was much louder than he had intended, causing the woman to jump.

"What are you doing in here?" she demanded in a trembling whisper without turning around. In protection of her modesty, she adjusted the neckline of her dressing gown.

He shrugged his shoulders, not showing the least bit of remorse for having barged right in. "I've come to see Kitty Tremaine. I assume that is you."

"Then you assume right! I am she!"

Ross took a step closer, glancing in the mirror to get a good look at her face. He found himself looking into deep copper eyes.

No, it couldn't be. He was seeing things. He passed his hand in front of his eyes, but the vision of loveliness did not fade away. His voice was choked as he whispered her name soundlessly. "Sabrina!"

At the sound of her name, Sabrina gasped. Her eyes met his in the mirror and she knew that she was lost. There could be no denying who she was. "Yes. Me!" A hodgepodge of emotions swept over her at the sight of Ross Sheldon. He was comely in his fringed buckskin jacket and trousers. His hair was just a bit longer than she remembered, brushing his neck as he moved his head. Though she had been expecting their paths to cross some day, she still wasn't prepared for the storm cloud of feelings he unleashed. Her masquerade was over.

"Sabrina James!" He couldn't have been more surprised had Kitty Tremaine turned out to be his long deceased mother. For a long moment, he merely stood there, bracing himself against the tent pole, staring at her in stunned surprise. Sabrina James a sharpshooter? "Sabrina?" he said again.

"What are you doing here?" Her expression grew hard, her soft mouth tightened. "Why have you come?" She tried to keep the quiver out of her voice by being overly stern.

"What am I doing here?" He grinned at her, his astonishment giving way to good humor.

It was just too comical. Enough so to inspire his laughter. It bubbled up from his throat, escaping through his mouth. Sabrina James! Sabrina! Damned if the whole thing wasn't insane. One of the reasons he had left her behind was because he thought her much too fragile and ladylike to travel with a Wild West show. Now here she was.

"You needn't laugh," Sabrina stormed, throwing down her powder puff. It was just too much to bear. He was amused. After all that he had done, he could stand there like that, deriding her. With stern resolve, she was reminded of the way he had just up and left. He had toyed with her heart as if it were a bauble. Won her love and then taken his leave. And now he was laughing. "Dear God, you sound like a braying jackass!" She put her hands over her ears to block out the sound.

"A jackass?" Ross choked on his laughter, instantly sobering as he realized just why she had resisted his attentions. "It's just that it's so amusing. You who are so very feminine, turning up here of all places. As a sharpshooter, for God's sake!"

"A woman does what she must to survive."

Standing there with her eyes flashing, she was the loveliest vision he had ever seen. Like the roses he had sent, her beauty had blossomed. His eyes drank in the sight of her, remembering how she felt in his arms. The smell of her. The taste of her.

"Sabree!" He stood towering above her. "I'm not laughing at you, but at my own stupidity." His easy smile was gone, his face drawn down at the corners.

"It's Kit now!" she snapped. "Sabrina James is dead. She died the night you so callously left her."

"I can explain." Could he? Were there any words to atone for what he had done? "Sabree—"

Seeing her again was like being dealt a physical blow. Ross felt his heart constrict in his chest with pain each time she glanced his way. He had been a fool for ever leaving her. Now it was too late to make amends. He knew she would never forgive him. Even so, he knew he couldn't leave it like this. He wanted her back.

"Sabrina, we were happy once." He took a deep breath, letting it out in a sigh. "We could be again."

"No!" Ross Sheldon was not the marrying kind, but she was. I will never be a man's lover again." When she gave herself to a man again, it would be in the marriage bed. Never again would she put herself in a position where a man could just up and leave her.

"Sabree . . ." His voice was husky and seductive. Bending down, he kissed the hollow of her neck.

Sabrina's flesh tingled with fire. Damn him! Damn herself. How could she be so weak as to feel the desire to react to his gesture. She wanted him to take her in his arms, carry her to her cot and make love to her. It was her deepest longing. That was why she pulled so violently away, her voice snapping, "Get out of here!"

"You don't mean that."

"I do!" Hastily she sought for something to say that would keep him at bay. "I'm . . . I'm marrying Jonathan."

"What?" He hadn't been prepared for this bit of information. "Jonathan who?" he asked sarcastically, as if he didn't know it would be that tall, lean, yellow-haired man she was paired with in the show.

"Jonathan Colt." She dug her fingernails into her palms to keep from crying aloud. "Jonathan asked me to marry him and I said yes." She hadn't, but she would at the first opportunity. Anything to protect herself from Ross Sheldon.

Ross tried to recover his poise. He didn't want her to marry him. The thought of any other man touching her now that he had seen her again was just too disturbing . . . yet his stupid pride was speaking when he said, "So what? We don't have to let a little thing like your being married come between us." An insensitive thing to say, but he couldn't hold his tongue.

"You bastard!" Sabrina could barely believe what she heard. He was an even worse cad than she had first thought. Any man who would knowingly seduce another man's wife was despicable beyond belief.

"Sabree . . ." He had regretted the words as soon as they were out of his mouth. He didn't mean what he said. Oh, how close he was to saying, "Please marry *me*." Reaching out, he touched her arm in a gesture he meant to be apologetic. "Sabree—"

Sabrina turned on him. Reaching for her pistol, she cocked the trigger and aimed it at his chest. "Get out. If you ever touch me again or come anywhere near me, I'll shoot you, so help me God."

"You wouldn't!"

Her expression was so fierce he wasn't at all sure she was bluffing. She had won this round of argument. Only a dad-blamed fool would face down an angry woman with a gun. Women's tempers being what they were, she might actually shoot him and then regret it later.

"I'm leaving, but this won't be the end of it! Nope, not by a long shot." He moved towards the exit in slow, even strides, turning as he lifted the flap. "I'll see you again. I never give up what's mine, Sabree. Just remember that." And then just as silently as he had come, he was gone.

Chapter Twenty-five

"Buffalo Bill proudly announces the marriage of the little lady with the rifle!" the handbills said in bright, bold red letters "Buckskin Kitty Tremaine has been spoken for. The nuptials are to be celebrated in great splendor at the next performance of "Buffalo Bill's Wild West Show." Jonathan Colt, of the gunmaking family, is to be the fortunate groom. Buffalo Bill himself will be the justice of the peace. Come one, come all, to join in the celebration. Watch your favorite sharpshooter say, "I do!"

So, Buffalo Bill wasn't above using anyone or anything at all to help him bring in a crowd, Ross Sheldon thought, as he crumpled the piece of brightly printed paper in his hand. A wedding! Sabrina's wedding.

He sought the quiet of a roadside inn to calm his jealous anger. My God, Sabrina was going to marry that tall, thin, pale-faced gunmaker, that leech who made his money off of her talents. He was a good for nothing, who made his living holding up cards and throwing tin cans into the air. How could she? How could she! It didn't make sense. "But then, women rarely did," he scoffed, speaking so loudly that some of the patrons raised their heads up from their beer glasses to stare.

"She loves me, not him!" he exclaimed to all who would hear. "Me!" He knew that she did, and repeated the words over and over to soothe his deflated ego.

He had been so sure that she would fly back into his

187

arms that he had wooed her with a vengeance, making a damn fool of himself in the bargain. He had tried to get in to see her again, only to be virtually thrown from the tent by some tall, scowling, irritating Indian. Undaunted, he had tried again, to suffer the same humiliation. He had even gone to the jewelers to buy her a ring, not a diamond, mind you, but a sapphire "friendship" ring. Finding a time when her Indian guard wasn't around, he had at last forced himself into her tent to present it, only to be rebuffed most heartily. She had another ring, she had coldly told him, one that spoke of the kind of commitment a man such as he was not capable of making. An engagement ring, the size of that diamond would choke a horse.

"A garish display of ostentation" he muttered in disgust. Undoubtedly bought with borrowed money.

"What will you have, mister?" asked a shrill voice, startling him out of his misery.

"Beer. Dark," he answered, looking up to find himself the object of severe scrutiny. Trying to soothe his injured pride and test his charms, he boldly winked, though the buxom miss was clearly not his type.

"Anything else?" She leaned over, affording him a look at the enormous breasts which seemed about to pop from her bodice. The gleam in her eye offered an invitation.

He ought to take her up on what she offered, he thought with a glower, yet just the thought of pursuing anyone but Sabrina was a troubling one. As he eyed this woman up and down, he compared her curves to Sabrina's delicately shaped breasts, so soft and alluring, and any passion he might have felt quickly cooled. Damned if he hadn't suddenly turned into a one-woman man. Sabrina had damn near ruined him for any other woman. Strange, he who had always considered himself a ladies' man.

"Nothing else! Just the beer!" he exclaimed, making his lack of interest plain to see. The tavern maid stalked away in silence, casting him a sullen look when at last she brought his beer. Taking a long drink, Ross had a notion to drown his sorrows. He felt totally consumed with his misery, helpless to stop the pain that even thinking of Sabrina in Jonathan Colt's arms brought forth. Not only that, but he had made a damned fool of himself before Buffalo Bill, his cast and crew, and most of all Sabrina.

"How can she even think of marrying Jonathan?" he muttered choking on the very thought. Not that there was anything really wrong with the other man. No. He was a bit self-centered, opportunistic, much too sure of his own importance, but all in all rather likeable, he supposed. But he wasn't Ross Sheldon! How could she even think of choosing pickled herring when she could have caviar?

"What did ya say, mister? Is there somethin' wrong with your beer?" The frowning barmaid put her hands on her hips, preparing herself for an argument.

"Nothing. Nothing at all. As a matter of fact, I want you to bring me another." In an exaggerated masculine presentation, he finished his beer in one long gulp. Jealousy. He had never felt the emotion before, and he didn't like it. The image of Sabrina lying in his arms came back to him, her golden hair spread about her slim body like angel wings. She had been all loving softness, how could he ever forget that night in his room? Their passion had been as shattering as an earthquake, a storm. How could he ever forget how wonderful their lovemaking had been?

"I won't do it!" When the barmaid brought him another drink, he pushed it aside.

"Do what, mister?" She was looking at him now as if she perceived him to be a troublemaker. "I won't get drunk." Right now he needed a clear head, not a befuddled one. He needed to think of just what he should do. "No, by God. She will not marry Jonathan!" Bolting up from his chair, he pushed past the astonished barmaid, mumbling beneath his breath as he stalked out of the inn. Sabrina belonged to him. He had to stop that wedding!

Ross paced about outside the inn's door, while he cleverly contrived a plan in his mind. It was bold. It was daring. But wasn't that what he was known for? Wandering among the oak trees, scratching his head and thinking, he worked out every detail. The timing had to be just right. He had to act quickly before anyone realized what he was doing. He had to make it appear to be part of the show, lest anyone intercede. Then, when it was least suspected, he was going to kidnap Miss Kitty Tremaine.

Chapter Twenty-six

It was a glorious May day. The arena was decorated like a primeval forest, with all kinds of potted shrubbery and flowers. The field was dotted with Western memorabilia. Beyond the bleachers, the tall buildings of Rochester acted as a backdrop, the only reminder of the city. The air sang with chanting as the Indians in the company finished their demonstration of dancing and made way for the ceremony that was to be the highlight of the day. Buggies, surreys, wagons, and other assorted vehicles funneled into the area disgorging the eager spectators who wanted to see an "authentic" Western wedding. It was Sunday, a day of rest and for the Lord, but these people didn't seem to pay it much mind. They were pushing and shoving, each and everyone there trying to get the perfect seat.

There were people still milling about the stalls for a bite to eat or something to drink who had not yet taken their seats when Ross rode into the arena. Carefully, so as not to be detected, he guided his horse to the end of the line of cowboys waiting for the parade. "Easy . . . I've got to act as if I belong," he warned himself, pulling his brown Stetson down low upon his forehead. Garbed all in buckskin from head to toe, he had dressed down purposefully so that he wouldn't stand apart from the other cowboys.

The band was poised and ready. The sky formed a

blue canopy over the assembled wedding party. Sabrina was astride a pure white horse, dressed all in white from her buckskin fringed jacket, short fringed skirt to her large-brimmed white Stetson. Even her boots were white, high-heeled in cowboy style. By contrast, Jonathan was attired in a red-embroidered gray leather vest over a red silk shirt, grey-striped trousers, and black leather boots. His Stetson was grey, as was his horse.

"You two look as if you came right off the pages of some dime novel," Sadie said, heartily congratulating the happy couple.

"I want Kit here to look just like the star that she is, and, of course, I want to look like a perfect mate for her," Jonathan replied, with not even a twinge of modesty. It was to be the wedding of the year, or so he said. Certainly the newspapers were making much of it, exploiting the fact that Buffalo Bill was an honorary justice of the peace and was going to perform the ceremony.

It was noisy in the arena until the members of the band picked up their instruments. The crowd stilled to a hush. The signal was given and strains of the wedding march, played by trombone, flute, trumpet, and saxophone sounded through the air. If the music was slightly discordant, well, those listening didn't seem to care.

As the bride and groom rode into the arena, a group of horsemen all dressed in white circled them three times then rode off leaving only the three participants — the bride, the groom, and Buffalo Bill. Bill was all dressed in black from head to toe, his long blond hair, which was quickly becoming his trademark, cascading to his shoulders.

"Ladies and gentlemen, welcome to this most solemn occasion," he intoned loudly. As if he and not the waiting couple was the star, he lapsed into a long, lengthy speech; then, with open prayer book in hand, he motioned to Jonathan. Dismounting, the grinning groom went to stand before him.

Ross made a hasty appraisal of the performers. None

of the people attending the ceremony were armed. There had been no need for rifles or revolvers. Besides, the bullets would have been blanks anyway. The coast was clear.

"Dearly beloved . . ." he heard Buffalo Bill say with all the solemnness of a preacher. Oh, he was milking this one for all it was worth. Indeed, Ross had heard that the finale was going to be quite a spectacle. A recreation of a prairie fire complete with a stampede of wild animals. A special steam curtain had been erected to give off smoke and make the enactment seem real. Solemn occasion, ha!

Dear God, Sabrina was beautiful! He knew he should have been watching Bill, but somehow he couldn't quite take his eyes off her. A lovely bride. Damn, if seeing her all dressed in white didn't begin to give him silly ideas — of marrying her himself!

Ross made sure of his timing. He wanted to be sure that no words were repeated to make Jonathan and Sabrina husband and wife, and yet he had to find a time when the coast was clear to make his escape.

It came just as Jonathan was looking at Sabrina adoringly, as if he wanted to devour her. It was more than Ross could bear.

With a yahoo, Ross swept down upon them, lifting Sabrina swiftly from the ground and depositing her none too gently across his horse's saddle. Sabrina was momentarily winded as her breath was knocked from her lungs. Splotches of darkness hovered before her eyes as she dangled precariously over the horse's back like a sack of grain. Blood rushed to her head, as she struggled. All she could think was that she wanted to feel her feet on the earth again. Thrashing her feet, she sought to get free, but Ross held her fast, maneuvering her around to sit in front of him. Oh, he was a strong brute!

So quick were his movements that there was no need to fire any shots from the pistol he held in a threatening manner. The assembled guests gasped in shock as Ross, with Sabrina clutched tightly in his arms and sitting in front of him, galloped across the field. Then they applauded, thinking it to be part of the show. Ross made his way through the open gate with a chuckle, wondering what Buffalo Bill thought of his performance. It amused him that not one move was made to stop him, at least until the addled groom ran after them shouting at the top of his lungs.

"Stop them! Somebody stop them!" He spouted off a string of violent oaths, calling Ross every name in the book, including "wife snatcher." Ross ignored the tirade, speeding off as if the hounds of hell were at his heels, which was no easy trick, considering the struggling, cursing, angry woman astride the horse with him. Several times her kicking and wiggling threatened to send them both toppling to the ground. All the while she raged at him.

"What do you think you are doing? You scoundrel, take me back! Ross Sheldon, turn this horse around right now." She was all too aware of him as they rode, though. His leg touched her thigh with a familiarity that troubled her.

He was equally aware of their bodies touching from shoulder to knee. "Hush, Sabree. You're glad I carried you off just now. Admit it!"

"I will not!" At least, she wouldn't admit it to him. In her mind's eye, however, she was secretly pleased. Wasn't this exactly what she had always hoped would happen? Her Western prince coming to take her away with him. In truth, this kidnapping was very romantic and exciting. What woman had not dreamed of being carried off by the man she loved? But where were they going from here? And what of poor Jonathan?

Chapter Twenty-seven

The road along which Ross and Sabrina traveled seemed to stretch endlessly eastward to the horizon, past fertile fields in shades of muted greens. The deep green of cedars and pines cloaked the gently rolling hills, contrasting sharply with the lighter hues of the grasses. Ross guided his horse down a slope to where it dimpled into a shallow valley and it was only then that he stopped.

"Well, what do you think, Sabree? Pretty little spot, don't you agree?"

It was, but she wouldn't have admitted it to him for the world, saying instead, "I don't know where we are, but I do know that you will deeply regret abducting me, Ross Sheldon."

"Y'know, I don't think so, Sabree." He chuckled low in his throat. Nope, he wasn't at all about to regret what he had planned. "Just wait until you see that big yellow moon rise over this place. No place closer to heaven than here."

"Than where?" Sabrina scanned the area, desperately trying to get her bearings. "Where are we?"

He didn't answer, just urged his horse into a slow trot down a winding pathway to where a small white cottage stood beckoning them like a luminous pearl. When he reached the small picket fence, he stopped again, this time dismounting. "Here we are," he announced with a wide sweep of his hand. "Home."

"What!" She suddenly realized just what he intended. "You can't mean to tell me that you plan to stay here? Just you and me?"

The muscles in his face danced with an expression of pure merriment. "That's the idea, Sabree."

"You must be mad!"

"There have been those who have said that I am." As he helped her down from her horse, Ross's hands lingered on the soft curves of her body.

"Don't!"

She tingled at his touch and that made her feel all the more frustrated, and vulnerable. Being here alone with him was going to be pure hell or pure heaven, only time would tell which. But oh, she was resolved to fight against the feelings he inspired with her very last breath, if need be. A man couldn't just ride out of your life and then think he could suddenly thrust himself into it again. Ross Sheldon needed to be taught a lesson.

"How do you know we haven't been followed?" she asked, casting a glance over her shoulder. Surely Jonathan and Buffalo Bill wouldn't stand for what had happened.

"I don't," was his reply, "but I'll cross that bridge when I come to it."

"Maybe Jonathan will come for me with a rescue party."

Ross took the liberty of patting her gently on the behind. "I would if it were my bride that had been stolen, but I'm not certain your intended bridegroom has the fortitude to come after me. From what I've heard, he's an all-too-placid fellow who just lets life come as it may."

Sabrina flushed. "He's a good man, a kind man. When I needed him he was there, not gallivanting off somewhere."

"Gallivanting?" He laughed at her language. How quickly she had picked up Western lingo from Bill and the crew. Yep Sabrina was certainly becoming "Westernized."

196

"You know what I mean, Ross Sheldon." Putting her hands on her hips, she glared at him as all the hurtful memories resurfaced "You just up and left me. Even you have to admit that it was a heartless thing to do."

"Yes, it was. I won't argue that. But I had my reasons, which I'll explain to you as soon as we get settled." He tugged at her hand. "Come on, Sabree. I intend our time together here to be a healing time. If we can't recapture what we once shared here in this romantic setting, then I guess we never will."

He sounded so soulful, so earnest, that for a moment she was almost tempted to forgive him, but the very thought of being so weak-willed rekindled her anger. There was just no excuse for what he had done. "It's too late, Ross. Too late." Even so, she followed him up the wooden steps of the cottage to the porch, pausing as she took a look around.

"Do you like it?" He could read the answer in her eyes. This ivy and vine-covered clapboard cottage had been a perfect choice as a hideaway.

"Yes, I do." There was no point in lying. In truth, it looked just like something out of a fairytale, complete with thatched roof and boxed windows that looked out on the rolling hillside. Each window was trimmed with bright green shutters that were cut out with designs that looked like lace. The cottage had been well cared for, at least outside, for it was not dirty nor was the paint chipped or peeling. It looked as if it had just been given a new coat of paint, in fact.

All around the porch was a well-trimmed hedge that blended skillfully with the rose bushes that seemed to grow in abundance everywhere. And there were trees. Apple trees, cherry trees, and those with just the tiniest bright red fruit. It was just the kind of place that Sabrina had always dreamed of having.

Ross could read Sabrina's thoughts and smiled, remembering her describing just such a place once in their conversation. He had filed the description away in his mind, but it had quickly resurfaced when he had ridden by while scouting out a place for his "love nest."

"There's a garden out back with all kinds of vegetables and flowers and more trees. There's a barn with a cow for milk and a henhouse with five or six chickens. And a smokehouse." He had made certain that it was self-sustaining, just in case they were in for a lengthy stay.

"Well, at least I won't starve," Sabrina said dryly, wondering just what it was Ross had in mind. What game was he playing? Seduction? Or was this something else?

Reaching in his pocket, Ross fumbled about until he found the key. "Come on, I'll take you inside." He put the key in the lock, turned it, then pushed the door open.

Stepping inside, Sabrina was surprised at how expansive the cottage really was. From what she could see, there were four or five rooms, cozy but comfortable. There was a square parlor with a table and four chairs, a large stone fireplace at one end. A horsehair-cushioned sofa, matching chair with wood arms and back rest, and a tea table made with deer antlers for legs and a round wooden top made the interior very Western looking, but then, what could she have expected from Ross?

"It looks a bit like a museum," she exclaimed, her lips curving up in a smile for the first time. Indeed it did. There was a mounted buffalo head on the wall beneath which were a collection of guns, bows, arrows, and lances. A war bonnet flanked the fireplace, colorful in its variety of feathers. There were leather pouches, some plain and some beaded, even a pair of moccasins.

"It is! I bought the place. I was hoping to share it with you."

"You what!" she exclaimed. "Never! I will never live here. When you left me behind I met Jonathan and formed a new life for myself."

Pulling a rifle from the wall, he looked at her. "I should throw this damned gun away and replace it with a Remington. It's a Colt. Never did like those damned guns anyway." Just as a precautionary measure, he added, "and if you have any ideas about pointing any of these at me, don't. They aren't loaded."

"Too bad!" The walls were covered with framed photographs. Sabrina leisurely strolled along, wondering who these people were with whom Ross was pictured. She recognized Buffalo Bill, but he was the only one.

"Wild Bill Hickok, Pawnee Bill, and a Sioux chief by the name of Sitting Bull. The one in the dark suit is an English prince who always likes to read my novels." Ross puffed out his chest with pride. "All friends of mine."

"And the women?" Jealousy tugged at her heart.

"A duchess, a madame, and an Indian squaw." He cleared his throat carefully. "Just acquaintances!"

"Mmm-hmm." She didn't believe him at all, but then, she really shouldn't care. What did it matter?

"Sabree." Ross shook his head, circling around and around her. "There's something I really must do." Before she could even protest, he had reached out and snatched the wig from her head. "I like you much better with your own golden hair framing that lovely face of yours. Yep, indeed I do." His face was so close to hers that for a moment she expected him to kiss her, but he didn't. Instead, he slowly removed the pins from her hair so that her blond hair fell down around her shoulders in soft yellow waves. "There, that's the way I like to see you. My girl."

"I'm *not* your girl," she answered, but her voice was breathy. She knew she was lying. Ross Sheldon would always have a claim on her heart, but she didn't want him to read that in her eyes, so she hastily looked away, pretending interest in the room. "Those books on the shelves, are they yours?"

"Yep!" He walked over to the bookshelf and picked up a few of the leather-bound volumes. "I know this will surprise you, Sabree, but I'm a very cultured man. Mark Twain, Sir Walter Scott, James Fenimore Cooper, even Shakespeare and Plato." He sat down on the horsehair sofa, scattering the books beside him. "So you see, a

199

man should not be judged too quickly."

Oh no? she thought. Right from the first when she had hit him with her wet mop, she had known him to be a scoundrel. Had she only listened with her head and not her heart she might have averted a whole lot of heartache. And happiness . . . Stealing a glance at him beneath her eyelashes, she had to admit that there had been many happy times. Perhaps the happiest moments in her life. But she was afraid to think about those times now for fear of falling right into his arms.

"I see there is a kitchen," she blurted out, trying to force her mind into different thoughts. "I hope it is well stocked. Men seldom think practically, you know."

"There's flour, sugar, and as many spices as I could remember my mother using. And coffee and tea."

Sabrina pushed through the door to explore and found the room to be bathed in sunshine. It was a bright room, decorated with blue and white checked curtains, with a matching tablecloth spread upon the small square kitchen table. Cupboards lined the walls and she hastily examined them. There were lots of china plates, with birds and flowers painted in the middle. Silverware. Cups, mugs, and glasses. Pots and pans, including a teakettle. One cupboard was stocked with canned goods, bought from the store and not done up by hand. From the kitchen, Sabrina could look out and see the pump just outside the screened-in back porch.

"Do you approve?" Ross asked from the doorway.

"You did very well for a man," she answered, not willing to even let him guess how charmed she was by this enchanting little place. "But it doesn't matter, for I am not going to stay here for long."

"Oh yes, you will, Sabree." His smile was the devil's own. "Until you say that you will come back to me."

"That will be never, Ross Sheldon!" She swept right past him exploring the other rooms with care. It annoyed her that there was only one bedroom, large to be sure, with a large brass bed in the middle, chairs, a bedside table upon which stood a lamp. She found the room threatening. An obvious mark of his intent. Well, she would never share his bed, even if she had to sleep on the floor. She would soon make that clear.

"I have a surprise for you." Coming up behind her, Ross put his hands around her waist, bringing her close against his body. The perfume in her hair wafted up to his nostrils bringing a swirl of pleasant memories to his mind. "Oh, Sabree!"

He was propelling her into the bedroom, and that was more than Sabrina would stand for. That big brass bed was just too unnerving, reminding her of how it felt to be nestled against his hard, strong body. "Keep your surprises to yourself. I won't go with you into that room."

He was amused by her reluctance, knowing very well that she was just as afraid of herself as of him. "My, aren't you the suspicious one." Taking her by the arm he whirled her around to face him. "Well, I can promise you one thing, Sabrina dear. I have no intention of ravishing you, if that's what you think. When you come to me, it will be of your own free will, because you've snapped to your senses and see that I'm the only man for you."

"The only man," she scoffed, forcing a sharp edge into her tone. "Hardly. The world is full of men."

"But none who love you as I do. Think on that, Sabree. For I do love you and I will claim that love once again." He took a deep breath, letting it out in a husky sigh. "Meantime, you'll stay right here, but don't worry, I've seen to your every need."

He gave her a nudge into the bedroom and it was only then that she noticed the boxes stacked beside the bed and the articles of clothing draped over the chairs. "What?"

"My surprise. I bought some clothes for you. Dresses, hats, shoes, even underwear." He took her hand, bringing it to his lips. Softly, lingeringly, he kissed the palm. "I want you to be happy, Sabree. And you will be if you

201

but give yourself a chance. You think you know me, understand why I left, but you will know all very soon."

Silence pervaded the room. Sabrina felt extremely uneasy. She had thought that she knew Ross Sheldon very well, and yet she had to admit that today he had been full of surprises. She was beginning to wonder just what to expect. Just what were his real reasons for bringing her here and most importantly, how was she going to get away?

Chapter Twenty-eight

The early morning sun streamed in through the window as Sabrina opened her eyes, flexing her sore muscles as she tried to forget the sleepless night she had just spent. The sofa certainly did not make a very comfortable bed! It was hard as a rock and the texture was prickly. But it was where she insisted that she sleep. She might have to share the cottage with Ross Sheldon, but she was adamant that she would not share his bedroom nor his bed. This time she wouldn't be so easy to win with soft words and caresses.

Slowly she sat up, swinging her legs over the side of the sofa, then sat staring at her bare feet dangling just above the carpeted floor. Last night while Ross was changing his clothes, she had tried to run away and might have been successful had she not tipped over a lamp. Now Ross had locked all the windows and doors so she was virtually a prisoner despite what he swore.

"A prisoner!" she grumbled, rising from the sofa. It was a fine way to woo a woman. Grimly she walked to the kitchen, using the wash basin to wash her face and hands and brush her teeth. She had been afraid to undress last night, thus she tried to smooth the wrinkles out of her dress, the one that she had designed herself for her wedding. She was surprised to see the coffee pot already upon the stove, bubbling and brewing.

"Good morning!" Ross peered from beyond the door,

looking especially cheerful. "Are you ready for breakfast?" When she nodded, he smiled broadly, took out a large iron frying pan, and settled himself in the kitchen with all the finesse of a chef. He fried bacon, eggs, and chunks of potatoes with onions and green peppers. A veritable feast. One thing Sabrina could say for him, rogue that he was, was that he wasn't at all lazy. With that thought, Sabrina washed the dishes.

"Were the dresses I bought you too big or too small?" Ross asked softly, stirring a bit of cream into his coffee.

"I don't know. I . . . I didn't try them on." Now that they were together in the same room again, a sudden shyness crept over her.

"Do you intend to wear that same buckskin dress day after day? Attractive though it is, buckskin often . . . well, how do I put it delicately? It has a way of . . . of . . . turning a bit rank . . . when worn—" He shrugged, not finishing the sentence, but she knew exactly what he meant and blushed furiously. He was right. She would have to take a bath and change her garments eventually. Being stubborn on the matter would make her uncomfortable, and not him.

"I would change my clothes if you give me your promise that I will be safe while in a state of undress," she shot back.

"Sabree, you wound me to the quick!" Throwing up his arms in a gesture of surrender, he opened his eyes wide in mock innocence. "You can use my bedroom as a dressing room, and I promise not to peek. Besides, I've got a bit of work to do on the barn out back. The roof leaks."

Sabrina cocked her head in surprise. It was hard to imagine Ross turning handyman. "And do you think you can trust me not to run away while you are working?" she asked sarcastically.

"No, that's why I've hidden my horse." He put the cup of coffee to his lips and drank to the last drop. "It's a long way from here to the next house, Sabree. I don't really think you'd want to try it. Besides, I'll have an excellent view of the cottage from the barn's roof."

"Watching over me like a prison guard!" In her anger, she dropped a cup, one on which a bright blue bird had been painted. "Oh no!" Reaching down, she tried to pick up the pieces, loathing her clumsiness. She hated to destroy anything so pretty.

He got up quickly and bent down to give her aid. Their fingers groped to retrieve the broken cup, brushing against each other's hands, unleashing familiar sensations. A quiver danced up and down Sabrina's spine as all her senses came alive in anticipation. For just a moment she nearly forgot all the reasons she should be angry with him as she looked up, focusing her attention on his perfectly chiseled mouth. It looked so firm, but she remembered that it could be very soft.

"Sabree!" His eyes held hers with a magnetic power as he watched the small beat of her pulse at the hollow of her throat. He touched her golden hair. "Sabree . . ." With gentleness and caution he took her face in his hand.

Sabrina drew in her breath. He was going to kiss her. Her body trembled at the very thought, yet somehow she didn't have the strength of will to pull away. She waited, gazing at him with a peculiar look of entreaty and sadness constricting her face. Her eyes were shadowed with a strange confusion, then suddenly were filled with tears.

She reminded him of a wild deer, a fawn, wanting to trust, yet still trapped by her fear. Had his leaving done that to her? Then if it had, he cursed himself and his stupidity. "Sabrina." He looked into her eyes and felt himself drown. There was nothing as potent as a woman's tears.

Ross put the pieces of the cup on the floor and stood up, thrusting his hands into his pockets. "Don't . . . don't worry about the cup, Sabree. I'll buy another." He wanted to comfort her, to draw her into his arms, but sensed that the timing was all wrong. He had wanted her so badly that he was pushing her, crowding her, when all the while she needed time to be alone. It was the hardest thing in the world to move his feet, to leave her, but he willed himself to do just that, heading for the door. "I'll . . . I'll be gone for at least two hours. Enough time for you . . . for you to see to . . . womanly things."

Sabrina watched him leave, feeling a sense of loneliness wash over her as soon as the door shut. Shakily she rose to her feet. "You have to get a hold on yourself, Sabrina James," she scolded. "You have to make up your mind about just what you are going to do. And no more crying!" Angrily she dashed away her tears. There was work to be done. She couldn't just stand around here like some statue. The least she could do was prove her worth to Ross Sheldon.

Filling the large copper kitchen sink, Sabrina gave herself a hurried sponge bath, still not certain she could be all that trusting of Ross. Going to his bedroom, he held up each dress in turn, looking thoughtfully in the mirror. She chose a green gingham dress with small white buttons, covering it with a white apron with green and white checked trim, then carefully folded the other articles of clothing and placed them in an empty trunk. She dragged the trunk out into the parlor, placing it beside the sofa so that she would have access to her new clothes.

The parlor and study were unmistakably a man's kind of room, but the kitchen was feminine and colorful and belonged to her. Sabrina wouldn't have admitted it for the world, but she really did enjoy woman's work. When she was living at her father-in-law's inn it had been a drudgery, but now she found it rather pleasant and it did help to take her mind off the situation in which she was.

She did in fact throw herself into her work, cleaning the inside of the cottage from top to bottom. Then there was baking to do, washing, and ironing. The exertion left her bone weary, too tired to do anything but sleep.

She found safety in her exhaustion. If she was asleep, she couldn't listen to Ross's practiced words, now could she? But she couldn't sleep forever.

"Tired, little gal?" To make matters worse, Ross was all thoughtfulness and concern when he came back. He even fluffed up her pillows and brought out extra blankets to make certain she didn't get cold during the night. Sabrina turned off the lamp, thankful when the room melted into darkness, but her ordeal was not over just yet. She lay in the dark, painfully aware that she could hear Ross undress. Dear God, she could even imagine just what his body looked like though her eyes were tightly closed. She heard the scrape of metal as he unfastened his belt, the rustle as he pulled off his shirt and pants. She knew he always slept naked and that thought brought forth memories of his well-muscled, perfectly shaped masculine body. Tossing and turning, she was besieged with all kinds of heated thoughts, but at last her fatigue won out and she faded off into a sound, if troubled sleep.

The next few days were painful, for though Sabrina longed to avoid Ross and the temptation he presented, the cottage was much too small to escape him for long. There was no way to avoid him. In these moments she yearned to tell him that she would forgive him, that she loved him still, only to be reminded of his betrayal. She wanted desperately to run away, to flee, to hide. How could she hope to escape this dangerous love that she carried in her heart for him when she was constantly reminded of her longing by Ross's presence? But though there might have been a way to get away she never tried, telling herself that she would wait another day.

Sabrina did, however, feel like a caged bird— trapped—albeit in a comfortable prison. And yet the alternative, of going away and never seeing him again, was even more disquieting. The love they had shared was embedded in her heart, her soul, her mind. She did not have to look at him to know just where he stood, what he wore, or the expression on his face — her senses told her. In spite of her common sense, her obstinate heart was consumed with yearning. She knew beyond a doubt that she didn't love Jonathan. Perhaps she never really could, especially not now.

Guilt stung her over the aborted wedding. She had left him, though not by her own actions. Even so, she had done to him exactly what she had vowed not to do. She had been the cause of his humiliation, his pain. Poor Jonathan. What was she to do? The answer buzzed about in her head, but she wouldn't listen. No, she wouldn't do to him what had been done to her. She had promised to marry him and by hook or crook she would.

The days seemed endless, yet time passed all too quickly when Ross was anywhere in the room. Then at night, alone and aching for his arms, she succumbed to her dreams. Though she had stubbornly insisted that she sleep on the sofa, she was all too troubled by the knowledge that his room was just down the hall. A comfortable bed. Warmth. Love. She wanted to be with him again, to be filled with him again, and she felt the burning fire within her so fiercely that she would awake moaning and perspiring.

Sabrina fought a battle within herself, but pride kept her away from Ross Sheldon's arms and from his bed. He had been the one to leave and she just couldn't forget it.

As for Ross, his patience was wearing thin. A week, that's how long it had been since he had first brought Sabrina to the cottage, and yet she still had not thawed a bit. Watching her now as she brushed her hair, he was overcome with the need for her. It was lonely in that damned big bed. He wanted her beside him. That's why he had bought the thing in the first place.

She stood before him in the airy room, her shapely body outlined by the light of the fire he had built in the parlor's hearth. He felt the overpowering thud of his heart against his chest and only managed by the slimmest strength to stand his ground.

"I like that dress, Sabree." This one was the black and white striped poplin that was draped and fit close to her figure in the current style, giving a long, thin silhouette. The high lace color emphasized the perfection of her face.

She turned her head, pausing in her brushing as she looked at him a long while. "I haven't really told you thank you for all the dresses you bought for me. I don't want to seem ungrateful. It's just that . . . that the circumstances . . ."

Ross laughed. "Well, the least a man can do when he abducts a woman is to make sure that she is well dressed."

It pleased him that she had voiced her appreciation at last. It was a beginning. Feeling a bit emboldened, he took a few steps closer, studying her profile. She was as flawless and perfect as a cameo. He was not at all certain that having known her, loved her, there could ever be another woman for him. Why hadn't he realized that before he had left her? It would have made his life so much simpler.

He saw her stiffen. "When are you going to let me go?"

"I've told you before." He hesitated, hating to keep the conversation centered on that topic. "When you promise to love me again, to give me a second chance, then I'll let you go."

"And not until then." She returned to her brushing, increasing the speed of her strokes. "And what of Jonathan?"

"To hell with him!" Let Jonathan Colt take care of himself. Besides, he was the wrong kind of man for Sabrina. Why couldn't she see that?

Ross had studied his rival man to man and found him wanting. Sabrina saw him as gentle, Ross saw him as weak-willed. Sabrina saw him as kind, Ross as indecisive. Sure, he had taken her with him when she had wanted to run away, but to further his own ends, not because he was any kind of hero. And Jonathan Colt had profited in the bargain by making use of Sabrina's talents and beauty.

"And that's all you have to say?" Sabrina shook her head in exasperation. "Well, I can tell you for sure that you could learn a great deal from Jonathan. Particularly how to treat a lady."

"Oh, I could, could I?" It was the straw that broke the camel's back. Jealousy goaded Ross. Slowly he moved toward her, reaching out to capture her shoulders in his hands. He pulled her toward him. "Sabree, you've got to listen to me." He'd tried over and over again to explain about that day he had left her, but every time he began the story, she turned her back and left the room.

"Why, so I'll believe some more of your tall tales?" She remembered how he had chuckled when first they'd met and she had naively revealed her belief in all the Western heroes. Well, she wasn't such an innocent any more.

"It's not a tall tale. Listen to me." Her lips looked so inviting, even pulled down in a frown. He felt a hot languid warmth melting his resolve, his self-control. "If I say that I love you, it isn't a lie. I did and I do." Ruthlessly his mouth came down on hers, engulfing him in the familiar sensations of passion. To kiss her once again, to feel his heartbeat against hers, was intoxicating.

For just an instant, Sabrina weakened. Pressing her body closer to his, she sought the warmth of his embrace. The softness of her lips responded. For a timeless moment they clung together, pressing closer and closer until a small cry from her begged him for release. If she let him touch her like this, she would be lost. Lost!

"Leave me be, Ross Sheldon." Tearing herself away, she stumbled backward nearly falling. Frantic. Panicked by how quickly she nearly responded to his advances, she struggled to get to Ross's bedroom and, closing the door, locked it securely behind her. She had

210

to get away, she knew that now. She had lauded herself for being so strong, but she knew that given time she would weaken. She must escape at the first opportunity.

Sabrina was given her chance when she saw Ross saddle up his horse and ride away the next morning. So what if she had to walk? Surely there would be a wagon or carriage somewhere along the way, someone who would give her a ride to the next town. The way Ross talked made it sound as if the cottage was on the moon, for God's sake, but this wasn't the West. It was the East where people were civilized and neighbors just over the hill.

Changing to her most comfortable shoes, low-heeled, high-button boots, Sabrina hurried about the cottage, assembling what supplies she would need for a short journey. Food, of course, enough for at least two meals, and matches just in case she needed to start a fire. And a blanket in case the worst happened and she had to spend the night outside. Forming the blanket into a makeshift sack, she felt proud of herself. It would do Ross a world of good to be thwarted in this matter. It would teach him humility.

Working at the lock with a hairpin, she was surprised at how quickly she had it open. Why in the world hadn't she done this sooner? It would have saved her a world of heartache. Stepping outside, she breathed in deeply of the morning's warm, fresh air. It would be a pleasant undertaking. Walking would give her a chance to really view the countryside. Somehow she would find her way. Looking back several times to make certain that she had not been seen leaving, was not being followed, Sabrina set off.

She walked until her legs ached and her feet were bruised and bleeding from the rocks of the pathway. Though the shoes she wore were of soft leather, the soles had all too quickly worn out. She cursed herself for not having worn her boots, even if they were high heeled. At least they were sturdy.

Past all logic, she aimlessly wandered, not admitting to herself that she was completely lost, that she didn't even know in which direction she was headed. Looking up at the sun, she tried to get her bearings. If only she could put as much distance between herself and Ross Sheldon, she would survive somehow.

"Going someplace?" an all-too-well-known voice growled behind her. Whirling around, she saw him standing there, a saddlebag thrown over each shoulder, a Colt rifle cradled in the crook of his arm. His horse stood grazing beside a brook.

"I was, Ross. I am." She could have run, jumped on his horse and ridden it bareback to anywhere that would have taken her away from him, and yet she just stood there. Perhaps she was just too tired, her anger and fear driven out of her by the fatigue of her journey.

"You got out."

"Hairpin."

"Ah, yes. I forgot just what a useful tool they are." He shook his head sadly. "But walking?"

"I would have saddled the cow if I thought she would have let me. I wanted to get anywhere away from here and you."

He threw his arms up in the air, his face suffused with unhappiness. "Sabree! Sabree! Why can't you just give me a chance? I'm really not a half-bad fellow." She didn't say a word. "Not talking, eh? Well, you'd better listen then. I just intercepted a carriage. Thought I'd get the scoop on what's been going on in Rochester. And I did. I did."

"Jonathan's undoubtedly put out a reward for my return," she interjected, her nose held haughtily in the air. "He'll want me back. So will Bill."

"Yeah, I imagine that they will. Course now they have a whole heap of problems so you might not be their only concern." At her puzzled frown, he explained. "Seems that the entire city of Rochester is under quarantine. A smallpox epidemic has broken out."

212

"Smallpox!" Sabrina turned ghostly pale.

"It's spreading like wildfire! Many people have died already. They have to bury them in mass graves."

"Oh no!" Her eyes widened as she shivered at the thought. "Sadie, my friend . . . and the others . . ."

"I heard that a few of Bill's people came down with it. Couldn't be helped, I suppose." Reading her thoughts, he said, "Bill's all right and so is Jonathan. But several of the Indians were hit very hard and over half of Bill's company was touched by it."

And she might have fallen victim to the outbreak, too, if Ross hadn't carried her off. Slowly Sabrina raised her eyes. Ross might have actually saved her life by carrying her off that way. She would never know.

"So . . . I don't suppose I have to tell you that escape won't do you any good. There just isn't anywhere that you can go, at least where it is safe. As I said, the area is quarantined."

She would just have to make the best of it here. There was no other choice.

"Perhaps now you'll listen fully to what I have to say. Will you, Sabree?"

"Yes." It was time. Slowly her stubborn pride left her. "I'll go back to the cottage and put some coffee on. Yes," she said again, "I will listen." Her copper eyes had a soft look, her smile was warm for the first time in a long while.

Chapter Twenty-nine

The room was heavy with an oppressive silence as Ross and Sabrina stood staring at each other. It was time for explanations, but neither one knew just how to begin. "Why did you leave?" Sabrina asked at last, really wanting to know, questing after the truth.

Ross poured himself a glass of whiskey, watching it slosh around as he tipped the glass back and forth. A sign of nervousness. At a time like this he needed something much stronger than coffee. He'd longed for this moment to exonerate himself, but now that it was here he felt strangely tongue-tied.

"Do you want the truth?"

"Of course I do," she said softly, looking up at him with expectation.

He downed the whiskey in one gulp, then came up coughing. He unbuttoned the top two fastenings on his shirt and leaned against the fireplace. "Just plain damned fear!"

"Fear?" Sabrina couldn't help but smile. Ross Sheldon wasn't afraid of anybody or anything. He was the very epitome of bravery.

"Not of any physical injury. Oh no! Hell, I've ridden through Indian-infested woods, shot it out with granite-faced men, used my fists and, when that wasn't enough, my guns, but . . ." He knew he could handle any life-threatening situation without even blinking an eye, but the matter of love was a far different thing. Just how could he explain?

"A man needs a woman, Sabree. It's in our natures to mate. But all my life I've escaped any serious entanglements as fiercely as I would a treacherous poison. I made it a habit to choose women who would understand when I just up and said good-bye."

"I see." Sabrina knew just what kind of woman he was talking about, and clenched her jaw in disapproval. "And, as I recall, you thought I was that kind of woman at first."

He shook his head. "Not really. I was just hopeful, knowing you were a widow and all. You did right in slapping me with your mop."

"But that wasn't the end of it." She inched towards the horsehair sofa, sitting down slowly. "You offered me genuine friendship. You made me feel alive again, Ross. That made it all the more cruel when you just up and left."

"I know. I know. Now." Ross put his hands behind his back, pacing back and forth across the floor. "I've been trying to sort things out in my mind these past few days and I've come to some startling conclusions." He paused before her, reaching down to take her hand. "But one thing I do know beyond a doubt. I love you. I think I probably did right from the start, from the first time you took that mop to me. But you scared me too, Sabree."

"Scared you?"

"Frightened the hell out of me, in fact." He reached in his pocket for a cigarette, lit it, then took a deep drag. "I've always been a man who valued his strength and independence. And freedom."

"And you thought I would threaten that." She was beginning to understand, to think beyond a woman's reasoning to the workings of the male mind. In a way they were just like little boys, rampaging around without anyone to whom to answer. Wild. Untamed.

"I *knew* you would." He took a long puff on his ciga-

215

rette, letting the smoke out slowly. "From the first moment I looked into your eyes, I started getting funny ideas. Ideas about settling down." He looked at her and grinned. "You'll never know how many times I packed my bags, determined to leave that inn, only to unpack them again."

"But you didn't leave," she said gently, fighting the compelling urge to cross the room and gather him into her arms.

"No, I just knew I had to get one more look at you, see you smile. And then that father-in-law of yours . . . well, he made me feel protective. I loathed the way he treated you—as if you were his servant."

"My father-in-law!" Sabrina paled at the reminder of Rufus James. What would Ross think if he knew that she had killed him?

"And then that night I saved you from that fat little man—"

"John Travers." Another unsettling reminder of that tragic night. Was he even now searching for her?

"Yeah, well, after that night I was hooked good." Suddenly tiring of his cigarette, he flicked it into the fire. "You became an obsession with me. I wanted to bring some happiness into your life, if only for a little while. At first I really did intend to leave you untouched, but I am only human. And then suddenly I was faced with a heaven I hadn't known existed."

"Yet you left without talking to me." She closed her eyes to the tears stinging her eyes. "Oh, Ross, a letter is such a very cold way to say good-bye."

"I'll agree. It was cowardly. But I knew that if I took one look into those big copper eyes of yours, I'd be lost. I knew I'd change my mind and beg you to come along with me."

"And I would have gone. I would have gone anywhere with you."

"I suppose you would have. But at the time I really did think it was in your best interests to stay." He told her

216

about the shooting incident, the trouble he had unearthed in his newly purchased Wild West show, his unrelenting decision that she was just not the type of woman who would be comfortable or happy on the road. "I wanted your happiness and at the time it just seemed that you would be better off without me."

"I was miserable! When you didn't come back to the bleachers I waited and waited, so long that I got into serious trouble with my father-in-law." She didn't tell him just how serious. Why? Why didn't she confide in him? Was she a coward too?

"I had so many other things on my mind, things that forced me into making a quick decision." He put his head in his hands. "Oh, Sabree, I never meant to hurt you. I just envisioned you with a different kind of husband. Not some two-bit wanderer like me. If only I'd known that you would just up and wander away with Jonathan I might have made a different decision." There was just a hint of reproach in his tone.

"I would have gone anywhere with you, Ross. Anywhere. To hell, if that's where you were headed. Because I loved you."

"Loved?" It worried him that she spoke in the past tense. "Don't you still?" At that moment he knew he would never be able to survive if she said that she did not.

She hesitated for such a long time that he almost ceased to breathe, then at last she nodded, saying in a tone of adoration that tore at his very soul. "Yes. Yes, I love you."

"Then marry me." He sat down beside her, stunned that he should make such a request. And yet to share his life with her seemed at the moment the greatest blessing he could ever be granted. The week they'd spent together made him realize there was much more to life than roaming.

"Marry you?" It was the answer to every prayer she had whispered in those days at the inn. To be Ross

217

Sheldon's wife.

"Marry me!" Ross drew her to him and kissed her long and hard, his heart pounding so loudly he could hear it drumming in his ears. "I love you, Sabrina. Please make me a happy man."

She touched his hair, but did not answer. Nevertheless, his elation knew no bounds because he read the answer in her eyes.

Chapter Thirty

The rhythmic ticking of the antique clock seemed to beat in time with his heart, Ross Sheldon thought as he waited for Sabrina. The fire in the fireplace crackled and sparked, the wick of the oil lamp was turned down to give off only a soft glow. Ross had brought the kitchen table out and set it before the fire, hoping to create a romantic setting. On the table was Sabrina's contribution, a roast chicken and all of the trimmings. Spread out on a white linen tablecloth was a veritable feast. Oh, yes, it promised to be quite an intimate celebration.

Understandably, Ross was impatient. He'd waited a long torturous time to claim Sabrina as his own. A time of thinking about her during the day, and dreaming about her the moment his head hit the pillow, imagining her slim legs parting invitingly for him. Soon, however, he was going to have his reward for unending patience. After dinner he was going to sweep her up into his arms and carry her off into that bedroom. Not before dinner, mind you, but after. He didn't want her to think he was too anxious. But he was! He was!

At last she opened the door to the bedroom and made her grand entrance. He looked at her and was starved for something other than food. She was beautiful in the lamplight, flawless and golden as an angel. The outline of her breasts where the bodice fell away made him long to reach out and touch her soft skin.

"I'm sorry I took so long," she said, sweeping up to take a seat in the chair he held poised for her.

"It was well worth the wait." Ross's eyes softened as he looked at her. "You're a beautiful woman, Sabree," he whispered.

She smiled in answer to his compliment, definitely pleased that all her attention to her appearance had won its reward. Sabrina had soaked in the brass bathtub for nearly an hour, feeling the hot perfumed water enclose her like a cocoon. She had debated over just which gown to wear, deciding on the cream-colored silk dress with the low neckline. Once she might have considered it much too daring, now she hoped that it was seductive enough. She didn't want to pass another night all alone on her horsehair bed.

"Would you prefer the white wine or the red?" Sabrina chose the Chablis and Ross tried to keep his hand from shaking as he poured it. Anticipation was making him as nervous as a bull about to be branded. "To us!" he announced, filling his own glass and holding it up. "And to that wonderful emotion called love."

"To love . . ." Sabrina's eyes met Ross's over the rim of her glass as she sipped her wine. Her eyes sparkled as she bubbled with talk of their wedding plans. Unlike Jonathan, Ross wanted to make it a quiet ceremony with only their friends in attendance, a plan which suited Sabrina to a T. Emotions were a private thing. It seemed that marrying the man that she so dearly loved should be quiet and reverent, not a spectacle. Besides, there was always John Travers of which to beware.

"And I'd like to get married in a church with a real preacher attending."

"A preacher it will be!" Ross said amiably. Anyone but Buffalo Bill. He was still smarting over Bill's betrayal. Before "Kitty's" wedding, Ross had gone to Bill, pleaded with him not to officiate at the wedding, told him that Sabrina really loved him, but Bill hadn't listened. He

220

was much too busy planning his grandiose ceremony.

Ross was hungry, but he picked at his dinner. He ate, but hardly tasted his food, drank of the wine, but felt much more intoxicated by Sabrina's glowing loveliness, her mouth so full and soft, her eyelashes so long that they cast shadows on her cheeks. For a long moment he sat perfectly still looking at her, watching the gentle rise and fall of her breasts. Desire for her raced along his veins and lit his nerves like quickfire. He could hear his own breath coming quick and rasping, and closed his eyes, clenching his fists as he fought for control.

Conflicting emotions took hold of Ross. One moment all he could think about was carrying her off to bed, the next moment a great tenderness welled up inside him, an urge to protect her from all the pain and unhappiness in the world. One thing he promised himself was that he would never be the cause of her heartache again.

Their dinner together was a merry one, an unqualified success of quiet talk and heated glances. Ross was jubilant. Soon his lovely Sabrina was going to be his wife. Did that idea frighten him? Surprisingly no, though he'd always thought that tying the knot would be scary as hell. His eyes were fixed on her face. She had piled her hair high on top of her head and all he could think of was how he wanted to free that lovely golden silk from its confinement.

As dinner progressed, he could sense that Sabrina was relaxing more and more. Her face was flushed with laughter and with wine, and she looked all the more lovely. Ross could not look away from her full, soft mouth. And her eyes. Were they brighter than usual? Such eyes, they were deeper and more alive than the eyes of any other woman he had ever known.

Reaching into his pocket, he took out two black velvet boxes which he opened slowly, teasingly. "Can you guess what is inside?"

Sabrina expected the smallest box to contain the sapphire friendship ring he had offered her once before, but she was wrong. He opened the box to reveal the most stunning ruby that she had ever beheld. "Ross!"

"I didn't want to buy you a diamond because you had already received one from Jonathan." He spoke his rival's name like a curse. "I wanted to give you something unusual, something to signify the fire you kindle in my heart." He succumbed to a rare bout of shyness. "Well, I hope you like it." Rising slowly from his chair, he went to her and slipped it on the fourth finger of her left hand. He was pleased that it was a perfect fit.

"Like it? I love it," she gasped, admiring its scarlet brilliance by the light of the fire. It was beautiful, but even if it had been a hunk of glass she would have cherished it because it came from Ross.

"There's more. An engagement present." His gaze raked her with heat that made her feel all quivery as he opened the other box. Inside was nestled a heavy gold chain that twinkled in the lamplight. Ross's fingers made a slow trek from one shoulder to the other, touching her in a way that made her heart pulsate at an alarming rate. She'd never thought her shoulders to be sensitive before, but surely he was doing things to her that were extremely stirring.

The metal was cold as it touched her throat, but Sabrina moved closer, leaning against his touch. "Ross, it's beautiful."

He clasped it around the slender column of her neck, then stepped back a little to admire it against the smoothness of her skin. "It was my mother's. I loved her very much. She was a great lady. And now it will be worn by another great lady." With a gentle nudge he propelled her towards the gold-edged mirror in the hallway. "It looks perfect on you, my love, as if it is just where it should be."

There were two reflections in the mirror—his and hers. "And right here is where *I* should be," she answered

222

softly. "With you." Sabrina leaned her head back, resting it on his shoulder. They stood there, molded together, a long time as if both of them were afraid to move and ruin the mood. Only when the fire went out did Ross turn away, with a regretful sigh.

Sabrina watched as Ross threw wood onto the grating. The fire leaped up, its flames dancing against the blackened stone. "There. We won't have to worry about being cold," he said, his wink showing that he had more than the fire in mind. Oh, he was so handsome, so virile.

Coming up to stand behind her again, his finger trailed downward to her breasts, stroking the valley in between. "I've wanted to do that all night."

"And I've wanted you to."

With a slow, sure touch he put his hand inside her dress, cupping her breast in a bold caress. Her body burned from his touch, with warm aching like a fever. He was a fever consuming her, igniting her with a sweet, fierce fire.

"And all night long I've been looking towards the bedroom door, wondering what you would do if I picked you up and took you there." He reached up, tracing a line from cheekbone to neck with his finger. "What would you do, Sabree?"

There was no thought of stopping him, no thought of trying to escape the inevitable. With a sigh of pleasure, Sabrina let her hands slip up along his hard chest, over his shoulders, returning his caress with equal intensity. He didn't have to carry her in. Sabrina walked into the bedroom of her own free will. Her fingers trembled as she reached behind her back to undo her fastenings. Then slowly, sensuously, she let the cream-colored dress slip down to her waist, her hips, her legs, to lie in a heap upon the floor.

Ross had been dreaming about this moment for several weeks, but nothing could have prepared him for the

223

moment he opened the door to the bedroom and saw her. Through the thin chemise and petticoat she wore he could see the silhouette of her curves, rounded in just the right places, tapering to slenderness.

"I want you. God, how I want you right now," he groaned. "Oh, Sabree . . ." His hand reached up to tug at the pins at her hair, scattering them all over the rug. The radiant glow of her silken hair, loose and gleaming, almost reached her waist. He turned her around to face him, drawing her into his arms again. His mouth fused with hers, his tongue exploring the softness of her lips. Sabrina met the open hunger of his kiss with a passion of her own.

Sabrina wound her arms around his neck, her hands grasping his thick, dark hair. It was all she wanted at this moment to be in his arms. How could she have thought that she could forget him?

"Oh, Ross, I want you too," she said at last. Erotic images flashed through her mind, memories of what it was like to be loved by him.

Possessively his gaze roamed over her as he reached up to loosen his black and red tie. "Then I guess if we have the honeymoon before the wedding, no one can blame us. Do you suppose?"

Sabrina walked slowly around the bed, her hand reaching out slowly to touch the wick of the lamp. Ross's eyes followed the gentle sway of her hips and lingered on her long supple legs. God, she was beautiful.

Ross said nothing as he moved toward her. Perhaps because his heart was trapped somewhere in the region of his throat. But he did give a whistle of appreciation. And when he came to her, enfolding her, kissing her mouth and hair, his gentle lovemaking did all the talking necessary. It told her that he loved her, that he desired her.

Sabrina warmed to his caresses, moaning softly, standing up on tiptoe to press herself closer to him, fitting her body to his in a sensuous dancelike motion that nearly drove them both beyond the limits of endurance.

"Sabrina!" Ross found his voice at last, calling out her name. He ran his lean, hard hands over her, sliding away the cloth of her chemise, stroking her breasts. He bent his head and sought her warm flesh, smelling the perfumed web of her sun-colored hair.

The chemise, her petticoat, and her drawers floated away with a soundless whisper. Ross lifted her up in his arms and carried her to the bed. He threw off his coat, unbuttoned his shirt, and worked his way out of his trousers with an unusual zeal. Standing above her, undressing, he felt fevered, dizzy.

With a groan Ross slid down on the bed beside her, gathering her into his arms. His legs entwined with hers as he kissed her, fusing their two naked bodies together. Sabrina felt the smooth hardness of his bare skin against her breasts and shivered. "Cold?" He tightened his arms around her, folding her even closer against him.

Ross's lips moved over her face and neck, down to her breasts. His lips were soft and warm and unbearably pleasurable. The sensations were incredible. Sabrina writhed as the old familiar feelings swept over her from head to toe.

His fingertips caressed the flat plain of her stomach in circular motions, slowly moving lower. It was as if every nerve in her body came alive. A sweet aching possessed her, a moan escaped her mouth at his touch, encouraging him to grow bolder. The sound of her pleasure excited him into a near frenzy.

"You are so beautiful." His hand slid between her legs, exploring her most private parts. She felt soft and warm. He could feel the warm wetness there. Ross was pleased. "The most potent aphrodisiac for a man is knowing that a woman wants him too," he said softly.

Sabrina moved her body against him, feeling the burning flesh touching hers. Reaching to touch him

225

with gentle probing hands, she marveled at the strength of his maleness. What a blessing it was that God had created man and woman.

Their loveplay was slow and leisurely, as though they had never made love before. Caressing her, kissing her, Ross left no part of her free from his touch and she responded with a natural passion that was kindled from her heart and soul. Her hands explored his body with not even a trace of shyness. This was meant to be. He was her mate, the man that she loved with all her heart.

Staring up into the mesmerizing depths of his eyes, Sabrina felt an aching tenderness for him. "I love you," she breathed.

Ross moaned his pleasure as she explored his hardened manhood yet held back his own hungry desires, lingering over her until she whispered in his ear that she wanted him inside her. It was all the invitation he needed. Sighing deeply, he cupped her buttocks and slipped hotly into her warm, satiny sheath.

Sabrina opened her legs to him, moving upward as he thrust his long length fully into her. She was so tight, so warm, so smooth around him that he gasped for breath. "Sabree . . ." he whispered, then covered her mouth in a searing kiss as he moved against her softness.

Locking her long, slender thighs around him, Sabrina moved with him, losing herself in the bursts of pleasure that rippled through her. Her body arched, surging up against his in a sensuous rhythm. She wanted to get closer. Closer. It was as if she couldn't get enough of him, blend deeply enough to him. She clutched at him with an all-consuming passion that made her wild.

"My God!" Ross had been with a lot of women in his lifetime, remembered what his lovemaking had been like with Sabrina before, but nothing could match this mating. Wordlessly he stared down at her as incredible sensations shook him. He didn't want it to end, wanted to move with her like this forever.

Welcoming his thrusts, Sabrina moved with him until they were engulfed by wave after blessed wave of the most incredible, unbearable pleasure she or Ross had ever known. It was a bit like being shattered into a million pieces, then falling back down to earth. For a moment they both hung suspended in time as her copper eyes met his piercing blue ones.

"Sabree . . ." Ross's cry was like a benediction. He buried his head in her hair, his teeth lightly nipping that sensitive place where her neck blended into her shoulder. "You will always be mine."

Sighing with happiness, Sabrina snuggled within the cradle of his arms, reluctant to move and break the spell. Her fingers threaded through his tousled dark brown hair, stroking gently.

Throughout the night they lay entwined, making love not once but twice more, then drifting off into sleep again. Ross watched her eyes as he brought himself within her, saw the wonder written on her face and knew within his heart that he would always love her. Pray God nothing would ever come between them again.

Chapter Thirty-one

Ross awoke, feeling bone tired and yet utterly content at the same time. For a long moment he simply lay on his back with his eyes closed, luxuriating in the sun streaming through the bedroom window, the rays of warmth dancing across his naked body. Weeks of frustration just seemed to melt away. She was his! At last she had granted him the glorious sweetness of her body.

Heaven. Her body had been pure heaven. Sabrina had made him the happiest man alive. "Ross, you tiger you," he mumbled to himself, smiling as he thought of her response to him last night. It gave him a heady feeling of power that he had been able to bring her such deep satisfaction. Not once, but several times during the night. He remembered her sounds of pleasure. He instinctively reached out for her. Sabrina wasn't there.

"Sabrina. Sabree!" For just a moment, he panicked. His pride suffered a painful flogging, thinking she had left him. No, it couldn't be. She had given herself to him with the same kind of wonder he had felt. They belonged together. She wouldn't, couldn't have left after last night. "Sabrina."

The sound of pots and pans clattering in the kitchen reassured him. She hadn't gone, nor would she. Now now. Not ever, if he could help it. If that meant tying himself down, well so be it. Somehow getting hitched to Sabrina seemed to offer its own reward. Let Jonathan Colt eat his heart out with envy!

"Jonathan Colt." He never should have even thought of the man. It was the only thing that threatened to ruin an otherwise perfect morning.

What if Sabrina had actually married that man? Ross pulled his knees up to his chest, trying to push the very idea out of his mind, thankful that he had taken a hand in the matter. He'd remind her to be properly thankful later, he thought, burrowing his head in the pillow. It was no use. He couldn't sleep now. An image of Sabrina danced before his eyes. Just the memory of her long legs, her breasts, the tantalizing way she had wound her legs around him, arching up to meet his thrusts brought a certain part of him very much alive.

"Steady . . . steady." Taking a deep breath, Ross forced himself to cool down. "All in good time." Running his fingers through his hair, he sat up chuckling. "Right after breakfast!" Oh yes, he was hungry all right.

Ross put his bare feet on the cold wooden floor one at a time, bending to retrieve his garments. His gray trousers, white shirt, socks, boots, vest, and tie were scattered on the floor in a haphazard manner, proof of just how anxious he had been to be rid of them last night. As he dressed, he whistled a cheerful little tune his mother had taught him once long ago. Happy days and the contentment he once knew were in his future. Now that he had Sabrina.

Golden sunlight filled the room. Sabrina was busy scrambling eggs when he popped his head through the kitchen doorway, humming merrily, in a mood equal to his. Ross grinned as she looked up, smiling shyly. "Good morning!" he greeted. There was nothing as good to the eyes as a joyful woman.

"Good morning." She blushed as she remembered

the passion of last night. She had said things, done things that nearly shocked her. And yet she wouldn't take back one caress, one kiss, one word of what she had said.

"Scrambled eggs and ham. Mmm, I really am a most fortunate man because I have a gal who can cook as well as—" Ross rolled his eyes suggestively, then pulled her into his arms.

"Ross, you really are a scoundrel," Sabrina teased.

"I am, but you like me that way."

"I do!" She gave him a kiss.

Ross whispered her name again and again, his gaze taking in the delights of her, one after another. She was wearing the pink and white polka dot dress, one that he favored. Her hair was hanging free just the way he liked it. Reaching out, he brushed away a renegade clump of hair that had fallen into her eyes. "Another kiss like that, and we won't have time for breakfast."

"Ross . . ." Her voice was muffled by his kiss, a fierce merging together of their mouths that quickly ignited passions. Ross moved his hand along the indentation of her waist, holding her closer as the hard evidence of his desire pressed against her.

"Have you ever made love in a hayloft?" he asked, smiling against her mouth.

Sabrina pulled away. "Never!"

"Then we will right after breakfast." It was a promise that he kept. Nestling with her in the cool, soft straw, Ross drew her down beside him, watching her eyes as he buried himself within her. With his hands, his mouth, and the strong yet gentle caress of his body, he showed her how very much he longed for her, declaring his love with every breath.

The next three days were spent loving, talking, loving, eating, and making love again and again. Ross knew just how to touch Sabrina, how long to linger, how to bring her time and again to the ultimate peak of pleasure. His hands learned every inch of her body, as well if not better than his own, and he in turn taught her the tempered strength of a man's desire. Always there was an exploding sensation, a wild passion between them, yet a great affection too. It was more than just a joining of bodies, much more. There was a deep caring between them, a blending of hearts and minds.

Ross had never realized before just how incomplete he was until that moment when he knew the shattering satisfaction of being whole. He had always been a loner. Disappointed with the world and the pain that could come from too much trust, he had erected a barrier around himself. Sabrina offered him devotion, a soothing balm to his bitter memories. Ross had been said to be wild at times. Stubborn. Restless. Sabrina's love tamed him, made him as docile as a bull in clover. Love. There could be no denying that was what it was.

Heaven! Pure unadulterated heaven, as Ross had said once before, that's what the precious moments together were to Sabrina and Ross. They talked for long hours, laughed together, worked together, contented themselves with long walks as they strolled along holding hands. Side by side, they knew the joy of just appreciating a sunny day, or huddling together during a rain storm.

Kissing and stroking each other, they delighted most of all in their mating. It was sometimes planned, other times spontaneous, always pleasurable. Ross taught Sabrina ways of making love she had never dreamed about, taught her how to accommodate his desires without feeling shy. He encouraged her to explore new paths of pleasure, different positions, ways of bringing each other to a heart-stopping ecstasy time after time. In the past Ross had eventually grown tired of a woman, and yet he found that the more he had of Sabrina the more he wanted.

For the moment, at least, the world ceased to exist for them. Living together at the cottage gave Sabrina a glimpse of what could be. Dangerously, she allowed herself to dream that someday she could get Ross to settle down. Was it really so impossible?

"What are you thinking, Sabree?" Ross asked her now, as they sat out on the front porch watching a mother sparrow build her nest. "Your mouth seems perilously close to a frown."

"That we are much too happy. I'm afraid that something is going to happen to end our contentment. We can't hide away here forever, as much as I would like to."

He drew her closer as if to reassure her. "Why not? We have just about everything we need here." He tried to sound cheerful, yet he knew that she was voicing his own thoughts. He had a show to run, and she had to make her explanation to Buffalo Bill. Three and a half weeks they'd been sequestered in the cottage, twenty-four days. Enough time for the quarantine to be over.

"We have to go back eventually." Undoubtedly both Jonathan and Bill were worried to distraction over what had happened to her. She'd have to face them sooner or later.

"Hush, let's not think about that now." The very thought of leaving was too much like being kicked out of paradise. Ross kissed the silken softness of her hair. "We have today and tomorrow and as long as we want and need." Or so he thought.

The sudden arrival of a visitor changed Ross's way of thinking. Stirring up a cloud of dust, a horseman rode his palamino mare all the way up to the door. Taking off his hat, he exposed a thick thatch of dark red waves. "Ma'am. Ross."

"Curly!" Ross was surprised to see the cowboy and obviously annoyed too. "What are you doing here? You're supposed to be looking after my show." Ross

232

leaped up as if he had been stung by a hornet.

"Had to see you. I rode all night and day."

"The quarantine, is it over?" Sabrina asked, curious yet at the same time fearful to hear the details.

"Yeah, it's over."

Ross was fidgety. "Was anybody I know stricken? Are all my people accounted for?" The intrusion of Curly seemed to bode ill, and he waited tensely to find out just why the man had come all the way up to the cottage. He had told him not to come anywhere near the place unless it was an emergency. "No one died, did they?"

"No . . . no. Weren't really as many casualties as was first expected there would be. Three children, two women, and one old man."

Taking off his hat, Ross paid his respects to the dead. "Six too many. God rest their souls." He was silent for a long while, then shook himself out of his sorrowful mood. "The show. That's what you came about, isn't it."

Curly nodded. "It's not my fault! You gotta remember that. I . . . I did the best—"

"What?" All the insecurities that had plagued Ross in the early days of his show came back to haunt him. "What's going on? Tell me." Curly was so flustered that it took a little while for him to be able to tell the story. Ross's none-too-gentle nudge prodded him to hurry.

"Somebody brought some bottles of whiskey in and . . . and liquored up some of the Indians."

"Damn!" Ross knew at once what an explosive situation that was. Indians and whiskey just didn't mix at all. Something different about the Indians' bodies he supposed. They were wilder. Liquor just seemed to bring out the savage in them. "What happened?"

"Four of them went on a rampage in the town. The same town that was quarantined. Tempers are short, Ross. People were agitated enough as it is. Anyway, the mayor is threatening to sue you, hang the Indians, and ban any more Wild West shows from ever appearing." He shook his head. "Damn fools are even trying to blame the Indians for that outbreak of smallpox."

"Ridiculous!" Ross's jaw ticked, indicating he was ominously close to losing his temper. His foot tapped an agitated rhythm on the wood of the porch.

"You know that and I know that but—" Curly shrugged his shoulders helplessly. "One of the Indians was . . . was your Indian chief!"

Grabbing one of the support posts, Ross encircled his hands around it as if ringing someone's neck. "When I get my hands on the man who gave the Indians that whiskey I'll . . . I'll . . ." The touch of Sabrina's hand on his arm calmed him down. "We've been so happy here, Sabree. But now we'll have to go. I've got to spring my Indians."

"I know." Sadly she looked around her. Some of the happiest days she had ever known in her life had been spent here. Her cottage of bliss! Now at last the world was intruding on their happiness.

Chapter Thirty-two

There was an old buggy inside the barn, nothing fancy, just a two-wheeler, but useable. It was a bit rusty, the seats were worn and cracked in places, the stuffing coming out, but Ross hitched his horse to it just the same. It would be a lot more comfortable than riding two on a horse over the long stretch of road he knew they'd have to travel.

"Do you have everything, Sabree?" She was loaded down with several boxes containing the new clothes he had purchased for her. Quickly remembering his manners, Ross lifted them up and hefted them into the luggage section of the buggy.

"I think so." Oh, how she hated to leave, but there was no alternative. She had commitments and so did he. Even so, she couldn't suppress a long, drawn-out sigh as she took one last look at the cottage.

"I know. I feel the same." Somehow the prospect of the journey back didn't inspire him. "But we'll come back just as quick as we can. Meantime, I've asked one of the neighbors to come by to look after things here. To see to the chickens and animals and keep it in tiptop shape until we have need of it again."

Bending down, he kissed her quickly on the lips, fearing that if he lingered at all in his lovemaking he wouldn't have the willpower to go, then, he helped her into the buggy.

Being together had given both Ross and Sabrina something beautiful to look forward to each day. They had crowded a lot of living and loving into a short amount of time. Now they had to face reality, had to go their separate ways at least for a little while. Sabrina had to return to Buffalo Bill's show and get things settled with Jonathan, and Ross had to free Indians of the troupe.

"Let's go—and hope this contraption doesn't fall apart on the road." With a flick of the reins they were off. "Well, at least the wheels seem to work all right despite the missing spokes."

Sabrina leaned back against the cushion, bracing herself against the jolt. Ross was right, the wheels did turn, but with an uneven rotation that threatened a bumpy ride all the way back to Rochester. Still, she had to admit that at least her legs and backside wouldn't be as sore as they might have been straddling a horse for hours at a time.

"This will give you something to put into one of your books," she said, glancing over at Ross with a smile.

"Yeah." Quickly an idea came to him. "Logan Hunter rescuing his ladylove from a marauding band of renegade Indians, when all of a sudden one of the wheels falls off. Plop!" He nodded his head sharply. "I can see it all now, yep. That scrappy devil keeping the buggy going with just one wheel, the two-wheeler leaning into the dust, the poor heroine hanging on for dear life."

"Oh dear!" Sabrina couldn't keep from laughing nervously at the vision he conjured up. For a long while she looked over the side of the buggy, keeping her eye on the wheel, then at last settled back, trying to make herself as snug as she could considering the circumstances.

The buggy rolled along at a brisk pace, its harness

rustling against the horse's back, its seats occasionally creaking. The hooves of the horse click-clacked against the hard dried dirt road. Ross held a rifle between his knees just in case of any trouble, and had his gunbelt strapped tightly to his hips. Though it was a reminder of danger, his manly presence also gave her a feeling of security. No matter what happened, she knew that he would protect her and that was a comforting feeling. She belonged to Ross, heart, soul, and body, always had perhaps, and now he had made the same pledge to her.

"Content?" Ross patted her knee.

"Mmm-hmm. Don't care where I'm going really, as long as it is with you."

"My feelings exactly."

As the buggy bounced down the rutted road, Sabrina tried to relax, going over and over again in her mind just what she would say to Jonathan to let him down easy. There had to be something she could say to make him understand. Or was there? No. It wasn't going to be easy telling Jonathan that she no longer intended to marry him, that she did in fact intend to marry Ross Sheldon instead. It wasn't a confrontation she was particularly looking forward to. Jonathan had been good to her and she didn't want to hurt him this way, yet she had no other choice.

"You're the only man for me, Ross Sheldon," she whispered.

"I better be." He leaned closer. "Cause you sure as heaven are the only girl for me."

As they rounded the curve near the creek bed, the sudden jolt caused her to be propelled upward. "Oh!" Frantically she put her arms around Ross, holding him close.

Ross urgently pulled the buggy to a halt. "Well now, if that isn't nice." Loosening the reins, he took her in his arms. "A man can always pause for a kiss.

237

Yes, sir." When she hesitated, he pointed to his lips. "Give me a kiss right here. I won't go another length without one."

Sabrina tilted her face up obligingly, flashing him her most seductive smile. Ross's lips were soft and gentle, his hands caressing her with infinite skill. It was a most pleasurable and stirring moment, ending much to their infinite regret.

A gust of wind upended his hat and he made a grab for it, laughing. "Whoosh. That kiss blew the hat right off my head. Potent, Sabree. Potent." He eyed the rocky terrain with a shrug. "Ooo. Sure as hell wish there was somewhere we could . . . uh . . . rest awhile. As it is, I guess we just have to keep going." With a regretful sigh, he plopped the hat back on his head and flicked at the reins again.

Ross was hard put to keep his eyes on the road. Again and again his eyes just seemed to stray in Sabrina's direction. He was acutely aware of the long, slender curves below that pink and white dress, the secret wonders of her body, now pressed close to his in the confines of the buggy. Damn Curly for intruding on his paradise like he had! He had trusted him to maintain at least a semblance of order while he was gone.

"Damn!" Ross's thoughts were rudely brought back to the problems at hand. Curly Davis's visit had completely shaken him. He blamed himself for what happened, because he had completely lost touch with what was going on in his show, and, though he had trusted the man he had left in charge, he was still immersed in self-recriminations. If only life were simpler, he thought.

It was a rough, time-consuming journey, made even longer by the fact that they had to stop the buggy to let a railroad train cross their path. The whistle tooted two sharp blasts. The huffing and puffing of the engine, the clicking and grinding of the wheels on the tracks, shattered the stillness of the countryside, reminding Sabrina that though it seemed as if they were the only two people in the world at the moment they were soon going to rejoin society.

"Well, I'll be. Take a look at that, Sabree." Ross took one look at the Barnum Circus logogram on the side of the railroad cars and gave forth a holler. "Gives me an idea. Why couldn't I transport my Wild West show by train?"

"The whole show?" It seemed a daring idea, corralling all the Indians, cowboys, buffalo, and horses into such a small space and yet, the wagons were really just as confining.

"Sure, the whole show." Ross pondered the matter over carefully, his pride prodding him to say, "If the circus can do it, so can I. And just think how much faster it would be to travel. Hell, there isn't anyplace a show couldn't go. The possibilities are limitless."

Sabrina could see him calculating all the profits in his head and laughed. "I know what you're thinking."

"Aw, honey, this thing about the Indians has me worried sick. But maybe I've just thought of a way to recoup my losses and keep one step ahead of whoever it is trying to ruin the show."

"But Ross, that might take you far away." Sabrina hadn't really thought about it before, but in a way the Wild West show was much like a rival lover.

"Not if you traveled with me." He hadn't wanted to mention the matter before, knowing as he did how guilty she felt for leaving Bill's show, but now that the subject had been broached, he knew they had to have it out. "I'm proposing that you join my show, Sabree. I can't keep following after Buffalo Bill's enterprise just so I can be close to you. I've got to think about my own investment."

239

"Leave Buffalo Bill?" She didn't have to think about it very long to know that it was the only answer. Ross had asked her to marry him and a woman's first responsibility was to her man.

"Well?" Ross raised his eyebrows in expectation, hoping it didn't come down to an argument.

"All right. I'll talk to him about it."

He gave her hand a squeeze. "That's my girl." Sabrina's decision put Ross in a much better mood as he guided the horse and buggy along the roadway. He'd get the Indians out of jail, atone to the mayor, and take matters from there. Somehow things would turn out all right. Certainly it seemed as if he was a man blessed by Lady Luck.

At last they could see the tents of Bill's camp across the river, the lights shining in clusters. "We're almost there."

"Yes, we are," Sabrina answered, trying to sound cheerful. Instead she wanted nothing more at that moment than to turn right around and go back to the cottage, but doing so would have only delayed the moment of reckoning. She couldn't be a coward.

As they drove up to the entrance of the camp, Ross saw a familiar figure standing by the hitching post. It was Buffalo Bill himself.

"Well, well, well, if it isn't Cherokee Ross." Bill strolled leisurely towards the buggy, his piercing eyes glowing under the shadow of his broad hat, his dark blond hair stirring in the breeze.

With a carefully expressionless face, Ross tried to judge just what Bill would do next. "Hello, Bill." He brushed his fingers against his gun just in case there might be trouble, but Bill grinned amiably.

"Thought you had a show of your own, Sheldon. Didn't have any idea that you wanted to be the star of mine. But you sure as hell were. The day after you left there were people just clamoring for more of

240

the same. Sold more tickets than I had seats."

"Yeah, I bet!" Ross mumbled, eyeing Bill up and down suspiciously. Something was up his sleeve. He was taking this matter far too much in his stride for Ross's liking. He'd expected recriminations and a scolding, at least.

"I'm deadly serious!" Bill winked good-humoredly. "Come on to my tent and we'll talk about making you part of my act."

"Very funny!" Ross gave Buffalo Bill a long, level unsmiling look, but Sabrina giggled.

Without waiting for Ross to help her down, she bounded from the seat, giving Bill an affectionate hug. "I thought you'd be angry. I'm so glad that you're not. Oh, Bill, if Ross hadn't done what he did I would have made the worst mistake of my life. I love him and not Jonathan."

"So I can see." Bill cupped her face in his large hand. "The signs of love are written all over you. Your face is flushed, your eyes sparkle, and that smile tilting up your lips speaks of a well-satisfied woman."

"Bill!" Her face turned a bright shade of scarlet.

Bill swept off his hat with all the courtliness of the finest Eastern gentleman. "Just speaking my mind, little Kitty Kat. Just telling it like it is." He looked at Ross and then at Sabrina and then at Ross again. "Course I'm trying to keep a good humor about the whole thing, but Jonathan is mad as hell!"

"Yeah, well that's too damned bad!" Ross challenged.

"Ross!" Sabrina put her hand on his arm, cautioning him from starting a quarrel. "You would have been angry too if you had been in his place."

Ross shrugged. "Yeah, I suppose." He had to be fair. It was just that there was something about Jonathan Colt that bothered him. Somehow he just didn't

241

like the man. Jealousy, he supposed.

They stood chatting with Bill for a while, curious to find out about the quarantine. It was a subject which piqued Bill's temper.

"Damned fool doctors wouldn't let me take my company and leave," Bill related testily. "Said I might spread smallpox all over the countryside. Hell, truth is not a one of my boys even came down with it. I gave them my antidote."

"Antidote?"

"Sulfur and molasses." For a moment his gray eyes softened. "My mother used to tell me it cured anything."

"Ugh." Ross made a face and groaned. "Well, if it worked He . . ." He wished Curly had known about the remedy.

The topics of conversation turned to other things, then returned to Jonathan. Though Ross told her that he would come with her, Sabrina knew it would be far better to meet Jonathan alone. Seeing Ross would only be a reminder of what had happened and she wanted to console him, not anger him.

"I owe it to Jonathan to make this as easy as I can on him. Please understand, Ross."

"I do." Bending down he kissed her on the lips, admonishing Bill to "take care of my girl." Ross turned to go, saying over his shoulder, "I have a few things to take care of myself, but I'll be back first thing tomorrow morning."

Sabrina watched as he walked away with that jaunty stride she had grown to love, feeling bereft as soon as he was out of sight. Biting her lip and steeling her nerves, Sabrina gathered control of her emotions and went in search of Jonathan. Bill told her that he was in his tent. When she arrived there, she pulled at the tent flap and stepped inside. A lantern was flickering, illuminating a figure who sat at the table, a half-empty whiskey bottle held in his hands.

"Jonathan?" she called softly. Looking up, he was startled by her entrance, but his face suffused with joy as soon as he recognized her.

"Sa—Kit! Kit!" Bounding to his feet, setting down the bottle, he soon smothered her in his embrace. "You're back." He planted wet kisses along her cheek, chin, and throat, and Sabrina couldn't help but notice that he smelled strongly of liquor. "You're back!"

"Yes, Jonathan. I'm back. Ross brought—"

"Ross!" The very name caused him to stiffen and pull away from her. "That bastard! Embarrassing me in front of everybody. Made me look like a horse's ass, carrying you off that way." He clenched his hands into fists. "Well, he'll be sorry! We'll have him put in jail."

"No!" She couldn't have that.

"Yes!" Jonathan was adamant. "There are laws that say a man can be punished for doing what he did."

"No, Jonathan!" she repeated in a fervent voice. "He . . . he didn't hurt me."

"He didn't? Are you sure?" Jonathan returned to the table, his hands shaking as he picked up the bottle and took a long, halting drink. When he set it down again, he looked at Sabrina slowly, lingeringly. "He didn't . . . you know . . . touch you . . . or . . . or force himself upon you, did he?"

Remembering how freely she had merged into his embrace, Sabrina shook her head. "No, he didn't force me."

Jonathan sighed with relief. "Good. Good! For that at least I thank him." He took her hand, pulling her down to sit across from him at the table. "Hell, Kit, we can just pretend that none of this happened then. I'll let bygones be bygones. I'm a civilized man."

"Jonathan . . ." She wanted to tell him all that had happened, but he reached across the table, silencing

243

her with his fingers.

"Everything will be rectified as soon as you say 'I do.'" He began rambling on about the new plans he'd made for an even grander ceremony. They'd make use of the Indians, he said, dressing them in brightly colored feathers. "Or even better yet, maybe we'll make it look as if you are going to marry someone else and then *I* can ride in and carry you away, ride out of the arena then after a significant pause, ride with you to the other side of the field. It will give it a sense of excitement. Gunshots, war whoops, the whole treatment. What do you think?"

It sounded terrible. Even if she hadn't been reunited with Ross, Sabrina knew she wouldn't have ever approved of the idea. Wanting to be diplomatic, however, she cleared her throat and chose her words very carefully. "Jonathan, you are the best friend any girl could ever have. I feel a great deal of affection for you. Honestly I do. . . . but—"

"But!" His eyes seemed to bore right through her. "But what?"

"But I can't marry you."

"Why?" He bounded to his feet, totally caught by surprise.

Sabrina spoke quietly and slowly at first, but then the story began to tell itself. She told him about first meeting Ross, about her heartache when he left, but about how her feelings were reignited spending all those days together at the cottage.

"I love him, Jonathan. I think perhaps I always will."

"You don't say." His tone was blatantly sarcastic. "That's just great. Yeah, just wonderful."

"Jonathan, please understand."

"Oh, I do understand. Understand just how manipulative you really are." He leaned towards her, his eyes flashing. "So all this time you were just leading

244

me on. Biding your time until *he* came back."

"No, Jonathan." She shook her head violently. "That isn't the way it was at all."

He mumbled on without even listening to her. "Using me, so that I'd help you get your starring role in Bill's little show here." His face was only inches from hers, his teeth a gleam of white against the redness of his angered face.

"That's not true!" Sabrina was indignant. "I never led you on. Never! I even told you how I felt about him that day we took the carriage ride. I was honest with you, Jonathan, and you pretended to understand."

"Well, I don't!" The effects of the whiskey made him unsteady on his feet as he began to pace about. "He was a bastard to you. Seduced you, then up and left. I showed you every consideration. Hell, I even made you a star and all the thanks I get is that at the first crook of his little finger you leave me flat on my butt and run off with him. And now you come back, but not to earn my forgiveness, oh no. You come back here to tell me you can't marry me."

Her voice was soft. "I can't. It wouldn't be fair to me or to you."

"Fair!" The word exploded from his lips. "Fair." Suddenly he grabbed her wrist, squeezing cruelly. Sabrina shrank from his touch, but he held her so tightly that she couldn't pull away. "Well, I have been making plans ever since you disappeared and I can tell you one thing. If you don't marry me, I'll sure as hell see that you never marry Ross Sheldon."

"I am going to marry him!" His attitude was slowly sparking her own anger, but she tried to maintain her good will. "Oh, Jonathan, I really didn't mean to hurt you. You have been very good to me and I'll never forget that. But Ross has told me that he loves me. I'm going to quit this show and join with his

245

and—"

"Over my dead body!" The small confines of the tent vibrated with his shout. "You won't leave here with him. If you think that I'll let you just waltz away after I took all that time to train you, then you're crazy."

"And you are crazy if you think I'll allow you to bully me this way!" With a burst of strength she pulled free of his grasp. The more he raved, the more she wondered if she had ever really known Jonathan at all. It seemed that he could be rough and pigheaded when the wind was not blowing his way. "Jonathan, please!" She wanted less tension, less antagonism between them. "Don't throw our friendship away."

"It's not me who is guilty of that, but you! You are being ungrateful. Hateful. Hurtful."

She opened her mouth to protest, but suddenly it didn't seem to matter anymore just what Jonathan thought. She had shown him her gratitude for all he had done for her. Not one day had gone by without her thanking him for his friendship. It was true that she had benefited from his tutelage, but equally true that in his own way he had also received his rewards. Not only had he gotten his own salary, but a percentage of her earnings as well. All because she felt beholden to him.

He continued, "Well, if you think you are going to leave me behind while you run off with your lover, think again. I simply won't have it, Kit. Or rather, Sabrina." The muscles along his jaw quivered, his expression became hard. Bitter. "Oh, no, I just won't have it at all." He paused a moment, then said triumphantly, "You murdered your father-in-law. Did you think I didn't know that? Did you think I wasn't wise as to just why you hid in my wagon?"

Sabrina's face turned pale and she clutched at the

tent's support post to keep from swaying. "I didn't mean to kill him. It was an accident. You must believe me."

"Accident?" He laughed and said smugly, "Of course it was. I saw the whole unfortunate episode while I was fixing my wagon. But if I just happen to say the wrong thing, no one will believe it. Certainly the circumstances are incriminating, what with John Travers babbling his version of the story."

"Jonathan, you wouldn't use this as blackmail—"

"Who said I wouldn't?" It was then that Jonathan revealed his ruthless side. If she left with Ross Sheldon, or even tried to see him again, he vowed angrily that he would betray Sabrina to the law. "I want you to stay in this show as my partner, even if you will not be my wife. But, as God is my witness, I will see you put in jail for murder before I let you see that scoundrel again."

"You wouldn't—" Sabrina breathed, but she knew in her heart that he would.

Chapter Thirty-three

After the long ride to his own quarters, Ross dusted himself off, fed and watered his horse, then strode toward the administrative office, a little house on wheels. Somehow things just didn't look good. He had an eerie feeling that there was something that Curly wasn't telling him.

He climbed the two steps, pushed the door open and walked into an empty room. Papers were scattered all over the room, empty desk drawers were open, chairs had been tipped over. The place looked as if a tornado had struck it. It had obviously been ransacked, but why and by whom and where the hell was Curly? He'd had more than enough time to return by now.

With a grumble Ross strode about the room, picking up the contracts, newspaper clippings, his notebooks, and the other documents littering the wooden floor. He was straightening up a chair when he heard a noise behind him. Turning around, he saw a short, squat, bald man leaning against the doorjamb, staring at him.

"If you're lookin' for your good friend Curly, you'll find him at the police station," the man mumbled.

"Oh?" Ross looked the man over from head to toe. Something in the man's manner made him wary. "And just who the hell are you?"

"Dan. Dan Steel."

Ross didn't remember ever seeing him before. "Dan Steel," he repeated. "And just what are you doing here?"

"Hired on about a week ago," the man answered, putting his pudgy hand on his rotund hip. He was too sure of himself, much too cocky for Ross's liking. "Curly hired me when two of your men up and quit. The quarantine spooked 'em so they just ducked out of town one night."

"That damned quarantine!" Ross fumbled in his pocket for a cigarette and put it to his lips, but couldn't find a match. The man named Dan Steel quickly came to his rescue, striking one of his own matches on the heel of his boot and holding it out for Ross's use. "Thanks."

"Always know how to please the boss," Dan Steel said gloatingly.

Ross put his foot up on the chair, leaning on one knee as he puffed on the cigarette. "Yeah, well, if you want to be real obliging, you'll give me some information on exactly what happened to my Indians."

Dan Steel shrugged. "Raising hell like Indians always do." He didn't sound the least bit remorseful. "Them redskins are nothing but savages."

Gritting his teeth, Ross hissed, "*My* Indians aren't. I've never had the least bit of trouble. Until some hairbrained ass gave them whiskey." Something about the man caused his temper to break. All his frustrations poured out as he asked, "And just who do you think that was?"

"Don't know. Don't care. Ain't none of my business." The sneer on his face angered Ross. It was apparent that he didn't give a damn about what had happened.

"Well, you damned better care!" With a lunge

Ross hurled himself forward, grabbing the fat little man by his shirt front. "You just better care one hell of a lot, because I have a gut feeling you know a lot more about this than you're pretending."

Obviously shaken, the man denied the accusation. "I don't know nothin'."

"Are you sure?" Ross pushed him against the wall. "Are you damned sure?" It seemed very odd that the man had shown up at the same time as the "whiskey incident."

"Does the name Hawthorne sound familiar?"

"Hawthorne?" His head looked as if were on a swivel, moving back and forth. "No. No."

Ross let him go. "I hope you're telling me the truth. I'd like to think that a man like you would keep better company." Folding his arms across his chest, he purposefully made himself look formidable. "But just in case you're not being quite honest with me and if you see him, tell Hawthorne for me that I'll never sell my controlling interest in this show. And that if he persists in causing me trouble, I'll nail his ass to the wall!"

Dan Steel shrank back. "I told you I don't know him."

"All the better for you." Ross decided to let the matter drop. "Now, suppose you saddle up two horses. I'll give you a chance to prove to me just what kind of a bargain you are and see if Curly made a good choice or a bad one in hiring you on."

"Saddle up?"

"Yeah, you're going with me when I spring my Indians." Ross didn't know exactly how he was going to do it, but come hell or high water he intended to get them out of jail.

Chapter Thirty-four

It was early evening when Ross and Dan Steel gal-loped out of Ross's camp at Fairport just a few miles from Rochester. It shouldn't take them long to ride on to Shortsville where the Indians had caused havoc, he reckoned. It was only fifteen miles away. They could get this mess cleared up and he would still have time to meet Sabrina early in the morning as he had planned, or so he hoped.

Ross kept to himself as he and Dan Steel rode out, galloping on a few feet ahead. He knew that he had quite a problem on his hands, but hadn't yet decided just how he was going to handle the situation. He had to do something, however. The whole thing reeked of bad publicity. All the advance men in the world couldn't rectify that.

"Damned nasty situation," he muttered to himself, looking over his shoulder at the man who followed.

Although he did not trust Dan Steel, he had de-cided to take him along just to keep an eye on him. He wasn't so sure the story he told was true and wouldn't until he'd had a chance to talk with Curly. It bothered Ross that Curly hadn't mentioned hiring anybody on, even though he'd ridden all that way to tell him about the Indians. And if Curly hadn't hired him, then what was going on? And just why had Dan Steel been hanging around the office wagon looking like a fox on the prowl?

I don't like it, Ross thought. He usually relied on his gut feelings about people, and his instincts were on alert where this new man was concerned. Ross liked a man who looked you in the eye when you talked to him, but Dan Steel always seemed to avert his gaze, and he displayed an awful lot of nervousness. Wasn't it possible that Steel was hired by Hawthorne to disrupt the show? What if he told the story of Curly having hired him just to cover his ass while Curly was away? What if he'd told Curly that Ross had hired him?

I'll soon know once Curly gets back, Ross thought, and we get this matter settled once and for all. Damn it all to hell! Why did this have to happen to him now when everything had been going so well? He was in a foul mood as they rode along. His grip tightened on the rein of his horse. He sensed Dan Steel's resentment, but made no special effort to draw the man out. Really wasn't much he wanted to say.

There was a damp chill in the air, and a sharp wind descending from the direction of Lake Ontario. Ross liked this location, because even though the evenings were cool in the summertime, there was a sense of peace and quiet. Instinctively he put aside his fears and anxiety. Soon he and Sabrina would be together to share their love forever. Somehow that thought cheered him and even made Dan Steel's companionship tolerable.

"We're almost there, Dan," he said, pressing his horse into a faster gallop. He was anxious to hurry up and settle this matter so that he could take care of other things.

"And none too soon if you ask me," the other man grunted.

Riding towards the town sprawled under the deepening blue of the night sky, Ross tried to get his bearings. He'd only been to the town twice before, but he thought he could remember where the main square was. The police station would most likely be located there.

Darkness had set in about a half-hour before, but the gaslights lit up the streets. Still, there were few people walking about. Ross thought he remembered something about a curfew having been issued because of the Indian situation.

"Damn place looks nearly deserted, doesn't it?" Dan replied, trying to catch up.

"Guess they're afraid of an Indian raid," Ross said sarcastically. He reined his mount to a halt and stretched wearily in the saddle. It had been a long day, and all he really longed for was sleep. For a long while Ross sat in silence and looked out at the night. A dog barked in a darkened yard and another across the street took up the call. Soon there was a whole chorus.

Ross pulled up at a tall, two-story building that bore a scrawled sign revealing it to be a tavern. It seemed to be the best place to start. In the past he'd found out that a man could learn just about any information he wanted if he talked to the right kind of people. And no one was as amiable as a man in his cups. Looping the reins of his horse around the hitching post, he pushed open the door and strode inside.

"Not your usual saloon," he said as he surveyed the inside. The floor was carpeted in shades of green and blue, the walls were brightly painted and hung with pictures and artifacts. The place reeked of class.

Three men in fancy suits leaned on the long bar that spanned one entire side of the cavernous interior. At the far end, a single bartender stood polishing glasses with a large dishtowel. It was towards him that Ross gravitated.

"Heard tell there was some trouble with a few Indians," he said, leaning against the bar, starting a conversation. As bartenders do, this one seemed to enjoy talking on and on about the matter. Ross learned that the Indians had been locked up, were being carefully guarded, and that a meeting was going on at the mayor's house at that very moment to decide upon just what was going to be done about the matter.

"Going to see that those savages don't cause any more trouble."

"You don't say." Ross thumbed his Stetson to the back of his head as he asked directions to the mayor's home. "I have an idea or two about how he should handle the matter," Ross said by way of explanation. "I'm quite experienced in what to do with Indians. I'll solve the mayor's problem for him."

With a nod and a smile, he bid the bartender adieu then went to find Dan Steel. It annoyed him that he found him sitting at a corner table, guzzling a bottle of whiskey.

"Long ride gave me a powerful thirst," he said, holding out the bottle towards Ross.

"Get up!"

"What?" His head snapped up and he glared.

"I said get up. As long as you are employed by me you'll do as I say. I didn't come all this way into town to watch you get drunk."

Resentment clearly oozed from every pore as Dan Steel got to his feet. Regretfully he pushed the bottle away. "You're the boss!"

"Yeah, just remember that." Ross led the way back to their horses, keeping his eye on the other man as they both mounted up and rode out. They sought that area of town where the houses were large, the grounds well cared for, and the street completely paved.

It was well after nine o'clock when the two of them

254

found the mayor's home and rapped upon his door. It was an imposing two-story building, built of lumber set on a foundation of mortared stone blocks. Its paint was shining with a new coat, the slanting roof showed no sign of disrepair, and the mountain of grass was as thick as a brand-new carpet. The lights were still on in one room of the house and they could see a group of men inside, sitting around the fire.

The mayor did not answer the first rap, so Ross rapped louder. When that knock wasn't answered, he knocked yet again. A tall, slim man with a receding hairline and graying temples opened the door. He seemed agitated to see Ross standing there, and Ross could only suppose that he recognized him from the show's flyers.

"What do you want at this hour of the night?" the man asked, regarding him with the utmost disdain. "We are trying to hold a council meeting here and don't want to be disturbed."

Ross tried to show restraint, realizing he was interrupting. "I am sorry but I'm afraid this interruption just can't be helped. I have some urgent business to discuss with Mayor Litchfield." He looked around. "Just where might he be?"

"I am Mayor Litchfield." The man drew himself up to his full six feet. Adjusting the spectacles, which balanced precariously on his nose, he took a long contemplative look at Ross and his companion. "What business do you have with me that couldn't wait until a decent hour? My downtown office is open from nine to five."

Ross tipped his head back and tipped his hat out of his eyes as he smiled. "Well now, this matter is of utmost importance to me and since I plan on doing some traveling first thing tomorrow morning, I wanted to get it settled. Couldn't wait until tomorrow morning, Mr. Mayor, sir."

"I see." The mayor's lips were sternly set, his eyebrows furrowed, forming a V.

Just in case the mayor didn't know who he was, Ross introduced himself. "I'm Cherokee Ross Sheldon, writer and owner of the Wild West show that's been playing in your town."

"I know who you are!"

"Well then, you'll know just what errand I'm on. Guess a few of my Indians got into the firewater and did a little damage to this town and I'd—"

"A little damage? A little damage!" Mayor Litchfield snorted. "They nearly frightened all the ladies into apoplexy, they broke windows and bottles, caused two wagons and a carriage to collide, and began a horse stampede."

"And I'm willing to make financial restitution." Ross reached in his pocket, withdrawing his money pouch.

"That's not enough" The mayor sniffed indignantly. "One of them threatened to scalp us all and would have if the entire police force of Shortsville hadn't interceded. Savages. Just like it says on those posters."

"No, not now." Ross sought to placate the irate man. "They're not, sir. They're peaceful. It's just publicity, all that talk about being on the warpath."

"So peaceful they were wearing feathers and war paint."

"Part of the act."

"Well, it doesn't matter. The whole damned bunch of them are in jail right now where they belong. Ought to hang every last one of them. Isn't that frontier justice? Just might do that, in fact. Heathens. Hollering savages." Seeming to think the interview ended, the mayor attempted to close the door, but Ross strategically placed his booted foot between door and doorframe.

All the while Dan Steel just stood as silent as a stone, shifting his weight occasionally from one foot to the other. Certainly he wasn't much help, Ross thought disgustedly.

"Savages? No, sir, they're not!" Ross was trying very hard to control his temper. "Besides, the real culprit is the man who gave them whiskey. It's a fact that Indians and whiskey just don't mix."

"Because they're more animal than human."

Ross was getting really riled. "That's not true! There are some things about their civilization that are far superior to ours. They are honorable and honest for one thing." Which Ross suspected the mayor might not be. He'd heard whispers of a scandal brewing.

"Bah! I know what I think. And I know that your show should be shut down for bringing such a menace into a quiet city. I never did like the idea of a Wild West show here anyhow. Noise. Unruly crowds. Gives pickpockets a perfect opportunity to steal."

Obviously the mayor had already made up his mind. The longer they stood there, the angrier Ross became. If there was one thing he couldn't stand, it was an unreasonable man. Although he had tried to be well mannered, intending to pay for the damages, this man was just too narrow-minded to be tolerable.

"Well, I can tell you this. I wouldn't want to bring my show around here again. Not where there are such ignorant people running the place."

"I beg your pardon!" Slowly, steadily, both men's voices were growing louder.

"I thought you would at least listen and give me a chance to rectify the situation, but I can see that along with my Indians you've already tried and convicted me. Do you call that justice?"

Several other faces appeared at the doorway as the other five men of the council entered what was quickly becoming a shouting match.

"Listen here, young man," one old codger with a florid complexion exclaimed. "You can't just come riding into Shortsville in the middle of the night and accuse Mayor Litchfield of injustice."

"Your mayor is not only unjust, he is rude and unreasonable as well," Ross shot back. His temper had always been his downfall and now it looked as if it just might get him into trouble again, but he couldn't help it. He wanted this man to at least try to see reason. Hell, how much more reasonable could Ross be? He'd said he'd pay for all the damages.

Meanwhile, Dan Steel stood back in the shadows, but that didn't keep him from being stared at just the same. "Hey, I recognize him," one man said, taking a step closer. "Sure, he was with the savages when they came into town. In fact, he was leading them."

"What?" Ross had suspected Dan Steel all along, but this was a startling bit of news. "So—" With a lunge, Ross grabbed at the other man.

"I can explain. I was trying to quiet them down." Trying to escape Ross's fury, Dan Steel pushed his way into the room, knocking over a small table. His clumsiness sent the lamp crashing to the hard marble floor, breaking it into several pieces.

"Stop him before he breaks anything else!"

As two of the councilmen came forward, Dan Steel raised his fist threateningly. "Don't touch me! Just stay away."

"Leave him be, I'll get him," Ross ordered, hellbent on giving Dan Steel his rightful punishment.

Unfortunately, none of the men took that advice. Pushing and shoving ensued, a free-for-all that ended with fists swinging. Ross parried one blow in self-defense, but in the process struck another man on the chin. "Christ!" he muttered. He hadn't wanted it to come to this. Now he'd made a mess of it.

Soon the group of men were out in the street along with Dan and Ross, shouting at the top of their voices. Hailing a policeman, Mayor Litchfield placed the blame for the ruckus on Ross's head. "We were having a peaceful council meeting, officer, when these two men pushed their way in." Feeling emboldened by the policemen's presence, he grabbed Ross's arm, as if he had bravely apprehended him.

"Troublemakers! You know how these Westerners are," one of the councilmen said. "Should stay out West where they belong and not bother peace-loving people."

"Violence is all they seem to know. Well, we don't handle things that way here." Mayor Litchfield nodded his head as if in some secret signal.

Ross started to protest, but at that moment all the policemen drew their guns as if they envisioned some kind of shootout. "Well, we'll see they mind their manners, sir. What do you want us to do with these two?"

"Take them both over to the jail and lock them up for disturbing the peace. Let them stay there until they learn a little respect for a man in my position." Like a strutting rooster, the mayor turned his back and returned to his house.

"A man in your position," Ross said beneath his breath. "I'll tell you just what that is." He grumbled a string of curses as he was dragged off to jail, his good intentions having blown up like a powder keg in his face.

Chapter Thirty-five

Summer storm clouds and sunlight competed for control of the morning. As she looked towards the tent flap, Sabrina watched as one of the dark wispy silhouettes of mist floated across the sun, blocking out the warm glow of the sunrise. Burrowing her head into her pillow, she thought how the weather matched the confusion and turmoil of her emotions. Flee or fight? Cry or shout? Give up or give in? Jonathan had her trapped, knew her darkest secret. What was she going to do?

Of a certainty she had spent a sleepless night, tossing and turning, so noisily that she was certain poor Sadie hadn't slept a wink. She had gone over and over in her mind the argument she'd had with Jonathan, stung by her disappointment. How could she have so acutely misjudged the man? Kind? Gentle? Caring? Not the man who had threatened to turn her into the law for something he knew to be a matter of self-defense, an accident. He was selfish, scheming, manipulative, she could see that now. His reasons for teaching her to shoot had been to acquire a position with Buffalo Bill as her manager. Her partner. He wasn't her friend at all, but a puppet master, a spoiled child who would rebelliously break a toy rather than give it away. How could she have been so very wrong?

"Oh, Ross!" Like the melody of a treasured song, the memory of their time together at the cottage hummed again and again in her mind. It had all seemed so clear to her then. She loved Ross, he loved her. It seemed only right that the two of them be together. But just when the world had promised rainbows, Jonathan's unreasonable, thunderous temper threatened to spoil everything.

Frightened, trembling, she had wanted nothing more than Ross's strong arms around her to give her comfort last night. Knowing that he would protect her, would tell her what she should do, she had tried to go to him last night with the intention of telling him the whole miserable story. But Jonathan had sensed her intent and when she had gone into the stable to borrow a horse, he had been waiting.

"Well, well, well, just look who we have here. Are you going to practice that trick shot from horseback that I told you about? Is that what you have in mind, Kit . . . uh rather Sabrina my pet? Is that why you are stealing one of Bill's horses?" He took out his pocket watch, clucking his tongue. "Oh dear, it is rather late for that. It's much too dark out to even see the practice target tonight." He grinned evilly at her. "Guess it will have to wait until morning."

"You know very well that I have no intention of shooting, unless I aim at *you!*" she had replied tartly.

"Me?" He pretended to be surprised. "Why on earth would you even say such a thing after all I've done for you?"

"You know why!" Thinking that perhaps she could make him listen to reason, she had bridled her anger and tried to talk the matter out with him. "Let me go, Jonathan. Please."

"And have to make it on my own again peddling my family's damned guns? Oh no. You're my meal ticket, Kit dear. I like being part of an act. I like the adulation — reflected glory though it may be."

"Find yourself another female sharpshooter. Teach someone else to shoot or . . . or talk to that Annie Oakley about signing with the show. You could manage her." If she could only convince him. "She is ten times a better shot than I'll ever be and . . . and she's well known because of her stint with the Sells Brothers' Circus."

"And she also has a husband, Frank Butler. He's her manager, remember?" Stubbornly Jonathan shook his head. "No, Kit. You're the one I want. We work well together, you and I."

"Because I didn't really know your true nature. You aren't a knight in shining armor at all, Jonathan. You're nothing but a leech!"

Angrily she had turned her back on him, but he had retaliated by grabbing her by the wrist. Wrenching her arm behind her back, he hissed, "Listen, you ungrateful little whore! All my life I've always had to do what everyone else said, but now I'm in control. If you even look as if you're going to run away again, I'll tell Bill, all the cowboys, and everyone within earshot that you murdered your father-in-law in cold blood. I'll fetch the law on you. I will, Sabrina James, just you wait and see. And what's more, I'll think of a way to get your lover involved in the trouble."

"Ross didn't have anything to do with what happened." All of Sabrina's protective instincts flared. She didn't want Jonathan's poisonous anger to harm the man she loved. "Ross wasn't even there and you know it."

"Then we'll just hope he has an ironclad alibi. Hmm, Sabrina dear? One that will stand up before a jury!"

Jonathan's threats had convinced her to run away. With seeming docility, she had meekly accompanied Jonathan back to her tent, making the promise that she wouldn't leave the grounds. She had tried to keep calm as she undressed for bed, but only the thought that Ross was coming for her in the morning gave her any comfort at all. Ross's last words to her were that he would return for her early the next day. Somehow, she had to believe that there was a way that Ross could get her out of this mess. He had told her that he loved her and surely the strength of his devotion was about to be tested.

"Get a hold of yourself, Sabrina Marie," she scolded quietly. Ross would work it all out somehow. Jonathan didn't know that Ross was coming for her. It was the one thing she had neglected to tell him, thank God.

I'll run away with Ross, she thought. And yet, did she even dare leave? Jonathan's manner was so hateful that she had little doubt he would make good on his threat to expose what she had done.

"I don't care!" she breathed into her pillow. "Ross will take me with him." And go where? asked a voice inside her head. Did she really want to make him a fugitive too? "At least I'll explain to him. I have to make him understand." Ross was her only hope, her one salvation.

Sabrina felt tense, confused, and deeply troubled as she rolled to the edge of her cot and got slowly out of bed. She didn't know exactly what to do, but knew that she had to be prepared for anything once Ross came. With that thought in mind, she moved quickly around the tent, packing up her things, throwing as many of her possessions as she could into a small blue and white carpetbag: her favorite buckskin dress and leggings, a few handbills with her name emblazoned across the bottom, and other souvenirs she just couldn't think of parting with, things Bill and some of her fellow performers had given her.

"For cryin' in a teacup, what's all the racket?" Sadie opened her puffy eyelids one at a time. "Can't we have a little peace in the early hours of the morning?"

"I'm sorry, Sadie." She hadn't meant to wake her.

"And well you might be." Turning over on her side, Sadie pulled the covers up over her head. "Why, it's not even light yet."

"It is, but the clouds are casting shadows. I hope that's not a bad omen," Sabrina murmured.

"Omen?"

"I think it's going to rain." All the better, she thought. Bill had said at dinner last night that he planned to pack up the wagons and move to their next location first thing in the morning. A storm would at least insure a delay in the plans and give Ross a chance to get here before the wagons pulled out.

"What in the hell are you doin'?" Sadie lifted her head and surveyed the scene. "Oh, that's right. Bill is antsy to get out of this place. Can't say as how I blame him, with the quarantine and all. Get while the getting is good, I guess he'd say."

Sabrina forced a smile, one that she hoped looked sincere. "Yes, I'm . . . I'm packing up so that I'll be ready when Bill gives the word to move out."

"Bill doesn't like to stay long in one place. Must have gypsy blood, I'd say. Ol' Rochester has worn out its welcome for him." With a grumbled oath, Sadie sat up in bed. "And I suppose for me. Well, guess I better take a hint from you and pack up things myself. Wouldn't want to hold things up."

"Oh, no. We wouldn't want that," Sabrina whispered with a wry smile, slowing down the rhythm of her packing. She moved in slow motion as she put things in boxes and trunks, quickly unpacking things when Sadie's back was turned so that she could pack them again. She had to stall for time until Ross arrived, then somehow she'd sort out her thoughts. Ross! His name was like a benediction on her lips, her only hope, her only escape. As long as they were together she could face anything!

"Was that thunder?" Sadie went to the opening of the tent and peeked out. "Naw, just someone being a smarty pants and firing off the cannon. In a farewell salute, no doubt."

"No doubt." Sabrina's fingers trembled as she fastened the carpetbag. "It looks as if it's going to storm. What do you think?" She knew how much Bill hated to travel in the rain. It might even hold up the wagons for another day. More than enough time for Ross to see to his own show and then come for her.

"Clouds look as if they're just sort of drifting away."

"Oh." She couldn't count on the weather then. But perhaps it was just as well. She wouldn't want Ross to get soaked to the skin on his way to Bill's camp. She'd just have to think of another way of delaying the departure.

A bugle tooted, signaling the start of the day, a habit Bill had acquired during his days as a scout. Suddenly the once-quiet morning was filled with a cacophony of sounds as the camp came alive. Horses neighing, feet shuffling, people chattering, the thump and bump of people milling about.

"Kit!" Pausing in her folding and bending, Sadie put her hands on her hips. "You started way before I did and look here, I'm nearly through. You're moving like a snail, gal. What's wrong?"

"Nothing. Just a bit tired all of a sudden."

Sadie grinned from ear to ear. "And I bet I can guess why. My, oh my, but it must have been exciting to have been carried off like that. Don't imagine you did much sleeping. I'm not surprised you're tired."

Sabrina sighed. "I'd be telling a lie if I told you it wasn't wonderful. I wish . . ."

"You wish what?"

For a moment Sabrina nearly confided in the woman who had become her friend, but cautiously she held back. "I wish I hadn't gotten up so early this

265

morning."

"So do I," Sadie sputtered.

Slowly Sabrina finished her packing, lending the men a hand as they loaded the baggage, boxes, and bundles on the waiting wagons. All the while her eyes scanned the horizon for sight of Ross's familiar form. Every buggy, carriage, wagon, and horse and rider was prone to her scrutiny, but none of them proved to be Ross. Morning. He'd said he would come for her the next morning and yet as the hours rolled by she knew it was quickly approaching noon. Where was he? Dear God, why hadn't he come?

"Get those tents down. Hurry. It's late. Haven't got all day. Get the wagons ready to roll," Buffalo Bill roared.

"Ross! Ross!" Sabrina willed him to hurry. Closing her eyes, she made a wish that when she opened them he would be there.

"Don't worry, you'll see him again!" Coming up behind her, Buffalo Bill paused in shouting orders to put his hand on Sabrina's shoulder, giving it an affectionate squeeze. "Ross Sheldon looked to me like a man in love," he whispered in her ear. "So much so that for a moment there I was scared you might want to up and leave."

"Leave?" Jonathan seemed to come from out of nowhere. "Why, Kit wouldn't even think of such a thing, would you, *Kit?* Would you?" His eyes glittered dangerously.

"No!" she answered quickly. "No, I . . . I just couldn't."

Bill was all smiles. "Good. Good. I might even think to offer you a raise, if you can do what ol' Jonathan says you can. Can you shoot while you're riding?"

"Not yet, Bill, but she'll learn. I'm going to see to her training myself," Jonathan said with a smug grin, speaking up before Sabrina had a chance. "You and me will make this the best Wild West show in the country. Yep!" He thrust a newspaper into her hands with a look of pure triumph. "It looks as if your competition has problems on his hands. Now is as good a time as any to leave Ross Sheldon behind in the dust."

"Ross?" Sabrina took the paper, scanning the front page story with a frown. Now she knew why Ross hadn't come for her. He wasn't able to go anywhere. Ross was in jail. "Oh no!" Her hopes crumpled with every word she read. In trying to free his Indians Ross had ended up in prison himself.

"Nope. Won't have to worry about him for awhile," Jonathan exclaimed, gloating. "Not for a long time I would suppose."

"The damned fool!" Bill mumbled, pulling at his beard. "He should have let things simmer awhile, but he always was impatient and just plain bull-headed!"

"Serves him right!" Jonathan shrieked. "He's no showman. Just a two-bit writer. He'll see that he's no match for the great Buffalo Bill! You'll have the field all to yourself."

"Don't want to be a winner that way," Bill replied, shooting Jonathan a scathing look. "Despite the differences between us, Ross is my friend."

"Then help him. Please." Sabrina's eyes were imploring.

"Can't. This is one thing Ross has got to handle himself," Bill answered grimly, though he did put his hand on her shoulder. "But he'll be all right. You'll see, Kit. I've seen Ross get out of worse jams." He chuckled as if remembering a few in particular.

"Then I'll do something!" she exclaimed, pulling away. She started towards one of the horses, but Jonathan blocked her path.

"I wouldn't if I were you," he warned.

"But he's in trouble."

"Mmm-hmm. He's in *jail*." And you will be too if

267

you don't do exactly as I say, his expression seemed to be telling her. Sabrina knew in that moment how truly ruthless Jonathan could be and that his were not idle threats. She was helpless. Completely at his mercy. All she could do was hope that Ross would be able to convince the town officials to show clemency. Once he was free he would find her. She had to believe that. Ross would come for her eventually.

When Buffalo Bill's wagons pulled out, Sabrina was in the caravan.

Part Three

A Portrait of Love
New England—1885

"Love is an Art and the greatest of the Arts."
Edward Carpenter, *The Drama of Love and Death*

Chapter Thirty-six

The steady pulsating rhythm of the train sounded like a metronome, nearly lulling Sabrina to sleep as she leaned back against the leather seat. "Buffalo Bill's Great Wild West Show" was boldly emblazoned on the side of the cars carrying performers, roustabouts, livestock, band instruments, wardrobe trunks, lumber, the painted canvas murals and more than enough weapons to start a new range war, or so Bill said.

The days were hectic ones. Buffalo Bill had elected to go from one town to another in a series of performances designed to increase his fame. And he had decided to transport his company in style, he had said, casting aside the wagons for a train and the usual tents for rooms in hotels. Now Bill's troupe was on its way to Hartford, Connecticut for a week's engagement.

Just like gypsies, Sabrina thought, hoping with all her heart that all this traipsing around wouldn't make it hard for Ross to find her. That is, when he settled his own difficulties. According to what the newspapers said, the matter of Ross and his Indians was far from settled. The ruffled mayor was even threatening to take Ross to trial.

Ross. The yearning for him grew stronger with every mile she traveled and she agonized over the situation she was in. She had hated to leave without even saying goodbye to him, but what else could she have done under the circumstances? Jonathan watched her like a hawk, his eyes ever threatening. All she could hope was that somehow Ross would sense that something was very wrong, that she had had no other choice but to leave and that he would look for her.

"I know what you're thinking, but you can forget it. That two-bit cowboy showman isn't going to try to find you, Kit." Jonathan's voice was nearly as grating as his presence.

"I wasn't thinking of him," Sabrina lied, "I was wondering why you've suddenly turned coward and refused to be the holder for my trick shots." She affected her sweetest smile. "Are you afraid I might make good on my threat and shoot you, Jonathan?"

Though Jonathan still shared the arena with Sabrina, he was no longer setting himself up as a target, perhaps because she had purposely missed his ear by only an inch a week ago in the arena. Jonathan had in fact armed himself with a gun and had started to do a few trick shots of his own.

"I'm not afraid at all." With a snort, Jonathan brushed at an imaginary fleck of dust on his white-fringed sleeve. "It's just that a man of my reknown should have his own turn at a little bit of glory."

"Oh, of course," she answered. "A man in your position." Blackmailer. Scoundrel. Conceited oaf. In emulation of Bill, Jonathan was even letting his blond hair grow all the way down to his shoulders. He wanted to be somebody, he said. It was amusing to her that Jonathan was increasingly jealous of her fame which he created himself.

Little did Sabrina realize when she first joined Bill's show just how quickly her reputation as a female sharpshooter would spread. Though there were other sharpshooters in the show, it was she who held the hearts of the crowd. Her appearance in any town sparked so much interest, in fact, that Nate, Bill's partner, decided to create a new persona for her. She was the daughter of an impoverished Prussian nobleman who escaped his enemies by fleeing to America, the story said. In search of opportunity, Kitty's father had taken his wife and daughter West only to fall victim to an Indian's arrow. Hiding in a cave, mother and baby escaped the same fate and in time were rescued by a kindly old trapper who married Kitty's mother and raised the child as his own.

Sabrina thought the story much too fanciful, and yet to her surprise the public fell for it "hook, line and sinker" as Nate had foretold. She had supposedly learned to shoot at the side of the old trapper, "Wildcat" Tremaine; when tragedy struck and he was killed by a bear, her shooting skills enabled her to keep food on the table for her mother and herself. Buffalo Bill had made her acquaintance on one of his scouting exhibitions, it was rumored, and had promptly put her in his show. It was there she had been taken under Jonathan Colt's wing whereby a romance had supposedly blossomed.

"Romance, ha!" Sabrina scoffed. Her feelings for Jonathan were more like those a prisoner had for a jailor. He was lucky she just didn't up and shoot him. Certainly it would have solved her greatest problem. All Jonathan ever did was watch her like a hawk, reminding her over and over again of her precarious position.

Sabrina sighed as she looked out the train window at the landscape, rolling hills in variegated shades of green, dotted with tall chestnut, poplar, birch, and maple trees. A lot of the area was used for farmland. The same scene seemed to be repeated every few minutes as if they were traveling in a circle or retracing their path.

"My father owns a firearms and ammunition plant near here," Jonathan interjected, breaking into Sabrina's peaceful mood. "Just think how surprised he'll be when he sees my name on those handbills." He pointed to the notices tacked to buildings and trees they passed by as the train slowed down. "Jonathan Colt!"

A sharp whistle interrupted him, signaling to the passengers that the train was reaching its destination. On the platform were several men, women, and children holding up signs that read, "Welcome, Buffalo Bill." The citizens of Hartford seemed to be an amiable lot, Sabrina

273

thought. Certainly it would make their stay more pleasurable.

"We're here, Kit dear. Now remember. Don't get any ideas. I'll be watching you." Jonathan gave Sabrina a look of warning as he stood up to stretch his legs.

"Why, Jonathan dear, I wouldn't even think of leaving your pleasant company," Sabrina shot back, following him ever so slowly as he made his way towards the door.

The train station was bustling with activity, the wooden platform groaning as heavy boxes, barrels, and trunks were wheeled over it. Men swore and grunted as they hefted a variety of items out of the railroad cars. The smell of sweat mixed with the smell of smoke permeated the air.

The first thing Bill did was to hire all the horses in the livery stable so that several of his men could ride around the town to advertise his show. Soon the streets were crowded with carriages, horses and people, the usual type of crowd anxiously trying to catch a glimpse of Buffalo Bill or his stars. In her buckskin dress, Sabrina was easy to spot. She was asked several times to autograph handbills, the ones which had her name emblazoned across the top and caricature drawings of her performing various shooting tricks.

"Look, Mama. Indians!" a young boy shouted, pointing as the feathered and buckskin-clad performers stepped off the train. A ripple of excitement swept through the crowd. Though there were a few in the crowd who hurled insults at the warriors and squaws, for the most part the people were congenial, flocking about the performers for anything at all that was a souvenir. One particularly bold woman even asked for a lock of Buffalo Bill's blondish hair.

"I hope no one asks for a lock of your hair, Kit dear," Jonathan whispered nastily. "How surprising it would be to find out that the famous brunette is really a blond."

Sabrina might have just shrugged his comment off had it not been for the fact that Jonathan had been overheard by a gentleman standing nearby. It made her uneasy, but she might have shrugged it off had the gentleman not stepped forward.

"Miss. Miss Tremaine!" He extended his hand, catching hers in a gentle clasp, raising it to his lips. "I've been waiting a long time to meet you."

"Have you, sir?" Sabrina studied the man intently, trying to identify him. He was a tall slender man she judged to be about forty-five or forty-six. Handsome, with dark hair turning gray at the temples, he wore a neat mustache peppered with gray. He was elegantly dressed in a three-piece gray pin-striped suit. One of Bill's many friends?

"It is an honor to have you with us. I hope you will make yourself at home in our fair city." Of solemn countenance, he was marked by that quality that spoke of a gentleman.

"It is an equal honor to be here." Sabrina remembered Bill talking about a British actor, a European prince, and a Washington dignitary meeting him at the train station and she wondered just which one this man was.

"You're beautiful. Bill really should use your image on his flyers as well as those sketches and your name. I'm certain that any man seeing your lovely face would come to Bill's show again and again." His eyes were riveted to hers. "I know that I will."

Sabrina stiffened. The last thing she needed was her picture being scattered around, but she said, "Thank you for the compliment. But there are many performers in the show."

"But none who look like you." He grinned a bit sheepishly. "Excuse me. Please. I have been very lax in my manners, Miss Tremaine. I'm Governor Ellis. Thomas Ellis."

"Governor Ellis." Sabrina remembered now that it was the governor who had used his influence to put Bill's troupe up at the very best hotel in town and that it was he who had arranged for the Wild West show to come to the state's capital.

"Please, call me Tom." His gaze caressed her with a familiarity that made her blush. Oh, she knew that look all

275

right and knew it boded ill. The men in her father-in-law's inn had stared at her with this same familiarity.

"I don't know you well enough to use your Christian name," she answered stiffly.

"I'm hoping that you will."

Sabrina might have protested right then and there had Bill not entered upon the scene. "Tom! You old dog! How have you been?" Bill was none too gentle as he slapped the governor on the back. "Long time since we rode those ponies together in the express." Chattering on excitedly, Bill related a string of experiences he and Tom Ellis had shared riding the mail through in the "early days."

"Careful, Bill." Ellis's voice held a tone of mock severity. "You'll make this sweet young thing think I'm old enough to be her father."

"You are, Tom. You are!" Bill grinned. "But that's never seemed to stop you before."

"Nor will it now!"

Before Sabrina could protest he had taken her hand and placed it in the crook of his arm as they made their way to his carriage, Bill in tow. Certainly it was proving to be an uncomfortable situation.

"Wait. Wait for me!" Just when Sabrina thought she had at least gotten rid of Jonathan, he scurried up like an annoying shadow, settling himself at Sabrina's other elbow.

"Miss Tremaine's partner," Bill said by way of introduction.

"And fiancé!" Jonathan announced stubbornly.

"I see." Despite that announcement Ellis seemed undaunted, saying in Sabrina's ear, "I've always been a man who enjoys a bit of competition. It makes the prize more worthwhile." His smile was most engaging as he gave Sabrina a hand up into his carriage.

Chapter Thirty-seven

It was hot in the windowless cell. Ross Sheldon had stripped down to his underwear in an attempt to make himself comfortable as he sat basking in the heat. Putting his feet on a small, round stool, he opened the first of two letters he held in his hand, hoping against hope that it was from *her*. It wasn't. It was just from his lawyer, Jason Roberts, a brief message telling him that everything was "under control."

Under control! Ross laughed aloud. It was easy for him to say. It wasn't Jason who was locked up, forced to eat disgustingly bland food, and made to suffer the damned boredom of this brick and stone jail. Nor have to face the knowledge that while he was locked up like some common criminal his world was slowly crumbling.

Running his hands across his stubbled beard, Ross was consumed by his frustration. He had promised Sabrina that he would come back for her, but this stupid situation had caused him to break his word. All he could hope was that she would read the newspapers and know what had happened to him. He wouldn't want her to think he had deserted her again. Not with Jonathan Colt waiting in the wings.

Tentatively he touched the second envelope, crossing his fingers to make a wish. Let this one be from Sabrina! His fingers trembled as he tore the letter open. The handwriting was scrawled and didn't look much like a woman's, but he held on to his hope anyway.

It was very thick. Inside were several folded pages, which Ross discovered to be newspaper clippings, articles about his predicament. The clippings were accompanied by a letter that was signed "Buffalo Bill."

"Why that sly devil!"

Bill had written that news of the "savages's trial" was scattered in the papers up and down the coast of New England. Some people were sympathetic, others angry, and still others just curious, he said. He expressed his concern and sympathies and told Ross to take care. Most importantly of all, however, he wrote that he would take good care of Ross's "gal." That revelation gave Ross hope that his luck was changing for the better.

"If I could only get Dan Steel to tell what he knows." He'd been the one to give the Indians whiskey all right. But who had been the one to give the order? Tom Kirkland? Apache Ed? Hawthorne? Or someone else? At that moment he would have given his two gold back teeth fillings to know. One thing that he had found out, however, was that he had been right in his suspicion. Dan Steel had told Curly that Ross had sent him so it wasn't surprising that Curly had taken him into the troupe. But Dan Steel wasn't overly intelligent. If given enough rope, he was certain to hang himself

"Hmm . . ." Ross thought a while. Somehow he had to make Dan Steel believe his own neck was on the line. If Ross didn't miss his guess, and he didn't think that he did, Steel would reveal the mastermind of this little episode if he thought the alternative was his own punishment.

"It will be like playing poker and bluffing," he said to himself. And he was an expert with a deck of cards. Was it any wonder then that he was smiling as he stood up. He knew just how he was going to get his Indians out of this pickle and absolve himself as well. He'd be certain that his lawyer made it obvious that he and his feathered friends were the victims and not the instigators of the trouble.

Ross's mood was vastly improved as he banged on the bars to get the attention of the four Indians huddled together in his neighboring cell. "I promised I'd get you out of here in one piece and I think I'm going to be able to keep my word, boys," he said. And when he was released himself he'd move heaven and earth to find out just exactly who was the culprit in this matter. And when he did, he'd give him a thrashing he'd never forget.

Chapter Thirty-eight

A soft breeze ruffled the curtains of the hotel room. Sabrina wandered to the window and looked out. It was beautiful here, she had to admit. She loved the village green, the riverside resorts and the fishing villages nearby. Governor Ellis had given them a short tour before he had brought them to the hotel where Bill's performers had been put up in red-carpeted third-floor suites which boasted velvet curtains, the softest beds, and a steady stream of eager attendants bringing chilled champagne.

She remembered how her eyes had widened the moment she had entered the lobby of the hotel. Her father-in-law's quaint inn was a far cry from the elaborately furnished splendor of beveled mirrors, art objects, cut-glass chandeliers, and oaken furniture with padded chairs. When she was a little girl she had dreamed of spending just one night in such a place as this, of being famous.

Sabrina should have been on top of the world, but instead she was miserable. She was haunted by her sense of loss, her yearning to find the contentment she had come so close to grasping. Ross was the only man she wanted. Not Jonathan. Not the governor of Connecticut. Not the king of the world. Ross! And yet right at this moment he was as far away from her as the stars.

Turning from the window, she looked in the mirror, regarding the woman who looked back at her. Sleep had been eluding her all these nights, marking her face with dark circles and frown lines. She had become paler and thinner worrying about how she was going to get away from Jonathan. She was distracted from her unhappiness during daylight hours when there was so much to do, but during the night her sense of restlessness returned.

"Miss Tremaine. Miss Tremaine." A loud knock on the door accompanied the voice. Answering the summons, Sabrina was surprised to see a young man standing there, his arms filled with bouquets and white and yellow envelopes.

She left the cards and telegrams in a large pile, unopened, and had the flowers taken away. It was too vivid a reminder of Ross and the time he had so enthusiastically tried to woo her. Without even asking, she knew who the flowers were from. Thomas Ellis. All the time she had been in the carriage he had stared at her, eloquently telling her how fascinated he was by her spunk, her daring, and her talents with a gun. He had even invited the entire troupe to attend a party in their honor tonight at his mansion.

But I don't want to go, she thought. Sabrina had been through all of this once before—at her father-in-law's inn. She knew just what to expect. The governor would try to get her alone and if he succeeded he'd pinch and he'd paw. Men were the same, whether young or old, rich or poor. Except Ross. When he had touched her it was as if the whole world had dropped from beneath her feet and left her balancing on the edge of a precipice. Sharply she remembered waking up in his arms, feeling his kiss upon her face, her hair.

She sighed, throwing herself full length on the red velvet bedspread, feeling a bit guilty that while she was enjoying such luxury Ross was languishing in jail, facing the same kind of confinement she would be subject to if she ever angered Jonathan.

Closing her eyes, she was troubled by a vision of Jonathan, dressed in the robes of a judge, condemning her to a life without the man she loved, a life all alone. And then as if to emphasize his control over her, she heard a footfall outside the door. She heard the sound of a key in the lock, a click, and drew in a long shuddering breath. Jonathan had locked her in. She really was a prisoner. Was she imagining it or did she really hear the soft sound of laughter before the footsteps continued up the hall?

There was a cold, sick feeling in the pit of her stomach, a feeling of being closed in despite the large size and lavishness of the room. She couldn't go on like this! The hatred festering inside for the man who had once been her friend threatened to poison her. Somehow she had to get free of him. And then suddenly the idea came to her. Lately Jonathan had taken to excessive drinking. Tonight, when he was disgustingly drunk, perhaps she might have a chance after all.

Just the thought of getting out from under Jonathan's thumb gave Sabrina energy. With renewed vitality she hurried to the closet and rummaged through her garments. She'd pick something pretty but durable, just in case she was successful in her attempt at escape.

Hurrying to the bathing room, a separate alcove that had as a permanent fixture a big brass tub with water that came from a faucet, she filled the tub, undressed, and with relief sank into the steaming water. She'd slip away to the train station and take the next train back to the small town where Ross was jailed. Somehow she'd create a diversion and spring not only him but his Indians. Ross had talked once or twice about taking his show to Canada. That's just what they would do. They'd go north to where no one could find them and Sabrina would be free of Jonathan's petty revenge.

"Canada!" For a long while she just lay in the tub imagining how it would be.

When she emerged from her bath, she dried herself and slipped on a silken wrapper, humming a rowdy song as she artfully styled her dark wig in a chignon, and darkened her lashes and brows. The dress she had chosen was of a sapphire blue, high necked but cut in a line that clung to her slender waist and gently flaring hips. She chose two pieces of jewelry, the ruby ring Ross had given her, and his mother's golden chain.

This time when she studied herself in the glass she looked younger, carefree. Like a mischievous child, a smile uplifted her face. Once at the cottage she had planned an escape, but her heart hadn't been in it. This time, though, Jonathan had pushed her too far. More than anything she wanted her freedom. If she didn't find it this time, she would, eventually. When Jonathan came to unlock her door, she smiled and was in such a pleasant mood that she even took his arm as they descended the stairs.

"That's the way I like you to be, Kit," Jonathan whispered in her ear. "Cheerful. Pleasant. Like you were once before. That's really all I want. Things just like they were before he came around. It's not too much to ask, is it?"

Thomas Ellis was down in the lobby waiting, dressed in very fashionable evening clothes. He promptly held out his arm for Sabrina, spoiling Jonathan's reverie and making it a very interesting situation as they all stepped into the carriage and headed for the governor's home.

An enormous velvety green lawn announced the boundaries of the governor's mansion, a graceful two-story building of painted brick and stone. Rectangular in shape, it reminded Sabrina of a southern plantation home she had seen once in a book, but without the pillars. It even had a black butler who answered the door on the very first knock. Thomas Ellis led Sabrina and Jonathan through the high-ceilinged entrance hall with its gold-framed mirrors to a room full of crystal chandeliers and marble busts.

"My predecessors," he said with a sweep of his hand.

Proudly Thomas Ellis took her on a tour of the house as Jonathan tagged along behind. "The wine cellar and storage rooms are down below the kitchen, along with the food cellar. I wouldn't imagine a lovely girl like you would have much interest in seeing the kitchen."

Thinking the kitchen or cellars might be a good place to hide if necessary, Sabrina nodded to the contrary. "Oh, I would. I once enjoyed cooking."

"Yeah, you sure did your fair share," Jonathan piped up, blatantly reminding her of her drudgery at the inn.

"You cook? A woman of many talents." Thomas Ellis seemed pleased.

The main wing of the house was divided into four rooms, the living room, sitting room, library, and drawing room, separated from each other by way of the long hallway and the front stairs. Each room was decorated in earth tones of greens, golds, and browns with carpet covering the floors and Victorian-style furniture artfully placed about. The far wall of the drawing room was covered with paintings.

"My private collection," the governor announced proudly. Sabrina saw several portraits, including one of Buffalo Bill. "Friends." He pointed to three paintings of very beautiful ladies. A woman with flaming red hair and an upturned nose who the governor said was an actress, a brunette with a provocative pout who danced ballet, a lady with black hair all dressed in emerald green. "And lovers . . ."

"I see." For the first time in a long while Sabrina was thankful for Jonathan's presence — for she knew beyond a doubt what might have ensued had he not been there. As it was, the governor was decidedly bold.

"And your portrait could very well be there." Drawing her aside, he whispered in her ear, "I'd like that, Kit. You are a beautiful woman. Such a painting would be a permanent reminder of your beauty."

"No!" She drew away, the idea alarming. She had even gone against Bill's wishes to have her image drawn for fear of someone recognizing her from the painting. She couldn't risk it.

"Please reconsider." The governor took her hand. "Think about it."

Jonathan's grin was treacherous. "She won't change her mind. Not my Kit. She just doesn't like her portrait done. Overly modest, I suppose." His eyes met Sabrina's in silent challenge.

Sabrina was relieved when they joined the rest of the company in the drawing room. The room was packed with Bill's performers, including several of the Indians. Leaving the governor's side, Sabrina sought the comfort of her fellow showmen. She moved around just listening to the conversation, not at all surprised that the topic was the show.

"Have you ever considered taking your Wild West show to Europe?" the governor was saying to Bill.

"Europe?" It seemed to be a far-fetched idea.

"England. I've heard the queen loves cowboys and thrills at the very word *Indian*. It would certainly be an interesting experience."

"England?" Bill's brows shot up as he mulled the idea over.

"England," the governor answered.

"I'll have to give that some thought." It was too early in the evening for Bill to be tipsy, but he was.

His eyes were not quite in focus. Though Nate usually kept him under control, it appeared that tonight was going to be an exception. Sabrina hoped that Jonathan would follow Bill's bad example.

The butler announced dinner and Thomas Ellis immediately returned to Sabrina's side, offering her his arm. He led her into the dining room, one of the grandest rooms she had ever seen. Over the white damask-covered rectangular table hung a huge chandelier, brilliant with candles that reflected in the ceiling mirror and marble floor. A tall centerpiece of fresh flowers decorated the table. Sabrina took her chair, to be sandwiched in between Jonathan and the governor.

"A toast. To Buffalo Bill!" Thomas Ellis's cry was echoed by all present. "And to Kitty Tremaine." Again the cry was echoed. "And to Jonathan Colt." Several of the other performers were mentioned by name to a rousing cheer. And each time the assemblage drank up. "You interest me greatly, Kit." Thomas Ellis's manner was direct. He didn't even pretend to be shy as he hinted very softly that he would like to make her his mistress. As tactfully as she could, Sabrina steadfastly refused. She wanted no man but Ross.

"Bravo! Well done, Sabrina!" Succumbing to his wine, Jonathan made a deadly slip, one which Sabrina thought might have been done purposefully because of his jealousy.

The governor's brows shot up. "Sabrina?"

"A middle name. All my friends call me Kitty or Kit," she quickly answered. She changed the subject, talking about the new rifle trick she was practicing, shooting from horseback.

The night continued on amidst delicious food, the best wine, and the buzz of conversation. Sabrina pretended to listen intently but her thoughts were on her escape instead. She had to create a diversion so that

286

she could slip out of the room and hide in one of the cellars until the coast was clear. This might be her only chance.

Sabrina raised her wine glass to her lips, tipping it just slightly before it reached her mouth. The red wine made a great stain on the white linen cloth. "Oh no!" She was acutely apologetic. "I've ruined it!" She rose from her chair, moving towards the door, but Jonathan was not as drunk as she supposed. His shrewd eyes studied her and seemed to see into her thoughts. Quickly he was on his feet, blocking the doorway.

"Don't trouble yourself, Kit dear. Allow me!" He bowed his head in gentlemanly fashion. Striding to the kitchen he brought forth a cloth, placing it over the offensive stain to soak the red moisture up. "Shame, shame, Kit. It's not like you to be so clumsy." His expression gave her clear warning that he was wise to her attempt at escape and that such a thing had better not happen again. For the moment Sabrina's hopes were dashed, but she tried to remain optimistic. It was a long evening. There had to come a time when the opportunity to get free of Jonathan would present itself again. She would just have to be patient and hope.

Chapter Thirty-nine

Night was the worst time for Ross. It emphasized his helplessness and loneliness. Aside from the snores coming from the other cells, it was much too quiet. It was dark in the cell, only a cracked lamp with a very short wick gave off any light. It was a time of contemplation and a time of agitation. He'd sent for Jason Roberts. Where the hell was he? Taking out his pocket watch, Ross marked the hour. Nine-thirty. If the lawyer hadn't come by now he wasn't coming.

Another five minutes went by, then another ten. Just when Ross's spirits were at an all-time low and he was preparing to settle himself down in his cot for the night, the jailor ushered in a man of average height with a prominent nose and white frizzled hair. Jason Roberts, Ross's attorney.

"It's about time," Ross grumbled.

"Patience my boy. Patience. You aren't my only client." Roberts was a man Ross had always trusted, a soft-spoken Southerner he'd known since he was a just a lad. The lawyer had handled Ross's affairs since he'd put his first sentences on paper, had guarded his finances as carefully as if they were his own, and since he was a silent partner, some of them were.

"No, but I'm your most famous." Ross's grin gave proof that being incarcerated behind bars hadn't totally destroyed his sense of humor.

Roberts sighed wearily. "Indeed." His tone was scolding. "Especially now that your name has been splashed in all the papers."

"Couldn't be helped."

Roberts sat his portly frame in the cell's only chair while Ross hunkered down on the hard stone floor. "You sent a message telling me to meet you right away."

Dan Steel was three cells away so Ross kept his voice down, raising it to just above a whisper. "I want you to find out some information for me."

"I'm a lawyer, not a Pinkerton agent." The attorney loosened his tie. "Besides, it appears to me that you've already taken a great many matters into your own hands."

"I couldn't just up and desert those men, even if their skin was red. I had to stand behind them. It was a matter of honor."

"You acted like a young fool!" Ross started to protest, but Roberts held up his hand saying, "If you'd kept your temper and used your head, you wouldn't be here. I'd be a lot happier if I didn't have to defend you on that charge of disturbing the peace. It's made matters worse."

"I suppose it has," Ross admitted in a conciliatory tone. "But I wouldn't have lost my temper if it hadn't been for what that councilman said about Dan Steel."

"Namely?"

"That he was the one leading the parade of my Indians when they came in to town. And the hell of it is that I'm not surprised." Ross threw up his hands in frustration. "Okay, you're right. I acted like a hothead. But it's because I really do care about what happens to White Feather and the others." Wrapping his long arms around his knees he sat in silence for a long agonizing moment. "And the worst of it is that this happened just at a time when I was very content. I'm in love, Jason. I guess I don't have to tell you that this sure puts a damper on all my plans."

There was compassion as well as shrewdness in those hazel eyes. "I'm sorry, my boy. But don't lose heart just yet." If anyone could get him out of this mess, Jason Roberts could.

"I want you to find out all that you can on Steel."

Ross was grimy and bone tired. There were deep circles under his eyes.

"You look exhausted. Can't we talk about this some other time?"

"No, I want to find out who he's worked for, any companions, employers, or other associations. I want to find out any of his habits. Does he smoke, chew, swear, gamble — you get the picture. Hell, Jason, I want to even know how often he visits the back house. Do I make myself clear?"

"Very. You wish for me to compile a profile of the man," Jason Roberts said patiently.

"I want to prove that someone is out to ruin me, that my Indians were set up to do just what they did. If there is a real culprit in all of this, it's the man who gave the Indians that whiskey and the man who paid Steel off. I want to find out just who it was and think of a way to use it at the trial."

"It's not that easy, I'm afraid. It will take witnesses or some kind of written proof to make this stand up in court."

"Then we'll find them. Do whatever you have to. For starters I want you to talk to some of my men. Curly, for one." Ross rattled off a list of all the members of his company whom he knew he could trust. Perhaps their testimonies all put together just might make this puzzle take form.

"Curly? Big Hands? Cactus Jack? Indian Joe? Arizona Charley?" Jason Roberts carefully took down notes, then when he was finished, held out his hand. His handshake was firm, his smile warm. "We'll do it, my boy." In all the days he'd known Ross Sheldon, nothing had ever defeated him and somehow Jason couldn't believe that anything would now.

Chapter Forty

The fire in the dining room's hearth had burned down to ash. The table had long since been cleared of its delicacies, but the smells from supper lingered, mixing with the potent odor of liquor. It was growing late. Sabrina judged it to be about midnight, but not one of Buffalo Bill's performers gave any indication that they intended to call it a night.

". . . We'd been hunting migratory herds for days, waiting for them to reach their destination. Then we seen 'em from a distance. The dark clumps of hair on those great hairy beasts were as thick as fleas on a dog." Bill was relating one of the stories of his great days as a buffalo hunter, his gray eyes gleaming with merriment. He'd been drinking steadily since his arrival, yet surprisingly his speech wasn't the least bit slurred.

"And you rode after them." Thomas Ellis pressed his knee against Sabrina's under the table, and she hastily pulled her own leg away.

"We took off in a gallop, heading down that rocky terrain until we were so close we could see the vessels in those buffalos' eyes! I waited until I was abreast of a cow at the front of the herd, then I raised my rifle and took aim." Bill's rifle was balanced against the back of his chair and he picked it up, balancing the butt against his shoulder. "I pulled the trigger and got her right between the eyes."

"An idea for a new trick shot for you, Kit," Jonathan said for all to hear.

"If I shoot anything between the eyes, it should be you," Sabrina whispered testily, still angered that he had second-guessed her a few hours ago.

"Now, Kit dear, be nice." All night long his mood had been changeable, from amiable to sarcastic and back again. "Have some wine," he said, pouring it. "It will relax you, make you smile."

"The only thing that will make me smile is being rid of you."

A muscle tightened in Jonathan's jaw, his eyes drew into slits as he squinted. "You'll never be free of me, Kit. Never!" Jonathan got up and threw another log on the embers and struck a match. The fire flared up, illuminating his face. At that moment he looked just like a monster, Sabrina thought.

"Why don't you just leave him?" Thomas Ellis's voice was soft, but startled Sabrina just the same. "It's obvious how much you dislike him."

Sabrina turned to find the governor regarding her intently. She flushed, embarrassed that he had overheard her conversation. "I can't."

Not unless she had a long headstart. Tonight she had been foolhardy to think it could be so easy. If and when she got away, it would take careful planning.

"Because you feel indebted to him." Thomas Ellis laughed. "Oh, I don't believe for a minute that story about you being raised by a trapper. The way I see it, you feel indebted to that young man and that's why you feel you have to stay. You think you need him, but you don't. You have me now. I'll see that you are taken care of."

That statement was far from comforting. "It's not as simple as that," Sabrina said curtly. "Jonathan won't let me out of his sight."

"I wouldn't either if you were my, uh . . . companion." His voice lowered to a whisper. "You're the most exciting woman I have ever met. And I am a most persistent man. I always get what I go after."

"Oh, do you?" Her discomfort increased with every minute that passed. There was something worrisome about this man, despite his ardent words and bold appraisal. She knew she might have used him to help her break free of Jonathan, but an inner voice told her that Governor Ellis would be far more dangerous than Jonathan could ever be.

"Yes, for example, I wanted to capture your images." He paused to take a sip of his wine. "And I have done just that tonight."

"What do you mean?" She could feel the quickening of her heart and hoped he wouldn't notice.

"All through dinner tonight you have been posing." He pointed towards the corner of the dining room where a short little man with dark hair, beard, and mustache sat quietly. Only now did Sabrina notice the pad and pencil in his hand. "Jacques is a friend of mine. An artist. While we were eating and conversing he has been making sketches of you, Kitty Tremaine."

She tried not to panic. "But I said that I—"

"False modesty."

Sabrina's neck and cheeks burned. She took a gulp of wine and tried desperately to laugh the matter off. So this artist friend of the governor's had made a few sketches. What would that hurt? There were drawings of her on some of the posters for the show. It wouldn't do any real harm. Her making a fuss over the matter would be far more detrimental.

"Don't try to tell me that you aren't pleased."

"Pleased?" Sabrina clenched her fingers in her lap, trying to ignore the strange tightening in her stomach.

Jonathan returned to his seat beside her, grinning from ear to ear. "Of course she's pleased. Aren't you,

Kit?" His fingers curled around his glass. He'd definitely had too much, but that didn't seem to bother him. With a chuckle, he poured himself another glass of whiskey. "Well, aren't you going to even ask to see the pictures, Kit?"

"Of course I'd like to see your work." Turning towards the artist, she remembered her manners. "Please."

"Madame." Standing up, the little man held the sketchbook up for everyone's appraisal, flipping the pages to show the various poses he had caught with his charcoal and lead.

"It looks just like you, Kit," Sadie exclaimed in amazement. "Why, those pictures look so real I'm nearly expecting them to speak." The others in the room laughed.

"I've always said our Kit is as pretty as a picture," Bill commented, putting down his rifle and leaning forward for a closer look at the sketch. "You're a good artist, Jacques. Might want to use you for my handbills."

The little man was offended. "Monsieur, please! I am a serious artist."

Sabrina's eyes widened and she frowned slightly as she looked at the drawing. "Dear God, that is me." He had captured everything about her, from the way she held her head to the slight uptilt to her nose, but he had taken liberty with the pose. She was standing, not sitting, her hands planted firmly on her hips as they often were after she had finished a performance.

"And you can imagine just how beautiful the finished portrait will be when the copper of your eyes and the pink of your cheeks and lips is added." His dark eyes held Sabrina's gaze and she read in his expression his determination. Obviously no one ever said no to Thomas Ellis.

"You do me too great an honor," Sabrina said cautiously. "I'm just an ordinary woman who just happens to shoot at things for a living. I don't belong up on your wall."

"You do!" He was too filled with vanity and self-importance to recognize her feelings. "And that's the last I'll say of it."

Sabrina tried not to panic. Hartford was far from New Hampshire. It was absurd to even imagine that anyone there would see the finished painting. Besides, the artist would paint her with dark, not light hair. Who then would ever connect her with a yellow-haired innkeepers' daughter-in-law? No one.

Everyone in the show agreed that their Kit was very deserving of having her face upon the wall for all to see, but soon the conversation turned to other things. Bill leaned back in his chair and joined Thomas Ellis in talk of their days as scouts for the Pony Express and about all the people they had met on the frontier—long lengthy tales that had Sabrina closing her eyes for long moments at a time. Then at last when the night was ended, Thomas Ellis walked Sabrina and Jonathan to the door.

"I hope all my jabbering didn't bore you, Kit."

"Not at all."

"Kit and I were balanced on the edge of our seats the whole time," Jonathan said in an effort to foster a friendship with the man whose lavish lifestyle clearly impressed him. "Damn near as exciting as being part of the Wild West show."

"I wasn't bored for a minute." Hardly that, Sabrina thought.

"Good. Good. Then you'll be delightfully agreeable when I call for you at your door tomorrow." It appeared that he had it all planned, from visiting the opera to long carriage rides Sabrina knew she wouldn't have a moment's peace.

Chapter Forty-one

The afternoon sun's blistering rays glared down upon the carriage as it moved slowly down the road, away from the hotel. It was the busiest time of day. Horse-drawn vehicles of all kinds — wagons, carts, buggies, and carriages all seemed to merge together in one spot, jamming the street with people trying to get where they wanted to go but standing still.

Inside the carriage, Sabrina frantically fanned herself in an effort to keep cool. Comfort was not at all easy considering the fact that she was sitting in between Thomas Ellis and Jonathan, whose every look seemed to scorch the governor with ill will. During the past six days, the two men had been forced to be companions, each vying with the other for Sabrina's complete and undivided attention, all the while pretending camaraderie. Behind his back Thomas Ellis laughingly called Jonathan "the shadow." Jonathan's name for the governor, on the other hand, was not quite as tame. It might have been funny at any other time or soothed Sabrina's vanity had it not been for her heartache at missing Ross.

True to his word, Thomas Ellis had spared no expense or lack of time in trying to show Sabrina a wonderful time. There were numerous days and nights of pleasures and distractions, yet Sabrina's strong feeling of restlessness persisted despite long carriage rides in the country, evenings at the opera, fancy balls and riotous parties. She was haunted by a sense of desperation, much like a bird in a gilded cage. Driven by the urge to get free of Jonathan's ever-watching eye, she was none-the-less thwarted at every turn. It was as if he had a sixth sense or could read her mind. Whenever she came close to making an escape, Jonathan was always there, his taunting look reminding her of the control he had over her.

Though she seemed to always be surrounded by people, Sabrina's yearnings and her fears could not be shared with anyone. Not even with Sadie for fear she might have to make explanations. Certainly not with any of the women she met — wives of councilmen, mayors, senators, and other men of politics — women who though they greeted her politely, looked down their noses at her profession. "Little better than an actress, I must say," she heard one velvet and feathered missis declare. Sabrina shrugged such twitterings off and kept herself aloof. She didn't need their friendship. There was only one person she knew she could count upon as friend *and* lover.

Ross. Where was he and what was he doing now? she wondered. Seeing a newsboy waving one of his papers, she fumbled in her purse for the right change and politely requested a copy, avidly scanning the headlines. There was an article on President Grover Cleveland, a story about the threat of inflation, a detailed interview with a new opera singer visiting the town, but nothing about Ross Sheldon. It seemed the scandal about his Indians was at last dying down.

"Anything interesting, Kit?" Jonathan was always alert to anything at all that might involve his rival.

"Nothing at all!" To emphasize that fact, she tossed the newspaper aside. Jonathan picked it up to use as his fan.

"Not even any gossip?" Thomas Ellis drew up on the reins of the carriage and looked over at Sabrina. "No stories about the governor and the mysterious Kitty Tremaine?"

"Not a word!" Sabrina had a cheery tone to her voice, having found that the one way to keep Thomas Ellis at arm's length was to treat the entire matter as a joke. It seemed to wound his pride and curtail his boldness, at least a little.

"Too bad. Better luck next time," Jonathan hissed, a malicious grin on his face. In the duel of sharp tongues, Jonathan was clearly winning.

Making its way through the throng of vehicles, the carriage at last broke free of the traffic and rattled over a small wooden bridge. The sun was dazzling on the water, claiming Sabrina's gaze. The pink mountain laurel was in full bloom, the robins were singing a welcoming to another day. On the other side of the bridge, a few top-hatted men strolled about in the sun. One man raised his hat to Sabrina as the carriage rolled by.

"I'm going to take you on a tour of this fair city and then I have a surprise," Thomas Ellis insisted, flicking on the reins.

"Another tour?" Jonathan purposefully made a sour face. "I can practically find each and every landmark blindfolded."

Sabrina ignored her one-time friend's comment, looking out the window at the scenery instead. The flowers were in bloom, the trees were covered with thick leaves, the sky was blue and shimmering. In some ways she was coming to feel at home in this quiet but oftentimes bustling town.

"I want to take you up on the hill where you can see for miles," Thomas Ellis whispered, urging the horses into a steady pace as they climbed. He pulled on the reins, stopping the carriage when it reached the top. Sabrina could see the river and an endless acreage of green, crisscrossed by roads and interrupted by the many buildings which looked like dollhouses from the distance.

"There it is. My city." The governor pointed out several places of interest. "That's my court house, that building taking up the whole square. That three-story brick building is the new hospital. And of course you can see your hotel."

Sabrina studied the Hartford landscape with eager eyes, taking in its beauty. Everything looked white and clean and tranquil. A place of peace, at odds with the turmoil in her heart. She counted the fireplaces and smokestacks on the brick and stone houses, saw the gardens, and wondered what it would be like to live in such a place. To stay put and settle down.

"Do you think you could be happy here?" Thomas Ellis asked softly.

"Yes." She could be if Ross were here, but she knew that wasn't what the governor meant.

"Kit can be happy anywhere for a short amount of time," Jonathan said quickly, "but she is a wanderer like me. Never stays more than a week in any town, nor will she!"

Jonathan's words broke the spell. With a disdainful sniff, Thomas Ellis guided the horses back down the hill, leading the carriage back among the busy, noisy traffic. It was obvious that he had had just about enough of Jonathan.

"Where are we going now?" Jonathan asked peevishly.

"You'll see." Ellis's voice was curt. "I said I have a surprise and I do." The carriage returned to the governor's home.

Thomas Ellis cleared his throat as they walked through the door single file, looking more than a bit annoyed. "I'd like to be alone with the lady if I might, Jonathan. I don't believe it's too much to ask."

"Now see here—"

"I want to show her something. *Alone!*"

Surprisingly Jonathan agreed, though he did position himself like a guard at the door, just in case Sabrina got any ideas, she supposed. Sabrina followed Thomas Ellis as slowly as she dared, suddenly apprehensive about what she was about to see, but he merely took her by the hand and led her into a small room which, from its books and desk, seemed to be the study. There was a long table in the middle of the room and she was surprised to see that it was littered with brushes, paint-stained rags, and palettes smeared with paint. Usually Thomas Ellis was extremely tidy.

"I let Jacques use this room," he said, noting her scrutiny. "To create something very special."

"A painting." But of whom? Sabrina knew all too well and braced herself for the shock of seeing her own portrait.

"Not just a painting, but a masterpiece." He led her towards the huge easel that stood in the corner.

"Masterpiece?" Sabrina craned her neck, but the painting was draped with a piece of white cotton cloth.

"I've kept it covered. I wanted you to be the first to see it, except, of course, for Jacques and me. A surprise."

"It's me, isn't it?" What had she expected? A landscape? Sabrina felt slightly foolish once the words were out. Jacques obviously had created a painting from his sketches.

"Yes, of course it is you. Pictured just the way I'd like to see you." Reaching out he gently touched her hair, his finger twisting a dark tendril as he inspected it closely. "Jacques is right, your neck is as long and graceful as a swan's, your eyes are expressive, your lips just the right fullness. But your hair. Much too dark. It doesn't go with your fair complexion." He

300

startled her with a question. "Why do you always wear that dark wig, Sabrina?"

"It's part of my costume, long dark braids Indian style, and . . . and it's easy. I don't have to worry about doing my hair," Sabrina quickly replied.

"Well, a minor point." Thomas Ellis smiled as if mollifying a child. "Jacques said that he enjoyed working on this portrait more than any of the others he has done. Partly because of the challenge, not having you to pose and all. He did say that you were by far the most beautiful woman he had ever painted, but also the most difficult to capture on canvas."

"Difficult?" She hoped it had been impossible.

"An exercise in memory. Many artists set themselves up to such a test, doing a painting without a sitting. But don't worry. I'm certain you will be pleased, just as I am. I think Jacques has captured the 'real' you. Part seductive temptress, part cherub." With a flick of his wrist he cast aside the drape, revealing the painting to Sabrina's eyes. "Behold—an angel!"

Sabrina gasped, gazing at the picture like someone in a trance. A lovely young woman clad in a gown of pure white, the bodice molded to the curve of her breasts, reclined against a scarlet pillow. Around her neck was a necklace of diamonds and pearls, emphasizing the creamy perfection of the neck and shoulders. The painting was exquisite, just as the governor had promised. The nose, eyes, arch of the brows, chin, lips, and shape of the face were so perfect that it was almost as if Sabrina was looking into a mirror.

"The hair!"

"Reveals the true you," Governor Ellis explained. "I heard Jonathan Colt talking to you that day and it was then I decided. I wanted to have a picture of Kitty Tremaine like no other."

Not Kitty Tremaine, but Sabrina James stared

back from the canvas. Sabrina put her hand to her mouth, biting her thumb to keep from crying out. Thomas Ellis had surprised her all right. He had chosen to paint her not as a brunette, but with golden hair.

Chapter Forty-two

A heavy damp fog had rolled in from Lake Ontario bringing with it a thick mist of humidity that made the heat nearly unbearable. It was hot, small, and cramped in the cell. To Ross, a man used to wandering around at will, it seemed even more stiffling.

He was angry and he was bored. They had no right to keep him in here. For the love of God, all he'd done was a little shouting. He demanded his rights and he demanded them now, or so he had told the grinning little man who acted as his guard. Mingled with a string of swear words, he had demanded to see his lawyer at the first opportunity. Ah yes, he asserted his rights. Ross was tougher, leaner, and more determined than ever since his prison stay.

"Damned leech!" He was perturbed at Jason Roberts for not having gotten him out of this mess. "All he's done is take my money and I'm still in here!" Ross lay sprawled on his cot, staring fixedly at the wall with unrestrained frustration. What hour was it? For that matter, what day was it? Time moved so slowly that there were times when he just lost track. And all the while his show was losing money. Curly was strong and loyal, but he wasn't smart. His business decisions were leading Ross into ruin. That and the scandal.

"Damn!" He had been as happy as a rabbit in its burrow until this whole episode had occurred. The Wild West show and his dime novels had produced enough income to set him and Sabrina up in style. The kind of life he wanted to give her, one rivaling a queen's. But all that had suddenly changed in the wink of an eye. Now he knew he'd have to draw from his life savings if he was going pay for the damages his Indians had done.

"White Feather, do you hear me?" he shouted out in sudden anger.

"Yes, I do. Loudly," the Indian answered from the neighboring cell where all the Indians were encamped.

"The next time you even look at a whiskey bottle I'll have your head. I swear it!"

"No more firewater! On that you have my word."

"Let's just hope we all get out of here so that I can hold you to your promise."

Ross knew the chief would keep his word. Unlike some of the white men, he knew the Indians were honorable. Which was more than he could say for the culprit who'd been the instigator of this unfortunate matter. Hell, it was against the law to give liquor to an Indian. He'd see just what the judge had to say about that!

And about all the other things that had been happening, he thought as he put his hands behind his head. When it was damp like this, his arm acted up, aching just a bit. A reminder of that time he had been shot. And what about all the little things he'd overlooked? It was clearly sabatoge. But by whom?

His musings were interrupted by a grating sound. The guard rattled the barred door. "Visitor." Standing by the iron bars, as if Ross's thoughts had conjured him up, stood Jason Roberts.

Ross jumped to his feet. "I hope you're here to get me out, because I've just about had it with this lace."

"I am." Jason Roberts held out a complicated document. "You're to sign this agreement. In it you agree to pay for the damage done to the town."

"The whole town?" Now that he'd heard the terms, Ross felt like reneging. It would mean an awful lot of money. Perhaps he'd be better off to take his chances at a trial.

"Yes, the whole town. Every overturned barrel, broken axle, smashed window, damaged door. And I've even agreed with Mayor Litchfield that you will buy four new horses to replace the ones that ran away."

"With what?" Ross asked with a wry grin. "This whole thing has nearly bankrupted me."

"It might have had I not set aside quite a large sum and invested it for you, my boy!" Jason Roberts made it obvious that he was overly pleased with himself. "I've looked after you as carefully as a father does his son."

"Let me see." Ross scanned the agreement, then signed the paper, feeling as if the weight of the world was suddenly lifted off his shoulders. "And Chief White Feather and the boys?"

"They'll be set free if you agree never to bring them anywhere near Rochester again. Within the radius of three hundred miles."

"Three hundred miles?" Ross could see by the look on his lawyer's face that there was no use in arguing. "All right. All right!" He signed his name to that section of the agreement. "You hear that, Chief? You and your boys are gonna walk right out of here with me."

Jason Roberts nodded to the jail guard who fumbled with his ring of keys. "Hurry. We don't have all day, sir. You've already kept this boy longer than I consider legal. Come on!"

The guard tried three keys, opening the lock with

the third one. The door swung open with a squeak "You're free." Jason Roberts walked into the cell, tugging on Ross's arm. "What are you waiting for Come on."

"Not so fast." It just wasn't as simple as that. Ther was more to this matter than just getting out of hi cell. "I gave you an assignment. Did you find ou anything?"

"Oh, yes. A great deal." The lawyer opened hi leather case and consulted his notes — methodica chicken scratchings as Ross called them.

"Well?" Ross was quickly losing his patience.

"Did a complete investigation on that man Da Steel. He's seemingly an honest man. No prison re cord. Before now he's never been in jail. Not eve once."

"Honest?" Ross was disappointed. He'd been s certain that Dan Steel was the key to all of this. "traveling preacher, no doubt."

"Not a preacher, but he did do a lot of traveling Used to work for a gun peddler as a matter of fact going from town."

"Gun peddler?" Ross grunted in disgust as Jona than Colt came to his mind. "Sounds suspicious t me."

"No, totally legitimate. Worked for a gunmakin company with a very reputable name. Colt. I'm cer tain you've heard of them."

"Colt?" Ross couldn't have been more stunned Jason Roberts had slapped him. "Colt?" he aske again.

"Jonathan Colt hired him on to drive one of hi father's wagons."

"Jonathan Colt." It certainly seemed to be a sma world or was there much more to this than was obvi ous? Ross plopped down on his cot, his head in hi hands as he thought it all out. No! His suspicion were only fueled by his sincere dislike of the man

There was no reason to suspect good old Jonathan. The man had no motive. Or did he?

"As for the man named Hawthorne, he's a reputable businessman whose offices are in New York City."

"Reputable?" Dan Steel was honest and Hawthorne reputable. Hardly the kind of men to be held accountable for mischief. "And he has no ties to Dan Steel?"

"No. As far as I can tell he never even met the man." Jason Roberts turned over the page in his notebook. "But he has done business with Jonathan Colt from time to time."

"Jonathan Colt?" Again that name popped up. "Hawthorne and Colt?" And Colt and Dan Steel. Coincidence? "And what about Jonathan Colt and Apache Ed?"

"He supplied the show with guns at one time." Jason Roberts gathered up his papers, putting them in his satchel. "Jonathan Colt, I mean."

"Colt, Colt, Colt." Suddenly the wheels in Ross's head started turning. Who was it who had been in the vicinity of Ross's show every time something strange had happened. Jonathan. Hell, he'd even been in the stands that day Ross had taken Sabrina to the opening of his new show. And thanks to Ross's obsession with Buckskin Kitty Tremaine, alias Sabrina, the two shows had practically been side by side. Colt would have had every opportunity to work his mischief. Could have, but did he?

There was only one way to find out, Ross thought. Frighten the information out of him. Goad him into a confession if he were guilty.

"Come on, Roberts, let's do as you say and get the hell out of here."

Ross was all smiles as he and his lawyer emerged from the jail but for very different reasons than Jason Roberts could have ever understood.

Chapter Forty-three

Ross glanced at the shadow of his horse and knew without even looking up at the sky that the sun was nearly at its zenith. It was hot. He was tired and thirsty, but he elected not to pause just now. He was riding straight from Shortsville to Hartford, only planning to stop when it was absolutely necessary. He'd learned from Dan Steel that Buffalo Bill's troupe was holed up in that Connecticut town, and Ross was determined to catch up with them before they moved out. He had some unsettled business to conduct with Jonathan Colt.

"Yes siree!" Ross should have been angry, but there was a sense of exultation pumping through his blood. Oh, how he'd wanted to smash his fist right into the smirking face of that gun peddler, yet he'd held back. Now he had an excuse.

Ross had been all good humor and smiles when he'd come back to the prison to arrange for his Indians to be freed. He'd visited Dan Steel's cell and with a great show of generosity had even let the man know that he was personally putting up his bail to get him out of jail. Like a spider luring a fly, he had suggested they drink to their freedom at a nearby tavern, then with his arm around Dan Steel's shoulder had cheerfully led him down a dark alleyway, slamming him up against a brick wall as soon as they were out of sight of any passersby.

"Talk, Steel!" he had thundered, grabbing the man by his shirt. "Tell me who put you up to getting my Indians drunk or I swear I'll beat you bloody."

"I don't know what you mean. I . . . I didn't get your Indians drunk. I told you I went along with them just to . . . to see that nobody got killed."

"Bullshit!" All the days of frustration, of being couped up in that cell, threatened to unleash Ross's emotions full force. His anger gave him the strength to lift Dan Steel off the ground until his feet were dangling. "Tell me the truth or I swear to you—"

"All right!" The fat little man's eyes bulged out of his head with fear. "All right! Don't know why I should cover his ass. Just put me down."

Ross did, with a thud that sent the other man sprawling. "Talk!"

"It was Colt who put me up to it."

"Jonathan Colt!" So he had been right, Ross thought, clenching his teeth together so tightly he could hear his jaw snap. "The bastard."

"Said you had it coming for running off with his wife, for having made an ass of him in front of the whole town of Rochester." Dan Steel slowly got to his knees.

"He was already an ass, I didn't have to prove it," Ross mumbled. "I just didn't know he was lower than a snake's belly too." Cautious, lest the other man get away, Ross stood hovering over him, his hands folded across his chest. "Question is, why'd you do it?"

"I owed him some money, an old gambling debt from when I drove his lousy wagon. He said he'd forget about it and call us square if I just did what he said." He started to scramble to his feet, only to feel the pressure of Ross's boot on his behind.

"Not so fast! I want to hear the whole story from start to finish. Now!"

Ross listened as Dan Steel told the tale of how a

chuckling Jonathan Colt had taken Steel into town to purchase a whole case of whiskey. The cheapest kind, but with enough alcohol to give quite a jolt. It was his plan to make it so rough on Ross that he would have to return, quarantine or no quarantine, and bring the young woman with him. And the plan had worked beautifully.

"Damn!" Steel further related that Jonathan had intended that the little man instigate himself into Ross's show to cause further trouble. "And you did, didn't you, you stupid son of a bitch. It's because of you I spent all that time in jail!" Anger pushed Ross to lunge, but the man's gasp and cowering cooled his temper. It wasn't so much this man as Jonathan Colt that he was infuriated with. Jonathan Colt. And now he'd pay his dues.

Ross rode through the sunlit afternoon with little thought to the scenery. Hunger pangs gnawed at his stomach, but even then he didn't stop, merely slowed down to eat his lunch in the saddle. Not anything appetizing—crackers, cheese, and some dried beef he'd picked up from a grocery store before heading out. He ate as the horse plodded along, then when his hunger was satisfied he stowed away the remainder of food and urged his mount into a brisker pace.

The more he rode, the more he thought, and the more he thought, the angrier he got. Oh, how he wanted to see that snake squirm! Giving liquor to Indians was a federal offense, one which just might get Jonathan Colt up to his eyebrows in trouble. Ross thought now of what fun it would be to see the expression on Colt's face when he threatened to expose him for his foul deeds.

"Which just might include having shot me," Ross thought with a scowl. Had it been Colt or one of his henchmen? Ross knew he wouldn't be the least bit surprised at anything he might learn.

Certainly he had a lot to think about. He'd

thought Jonathan Colt to be nothing but a lazy, stupid, restless fool, but now he knew he could add spiteful, nasty, and cunning to the list. Even so he was surprised at what he had found out. All this time he had thought Hawthorne or Apache Ed to be the culprits.

"But it was Jonathan Colt." As he rode along he pieced together the fragments he knew to try to come up with the finished puzzle. Jonathan Colt was a restless, money-hungry man, this he had already known. A man whose vice was gambling. He had spent money in riotous excess until his father had practically disowned him and had cut his allowance in half. It was probably then that he had decided to take up with Sabrina. A lonely young widow seemingly would be an easy target.

Ross winced at that thought. Hadn't that been his own line of reasoning? It had been. At least until he had gotten to know the true worth of the young golden-haired woman. But even then he'd hurt her.

"But that's all behind me!" he vowed. From now on it was going to be a bed of velvet and roses. He'd make Sabrina James so happy, so content, she'd never even look at any other man.

Ross guided his horse eastward, following the train's rails, wondering why he hadn't had the good sense to just take the train. It would have been faster and sure as hell more comfortable. But then he'd been in such a dither he hadn't been patient enough to wait until the train came into the station. Now his backside was paying for that impatience and, worst of all, his horse was being driven much too hard.

"You need a rest even if I'm too pig-headed to admit that I do," he said, patting the animal on the flanks. As soon as they reached the next town, Ross saw to it that the stallion was properly cared for at a stable, then he found a hotel to spend the night. Nothing fancy, just a bed and a chair. At dawn he renewed his journey, annoyed at how easily his thoughts turned back to Jonathan Colt. How had Sabrina ever been saddled with that fool in the first place?

He seemed to remember her telling him that Jonathan had asked her to go along with him in his wagon. But why had she left? Because Jonathan Colt talked her into it, he supposed. A smooth-talking con man wanting a pretty young woman to keep him company.

Ross could nearly imagine the scene as he rode. At first Jonathan would have gained her sympathy with his mewling tale of how his father had abused him, then he would have flattered her ego with his talk of making her a star. He remembered how eagerly Sabrina had listened to his own stories about the Wild West. And Jonathan Colt had known just what words to say: Buffalo Bill!

"Oh, he must have made some dandy promises!" But all the time all he wanted was to hitch his wagon to someone who could be a star. Sabrina was young, pretty, and vulnerable. The perfect Kitty Tremaine. The more Ross thought about it, the more certain he was that Jonathan Colt had planned the whole thing right from the first. But then Ross had entered the scene and Jonathan must have been frantic. He had either paid to have Ross shot or had shot him himself. It was probably the only way he could figure out to get rid of him. But he hadn't, and that was the only part about this whole thing that made Ross smile. He'd won out after all with his daring abduction of Sabrina and he would again when he waltzed right into Hartford and took her away with him.

He was approaching that town now, or so he saw by the sign. It had been a long journey, but now he knew it to have been a rewarding one. His arms were tired, his legs cramped, his eyes gritty and bloodshot, but adrenalin pumped him up when he might have otherwise sagged in the saddle. He'd settle his score with Jonathan Colt, then take Sabrina away. Somehow they could recoup his losses. Hell, together they could do anything.

Hartford, Ross thought surveying the area. On the edge of the Connecticut River. A pretty spot for his reunion with Sabrina. A seemingly perfect place for a honeymoon. Hell, they'd get married that very day. Why not? A town this size would have more than its share of preachers.

It didn't take many questions to find out just where Buffalo Bill's company was staying. Ross made straight for the hotel without even bothering to change his clothes or to shave. He'd have time for that once he'd taken care of the business at hand, he thought with a smile, pulling his mount to a halt. He rode right up to the rail in front of the impressive brick building, dismounted, and tied the reins.

"Fancy. Real fancy." A carefully trimmed lawn stretched more than a hundred yards from the structure on all sides. Old Bill had certainly done himself proud in setting himself up in this place, Ross thought with a grin. Well, at least Sabrina hadn't been languishing while he had been gone, but had been living in style.

Ross mounted the steps and was just reaching for the door when it swung open and a tall, well-dressed, dark-haired gentleman strode out. "That's the governor!" a portly man behind the desk hurriedly told him in hushed tones.

"You don't say!" Ross shrugged. He'd met so many people of consequence that he wasn't impressed. Hell, he'd even met two presidents once—Hayes and Arthur. "I want to pay a call on a Miss Kitty Tremaine," he insisted, but before he could ask for the number of her room, the desk clerk was quick to inform him that she was the governor's new "ladyfriend."

313

"What?!"

"He's been paying court to her all the while she's been here. Smitten. Even had her portrait painted to hang on the wall in his mansion."

"I see!"

Ross felt the heat of jealousy creep up from his toes to the top of his head. Seemed as if he'd come just in time. Well, Sabrina wouldn't have any need for any governors now that he was back. But perhaps it would be better to settle his score with Jonathan first and then go to see her. And perhaps he would clean up a bit. That way he could just sweep her up in his arms and carry her away before she could make any protestations.

"What's the number of Jonathan Colt's room, please?"

"Three thirteen."

Ross took the stairs two at a time in his hurry to get there. His rap at the door was far from a gentle tapping, and echoed in the stillness of the hallway.

"Go away. I didn't want anything," came a mumbled voice from beyond.

Ross knocked again, louder this time. The door was yanked open. "For God's sake, don't break the door down." Jonathan then made a disgusted sound low in his throat when he saw who stood out in the hall. He started to close the door, but Ross's foot acted as a door stop. "What do you want?" he asked brusquely.

Through the open door Ross could see into the room and noticed the high-backed chairs and an upholstered divan. A table near a marble fireplace seemed to be able to seat a dinner party of eight. Certainly Jonathan was living in the lap of luxury, and all thanks to Sabrina's talents.

"I came to see you, Colt." Ross pushed his way in despite Jonathan's protestations.

"Now, see here. How dare you come barging in

314

here like some ruffian. I'll see that you are thrown out. I'll—"

Ross closed the door with his foot. "Came to talk with you on a little matter of liquor and Indians. I've been speaking with a friend of yours. A man named Dan Steel."

Ross's words were as effective as a magician's spell in silencing Jonathan. He became as still as a statue. Clearly he was stunned that Ross was onto his game. At first Jonathan's face paled, but then an angry red flush crept up his neck and spread to his face.

"Don't bother to deny knowing him, or try to deny what you did. I got a confession out of him after I posted his bail." Oh, how Ross was enjoying this. Jonathan's arrogance was deserting him and he was being shrunk down to his proper size.

"He's a liar!"

"I don't think so and I'm willing to risk my reputation just to prove it." Ross gloried in the fact that he had Colt by the throat. Now he moved in for the kill. "I'd just be willing to bet that I could find witnesses who could testify that they saw you buy a case of whiskey. And I know for certain that one or two Shortsville councilmen can point out Dan Steel as a culprit. You'll be guilty by association, not just by what Steel himself has to say. Hope you like bars, Colt, because you'll be seeing the sunrise from behind them when I have my way."

"You wouldn't!" Like a cornered rat, Jonathan's eyes darted from side to side, but then suddenly he seemed to relax. "Do what you will, Sheldon," he snorted. "I have an ace or two up my own sleeve."

"You're bluffing!" Ross exclaimed.

"I assure you that I am not." It was then that Jonathan Colt related the story of a young woman fighting off the advances of her overly aggressive father-in-law. He told of how she struggled. How she hit her attacker on the head with a rock. How she

315

tried to get away, only to be cornered again. How she had picked up a poker and struck him again. "He's dead, Sheldon. Dead. And she killed him."

"No, I don't believe it. Sabrina wouldn't kill anyone." He hurried to defend her. "And besides, even if she did, it was an accident. Self-defense!"

"You know that and I know that, but I plan to tell a different story if you force me to." His meaning was all too clear.

"Let me make certain I understand you, Colt," Ross said, suppressing his anger and choosing his words very carefully. "You're telling me that Sabrina killed her father-in-law and that you witnessed the deed. And that you would be skunk enough to turn her into the law if I don't play this game your way?"

"Precisely." Jonathan looked just like the cat that swallowed the parakeet. "First and foremost, you are not to harass Sabrina, or should I say 'Kit.' I don't want to see you talking to her or see say you anywhere near her. Like it or not, Sheldon, she is mine to do with exactly as I please . . ."

"Careful! She's a lady." Ross took a threatening step forward. "I won't have you hurt her—"

"Oh, you know what I mean. I'm not after her charms, interesting though they might be. I want her to stay in the show with me as her manager. That's all."

"Of course you do." Ross's face suffused with anger. "Without her you're just a two-bit gambler, a gun peddler. With Sabrina you're an important man, or at least so it appears. But you and I know what you really are, Colt."

"Watch it!" You might really rile me and bring a whole lot of trouble upon Sabrina's head." Jonathan Colt laughed loudly, forced laughter but annoying nonetheless. Edging toward the door, he pointed to the portal with an exaggerated gesture. "Now, I'm tired of standing here jabbering with you. I want you out."

Ross hesitated. He wouldn't let this lowdown, bloodsucking worm order him around. "I'm not through talking this over yet."

"Oh, yes, I think you are through." Again the room was filled with shrill laughter. "Quite through. Shall I prove it?"

Ross knew he couldn't take any chances. "No!" But oh, how giving in—even for the moment—hurt his pride. Still, he had to protect Sabrina.

"I knew you would see it my way." Jonathan Colt's voice oozed with smug cordiality. "Have a good day!"

Oh, he is getting satisfaction from all of this, Ross thought with a burst of anger. He wanted to lash out at him, but the threat he presented to Sabrina kept his hands tied. Like it or not, Jonathan Colt did have the upper hand and until the cards were redealt, Ross knew he'd have to use caution and do exactly as the man wanted.

Chapter Forty-four

Sabrina paced the carpeted floor of her hotel suite like a restless, prowling cat, still troubled by the governor's "surprise." Only a blind man couldn't recognize her by the image painted there. A blind man or a fool. The longer the troupe stayed in town and the more people saw the show, the more dangerous the situation became. Somehow, someway, she knew that the portrait's existence was going to change her life.

"Perhaps it would be for the best," she whispered, moving to the window and staring through the glass. Every morning when she looked in the mirror, she wondered how much longer she could keep going. Certainly she couldn't be any more confined had she been in prison. There were days when she wondered if it wouldn't be better to just surrender to the inevitable.

It was a beautiful day and she wanted to be free. Wanted to breathe in the fresh air and feel the sun on her face. Instead she was like some pampered, treasured pet, allowed only to go for a walk or take the morning air when her "master" was along. What made it all the worse was that the others in the Wild West troupe, and Thomas Ellis too, thought that Jonathan was always by her side because she was so devoted to him.

"Devoted. Ha!" She clasped her hands so tightly

together that her fingernails etched the flesh. If the truth be known, she was growing to hate him more with each day that passed and that all-consuming resentment was threatening to destroy her. Thoughts of revenge on Jonathan whirled around in her head.

Jonathan, she thought. With each day his temperament grew worse. He drank to excess, then quarreled with nearly everyone in sight. Thomas Ellis. Sadie. The hotel workers. Even Buffalo Bill himself. Just a moment ago she had heard him raising his voice to someone. Arguing in that whining tone of voice only Jonathan possessed. Whoever was the butt of his tirade, she didn't envy. With a long-drawn-out sigh, Sabrina sat upon the settee. Resting her head against the back, she closed her eyes.

Why hadn't she tried to get free of Jonathan again? Had she just given up? Or was it just that she realized that even if she did get free there would be no place to go? Not really. Except for Jonathan, she was happy in Bill's troupe, she had to admit that. Bill had been good to her; Sadie was perhaps the only female friend she had ever had. It was as good a place as any to wait for Ross. And most importantly of all, it was where she knew Ross would come for her when he at last got out of jail.

"Oh, Ross!" It seemed that he was always on her mind. During the day she thought of him constantly, at night she would hug her pillow, imagining it to be his body in bed with her. She wanted him so much that her entire body ached, her breasts throbbing for his touch, her inner core heavy with need. She missed his devastatingly wicked grin, the way his brows shot up when he was telling a story, his voice, his laughter.

A tapping sound caused her to open her eyes with a start. Jonathan! Come to annoy her with talk of the new trick she was going to do tonight. He had insisted that she copy one of Annie Oakley's shots, shooting at a glass ball suspended from a rope that one of her assistants twirled around his head. Sabrina knew that her timing was off just enough to make the shot too risky, but though she'd argued and argued with Jonathan, in the end he'd had his way as always.

"Jonathan?" With a start she realized the sound wasn't coming from the door at all, but from the window. The window? A bird perhaps, tapping on the pane.

She hurried to the window, clutching at her throat as she saw it wasn't a bird at all. "Ross!" she breathed. He had used a rope to lasso the flag pole and had thus been able to pull himself to the third-floor ledge, but his frantic attempts to get her attention made it obvious that he couldn't hang on much longer.

Sabrina hurried to him, sliding the window up, helping him from the ledge, into the room. She collapsed into his arms with unrestrained gladness, feeling the same excitement she always felt when Ross was with her.

"You're out of that terrible jail. You're free!" She nestled in his embrace. "I knew you'd come for me."

"Sabree!" Oh, how he wished he had better news. "I . . . I talked to Jonathan."

Her face went pale. "Then you know!"

"I do."

All her control burst in a flood of tears. "I didn't mean to kill him. I didn't. But I couldn't stand his . . . his hands on me!"

Ross stroked her hair, her tears causing his own eyes to sting. "I know, darlin'. I know."

Between sobs Sabrina told him about Jonathan and how he had revealed to her that he knew her terrible secret. "He . . . he said he'd turn me in if I dared to leave the show and him."

"I have no doubt whatsoever that the bastard

would make good on his threat," Ross confided. "If I didn't think so, I'd take you by the hand and walk right out of here. But we can't take the chance." He noticed how longingly her eyes caressed the door, knowing instinctively just what she was thinking. "Nor can we just up and run away. Hell, Sabree, I'd like nothing better than that, but we'd be running for the rest of our lives, always looking over our shoulders."

"And so Jonathan wins the game after all." She had been so certain when Ross had climbed through that window that all was well, that he would somehow save her. She had imagined it like a fairy tale. Rapunzel's prince taking her away from the tower.

Ross hastened to reassure her. "He hasn't won. Not yet."

"But he will." Pulling free of his arms, Sabrina walked to the window, staring out at the sunshine with a feeling of total helplessness. Frustration. Jonathan had her trapped.

Ross watched Sabrina uneasily. She was standing at the window with her back to him, her demeanor mirroring her restlessness, her discontent. Walking to the window, he put his arms around her, kissing the tendrils of golden hair that tickled her neck.

"Sabree . . ." he said softly. When she didn't answer him, he repeated, "Sabree, I love you." Gently he turned her in his arms so that she was facing him. He took her chin in his hand and lifted her face to his. "Jonathan won't win out. I won't let him. I promise you that when he tangles with me, when I gain the upper hand again, he'll rue the day he did this to you."

"What are we going to do?"

Ross was silent for a moment then said, "Well, we could always shoot him!"

Sabrina looked at him in consternation, until she saw that he was only teasing her. His eyes were twinkling, the corners of his mouth twitching. "How can you be in a jovial mood after what has happened?" she asked with just a hint of censure in her voice.

"Because we're together and no one can keep us apart for long. Sabree, we'll find a way." He planted small, swift kisses on her nose, brow, and chin. "And until then we know we love each other."

"Yes, we do. And we are together now." Putting her arms around him again, she hugged him tight, her fingers digging into the heavy muscles of his back as she rose on tiptoe to fit herself against him.

"Sabree . . ." He tried to control his desire, but it knotted his stomach. The taste of her, the velvety feel of her under his hands, the intimate embrace — all acted with a potency that swept through him. Even so, he didn't want to fall upon her like some passion-sick fool. He took a deep breath. "Sabree!" Putting distance between them, he walked to the middle of the room, sitting down with a thud upon the settee.

She followed him to the sofa and sat beside him, taking his hand. A warm intimacy was slowly, sensuously surrounding them as they sat side by side. Their eyes met and Ross reached out to touch her face. The love and desire she felt at that moment made her glow with radiance. At that moment he knew that she wanted him as much as he wanted her.

"Sabree. Oh, God!" He came to her then, enfolding her in his arms, kissing her mouth, her eyes, her hair, and she warmed to him, making small incoherent sounds as she fit her body to his in a sensuous dancelike motion she knew aroused his passion.

"Oh, Ross, I want you so! Remembering how it was between us is all that has kept me going."

"It's all right now." He bent his head and his mouth closed over hers, hard and hungrily. Ross kissed her and desire as fierce as the sun's fiery rays flowed through them. He ran his lean, hard hands over her, stroking her neck, her shoulders, and the firm softness of her breasts.

Sabrina felt every nerve within her body quiver in response to his touch. Her fingers clenched in his hair as she savored his kisses. When she felt Ross's hands fumbling at the fastenings of her bodice, she lent her own fingers to his quest, freeing herself of the cumbersome material. In moments, the rest of her clothes lay on the floor.

"I haven't forgotten how very beautiful you are."

Standing above her, he was impatient as he undressed, dropping his own clothes heedlessly to the floor. His skin felt hot, as if he had a fever. Perhaps he did, he thought.

"Sabree . . ." His voice was low and husky with desire as he knelt down beside her.

His hands explored the satiny expanse of her bare back and traced the gentle curve of her waist and hip, then with a groan he lowered his face to hers and took her mouth again in a starved, demanding kiss, then he whispered her name, the sound of it muffled against her flesh as he moved his head to her breasts. His tongue sought the already tightening peaks, tasting her sweetness.

Sabrina could not get close enough. She burrowed into him, holding him as close as she possibly could. "Oh, Ross, I love you so!"

Caressing her, kissing her, he left no part of her free from his touch and she responded with a natural passion born of that love. At the sighing sound of her breath, he kissed her again, a long soul-searching kiss that made her tremble.

Suddenly the spell was broken as she heard Jonathan's voice calling her name from beyond the door, and stiffened. If they were caught together now she knew it would bode ill.

"I'm tired, Jonathan," she called out. "Go away!"

"I want to talk with you, Kit." His voice held that stubborn tone she had come to know so well.

323

"Not now. I'm resting. If you want me to be able to shoot straight, then I suggest that you save whatever it is you want to discuss with me until later." She sucked in her breath, waiting tensely. She heard the door latch rattle, but assuring himself that the door was locked, Jonathan proceeded on his way.

"Close call," Ross whispered in her ear.

"Very. But I think we have at least a bit of time." She stretched her arms and looked up at him, enjoying the familiar sight of his lean, muscular body. Reaching up, she clung to him, drawing in his strength and giving hers to him in return. She could feel his heart pounding and knew that hers beat in matching rhythm.

"Love me. Love me now, Ross," she whispered.

Their bodies seemed almost desperate in their haste and this very desperation seemed to heighten their pleasure to the agonizing edge of excitement. Sabrina's quickening body answered his with an almost unendurable joy, a heightened frenzy. She could not even contain the husky cry that escaped her lips as he thrust into her softness. Sabrina locked her slender thighs about him and for just one wonderful moment there was no Jonathan, no people in the world to do her harm, no turmoil. Only this man filling her, loving her.

Welcoming his thrusts, she moved with him until they were engulfed by wave after blessed wave of ecstasy. Sabrina felt sensations so startling, so acute, that she lost awareness of everything but the glory of this all-encompassing tide that swept over her. But time could only be suspended for so long.

Ross's features were softened from their lovemaking, but nevertheless he had to break the spell. "I must go soon, before Jonathan comes to check on you again," he whispered, surveying his clothes and hers scattered about the floor. At the moment leaving her was the furthest thing from his mind, but he had to get a grip on himself. He had to protect her.

"Yes, dear old Jonathan." She knew Ross was right and that they had to hurry. Even so, he felt bereft as she once more became a separate being.

Gently he detached his arms from her body and got up from the settee. Sabrina watched him move about the room as he dressed. Rising, she bent to retrieve her own discarded garments. There was a performance this afternoon. She had to get ready.

She heard the window open and shut, heard the creak of his boots, the rustle of his clothes as he climbed out the window, but lay still on the settee. She was afraid that if she moved, her emotions would erupt with a force that could not be controlled.

Chapter Forty-five

Ross stared out the window, looking searchingly up at the sky as if it was from there he could get the answer to this predicament. If you give a man enough rope, he'll hang himself, Ross thought, remembering an old saying. And that was just what he intended to do with Jonathan. Somehow that fool would slip up and then Ross would pounce. In the meantime, he had sent a telegram to his lawyer, instructing Roberts to do a bit of looking into the matter of Rufus James's death. There had to be a way to clear Sabrina, there just had to be.

Ross's single-minded purpose, his determined goal was to find a way to get Sabrina out from under Jonathan Colt's thumb. Somehow he'd do it, if he had to work a miracle, he thought. There had to be something or someone that could prove that Sabrina had only been defending herself when she had bonked her father-in-law on the head.

With a coolness of nerve that he most certainly didn't feel, Ross was determined to keep his poise for Sabrina's sake, keeping a watchful eye on her, yet in a way that didn't arouse Jonathan Colt's suspicions. He'd checked into the hotel, but under an assumed name—Logan Hunter. A private joke, as it were. One he'd share with Sabrina as soon as they were together again. And they would be together. Somehow he'd find a way to meet with her in her suite.

"Might make for a whole heap of climbing," he thought, but a woman like Sabrina made the most daring task seem worthwhile.

A pigeon, flying right outside the window, seemed to emphasize that thought. Winging through the air, the bird was dauntless in his effort to at last reach his ladylove, joining with her at last to bill and coo on the window ledge.

"Love!" Ross said with a grin. "It really does make the world go round." That was the thought that ran over and over again in his head as he bathed, changed his clothes, and shaved. "Hell, if I had enough time I'd train those pigeons to carry messages back and forth from my room to Sabrina's."

Instead, Ross bribed one of the hotel maids to carry a message in the laundry basket to Sabrina's room. In it "Logan Hunter" expressed his admiration for her beauty and her skill and told her he would be at the afternoon's performance. He also stated that she would probably not recognize him, hoping she would realize that he meant he would be in disguise. Just in case Jonathan was keeping his ever-watchful eye. Keeping to the shadows, he made his way down the stairs.

Bill won't mind at all if I just "borrow" something from one of his prop wagons, he thought with a wry grin. A tie-on beard and mustache was just what he was after, and he knew he'd find it there. The very thought amused him. Maybe he'd even try it out by walking right under Jonathan's very nose.

He was immersed in the thought as he made his way, but not so much so that the sound of a familiar name couldn't bring him back down to earth.

"How are things progressing with that pretty little Buckskin Tremaine, Tom? Have you made any time with her yet?" he heard a man's lazy, drawling voice ask.

Ross attuned his ears, glancing sideways at the man who asked the question, a shifty-looking character if ever he'd seen one. Standing beside him was the man he recognized as the governor. It didn't seem that the governor was very picky in his choice of friends, Ross thought with a shrug of his shoulders.

"How can I make any time when that fool manager of hers always clings to her shadow?" The governor did not seem to think the matter very funny.

"Why, he's only acting as a proper chaperon. Perhaps he can read your mind and knows just what thoughts are running around in that head of yours, Tom. Hmm?" There was a great deal of laughter, which was not shared by the governor.

Chaperon, Ross thought. Well, at least he could be thankful to Jonathan for that. Perhaps his constant hovering wasn't all bad.

"Shut up, you fool!" The governor's voice exploded in outrage. "What on earth do you know about the matter. I intend to ask that little lady to marry me, in fact!"

"Marry you? Marry you? Well, that might be the only way you're ever going to get in the famous Kitty Tremaine's pantalettes! If she wears any, that is!" That statement only made the governor's companion laugh all the louder, but he paused to ask, "But how can you get married when you already have a wife?"

"A moot point." The governor took out his handkerchief and dabbed at his nose. "Miss Tremaine doesn't know that." This time the governor joined in the laughter.

"Bastards!" Ross hissed beneath his breath. His dearest wish was to put his hands around the governor's neck and squeeze. The very thought of what the man planned, even though it would not be successful, was enough to make him livid. Only with the greatest effort was Ross able to control his rage. Hurrying

328

towards the back door of the hotel he was even more anxious to find what he needed in Bill's wagons. The urge to protect Sabrina burned in his breast. She needed watching out for even more than he had imagined. And he was just the man to do it! Anyone thinking to trifle with her had better beware.

Chapter Forty-six

Sabrina felt the warmth of the sun through her
dress of fringed buckskin as she stepped out into the
edge of the arena and turned her face up towards the
sky. It was a wonderful day. All the misgivings and
worry about the past had just seemed to vanish. Ross
was nearby, watching over her protectively and that
knowledge gave her hope.

"And now the moment you have been waiting for.
The damsel of daring herself, Miss Buckskin Kitty
Tremaine!" She heard the voice ring out, heard the
thunderous applause, but it took her a moment to
react. Then with a slow, measured stride, she made
her entrance.

Moving as if in a trance, she went about her familiar routine with surprising accuracy, considering the
fact that shooting at targets was the farthest thing
from her mind. Ross had been watching over her
from a distance and she couldn't help but wonder if
he was in the crowd, if at this very moment he was
watching.

Three clay pigeons flew, the last two at once, but
Sabrina was ready. "It's a hit!"

More targets sailed in the air, but because of Sabrina's keen eye they all exploded obligingly.

"And now, Miss Tremaine will attempt something never even dreamed of before."

The glass ball trick, she thought. Nearly impossible, and yet somehow she knew she could do it. For Ross! More than anything she wanted to make him proud of her.

"My reputation is banking on this, Kit. You had better do it right!" Jonathan hissed from his place behind her, but even his cajoling didn't rattle her nerves.

"Go ahead, Andy!" she instructed to the lad who was her new assistant in the act. "We can do it!" She granted the youngster her most genuine smile.

"Okay, Miss Tremaine." The boy drew a blue glass ball from a pouch and after a walk around the arena, holding it up for all to see, he made great show of tying it to a thick string, lowering it to hang at a level near his waist, then slowly whirling and twirling the globe higher and higher.

Sabrina drew one of her Colts, took aim quickly and fired just as the ball reached the highest point in its trajectory. It burst, glittering with tiny fragments that floated to the ground.

"Bull's-eye!" By the tone of his voice, Jonathan was astounded but triumphant. As if he had been the one to hit the target. He joined her as she curtsied to the audience. "And now from horseback," he stated.

Sabrina slipped upon her horse's back with grace and ease. She tied the reins over the pommel of her saddle, confident the horse would respond to the pressure of her knees. Slowly she led the animal into a slow canter around the arena.

All eyes were upon her as she raised her Colt in both hands and took aim as two targets were thrown into the air. "It's all right, girl" she cooed, soothing her horse to alert her to the coming repercussion. The shot rang out, and the china plate exploded into shards. She'd done it! Sabrina's satisfaction was complete. At least she'd leave the town of Hartford in a blaze of glory. Whatever happened now at least she would have that.

"Good girl! Good girl," she cooed to her mare, patting the animal's sleek neck. Reaching into the pocket of her buckskin dress, she produced a lump of sugar as a reward, then rode around the arena to bask in a thunderous clapping.

"Bravo, Kitty!" From his place of honor in the stands, Thomas Ellis applauded her. In a gesture of sincere affection, Sabrina threw him a kiss.

"And now, ladies and gentlemen, we ask you to stand and join in with us at this final finale, the grand parade which will signal our farewell to your lovely town."

"Kitty, ride by my side!" Buffalo Bill, resplendent in buff-colored buckskin, knee-high black boots, his hair flying from beneath his wide brimmed black Stetson, gave her a complimentary tribute.

The crashing sound of heavy hooves accompanied the music from the band as the performers in the Wild West show began their final parade around the ring.

"You've been about as reclusive as if you were in hibernation. Is anything troubling you?" Bill asked as they rode. "Keeping to your hotel room and not mingling with the others, even Sadie, just isn't like you. I haven't said anything, but I've noticed." Belying his conversation, he smiled at the crowd and lifted his hat up in greeting.

"I've wanted to be alone with my thoughts. And then the . . . the governor has been keeping me busy."

"So, I've noted." Bill chuckled. "Tom Ellis, you, and Jonathan have made quite a threesome that have raised more than a few brows. What about poor old

Ross?" As his eyes swept to the other side of the arena, he took note of her expression. "So, it's him you've been thinking about, huh?"

"Yes." There was no reason to lie to Bill. "I wish with all my heart that we could be together." Passing by a group of children, she bent down to touch their hands as they cried out to her.

"I've been reading the papers. He's out of jail, Kit. He'll come back for you. If I were selfish I'd worry about him taking you away, but I want your happiness above all."

"I know!" At that moment she dearly loved the smiling showman. "I am happy!"

As she rode around the ring, Sabrina scanned the crowd for Ross, trying to recognize him, though he had told her he'd be in disguise. She thought she sighted him wearing a phony black beard and mustache with a tan hat pulled low on his face, but she wasn't sure. She'd tease him tonight about it when he came to her and tell him how easily she had been able to spot him. Somehow the heart just seemed to know. That thought made her smile as she tipped her hat, but her lips suddenly froze as an all-too-familiar face hovered before her eyes.

"No!" She gasped, feeling as if she were suddenly strangling. For a moment she feared she just might faint. It couldn't be. He was dead, and yet for just a moment she had nearly imagined that she had seen her father-in-law's face in the crowd. Staring.

Dear God, what was the matter with her? She wasn't the type of person to see things that weren't there. Rufus James was dead! But Jonathan's constant taunting might have resurrected him in my mind, she thought. Guilt. Fear. But, oh, how she wished that ever-frowning, stingy man were still alive.

"Kit, you look as if you've seen a ghost!" Not allowing her to bask by Bill's side in her glory for long, Jonathan caught up with her.

"A ghost?" Sabrina looked at him, forcing herself back to calmness. "Maybe I did, Jonathan. Maybe I did." Then nudging her horse with her knee, she concentrated her attention on the parade.

Chapter Forty-seven

Ross was in a somber, restless mood as he sat in the hotel dining room. With the first light of the next day's sun Buffalo Bill was going to at last pack up and leave Hartford and Ross still hadn't been able to think of any way to help Sabrina. What made it a difficult situation was that unlike at the hotel where he could watch over her from afar, he wouldn't be able to tag along with Bill's company. He'd have no excuse to be hanging around the tents. No reason at all.

"Unless I join up with Bill's show," he thought with a half-smile. The way his own finances were going, it didn't sound like a half bad idea. Certainly "Cherokee Ross Sheldon's Wild West Show" was close to folding, that is if he didn't come up with some quick ideas on how to attract a large crowd. But no. Closing the show would be admitting defeat and that was one thing Ross just wouldn't do. Somehow he'd pull out of this.

He poured himself a glass of whiskey, looking at the menu as he leaned back to relax, smiling as he saw that the hotel had named some of their special dishes after members of the show. Buffalo Bill Beef Stew. Utah Frank Broiled Chicken and Dumplings. Jim Lawson Boiled Roast Beef with horseradish sauce. Kitty Tremaine Wild Pigeon Pie, under glass.

335

Kitty and Sabrina. Two women rolled into one and he loved them both. He adored the softness and golden beauty of Sabrina, yet admired the spunk and daring of her alter ego Miss Tremaine.

God, how he had been proud of her this afternoon. Ross didn't think even he could have made those two shots she had done without blinking. Shooting from horseback. And the spinning globes.

He remembered the very first time he had met her when she had wielded that mop, pretending it was a gun and she one of the heroines from her favorite books. He'd never imagined that she would become a renowned celebrity in her own right, one who would make even Hurricane Nell pale by comparison.

"Have you made your decision, sir?" A young waiter seemed impatient to take Ross's order.

"I'll have the Kitty Tremaine Wild Pigeon Pie, if you please. And I hope that you didn't shoot the poor lovers outside my suite window."

"Beg your pardon, sir?" The waiter looked bewildered.

"Nothing." Ross repressed a smile, knowing very well that the pigeons in the pie would be passenger pigeons, said to be related to the quail.

"And would you like coffee, sir?"

"No, thank you." Ross changed his mind. Maybe it would be a good idea to have a cup, the better to keep him awake tonight. He still hadn't given up hope that some plan or another would come to his mind. "I think I was right in the first place," he mumbled, thinking of Jonathan. "I think we should shoot him."

"Sir?"

"I said I was going to do a bit of shooting. The coffee will be just fine." Ross settled back to his musing, stiffening slightly when he saw the governor and another man enter. Jealousy sparked through him like a forest fire. Marry Sabrina! Ha! If the man

336

even dared to ask for her hand he'd cause a ruckus.

"You know, George, I never really realized just what a commotion that portrait would cause when I had it painted," he was saying. "I mean the young woman is obviously pretty, but you should have seen the expression on that fat gentleman's face when he saw it hanging on the wall a few days ago. His eyes literally bulged out of his head. He asked me question after question, then hurried away saying that someone was going to be very glad to know just where 'she' was. Strange."

"But not surprising. If you ask me, there is something very odd about that woman."

"Perhaps, but that's just what makes her so interesting."

Ross attuned his ears to the conversation, but just then a loud, chattering party of two men and four women took their places at the table next to him and so he just settled back to finish the rest of his whiskey.

I wonder what would happen if I countered Jonathan Colt's testimony and said that I witnessed Rufus James's death myself, he thought. A lie for a lie. But no, there were those in his own troupe who knew he was with them that night. Saying things that just weren't true could get a man, and perhaps Sabrina, in a whole mess of trouble.

"I'll just have to rely on old Roberts," he sighed, picking up his fork when the waiter brought his food.

"I hope you enjoy this, sir."

Ross poked the utensil into the crust and came out with a large piece of meat. Blowing on it to cool it, he lifted it to his lips. "Delicious!" He was starved and the pie was awfully small for a man with a hearty appetite. He'd remember to tell the hotel manager when he saw him.

"Excuse me, sir. I nearly forgot." He eyed Ross a bit warily. "You are Logan Hunter, aren't you?"

337

"Yes, of course I am." Reaching up, Ross felt for his beard, discovering that it had slipped a bit, no doubt the reason for the young man's scrutiny. "I'm Logan Hunter."

The waiter seemed flustered as he reached in the pocket of his apron. "A telegram arrived at the front desk for you. A very special delivery."

Ross practically ripped the envelope from the young man's hands, he was so excited. It was from Jason Roberts. Well, he certainly hadn't wasted any time, he had to give the lawyer that. His fingers trembled as he began to read, but noticing that the waiter just stood there staring, he reached in his wallet for some money and handed it to the young man.

"Thank you, sir."

Hastily Ross read the thick black type. "Inquired at the coroner's office. Stop. No murder. Stop. Rufus James not dead. Stop. Injured only. Stop. Recovered."

"What's this?" Ross was stunned. Fearing he might be imagining things, he read the words again. Rufus James not dead. *Not dead.* Throwing down his fork, he bolted from his chair. He had to find Sabrina and tell her the wonderful news. She was free! Free! And woe be to Jonathan!

Chapter Forty-eight

Like a hound hoping to corner a fat cat, Ross lay in wait near the stairs to the third-floor landing. For a measureless time, Ross was beyond all reasonable thinking. Rage boiled in his veins as he thought about what Jonathan Colt had done to him and to Sabrina.

"The little weasel." He was worse than that. Much worse. He was a blackmailing son of a bitch. A trouble-maker. A liar. Now he was about to pay the piper.

Ross's breath was ragged; every muscle in his body was tense as he waited in expectation. Clenching his hands into fists, he willed himself to calm down. Sabrina hadn't killed anyone, but feeling as he did at this moment he just might be capable of murder — Jonathan's. He'd break every bone in that skinny skunk's body, and that would be just for starters.

Ross forced himself back into a calmer mood as he waited, counting off the minutes by making a mental list of the things he would do to Jonathan. All sorts of punishments came to mind. Stripping the fool naked and making him run through the hotel lobby, showing off all of his shortcomings. But no. That wasn't harsh enough. Using his face as a punching bag? Too violent. Breaking both his arms? No, it would only make Jonathan a sympathetic figure in everyone's eyes. Locking him in his hotel room and throwing away the key? It was suitable, but somehow didn't show enough imagination. Blackening his eye? Too quick. Using him for target practice? Now that had merit.

Laughter sounded from the landing below and Ross

drew back, ducking behind a pillar. Jonathan's laughter. He'd recognize it anywhere.

"It was my idea for Kit to shoot from horseback and to shoot at those little glass balls. Remember that, Bill old friend," Jonathan was saying. "And while we're on the subject, just when are you going to pay Kit what she's worth?"

"Jonathan, you're nothing but a highway robber. Always pushing. She already makes more than just about anybody else. Shall I make her a partner?" Buffalo Bill's voice was sour with sarcasm.

"Bill. Jonathan. Please." Sabrina sought to be the peacemaker. "Please don't spoil our last night here by arguing. We were all a success. Let's just remember that."

"Hats off to the lady. Not only is she a crack shot and beautiful but she has a lot of charm and common sense." Pausing by Sabrina's room, Bill kissed her on the cheek. "Good night, Kit. Remember, no lazing about tomorrow morning. Back to the old grind again. We're going all the way to Chicago, so I want to get an early start." He paused for a moment as if wanting to say something more, but with a shrug hurried on his way.

"Are you going to ask me in for a drink, Kit?" Jonathan's weaving clearly proved that it was the last thing he needed. Undoubtedly he'd been the first to tip his glass in celebration of tonight's success, Ross thought with annoyance.

"It's . . . It's getting late, Jonathan. Bill said that we should be ready—"

"Bill says. Bill says. Who the hell listens to him anyway? He's not the star of the show!" As if to prove that he was the one who had the final say, Jonathan took Sabrina roughly by the arm and pushed her inside the room. It was then that Ross lost any semblance of self-control. With a cry that sounded more animal than human, he launched himself at Jonathan.

"Ross!" Sabrina was clearly stunned, but not as much as Jonathan.

"Sheldon. What in the hell are you doing lurking

around here?" Reaching for the door knob he started to close it, but Ross moved faster. Before it closed in his face, Ross maneuvered himself inside the suite. "What on earth do you think you are doing?"

"You'll find out" Ross bared his teeth in an evil smile.

"Ross! Why?" Sabrina looked at him as if he had suddenly lost his mind. "He'll . . . he'll . . ."

"Open his mouth and spill out the *lie* that you killed your father-in-law, Sabrina?" Ross shook his head emphatically. "I don't think so. I don't think even Jonathan Colt is enough of a fool as that. You see, Rufus James is alive!"

"Alive?" Jonathan's voice squeaked.

"So, you didn't know. Well, I have it on word of my lawyer that he is." Ross produced the telegram, dangling it in front of Jonathan's nose. "So, Sabrina is free of you at last and I will have my revenge for what you did to White Feather and his braves."

Looking at Ross's face as he, with an unnerving quietness, slammed the door behind him, Jonathan whimpered, "You can't just barge in here and manhandle me. This isn't the Wild West. People are civilized here."

"Civilized. I intend to be that." Ross didn't touch Jonathan, but he did take a step forward, standing nose to nose with him. "Otherwise I'd kill you! But I might hang you."

Swallowing convulsively, trying helplessly to maintain at least a bit of bravado, Jonathan stood his ground. "You wouldn't. You're only bluffing."

"Am I?" Ross had a length of rope hanging from his belt, the same rope he had planned to use for his late-night visit to Sabrina's suite. Now he ran it through his hands slowly, lingeringly. "I don't think so."

Jonathan looked into his adversary's eyes and knew his time had come. "No!" With a gasp he made a mad dash for the door, but Ross's outstretched leg tripped him. The blond man went sprawling to the floor. "Sabrina! Kit! Don't let him hurt me. I taught you how to shoot. I made you a star. You owe me for that."

Sabrina might have felt sorry for Jonathan once, might

have interfered, but her heart was cold as she remembered the past several days. "I paid my dues twice over, Jonathan. I consider that we're even."

Jonathan Colt's eyes were dilated with fear, his entire body convulsed with an uncontrollable trembling as he reached up to touch his neck. "You can't hang a man for doing what I did. It would be murder, Sheldon."

Ross's smile was mysterious as he made a loop with the rope. He moved forward, winking at Sabrina as he did so, then quickly slipped the lasso over Jonathan's feet. The free end of the rope was tossed over the base of the large chandelier. With a tug, he pulled Jonathan up, up, up to dangle like a hooked fish from the ceiling, securing the rope tightly so that no matter how much he kicked and squirmed, Jonathan couldn't get back down.

"Now, shall we go, Sabrina dear?" Ross kissed her lovingly on the cheek. "We'll go to my room and celebrate your freedom and our engagement. I'll have a bottle of chilled champagne brought up and . . . and we'll think of something to occupy our time." Putting his arms around her waist, he gathered her close. "You were fabulous this afternoon." He grinned. "Did you see me sitting in the stands?"

"With your black beard and mustache? Yes." Reaching up she rubbed his bare chin. "And must say I'm not so certain you shouldn't put it back on. It made you look like a real Western man."

"Oh, it did, did it?" Ross nuzzled her neck, taking great delight in plucking off her wig. "You won't have to wear this ever again." He tossed it over his shoulder, then picked her up in his arms like a bride about to go over the threshold. In four bold strides he reached the door. "Too bad you can't help us celebrate, Colt. Too bad you're all tied up. We'll miss your company. We really will." Ross kicked the door open with his foot. "I guess we'll just have to make do without you." With a laugh as carefree as a young boy's, he walked out into the hall, then with Sabrina in his arms he headed straight for his room.

Chapter Forty-nine

Ross and Sabrina were flushed from their delightful and passionate night of lovemaking as they left his hotel suite. Together they went to Buffalo Bill's room to give him the news that Kit, or rather Sabrina, was going to leave his show.

"He'll be expecting this news. We won't take him completely by surprise. Don't worry, Sabree!" Ross's knock was jaunty as he stood before the door.

She wasn't worried, only a bit sad at the thought of leaving him high and dry without another performer to take her place, but it couldn't be helped. She loved Ross and her place was at his side. Somehow she'd make Bill see that.

Buffalo Bill answered the door in his underwear without even a sign of embarrassment. His gray eyes twinkled merrily when he saw Ross in the doorway. "So, you did come back. I thought that you would. And from that smile on your face I don't even have to ask if you've seen Kit."

Ross grinned a bit sheepishly as he gently pulled Sabrina towards him. "Yep, I've seen her." Not wanting to beat around the bush, he blurted out, "I've come to take her with me, Bill. As my wife."

"Mmm-hmm. I'm not at all surprised," Bill exclaimed.

Impulsively Sabrina took Buffalo Bill's hand. "I hate to leave you right before you head for Chicago. It seems so ungrateful of me. Please understand . . ."

"I do." He looked at Sabrina and his eyes were gentle. "She loves you, Ross. Wouldn't even give the governor a kiss, though he tried. He tried." Bill chuckled. "She's quite a woman."

"I know. She's one of a kind."

"And so are you!" Bill whispered behind his hand. "Just what did you think you were doing, hanging Jonathan Colt up there by his heels like that? He's threatening to have you skinned alive. Lucky for you he hollered so loudly that the hotel manager found him before he was there very long, but I think I'd hasten out of town, if you know what I mean." Bill winked conspiratorially.

"Believe me, he had it coming." Ross started to tell the story, then thought better of it. What did it really matter? Everything had turned out well in the end.

"Good-bye, Bill." Sabrina couldn't keep the tears from streaming down her cheeks. "Being in your show was like a dream come true. I'll never forget you."

"Nor I you." Bill gathered her into his arms for a bear hug. "Take care of yourself, honey. And don't let old Ross there cheat you any, just because he makes you his wife. You're a great sharpshooter. Make him pay you what you're worth."

She gave Ross a playful nudge in the ribs. "I will!" Sabrina paused then looked long and searchingly into Bill's eyes. "But what about the show? Do you have anyone to take my place?"

"No one can ever take your place, Kit. You should know that by now, but I just might go visit the Sells Brothers' Circus. There's a little gal there who I'm told is quite good with a gun. Phoebe Anne Mozee is her given name, though she goes by Annie Oakley."

"Annie Oakley!" Sabrina remembered the dark-haired girl — it was she who had given her the idea to shoot in the first place. "I saw her shoot once. She's very good. Much better than me. Somehow I think she'll do you proud, Bill."

344

"We'll see." Bill might have said more had a young blond woman not come out of the bedroom to see who was at the door. She was very pretty. Her hair hung well past her shoulders and she was wearing the skimpiest of nightgowns. "Laura Mae, meet Kitty Tremaine and Ross Sheldon. Friends of mine." Now it was Bill's turn to look a bit sheepish.

"Pleased, I'm sure." Laura Mae was all teeth as she smiled in Ross's direction. "Any friend of Bill's is a friend of mine."

Sabrina looped her arm through Ross's, just to make certain this young woman knew he was taken. "I'm glad that you're so friendly," she said sweetly, then turned to Bill. "Take care, Bill. I'll never forget you." Turning away before she completely succumbed to her emotions, Sabrina preceded Ross down the stairs.

"I need to take care of my bill, Sabree, and gather up your luggage, but I've already hired a carriage." He sensed that she needed to be alone for just a little while. "Why don't we meet in the carriage house?"

Sabrina agreed, making her way to the brick and wood building without looking back. From now on she would be looking ahead to a new life with Ross by her side. At last all the obstacles to their happiness had been swept aside. It was a thought that caused her to cry again, only this time the moisture in her eyes was from joy.

Stepping through the door of the carriage house, Sabrina wiped at her eyes, then stiffened. Suddenly she had an all-consuming feeling that she was not alone. Someone was watching her. Whirling around, she was too late to escape as an arm gripped her about the waist, nearly squeezing the breath out of her. Struggling frantically, her eyes strained in the dim lantern light for the identity of her captor.

"My God!" It was a face that came whirling from her past. Rufus James!

"We meet again, my dear. How pleasant. I come face to face with the famous Kitty Tremaine and find it to be

345

my dear departed son's wife. My daughter-in-law. I thought when John Travers told me he had seen your painting on the governor's wall here in Hartford that he was hallucinating, but I see that he told me the truth."

"Let me go!" Sabrina was not the same terrified young woman he had badgered at the inn. She'd made a new life for herself and that had made her strong.

"Not until I make you see reason, Sabrina dear." He screwed up his face in the expression she remembered all too well. It reminded her of a prune. "There are rumors abounding that the governor intends to — how shall I say — make you an important woman in his life. When he does I want to be assured that you remember me."

"I remember you all too well." If he thought that he could strong-arm her into submitting to his will he was sadly mistaken. "You made my life a living hell, a misery."

"I gave you food, clothes, and a roof over your head. You owe me!"

"I owe you nothing!" Sabrina was adamant. "Let me go!" She pushed at the hands which held her, looking frantically for anything she could get her hands on. "Oh, haven't you learned?"

"Indeed I have." He guessed her intent in an instant and wrenched her arm behind her back. "You gave me quite a goose egg. I was flat on my back in bed for three weeks, out like a light."

"I . . . I thought you were dead."

"So did quite a few of my customers, but as you see I'm still among the living, for which you should be glad." His eyes glittered dangerously. "Very much among the living." He licked his lips and bent his head towards her, revealing his intent and Sabrina remembered that other time which seemed so long ago.

"No!" Lifting up her knee, she aimed between his legs.

"Oooohhh!" Doubling over in pain, he let her go, but his flailing arms knocked over the lantern. Sabrina watched in silent horror as it fell to the ground, the oil

346

and sparks igniting a small pile of straw with flames. Like a tinderbox, the carriage house was soon on fire.

"You little fool. See what you've done!" Rufus James stumbled to his feet, blocking her escape.

"What *I* have done?" Sabrina tried to move past him, but he wouldn't get out of her way. "For God's sake, are you mad? We'll both be killed if we don't leave immediately."

Already the smoke was beginning to choke her. It was like a nightmare, a terrible recreation of the past, only this time it was even worse. There was a fire now. This time her very life was in danger.

"Move aside!" Taking in a deep breath, Sabrina let out a scream of anguish and of anger. She wouldn't let this horrible man ruin everything just when her happiness had begun. Pushing him aside with a strength that surprised her, she frantically searched for a way out of the raging inferno.

"Sabrina! Oh, my God!" Ross's voice was the dearest sound in all the world at that moment. Ignoring his own danger, he pushed through a wall of flames and picked her up in his arms. He moved towards the door, but Rufus James stood in the way. Using his muscular body as a shield, he pushed James to the ground, carrying Sabrina like a rag doll out of the burning carriage house.

"Water! Water!" came the cry. Bill's people. They knew they had to put out the fire before it threatened the hotel. "Hurry!"

Several Indians and cowboys reacted, carrying buckets of water to fight the fire.

"My father-in-law!" Sabrina's hand trembled as she pointed towards the fire. Rufus James was still in the carriage house.

"I'll get him, though if you ask me he isn't really worth saving," Ross sputtered. He didn't have to have been there to know what had happened. That bastard was responsible for this. Nevertheless he fought against the flames to come to the man's rescue, tugging him through

347

the sheets of spitting red, orange, and blue. He deposited him none too gently on the ground, hovering over him with a fiercesome scowl. "Listen, you bastard! Sabrina is going to be my wife, and if you ever come near her again, or bother her in any way, I swear before all that I'll grab you by the balls and squeeze so hard your voice will change. Do you understand?"

Rufus James nodded. For once the smirk was gone from his face. Not only was he fearful of Ross, but it seemed that he realized just how close he'd come to death. "I understand!" he croaked.

Ross bent down to comfort Sabrina. She looked so fragile, like a flower. "I love you, Sabree. I thought I knew how much, but I didn't really until this moment. Until I almost lost you." He shuddered as he imagined what might have happened.

The smell of smoke permeated the air, but the steady stream of men carrying buckets promised that the fire would be out soon. But one flame Ross knew would never be extinguished was the one burning inside him for Sabrina.

Epilogue—1889

It was a beautiful May day. The flowers in the cottage's garden were in full bloom, filling the air with a marvelous perfume. Sabrina bent over, scissors in hand, with the thought in mind of cutting the perfect bouquet. It was Ross's birthday and she wanted to make the table look festive for his party. Just a small gathering, really: Curly, Jason Roberts, Moe and Buck, and of course little two-year-old Billy, named after Buffalo Bill. Perhaps he'd be the most important guest of all, this dark, curly haired son who was so much like Ross. Right down to his temper, wild streak, and fierce independence.

"A chip off the old block," as Ross would say.

Had it really been four years ago when she'd toured as a sharpshooter with the famous Buffalo Bill? Sabrina smiled at the thought, wondering where the years had gone. Did it matter? They had been precious, each and every one, for she'd been together with Ross. Mrs. Ross Sheldon. Of all the names she'd had, she liked that one the best.

"I am very, very happy now," she thought. Content.

And she and Ross had earned every minute of their tranquil peace. Side by side they had worked long and hard hours, in trains and in wagons, to make his Wild West show a success again. And it had been! Second only to Buffalo Bill's, Ross's show was the most famous in the country. Sabrina had thought Ross would want to travel the road forever and then, just when she was least expecting it, he had up and decided to settle down. Remembering their special cottage, he had brought her back and it was there that they'd started their family.

"You should have seen Bill, Sabree." Ross was the very picture of the proud father as he strode into the garden, tugging his little son by the hand. "Already he's a crack shot with that slingshot I gave him. You know, I think he takes after you." He bent down to give her a kiss on the cheek. "Might even put him in Bill's show as the youngest sureshot in the world."

"Not now, darling. But maybe in a few years." Remembering the clippings she cut from the paper, she took them from her apron pocket. "You know Bill's opening up his show in Paris." Only a few weeks before the whole company had left New York for the group's first European tour, celebrating the hundredth anniversary of the French Revolution. "Bill writes that the French are a very strange lot. Why, they've even built the strangest-looking building for the exposition. The Eiffel Tower, they call it."

"You don't say!" He was quiet for a moment, then he asked, "Sabree, you're never sorry, are you, that you let Annie Oakley take your place. It could be you basking in all that adulation."

She answered him very quickly. "No. I'm never sorry. You and Billy are my whole life." With a smile, she wound her arms around him. "Besides, I'm much too busy giving you competition." In the past year Sabrina had tried her hand at writing, creating a character that even rivaled Logan Hunter's daring. "Sureshot Sally," a woman she based on her own experiences, with a dash of imagination thrown in.

"But if you had the chance?" He cocked his head, studying her expression.

"I wouldn't trade my life here for all the money and

glory in the world." She smiled mysteriously. "Besides, I have a little secret."

"A secret." Ross knew exactly how to make her tell. There was a sensitive spot right below her left earlobe which was just where he kissed her. "Tell me!"

Sabrina felt as quivery as she had on her wedding day. "I'm going to make you a father again."

"A baby? Sabree!" Ross thought of all those years when he had refused to settle down, and laughed aloud. If only he'd known what he was missing, he'd have taken Sabrina James to the altar much sooner. Being married to her was even better than he had dreamed.

"Then you are happy?" Sabrina remembered a time when she had been worried about how Ross would accept fatherhood, but he had pleasantly surprised her.

"Happy isn't the word!" Just to show her that he meant it, Ross's mouth found hers, delighting in the pleasure her love always brought him, and giving to her in return. Love was the secret of life. As long as Sabrina was by his side, he knew he'd be on top of the world. Ross Sheldon, you lucky dog, he thought. You've got it all. And he did. Most importantly, he knew it.

Note to Reader:

The name Annie Oakley is usually thought of when thinking of sharpshooters and Buffalo Bill's Wild West show. However, she was not the only female to follow such an exciting calling. May Lillie and Lillian Smith are just two of several others. There were also other women prior to Annie Oakley whose names have been forgotten.

Annie Oakley and her husband Frank Butler did not join Bill's show until 1885. Before that they had an act with the Sells Brothers' Circus. She outdistanced the others in popularity and notoriety only after the show's sojourn in Europe. The crowned heads of England,

France, and other European countries adored her, possibly even more than they did Buffalo Bill himself. They admired the spunk of the small young woman and her ability to outshoot even some of the best shots in Europe.

Through the years the life and legend of Annie Oakley have been immortalized in movies, books, and television. She has emerged as a genuine folk heroine, a pretty, talented, and gentle woman who excelled at what was considered a man's skill without losing her femininity.